THE LIBRARIAN AND THE ORC

FINLEY FENN

The Librarian and the Orc

Copyright © 2020 by Finley Fenn

info@finleyfenn.com

Cover artwork of John-Ka by Helena Nikulina

Cover design by Sylvia at The Book Brander

Visit www.finleyfenn.com for free bonus stories and epilogues, delicious orc artwork, complete content tags and warnings, news about upcoming books, and more!

ALSO BY FINLEY FENN

ORC SWORN

The Lady and the Orc

The Heiress and the Orc

The Librarian and the Orc

The Duchess and the Orc

The Midwife and the Orc

The Maid and the Orcs

The Governess and the Orc

The Beauty and the Orcs

The Widow and the Orcs

The Artist and the Orc

Offered by the Orc

Tryggred by the Orc

Yuled by the Orcs

ORC FORGED

The Sins of the Orc

The Fall of the Orc

THE MAGES

The Mage's Maid

The Mage's Match

The Mage's Master

The Mage's Groom (Bonus Story)

ABOUT THE LIBRARIAN AND THE ORC

He's a cruel, terrifying orc. And he's reading a book in her library...

In a world of recently warring orcs and men, Rosa Rolfe leads a quiet, scholarly life as an impoverished librarian—until the day she finds an *orc*. In her library. Reading a *book*.

He's rude, aggressive, and deeply terrifying, with his huge muscled form, sharp black claws, and cold, dismissive commands. But he doesn't *seem* truly dangerous... at least, until night falls. **And he makes Rosa a shocking, scandalous offer...**

Her books, for her surrender.

Her ecstasy.

Her enlightenment...

Rosa's no fool, and she knows she can't possibly risk her precious library for this brazen, belligerent orc. Even if he *is* surprisingly well-read. Even if he smells like sweet, heated honey. Even if he makes Rosa's heart race with fear, and ignites all her deepest, darkest cravings at once...

But surrender demands a dangerous, devastating price. A bond that can't easily be broken. And a breakneck journey to the fearsome, forbidding Orc Mountain, where a curious, clever librarian might be just what's needed to stop another war...

To Jennifer N.
With gratitude for your encouragement, generosity, and utter
brilliance!

1

There was nothing more Rosa Rolfe wanted, in this moment, than to throw a book at Lord Kaspar Sippola's handsome, smiling face.

A good fat hardbound book, she thought firmly, as she gave a low curtsey, her blonde head bowing. An encyclopedic tome, perhaps. Something like the *Annals of the Realm*, full of pomp and blather and *lies*, just like Lord Kaspar himself.

"A very good afternoon to you too, my lord," Rosa said instead, forcing the smile to her mouth, the smoothness to her voice. "And to your esteemed guest, as well. Welcome to the Dusbury Library, ma'am."

She had to drag her eyes to the lovely, well-dressed woman who stood at Lord Kaspar's side, clinging to his arm with an easy, entitled familiarity. She was wearing the latest in high fashion, her taffeta day dress cut close to her ample curves, her shiny brown hair piled intricately atop her well-shaped head. And her replying glance toward Rosa was distant, and then increasingly disapproving, as though Rosa were a piece of offal stuck to her delicate, pointy-heeled shoe.

"Indeed," the woman said, clutching her manicured hand

tighter against Lord Kaspar's arm. "Does it always *smell* like this, Kaspar darling?"

Her disdainful gaze swept across the library, as if to condemn all its failings in one fell swoop, and Rosa felt her own back go rigid, her smile almost painful on her face. The Dusbury Library was a true little treasure, comprising an eclectic, highly valuable collection, and the building itself was cramped but welcoming, with tables and chairs scattered about, and large windows studded along the walls. There was nothing else like it in all of Sakkin Province, perhaps in the entire realm, and how *dare* this grand lady behave as though it were a vermin-infested *hovel*.

But Lord Kaspar only gave a loud, hearty laugh, and a cheerful response that Rosa couldn't hear through the rising, clanging ringing in her ears. And when he guided the lovely lady toward the tall stacks, clearly intending to give her the full tour, it was all Rosa could do to hold herself in place behind the lending desk. Especially when—her whole body twitched—Lord Kaspar turned his head, and shot her a swift, surreptitious wink over the fine lady's shoulder. Hinting, maybe, at just last night, when he'd hiked up Rosa's dress, bent her over this very desk, and...

Rosa's cheeks were furiously heating, but she somehow kept the painful smile plastered to her face until the happy couple was fully out of sight. Until she could finally sag her badly trembling body against the desk, scrubbing her face with her hands, and gulping back deep, dragging breaths.

The bastard. The complete and utter *bastard*.

But curse her, Rosa had *known* this was coming, hadn't she? Lord Kaspar was only the second son of Preia Province's vaunted Duke Warmisham, so despite his lordly title, he was lacking any proper estates, and the associated income. And instead, he'd set himself up here, in Sakkin Province, as one of

Dusbury University's most prestigious gentlemen scholars, and as Grand Patron of the Dusbury Library.

All of which meant, of course, that Lord Kaspar was perpetually in need of funds—and thus, naturally, on the hunt for a rich wife. And the rumours that had been swirling for weeks had clearly been all too true, and this lovely woman had to be none other than Lady Scall, the recent widow of one of the wealthiest men in the realm. And a clever woman, they said, with many advantageous connections, to boot.

"Who's the *girl*?" came Lady Scall's high, cultured voice, carrying easily over the stacks, loud enough to make Rosa wince. "The university hasn't honestly hired *her* as a *librarian*?"

There was an instant's hanging stillness, and then a too-light laugh from Lord Kaspar. "Oh, she's only an assistant," his cool voice said. "Helps Southall with fetching, and shelving, all that sort of thing. A charitable appointment."

Rosa's hands were gripping hard against the lending desk, the roaring rising again in her ears—but she leaned forward, and sucked back a silent, bracing lungful of air. She had to know. She *had* to.

"Quite well-dressed for a charitable appointment though, wouldn't you say?" came Lady Scall's reply. "That dress looked like Madam LeTourney's work, to my eye."

"Does it?" Lord Kaspar said, with creditable vagueness. "Perhaps it's some kind of cast-off. Surely those charities are swarmed with old things."

Lady Scall didn't answer, but Rosa's heart was truly hammering now, pounding desperately against her ribs. If Lady Scall was already suspicious—with good reason—what would come after, once Lord Kaspar proposed to her, once they *married*? Would Rosa be fired? Cast out? Kept away from her precious library, *forever*?

Her hands were sweaty and shaking, clutching uselessly at the desk, and she abruptly shoved herself out from behind it, grasping a handful of books from the nearest table. If her job was supposedly only shelving, then she would shelve. She would do anything. *Anything.*

Lord Kaspar's grand tour went on for another full hour, and included a good stretch of conspicuous silence from the very back of the library. Clearly some kind of hanky-panky, no doubt an attempt to prove his desire for his fine new lady, and his utter disregard for his tarted-up assistant. And by the time Lord Kaspar finally ushered Lady Scall out the door, and then strode back to find Rosa still shelving in the stacks, she was so enraged that she could scarcely speak.

"My lord," she said, through gritted teeth, as she thrust her books down onto the nearest table. "Did Lady Scall enjoy your tour?"

Lord Kaspar was looking distinctly ruffled, and he absently ran a hand through his wavy brown hair, giving Rosa a sheepish, indulgent smile. "Quite, I think," he replied. "Don't tell me you're jealous, Rosa darling? Or perhaps"—his head tilted—"you're afraid she'll be jealous of *you*?"

Rosa couldn't help a betraying wince, and in reply Lord Kaspar huffed a low, knowing laugh. "Don't concern yourself, darling," he said, as he came an easy step closer. "It'll take more than a jealous wife to make me give *you* up, my clever little bookworm. Especially when"—he brought up an elegant, long-fingered hand to pat lightly against her cheek—"I have a new research project for you, love. A *crucial* one."

A crucial new research project? Rosa couldn't deny the traitorous flare of interest that surged through her thoughts, and Lord Kaspar's smile widened as he again patted her cheek. "I need you," he said, "to find a way to finish off the *orcs.*"

The orcs. "The *orcs*, my lord?" Rosa asked, frowning at his satisfied, expectant face. "The orcs with whom our province just signed an extensive *peace agreement*? No aggression, no retaliation, from either party, under threat of severe and lasting consequences?"

"Yes, yes, of course," Lord Kaspar said, with a trace of impatience in his voice. "*Those* orcs, love. I've been tasked with finding a way around that damned new peace-treaty, without getting our hands dirty, or spending any more of our limited resources. We need to wipe out those bastards once and for all, and actually be *clever* about it this time."

Rosa's brain was already churning—who would have possibly given Lord Kaspar such an alarming task, maybe his duke father, maybe the realm's powerful Council of Lords?—and despite herself, she felt her head give a quick, twitchy shake. "But for a project of that calibre, my lord," she said, "you need actual lawyers. And military strategists, and the like. Not"—she took a breath—"*me*."

But Lord Kaspar's mouth had curved up into another cool, assessing smile. "On the contrary, darling," he countered, "you're *precisely* what I need. The legal and martial avenues have already been thoroughly investigated, and found currently—*undesirable*, at this point, and far too costly. What we need now is something *new*. Weaknesses. Scandals. Shocking atrocities. Some surefire means of inciting the masses to march upon that foul Orc Mountain with pitchforks."

Oh. So Lord Kaspar wanted to provoke a *peasant rebellion*, then. So he didn't have to pay for his own damned war. And while Rosa held no particular fondness for orcs—by all accounts, they were wild, dangerous, brutal beasts, who stole away women in order to sire their huge, deadly sons upon them—this peace-treaty between men and orcs had been signed only six short months ago. And the original signed agreement, complete with a lengthy, detailed endorsement by the well-respected Lord Otto, had been filed here, at the Dusbury Library.

Rosa had of course read it—in her nine years working here

at the library, she'd read nearly every new tome and file that came in—and she'd found it surprising, and perhaps disconcerting, too. Claiming that the vicious, violent, warmongering orcs truly longed for *peace*. With peasants, as well as lords. With *all* humans.

"Well," Rosa said, glancing helplessly toward the stacks, "why not ask the university to help you? Surely there are any number of actual students and scholars who could suffice?"

"Absolutely *not*," Lord Kaspar replied, voice clipped. "This project is top secret, and the results need to come from me alone. Besides, most of those students are far too imbecilic to take on such a task. I need real cleverness, and enough imagination to isolate the most promising possibilities. Some insight into the common peasant brain is essential, as well."

Rosa swallowed, her gaze dropping to the floor between them, and while she knew she was now required to speak, to eagerly agree to such a prestigious project, nothing would seem to come. Lord Kaspar and his fellow nobles wanted to start a *war*. And worse, they wanted to manipulate innocent, impoverished people into fighting it for them. *Dying* for them.

There was an instant's hurtling silence, during which Rosa could almost *feel* Lord Kaspar's disapproval, boring deep into her skin. And then that touch became truth, with cold, hard fingers gripping at her chin, and tilting it up toward him.

And curse him, but despite being well over a decade older than Rosa's twenty-four years, the pompous, marginally clever, disgustingly privileged Lord Kaspar was also unfairly, breathtakingly handsome. With those dark curls and thick eyelashes, the clean-shaven square jaw, the shadows under his grey eyes that spoke of too many late nights spent reading. And his long fingers on Rosa's face were strong, familiar, as though he had every right to touch her, to do with her whatever he pleased.

Which, of course, he did. And Rosa saw the exact moment

when he remembered it, the heat and the determination flaring across those lovely grey eyes.

"You *will* do this for me, Rosa," he said, his voice lower, smoother. "Won't you, my clever little bookworm?"

Rosa could only seem to stand there, blinking at those eyes, and Lord Kaspar smiled again, chilly, amused. "Don't second-guess your abilities, darling, if that's what you're thinking. I know you possess a thorough understanding of this library's current resources on the subject, and you do not lack in reading comprehension or imagination. And, thanks to your background—"

He at least had the courtesy not to say it, to point out Rosa's common peasant brain, or her inferior education at the Charitable School for Girls. But Rosa knew he was thinking it, all the same, and his smile was almost apologetic this time, his fingers gripping tighter on her chin.

"You *will*, Rosa," he said firmly. "You will use this library's plentiful resources to help you, and you will speak with Southall to obtain the report's full requirements, and any extra sources you may need. And when I return from my travels in three weeks, you will have my finished proposal ready and waiting, full of shocking new revelations about those dreadful beasts. You do *not* want to disappoint me on this, darling. Not now."

His eyes had darted a brief, meaningful glance toward the door—toward *Lady Scall*, oh gods. Lord Kaspar had meant that as a *threat*. And suddenly the terror was shouting again, spattering wide across Rosa's thoughts, would she truly start a war, to keep her job, her library, her livelihood? *Everything*?

"But, my lord," she heard her plaintive voice say. "What if I don't wish to be part of a war?"

There was a flash of undeniable rage in Lord Kaspar's eyes, enough to make Rosa flinch—but then it faded again, twisting away into something she couldn't quite read, or follow. "You're not, darling," he said, his voice oddly flat. "You're only serving your lord, who has been *extremely* generous to you these past nine years. And surely, by now you know that pleasing me on such an important project can only benefit you. Not only financially, but personally, as well."

Financially. *Personally*. And it was that last one that finally caught, held, gripped onto something deep inside. Something that hurled a hard shiver up Rosa's spine, and she squeezed her eyes shut, drew in a breath, courage. She could say it. She could try again. She could...

"Personally?" she made herself ask. "Like you finally sponsoring me as a student, my lord? Publicly? At the university?"

Her voice came out sounding too loud, too presumptuous, echoing painfully against the stacks, against Lord Kaspar's sudden silence. And when Rosa blinked back up at his face, it was far too easy to see the same old tired arguments, flitting one by one across his flat eyes. *Women don't belong in a university. Women can only be admitted under exceptional circumstances. I've already gone above and beyond to secure you this position here at the library, even this role should by rights belong to a man...*

But Lord Kaspar didn't speak any of it aloud. Hinting, perhaps, that the entire situation was far more dire than he'd first indicated, and Rosa held herself tall before him, held her gaze on his pale face. "Because that is what I want, my lord," she said, her voice a whisper. "More than anything. *Please*."

There was another instant's stillness, the unease and the irritation warring behind Lord Kaspar's lovely grey eyes, until finally he dropped his hand from Rosa's face, and gave a heavy, exasperated sigh.

"Very well," he said, voice thin. "If you impress me with this project—if you impress me very, *very* much, enough to achieve our ends—then I will request an exemption for you. In the fall."

Rosa's heart leapt, hammering bright and wild, and she

couldn't help a broad, genuine grin up at Lord Kaspar's face. "Thank you, my lord," she breathed, clasping both hands to her chest. "*Thank you.* I'll impress you, you'll see. I'll blow your damn *mind.*"

The irritation had faded slightly from Lord Kaspar's eyes, replaced by a familiar, tolerant amusement. "I'm sure you will, darling," he said, with that low, telltale lilt to his voice. "In the meantime, perhaps you can find something else to blow?"

Gods curse the bastard, but his arched eyebrow had already quirked up, his hands moving down to unfasten the front fall of his trousers. Knowing full well that Rosa would never refuse, especially not now, not with an offer like *that* on the table.

But even so, for a brief, hanging instant, there was again the miserable, overpowering urge to throw an enormous book straight into his smug, handsome face. To shout at him, *No, you great lazy snake, why don't you write your own damned proposals, start your own damned war. Get Lady Scall to suck you off, if she's so gods-damned important to you...*

But Rosa desperately needed this job, and the occasional clothes it provided, and its meagre salary. She *needed* this library. And if there was even the faintest chance of finally, *finally* becoming a real scholar, after all these years—then she needed to suck it up. In every way possible.

So she nodded, with only the slightest hesitation, and even managed another smile up at Lord Kaspar's pompous, satisfied face—before she dropped, hard, to her knees on the floor before him.

"Of course, my lord," she said, through gritted teeth, as she took him firmly in hand. "I'm most delighted to serve."

2

Three days later, there was an *orc*. In the *library*.

"An orc?" Rosa repeated, toward Susan's white, wide-eyed face. "*Here*?"

Susan nodded frantically, waving with her visibly trembling feather duster in the direction of the far corner. Well beyond the tall stacks, and Rosa glanced toward it, and then back at Susan again. Susan was the Dusbury Library's regular morning maid, a scattered, elderly woman who held a deep-seated fear of fairies and the underworld, and who more than once had claimed to see ghosts floating among the stacks.

"Are you certain it was an *orc*?" Rosa asked, though she felt her voice lowering, her eyes darting another wary glance toward the far corner. "How did he get in? I locked the door last night, and I'm quite sure I did it properly."

"It was locked when I arrived," Susan said, with feeling. "But then—*him!*"

Him. Her hands were still shaking, her eyes blinking around the room, and she took a step backwards, toward the door. "Maybe he dug a tunnel into the cellar," her breathless voice continued. "Or maybe he used the orcs' nasty black magic. Or maybe he's here"—her voice dropped to a whisper—"for *you*."

For you. The words sent an undeniable shiver down Rosa's back, and she drew in a deep, fortifying lungful of air. No one but Mr. Southall, who served as both the library's director and Lord Kaspar's secretary, knew about Rosa's orc research—*surely* no one else knew—but the fact that an orc had shown up *here*, in person, only days after she'd been tasked with it...

And thanks to Rosa's three days of copious reading, she now knew more than she'd ever imagined about orcs. They were cruel, bloodthirsty beasts. They used their dark, dangerous magic to steal away hapless, terrified women, drink their blood, and infect them with their huge, violent sons. Their sons were a death sentence, their massive Orc Mountain was a death trap, their ways were foreign and senseless and *wrong*. They were a scourge upon the realm, and they deserved to be crushed underfoot, and burnt alive, and their mountain reduced to ash and smithereens.

And until this very moment, it had seemed like complete bollocks. Utter, unproven, laughable *bollocks*, with barely a primary source—and not a single genuine orc source—to be seen.

But now? Now that there was apparently a real-life orc, here, in the *library*?

"You'd best tie up your hair, young lady," Susan cut in firmly. "And find something to bind your bust with. And you *are* wearing proper undergarments, aren't you?"

What? Rosa blinked stupidly at Susan—she'd in fact gotten out of the habit of wearing proper undergarments to work long ago, in order to better address Lord Kaspar's all-too-frequent needs—but then she gave her head a hard, bracing shake. Oh. Of course. The orc might be here for—*that*. Kidnapping. Forcing. *Ravaging.*

"Um," Rosa managed, around her oddly tangled tongue.

"Surely not, Susan. The signed peace agreement, in section four, it says—"

"Who cares what it says," Susan interrupted, with new urgency in her voice. "We need to get rid of him at *once*. I'll go call the town guard now—a dozen men should be enough to deal with him, don't you think?"

Wait, wait, wait. A dozen men? Fighting an orc here, in the *library*?! And well above the rest of the mess currently plaguing Rosa's thoughts, there was the appalling, bone-chilling vision of knocked-over shelves, volumes torn and trampled, blood surging and gushing about all over—

"*No*," Rosa hissed, grasping at Susan's arm. "Orc or not, there will be *no fighting in this library*. If you *dare* call those men in here, Susan, I'm sorry, but I *will* have you released. Permanently."

The flash of fear across Susan's eyes was almost enough to make Rosa regret her threat, but not quite. This library's collection was absolutely priceless—many of the volumes were hand-copied and utterly irreplaceable—and like *hell* was a brawl happening here under Rosa's watch.

"Then what are you going to do with him?" Susan wailed. "You can't just allow an *orc* into the *library*?"

It was a valid point, and Rosa took a thick, unsteady breath. There was an orc in the library. She was entrusted with this library. And she was finally, *finally* about to become a student, and no *way* was an orc ruining all that. Not now.

"No, the orc has to go," Rosa said firmly. "So I will tell him to leave."

And before she lost the nerve, she spun on her heel, and strode into the stacks toward him.

3

Gods curse her, but Susan had been right.

There was an orc, in the library.

Rosa had half expected to find nothing whatsoever in the back corner, only more proof of Susan's overactive imagination—but when she strode around the last shelf, toward the table she knew to be tucked behind it, she felt her body lurch to a halt, her heartbeat pummelling against her throat.

There was an orc. In the library.

He was sitting at the table, his dark head bent over an open book, his face hidden in shadow—but there was no mistaking his massive size, or the deep grey tint to his skin. Or—Rosa shuddered all over—the long, pointed black claws at the tips of his fingers, one of which slowly, casually, flipped to the next page in his book.

Rosa couldn't help a shocked, strangled gasp, and at the sound, the orc glanced up. And his face, his face was harsh and frowning, his bones angular and uncompromising, his mouth a cruel thin line. And his eyes were a deep, bottomless black, long-lashed and blinking, and at the sight of them Rosa's hand fluttered to her heart, her feet stumbling and staggering backwards.

There was an orc. In the library. Reading a *book*.

Without at all meaning to, Rosa felt herself spin around, and rush back through the stacks. Back toward Susan, and safety, where the world made sense. Where orcs didn't read books, in libraries.

"So?" Susan demanded, once she caught sight of Rosa. "What happened? Did you tell him to leave?"

Rosa's brain felt trapped in a fog, swimming aimlessly round and round, and she grasped for the book she'd stashed longingly under the lending desk. *The Lady Bright*, it was called—it had been a thoroughly delightful adventure, until Rosa had had to abandon it in favour of Lord Kaspar's project—and she clutched it to her chest, breathed in the familiar, reassuring scent of paper and ink and dust. There was an orc. In her library. Reading a *book*.

"No," she said, her voice coming out curiously hollow. "He was—*reading*."

"So what?" Susan countered, with even more belligerence than before, suggesting that perhaps an orc reading was just as inappropriate as one running about maiming and murdering. "Why didn't you tell him where to go? Should I call the guard after all?"

The panic surged again in Rosa's chest, and she clutched the book tighter. No. There could be no fighting, the orc had to leave, it didn't matter whether he was reading or not. He had to go.

She whirled again toward the stacks, keeping *The Lady Bright* close against her chest, almost as though it could defend her from the vagaries of a reading orc. Who would have ever fathomed that orcs could read, or maybe he was only pretending, waiting until Rosa was alone. And then, he would overpower her, trap her, *bite* her, carry her away. Or worse, demand she abandon her research, and ruin her chances of becoming a real scholar forever...

But when Rosa halted before the orc again, lifting her chin, he didn't seem at all interested in demanding, or trapping, or kidnapping. In fact, he didn't seem the least interested in her whatsoever, and only frowned down at his book, turning another page with a sharp black claw. He was biting his lip this time, showing just a hint of a pointed white fang, and Rosa couldn't help a furtive, disapproving glance down at the book's spine. It was a bit much, really, for an orc to thoroughly ignore a young, blonde, decently attractive woman, who also happened to be actively researching his people's demise, in favour of reading a—*Antidotarium and Other Medical Recipes*?

"Excuse me," Rosa finally said, her voice coming out a croak. "Sir."

The orc's black eyes glanced up again, a furrow appearing between them, and he lowered the book slightly. "Yes, woman?"

His voice was low and smooth, drawing something tight and strange in Rosa's belly, and she took another deep breath of her book, still clutched close against her chest. "I'm afraid," she said, "I must ask you to leave this library at once."

The furrow between the orc's brows deepened sharply, and he set down his book on the table—taking care, Rosa distantly noticed, to keep his claw in his place on the page. "Why must I leave?" he countered, his low voice lilting with a faint, unfamiliar accent. "There is no one else reading here, and I cause no harm."

Rosa gulped for air, for rational thought. "This library," she choked out, "is meant for *humans*."

There was a scornful curl on the orc's lip, showing more of that pointed white fang. "This library *was* meant for humans," he said, with heavy emphasis on the *was*. "But of late, you humans have signed a new treaty with my kin. And this treaty states that orcs may freely enter and utilize all public places within Sakkin Province, provided they follow all applicable human laws and commonly held practices while doing so."

It was a direct quote from the written treaty, Rosa noted with a grimace, and she fought to grasp at her scrambling thoughts. The library *was* technically open to members of the public, yes, as long as they didn't take out any books—but the Dusbury University would *not* approve of an orc using their library, treaty or not. And despite this research project of his, Lord Kaspar would be the loudest detractor of all. He would be shocked and appalled, he would question Rosa's judgement and sanity no matter the quality of her research, she would be throwing away her chances of becoming a student before they'd even begun...

And most terrifying of all, Rosa would surely be throwing away this job in the library, too. Proving herself unfit, unwise, far too foolish to properly guard such a valuable collection. And even if she had the deepest throat in the realm, it still wouldn't do a lick of good once Lord Kaspar found out.

Rosa squeezed her eyes shut, fighting to block out the rapidly spiralling visions of her ruined future—but the orc just kept on speaking, now with thinly veiled contempt. "Is this library not a public place? And do I not follow your laws and practices?"

The panic kept clanging louder through Rosa's brain, and she blinked her eyes open to glare at the orc's angular grey face. "Well," she managed, "you broke in while we were closed. The door was locked. And, breaking and entering"—she drew in a breath—"is illegal. So there. You broke the law, and as per the agreement, now you leave."

The last bit came out with a vindictive-sounding

satisfaction, but Rosa's triumph was short-lived. Because rather than immediately arguing—or leaving—the orc visibly winced, his claws clenching against the page of his still-open book.

"Ach," he said. "You shut this library at night? And this latch on your door was truly meant as a *lock*?"

Rosa jerked a decisive nod, and the orc winced again, now frowning down at his book. "This lock," he said flatly, "would keep out no one. You ought to better guard a priceless place such as this."

His clawed hand had given a fluid wave toward the rest of the room, and his eyes flicked up to frown at Rosa again, as though she were personally responsible for such a vast over-sight. An implication that deeply rankled, and Rosa pulled herself taller, and glowered down at his disapproving face.

"If you must know, orc," she snapped, "I have been asking for a new door and better locks ever since I started working here. As well as mitigation strategies for fires and floods. But what I want matters very little around here, and if my patron ever found out I was allowing an *orc* to read in this library"—her voice cracked—"I would lose my job here, and likely my access to the library altogether. *Forever*."

The frown on the orc's face didn't budge—if anything, it went even deeper—and he glanced down at his book, and back up at Rosa again. "So you shall break your own treaty," he said, his voice hard. "You shall call armed men, and they shall force me away from my book, so that your—*patron*—shall remain pleased with you."

There was a rising pounding behind Rosa's eyes—*would* she break the treaty, subject her precious library to destruction, in order to force this orc away from his book? A real, honest-to-gods reading orc, dropped straight into Rosa's lap, almost immediately after she'd been tasked with researching the orcs' weaknesses...

Her thoughts darted back to the stack of resources on the lending desk, including the eighteen entire books she'd already read, along with many more pamphlets and treatises. And apart from the occasional outlier—usually couched in the words of a supposedly unreliable female witness—the sources had universally agreed that orcs were violent, wicked, depraved. Bloodthirsty, licentious, kidnapping warmongers, all too eager to thrust themselves upon their unsuspecting victims, to capture and ravish as they pleased...

But this orc was looking longingly down at his book again, trailing his clawed finger down the page with a slow, careful reverence. And for the first time, it occurred to Rosa to look about him for weapons—orcs were always extravagantly armed, weren't they?—but a swift glance up and down his bulky seated form showed nothing of the sort. His beige tunic was close-fitting, laced at the neck, betraying broad shoulders and a flat waist, and his trousers, just visible to Rosa's peering eyes, were tied up by a string, with no weapons belts or sword hilts to be seen. Only a hint of his powerful thighs under the table, and Rosa felt herself swallow hard, her eyes snapping uncomfortably back to his still-frowning face.

"Well, woman?" he demanded, with even more contempt than before. "Shall you call your men?"

Rosa's throat made a noise not unlike a growl, and she rubbed at her aching head. "Look, are you armed? Do you have a sword? An axe? A mace?"

The orc blinked, once, before his face settled into its frown again. "No," he snapped back. "I would not bring weapons into a library. A battle here could endanger many priceless tomes."

Well. Rosa felt her shoulders sagging, and she shot a quick, uneasy glance over her shoulder, to where Susan was, hopefully, still out of earshot. Rosa needed to impress Lord Kaspar. She needed to succeed at this damned research project. And this—perhaps this was an opportunity. Or even a gift from the gods. A real live orc, here in her library, precisely when she most needed one...

"Oh, all right, *fine*," she said to the orc, dropping her voice. "Stay if you wish. But you need to move. Into there."

She'd waved at one of the nearby closed doors—the entrance into Lord Kaspar's private back room—and the orc's brief look of surprise was immediately replaced with suspicion. "You seek to lock me in there," he countered, "and then call your men."

Dear *gods*, this *orc*, and Rosa rolled her eyes toward him, earning an odd, visible flinch from his big body in reply. "No, orc," she shot back. "I wish to keep you out of sight. If anyone else walks in here and sees you, you'll be leaving whether I want you to or not. Surely you can understand that?!"

Those long-lashed eyes blinked at her, but he didn't speak. And when Rosa gave an exasperated wave toward the door, he finally shoved back his chair, picked up his book, and smoothly rose to his feet.

And. For a fleeting, frozen instant, it was like the room had stuttered, catching itself on the bizarre, inexplicable sight of it. A tall, broad, grey-skinned orc, with his long braided hair and harsh face and square jaw—and *pointed ears*—was standing across the table from Rosa, holding a book in his clawed fingers, looking down at her with bottomless black eyes.

And for perhaps the first time today, Rosa was briefly, acutely aware of her own appearance. She'd stayed up late into the night researching, and had only had time to hurriedly wash up and dress this morning—in one of her own shabby, comfortable dresses, rather than the fancy, tight-fitting ones Lord Kaspar provided—before rushing over to work in the rain. Which meant that her long blonde hair was still wet and straggly, her dress baggy and rumpled, and *why* was she thinking these things, he wasn't Lord Kaspar, he was an *orc*—

"Get in," she ground out, and finally, thank the gods, the orc turned, and went. Opening the room's latch with an easy flick of his hand, and striding inside with long, graceful steps before shutting the door tight behind him.

It left Rosa standing there alone by the table, dragging in deep breaths, clutching her book closer to her chest. It was fine. She'd managed the situation. This was an *opportunity*.

And when she walked back out toward Susan, it was almost easy to smile at her suspicious face, and set *The Lady Bright* down on the desk. "It actually worked," she said, as brightly as she could. "He's gone. I sent him out the back door, so as not to further alarm you."

Susan's relief was so palpable, she actually dropped the feather duster, and by the time she'd collected it again, she was already happily chattering, back to her usual self. What would her neighbours say when they heard she'd seen an *orc*, had he truly still pretended to be able to *read*, and had Rosa managed to avoid giving away her scent, so that the orc wouldn't follow her home to the boarding house and kidnap her afterwards?

"Oh, I don't think he was interested in me in the slightest," Rosa said, her voice coming out strangely flat. "He only cared about his book. An *Antidotarium*."

Susan clucked and protested at that, kindly recalling the various men who had lost their heads over Rosa, and if only Lord Kaspar wasn't so entangled with Lady Scall, Rosa might yet have a chance of landing him for good, perhaps?

Rosa didn't waste any breath correcting Susan of that delusion, and instead nodded and smiled at the appropriate pauses. Until Susan finally stopped talking and took her leave, shutting the door behind her with a self-satisfied bang.

And finally—*finally*—silence. Enough that Rosa could finally breathe again, despite her too-present awareness of that closed back room, with that tall, disconcerting orc inside it. In her library. Reading a *book*.

But there was no actual sign of him, only the silence,

spreading wide and close and familiar. It was likely to be a quiet day, what with the unpleasant weather outside, and Lord Kaspar was sure to be away for at least another two weeks.

And in the meantime, Rosa would make a plan for this orc. She would impress Lord Kaspar. And no matter what it took, she would start this damned war.

4

Rosa spent the rest of the morning frantically working at the lending desk, sketching out a plan.

She needed to get beyond her sources, and all their useless, unverifiable bollocks. There had already been an endless war between orcs and men, driven by all those tired, familiar claims—and as much as Rosa hated to admit it, Lord Kaspar was right. To start a new war, he needed something new. Weaknesses, he'd said. Scandals. Shocking atrocities. Something compelling enough to incite a full-scale rebellion.

And it wasn't like this orc was going to offer up such damning information on a platter, of course. But Rosa could try. She could attempt to make conversation. Build a rapport. The orcs were supposedly drawn to women, wanted women—and Rosa had extensive experience in giving powerful males exactly what they wanted. Didn't she?

By the time she'd filled her sheet with her increasingly cramped writing, her hand felt shaky and clammy, her heart beating erratically against her ribs. But she nodded as she scanned her neat script, and mentally reiterated the main points. Introductions first. And then offers of help. And then, perhaps, admitting a partial truth of her research, asking for some guidance on some non-offensive questions. And then...

She set aside the quill with quavery fingers, and again reached for *The Lady Bright*, clutching it close against her chest. It was a good plan. It was the best that could be expected, under the circumstances. It was an opportunity.

She turned and strode with quick steps toward the back room, her eyes fixed on the floor, her heartbeat echoing even louder in her ears. And before she lost the nerve, she raised her hand, and rapped firmly upon the still-closed door.

"Hello?" she called. "Are you still in there?"

There was a sound much like a grunt in reply, so Rosa swung the door open. Only to find the orc again sitting and reading, this time at the little table beneath the room's small window.

His big frame looked almost comically large against the table, and he seemed to be perched rather precariously on the stool—but he also managed, somehow, to yet make the pose look easy, languid, relaxed. He hadn't yet finished his book, perhaps now halfway through, and he was still intently reading, his eyes scanning steadily across the open page.

And now that the initial shock of seeing him had passed, Rosa could admit that his appearance didn't at all match her sources' descriptions, either. Orcs were supposed to be hideous, crooked, fleshy, broken. Their skin was supposed to be rough and scarred, their hair chunky and matted, their bodies hulking and coarse and displeasing.

But this orc—Rosa's eyes flicked up and down his seated form—was none of that. His face was strong and angular and sharp-looking, yes, his braided hair long and black, his skin that disconcerting grey—but it was all smooth, balanced, unmarked by scars or disease. His nose was straight, his jaw square, his ears tapering to those elegant points against his thick, shining hair.

And despite its size, his big body was just as well-formed, broad and strong-looking, the hard ridges of muscle clearly visible beneath the thin fabric of his tunic. And Rosa felt her eyes lingering, first on his corded forearms and wrists, and then his too-large hands. Noting how long and graceful those clawed fingers were, as they closed the book between them, again taking care to mark the page.

Something twisted deep in Rosa's belly, powerful enough to bring a quiet, heated gasp to her mouth—and when her eyes finally, belatedly darted up to the orc's face, she was suddenly, intently aware that he *knew*. And perhaps even *approved*, his sharp tooth just visible against his lip, his black eyes sweeping swift and strong up and down Rosa's trapped, trembly body.

But then, inexplicably, the orc's gaze flicked purposefully across the small room, toward Lord Kaspar's empty cot. Lingering there for a long, twitching moment, before sliding back to Rosa again. And this time, there was only a determined wariness in his eyes, and maybe even disapproval.

"Woman," he said, voice flat. "For what do you wish now."

He spoke as though Rosa had been harassing him all morning, and she mentally grasped for composure, for her plan. "We didn't actually meet properly, did we?" she said, with an attempt at a smile. "Hi, I'm Rosa. Rosa Rolfe."

The orc only kept frowning at her, and she could see his claw tapping lightly, irritably, on his closed book. "And?" he asked. "Is this all you wished to address?"

Rosa's own irritation was already returning in force, and she clutched *The Lady Bright* closer against her chest. "No, of course not," she replied, as smoothly as she could. "It is also my job to supervise patrons of this library. I needed to ensure you're still keeping to our rules."

"Else you shall call your men to kill me," the orc said dryly. "Very well, woman. I sit here, as you asked of me, and I read. Does this not keep to your *rules*?"

Rosa's mouth opened and closed uselessly, and she cast a helpless glance around the small room, with that cot, and the shelf of Lord Kaspar's private books. She wasn't even supposed to be in here without him, there certainly wasn't supposed to be an *orc* in here without him, gods, she needed to get it together, focus on the plan, this was her chance—

The orc was still frowning at her, the disapproval still far too clear in his dark eyes, and Rosa hauled in a breath of the room's too-warm, oddly sweet-smelling air. "Well," she said, "um. I—was hoping you might be willing to countenance a moment's interruption? To chat?"

The orc's eyes kept gazing at her, his lip betraying a faint, sneering curl. "Is this not what you do already?" he asked. "Have you even more *interruption* yet to complete?"

Rosa's thoughts flailed unpleasantly, and she gripped her book tighter. "Yes, I do," she said, her voice only slightly wavering. "I've been doing some reading on orcs recently, and I was wondering if you might be willing to answer a few basic questions for me?"

Those eyes blinked, once, and Rosa didn't miss the sight of that big clawed hand clenching against his book. "Questions," he repeated. "To inform what?"

Rosa fought to assume her brightest, most innocent smile. "My curiosity," she said. "About your culture, your history, your home. It's all very fascinating, and our library's sources are excessively one-sided, and we as humans are very woefully uninformed about orcs, in general."

She'd been speaking very quickly, her voice rising, and in reply the orc's frown only deepened, his big hand giving a vague wave at the library around them. "Are you not the one at fault for filling this library with these one-sided *sources*?" he demanded. "Why must I correct your oversight? Your humans—and your *curiosity*—should be far better served by better efforts, on your part, on behalf of this library."

Rosa's mouth had fallen open, but she snapped it shut again, before her waiting retort could hurtle out of it. "I am not wholly responsible for this oversight," she said thinly. "The job of building the library's collection lies with the university, and the library's director, and my patron."

The orc's eyes had again flicked, inexplicably, over to Lord Kaspar's cot, and then back to Rosa again. Looking even more disapproving, more contemptuous than before, and with it was a hint of a low growl, deep in his throat.

"And you hold no sway with this *patron* of yours?" he said flatly. "Do not speak false to me, woman. The scent of your mating with this man fills this room, and indeed, the whole of this library."

What? Rosa's face flushed sudden and scarlet, and her heart jolted uncomfortably, her eyes helplessly catching back on that cot, envisioning all the things she and Lord Kaspar had done there. Gods *curse* her for putting this orc in here, she should have realized he'd smell such things, all those damned sources hadn't even *hinted* at such an appalling fact—

"My personal life," she gritted out, "is none of your business, orc."

The contempt flared again across those eyes, and with it, something almost like satisfaction. "No," he said. "And thus, neither is mine any of yours, woman."

Rosa could only seem to stand there and stare, while the shame and the frustration soared and pounded through her head. This awful orc was judging her. Mocking her. And even worse—she swallowed, and raised a hand to rub at her aching temple—he was refusing to help her. Wasn't he?

"So you won't answer any of my questions?" she managed, her voice coming out thin, almost plaintive. "Not even a few? Not even to help correct some misconceptions about your people?"

Something dark and dangerous seemed to settle into the

orc's coiled form, and the smile that curled across his mouth was cold, vindictive, cruel. The smile of a brute, a beast, a *monster*.

"No, you foolish, silly, *useless* little woman," he growled. "I shall not. And if you truly wish to be some help to my kind, you shall go away at once, and leave me in *peace*!"

5

Rosa stormed back to the lending desk in a blind, bitter rage.

How *dare* an orc mock her and insult her like that. How dare he speak so rudely to her, after she'd so kindly allowed him to stay. How dare he blame her for a whole university's choices, when she wasn't even permitted to become a gods-damned *student*.

She slammed open the cover of the nearest book—*Orcs Run Amok*—and frantically, furiously began to read. All the while fighting the rising, overpowering urge to either hurl the book across the room, or go back and shout at that awful orc's awful face.

I'm not foolish, she wanted to holler at him. *I'm not useless. I'm just doing my fucking job.*

But no. *No.* She would stay put, keep reading, and find Lord Kaspar's shocking atrocities. She would get him his war. She would help him rid the world of cruel, unnerving, and horribly ill-mannered orcs.

But the longer she read, the more desperate and futile it felt. It was all the same rubbish, couched in slightly different terms, and finally Rosa slammed the book closed again, and glared down at her neatly written plan. Attempt a rapport. Ask some questions. And then...

She crumpled the plan up into a tight ball, and then ripped it into pieces for good measure—but the whisper was still there, quiet and terrifying in her skull. The orcs were supposed to like women. The women had been the only outliers in the whole of her research. And truthfully, despite his abominable personality, the orc hadn't been nearly so hideous or unappealing as she'd expected. And so...

Rosa combed through her hair with her shaky hands, and smoothed out the front of her shabby dress. And then, once again, she walked down the aisle toward the back room, every step slower and heavier than the last. If she succeeded, she would become a student. A real student. A *scholar*.

She didn't wait for an answer to her knock this time, but instead just opened the door, and stalked inside. Back into the quiet, sweet-smelling warmth, into the already-lowering truth of an orc who still just kept on reading, not even sparing her a single glance.

"I yet keep to your rules," he said distantly, his eyes flicking across the page. "Your *work* is well done, woman."

It was sarcasm, he was *mocking* her again, and Rosa gritted her teeth, took a breath, and strode further into the room. Over to sit down on Lord Kaspar's cot, where she clamped her knees together, and gripped her jittery hands against them.

"Your mockery is not appreciated, orc," she said thinly. "I did you a kindness, by allowing you to stay here, when it could cost me my job. The polite thing to do would be to return the favour."

She was looking at the orc's profile, now, at his perfectly straight nose, his sharp square jaw, flexing under his skin. "It is my right, by law, to read in this library," he countered, without even glancing at her. "I owe you no debt."

"You do owe me," Rosa shot back, the frustration edging into her voice. "You broke in. You broke the law."

"And thus I must share with you deep truths of my kin?" he demanded, as he finally looked at Rosa again, his eyes glinting, disapproving. "Very well, woman. Here are some truths for you. I am an orc. I live in the place you call Orc Mountain. I bear sharp claws, sharp fangs, and tapered ears. Your people have long waged a cruel and unjust war against mine. I cannot even peacefully read in a library without question and blame. Does this repay my debt to you?"

Rosa's empty stomach shifted uncomfortably, and she glanced away from his unnerving, prickling gaze, toward the wall opposite. "Look, I'm not trying to—to oppress you," she said, wincing at the words. "I'm only asking for your insight. Your help."

But even that sounded hollow, brittle on her lips, and across from her the orc made a sound that might have been a laugh, hard and scornful. "My *help*," he repeated. "I fully fail to follow, woman, why I would freely grant you this."

Rosa bit at her lip, stared down at her knees. She could do this. Whatever needed to be done, to become a student. A real student. A scholar.

"I could offer payment," she said, to her knees. "If that might be any incentive."

There was an instant's empty, hurtling silence, and when Rosa risked a glance up, the orc was again staring at her, his gaze bright with disbelief. "What payment?" he demanded. "I smell no gold or trinkets in this library, and no food, also. What might you offer me? Goods? Books?"

His head tilted at the last, his eyes glancing toward Lord Kaspar's small shelf of books, almost as though he might actually consider trading for those—and Rosa frantically waved her hands, whipping her head back and forth.

"No!" she replied. "No books, of course not, the books are

priceless, and they aren't mine to offer. I could *never* enable book theft. I meant—"

The orc was staring at her again, mouth pursed, eyebrows raised—so Rosa gulped away the constriction in her throat, and clutched her shaking fingers to her knees. "I meant," she continued, her voice almost a whisper, "I could, um, please you. Bring you satisfaction. Um. Physically."

The stillness felt like a slap, suddenly, jarring and painful between them—and even worse was the orc's abrupt, hoarse laugh. "Ach, woman," he said, grating, thin. "I am an orc, and thus you think I shall trade away all the truths of my kin, for a few shallow thrusts in your weak little mouth?"

Rosa's face was furiously burning, enough that she had to bring up her hands to rub against her cheeks. "It wouldn't be shallow, I'm good at—" she began, before tightly scrunching her eyes shut. "I mean, it could be—something else. If you'd rather."

There was more unmistakable astonishment, juddering through the too-small room—and then another barking laugh, loud and deep. "You wish me to *mate* with you?" he demanded, his voice cold, incredulous. "You cannot truly be this foolish, little woman?"

Rosa swallowed hard, but forced her chin to lift up, her eyes to hold on his taut, mocking face. And she could see something change, flicking across those dark eyes—and then, a telltale flare of his nostrils, a slight arch of his head. Almost as if he were smelling the air. Smelling *her*.

And for the briefest of instants, all Rosa's plans and goals dissipated into emptiness. Lost in the dark glint of those eyes, the deep inhale of that broad chest. The slow, inexplicably compelling sight of a sinuous black tongue, slipping out to leisurely brush against his parted, sensuous lips...

It was like a compulsion, an immovable force, drawing Rosa up onto her unsteady feet. Moving her one step nearer, and another, until she was standing close before him, looking down into watching, half-lidded black eyes. And her hand, her hand had somehow lifted between them, her quivering fingers drifting through the heated, sweet-smelling air—and then coming to rest, impossibly, against those warm, parted lips.

The orc breathed in again, long eyelashes fluttering, and as Rosa watched, taut and caught and frozen, that slick black tongue flicked out, swift and purposeful, to curl against her fingers. Hot and wet and shockingly arousing, and there was nothing she wanted more, in this instant, but to slip her fingers between his lips, to feel the warmth of his liquid beautiful mouth, sucking sweetly against her skin...

The world jerked and twisted all at once, sending Rosa staggering backwards, hot strong hands gripping against her shoulders—and when she found herself again, she was standing back beside the cot, shivering all over, while a huge, threatening orc loomed over her, his lips snarling, his eyes flashing with bitterness and rage.

"*No*, you deceitful little human," he hissed. "You shall not use me for your own aims. I may be an orc, but I am not a fool. Now leave me in peace. As I have asked you. Again, and *again*."

Rosa could only seem to blink at him, while the chagrin pulsed and swerved in her skull. "I wasn't trying to *use* you," she began, and perhaps that was even true—was it? "I just wanted—"

You, she was about to say, and good gods, what was wrong with her today, she did *not* want an orc, she would *never* want an orc, especially one as cold and cruel and terrifying as this one—

But the denial wouldn't come, nothing would come, and the orc's long arm had raised to point toward the door, slow, purposeful, a threat. "I care not what you want, fool woman," he growled. "Leave me."

Rosa still couldn't move, couldn't think, his rage was hers, it was bending the room around him, it was swallowing her alive...

"Get out!" he roared. "Now!"

And thank the gods, finally, Rosa's feet staggered back to life—and with a sharp, miserable little cry, she ran.

6

The rest of the day passed in a tremulous, twitchy blur. With Rosa standing back in her place behind the lending desk, fighting for composure, while visions of that orc—and his sweetly caressing tongue, and his loud furious shouting—whirled and scraped through her brain.

I owe you no debt. You shall not use me. Leave me in peace. As I asked you, again, and again.

The words felt so wrong, so bitterly uncomfortable, almost as if Rosa had somehow been the aggressor toward *him*—but she hadn't, had she? He'd owed her a favour. It wasn't her fault that orcs were vile kidnapping killing monsters, who'd taken hundreds of years to finally end their stupid war. Right?

But Rosa's discomfort only grew with every endless moment that passed, and with the sinking, frustrating reality that she couldn't even risk leaving the library. Even without the orc, she was expected to keep proper hours, and Southall was sure to find out—and report to Lord Kaspar—if she closed a moment too early. She was trapped here, alone with a rude, accusing, dreadful orc, until nightfall.

At least there were no students or patrons to contend with,

thanks to the still-driving rain outside. So there were no inter-ruptions, no distractions, no reasons to leave the lending desk, and Rosa forced her blank, blinking eyes to finally scan through one book, and then another. Only half-reading the words, page after page after page, more endless biased *bollocks*, until the light through the windows slowly faded into darkness.

When it was finally sunset—the permitted closing time—Rosa shut her most recent book with a shaky, resigned sigh. It had been a terribly written, terribly argued *Homily Against the Dire Swivings of the Orc*, and as much as she currently wanted to agree with its furious, familiar rhetoric, it was still nothing new. Nothing compelling. Certainly nothing shocking enough to start another war.

She carefully placed the book on top of the pile, squared her shoulders, and then, for good measure, yanked out her copy of *The Lady Bright*. And before she could think better of it, she stalked to the back corner, and thrust the door open.

"It's time to close for the night," she announced into the dim, sweet-smelling warmth. "You need to leave."

It was harder to gauge the orc's expression in the twilight, but she could almost taste his familiar disapproval, swirling through the air. "Why must I leave?" his deep voice replied. "I wish to stay, and keep reading."

Rosa's head was already beginning to ache again, but she held herself tall, gripped her book closer to her chest. "You can't stay here alone," her unsteady voice said. "It's against the rules. You're not supposed to break the rules. Remember?"

She could just make out those black eyes studying her, glinting in the dim light. "Then can you not stay here also," he said, "whilst I read?"

"No," Rosa shot back, "I can't. I've already given you far too many accommodations today, I'm tired, it's time to close, and I need to go back to the boarding house and *sleep*."

If the orc was swayed by such logical arguments, he gave no

sign of it, only gazed at her with those unreadable eyes. "You can sleep the night through here," he said, with a twitch of his head toward the cot. "I can smell that you have oft done this, with this man."

The contempt had crept back into his voice, and Rosa fought down the responding flare of compulsive, wrenching misery. "*No*," she replied. "And honestly, orc, why in the gods' names would I grant you such a concession, when you have only returned my kindness today with judgement, and insult, and aggression, and mockery?!"

Her voice came out sounding uneven, frayed, as though this horrid orc's actions today had actually *hurt*, for some ridiculous, unfathomable reason. And before she could betray herself any further, she turned and strode back to the lending desk, snapping her book down upon it. She would give him a quarter-hour to get out. And that was all.

There was an instant's stillness all around, broken only by Rosa's heaving breaths—and then, suddenly, by the chilling, telltale sound of the floor creaking. *Directly behind her.*

Rosa whirled around, far too late—and found herself faced, once more, with the orc. Except there was no reassuring table between them this time, no reassuring book, and instead—she swallowed hard—there was only that too-thin beige tunic, those broad shoulders, the critical black eyes, glinting down toward her.

Gods, he was big. And Rosa had never been a large woman to begin with, and in this shocked, stilted instant, there was the sudden, blaring certainty that this orc could so easily lift her up, carry her away, lock her into that back room whether she wanted it or not...

"I wish to stay, woman," he said, calm and authoritative, as though his very tone settled the matter. "There is much truth in these books I must learn, to take back to my kin."

"Then maybe you should have thought of that earlier,"

Rosa countered, her voice quavering. "Before you decided to yell at me, and mock me, and *humiliate* me!"

There was an odd, compulsive-looking twitch of the orc's big body before her, a slight tilt of that dark head. And most unnerving of all, that faint, familiar hint of a long, sinuous tongue, coming out brief and black against his curling, mocking lips.

"Ach, little woman," he said slowly. "I have bruised your pride today, by sending you away as I did. Have I not? You thought yourself too pretty for any orc to refuse?"

What? Rosa felt herself bristling, her shoulders squaring, her eyes narrowing at his infuriatingly appealing face. "I was only offering a—a mutually beneficial *business arrangement*," she snapped. "Which was, in retrospect, indeed a foolish mistake on my part. You have been nothing but rude, insulting, and belligerent toward me, and I have *no* desire to grant you any further favours whatsoever, or spend any further time in your odious, highly disagreeable presence!"

The orc's eyes kept studying her, his big body still far too close, and his lip twitched up, showing a glimpse of a sharp white tooth. "Ach, I *have* harmed your pride," he said, with a cool, enraging satisfaction. "Not only did a lowly orc refuse your mouth and your womb, but he refused your silly questions, also. This vexed you most of all, did it not, little woman?"

The unfair acuity of that caught Rosa up short, for an instant too long—and the orc let out a low, sardonic chuckle. "You wished to hear of blood and death and cruelties, did you not?" he continued, his voice smooth, almost caressing, on the words. "You wished to hear of a deadly, filthy mountain, full of black armies and human skulls. You wished to hear of women forced and swollen and screaming. You wished"—his mouth twisted—"for a grim, fearful tale to spew in these dark times, to raise more hate and swords against me and my kin."

Rosa's body had pressed itself further back against the

desk—wait, this cursed orc couldn't truly *know* the extent of her research, could he?—and it took nearly all her willpower to keep her gaze from darting over her shoulder, toward her pile of sources behind her.

"I did not wish for any such thing," she managed, far too late. "I wanted to know the *truth.*"

There was another mocking sound from the orc's throat, a flare of something unpleasant in those bottomless eyes. "Do not speak false to me, little woman," he hissed. "You seek no truth in this. You think I have not seen this stack of lies you read so fiercely?"

Rosa winced before she could help it, earning another insolent twist of the orc's mouth. And then, in a swift movement, his big hand reached behind her, directly toward her research pile. Tracing a sharp claw down the neat edge of it, gently ruffling the paper and vellum as he went.

"You humans wish for these lies," he said. "You wish for just cause to wreak your cruelties. You *wish* to be afraid."

Rosa didn't, of course she didn't—but this damned orc somehow saw too much, knew too much, his eyes fixed to hers with a narrow, powerful intentness. And then—Rosa gasped aloud—that big hand slowly lifted again, and carefully, gently, brushed a warm finger *against her neck.*

Rosa's entire body froze at once, and she felt herself swallow, her throat spasming against that audacious, lingering finger. But she didn't otherwise move, or seek to push him away, and *gods* he was so huge, so *close...*

"Do not deny this to me, silly woman," he breathed, and that—*that*—was the unmistakable, heart-stopping feel of his finger's deadly claw, tracing gentle against delicate skin. "The strong scents of your fear and your hunger have swarmed me all this day. You wish for me. And you wish to be frightened."

Rosa's mouth opened to speak, but nothing came out, and that finger kept skimming against her neck, leisurely, deliberate. "So heed this, woman," he purred, his eyes shifting, flaring, settling again. "I shall grant you this bargain you asked for, but upon *my* terms, rather than yours. Should you grant me leave to stay here—tonight, and as many more nights as I should wish—I shall now sate your fear, *and* your hunger."

He would—*what*? Rosa could only seem to gape up at him, her heartbeat clanging wild against her chest—and if there had been any uncertainty around his meaning, it was immediately thrown to waste by the feel of that finger, slowly giving way to his whole *hand*. Sliding strong and smooth against her throat, in a movement that should have been a threat, but felt like something else entirely.

"I shall only offer this to you once," he murmured. "And you shall not have my seed, in this. And, you must swear to never speak to any other of me, or what we have done. Ach?"

Good *gods*. "Th-that is completely *ridiculous*, orc," Rosa stammered, her voice coming out choked against the close, thrilling, terrifying touch of that hand. "Look, I didn't make you that offer because I really wanted *you*. I only wanted—*knowledge*. And that was *before* you proved yourself even more of an arrogant, self-righteous arse than I already thought you to be."

There was an instant's still silence—and then the shocking, heart-stopping feel of the orc's hand on her throat clenching, just slightly. Drawing a hoarse, furtive gasp from Rosa's mouth, and surging heat deep into her belly.

"You lie, woman," came the orc's smooth reply. "You have hungered for me since the first moment I stood before you. It has been all I have smelled in this library, all this long day."

The hell? Rosa sputtered again, flailing against the touch of that hand—but another gentle flex of those fingers on her throat jolted her back to stillness, and there was an odd flash of those eyes in the dim light.

"You shall speak no more falsehoods to me, woman," he

said, his voice silken, soft, dangerous. "I have learnt much of your kind, and I am not fooled by these lies and games and tricks. I wish to use your library; you wish to be used by a fearsome orc. All that remains is whether you shall swear to my terms, and"—he came a small step nearer, his body looming close and massive over her—"how you wish this to be done."

Rosa's clamouring heart felt like it would escape her chest, her eyes wide and searching on the orc's harsh, frowning, uncompromising face. He meant all this, he really, really meant this, after what he'd said earlier, after *everything*?!

"B-but you," Rosa began, and then took a deep, desperate breath. "Earlier. You yelled at me. Told me to get away from you, and stop oppressing you. You said you didn't care what I wanted. Remember?"

The orc's mouth betrayed an unmistakable grimace, his gaze flicking to the wall behind her. "I did not *care*," he said thinly, "to be toyed with by a foolish little human, who only sought to use me for her own selfish ends."

Rosa somehow managed a snort, and even a creditable roll of her eyes. "And now that *you're* the one doing the toying, for *your* selfish ends," she gritted out, "you're completely comfortable with that?"

There was a new, unfamiliar twitch at the corner of the orc's thin mouth, a sidelong glance at her face. "I am," he said coolly. "Are you not, also?"

He'd raised his eyebrows at her, taunting, *amused*—and gods curse her to hell and back, but Rosa felt her own mouth twitch up, too. While something seemed to flare and hold deep inside, burning bright and strong and strangely mouthwatering. Warmth. Understanding. *Longing*.

But no, no, he was an orc, he was *awful*, Rosa couldn't possibly still want this, it had been sheer madness earlier to even offer such a thing. And so much worse now that this orc was admitting to *using* her, he was fully admitting that he was a selfish calculating *prick*—

But then it occurred to her, sudden and incongruous, that clearly her sources had been partially correct, after all. Clearly orcs truly *were* ravaging insatiable beasts, to some degree, no matter how peaceful they pretended to be. And was this not still knowledge, and perhaps just as useful? Perhaps *this* was the way to ultimately discover those weaknesses, scandals, shocking atrocities?

And Rosa *had* to impress Lord Kaspar. She *had* to seize this once-in-a-lifetime chance of becoming a student. And that meant—yes, yes—once again, she needed to suck it up. Get on with it. Do whatever needed to be done.

The orc's eyes were very intent on hers, still waiting, that big hand still curved against her throat—and again, for an instant, there was the shuddering, uneasy fear that perhaps he could even follow her thoughts. Perhaps he'd guessed about Lord Kaspar's war. Perhaps he *knew*.

"Oh, all right," Rosa blurted out, before she could stop herself. "I accept. Your terms, I mean."

The orc's eyes fluttered, again betraying just a trace of amusement, of warmth—but then he stepped closer, solid, strong, steady. His hand big and warm, so oddly reassuring, and as Rosa blinked up at those watching eyes, his other hand came up, tracing slow and careful and quiet against her cheek.

"Clever woman," that low voice breathed. "Now, how do you wish this to be done."

Rosa's whole body shuddered again, her mouth letting out a harsh, shaky gasp—and in reply that hand on her cheek slid to her mouth, his thumb brushing light against her parted lips. And gods, the smell of him was mouthwatering, all musk and sweetness, and the books hadn't said that either, they hadn't said anything, *anything*—

"Speak to me," he purred, hurling another clenching flare

of heat deep into Rosa's belly. "No falsehoods. For what do you wish."

Rosa couldn't answer that—she wouldn't—but the orc's shifting watching eyes seemed to know that too, his thumb still brushing gently, almost absently, against her mouth.

"Ach," he said, his voice a low rumble. "Then, mayhap, you wish me to take you as I choose. You truly do wish to be forced and frightened by a fearsome orc, and used as a silly little plaything, however I should wish."

Another shudder wrenched down Rosa's back, her breaths coming out hitched and shallow. Of course she didn't wish for that, even the idea was entirely appalling, but if it was for research, perhaps, perhaps—

"No falsehoods, woman," that voice insisted, velvety, desperately thrilling. "Shall I be this orc, for you? Shall I frighten you, and take what I wish from you?"

It was a shocking question, an impossible unanswerable demand—and one that was made worse, damnably so, by the orc taking a swift, graceful step backwards, and reaching for the bottom of his tunic. And as Rosa stared, stunned, struck still and silent, he drew the tunic off over his head, and dropped it to the floor.

And. His chest was broad, grey, muscled—but unlike his untouched face, it was marked by many scars. They were deep, ugly claw-marks, and combined with the huge breadth of him, they made him look dark, dangerous, deadly. And then—Rosa stifled a hoarse, inexplicable groan—the orc seemed to shake out his big form, easy and graceful, while his claws almost seemed to snap out even further than before, sharp and black and gleaming.

And then, one of those claws came up to his thick black braid. Yanking hard upon it, enough to jerk his head sideways—but then he was shaking his hair out too, tumbling it loose and shining over his muscled chest and shoulders. And

Rosa very nearly whimpered at the sight, her entire body aching and choked and yearning, both hands come up to press against her powerfully surging heartbeat.

The orc was looking back at her, sweeping those suddenly blazing black eyes up and down her form, and his smooth step toward her was a flare, a blow, a terrifying, mouthwatering gift from the heavens.

"Well, woman?" he growled, raising a clawed hand before her eyes, and baring those sharp white teeth. "Is this what you wish for?"

Oh gods, it *was*, and Rosa's traitorous, betraying mouth moaned aloud, her body finally giving way to full-blown trembling. While the orc's eyes flared with triumph, and that clawed hand came back to its familiar place on her throat, circling close, beautiful, *everything*.

"Speak this, woman," ordered the menacing, breathtaking beast before her. "This, for your library."

Rosa couldn't think, couldn't follow, could only stare and choke and breathe. Lost in this moment, in this twirling shouting vision before her sparking eyes. He was going to make it truth, he would, this, for the library—

He'd come even closer, that big hand convulsing against her neck, that scent of him swirling raw and reckless and delicious in her mouth. "Speak, woman," he commanded, lower this time, those eyes hard and intent on hers. "No falsehoods."

And in that desperate, hanging moment, there was no thought of falsehood, of dissembling, of searching or secrets or war. Only a craving, furious longing, a promise, a question, a truth. Speak.

And without thought, without intention, Rosa raised her chin, pressed her throat closer into those warm safe fingers, and spoke.

"Yes, my lord," she whispered. "Frighten me."

7

Rosa's words landed like a stone, rippling through the hollow, aching silence. *Yes, my lord, yes, my lord, yes.*

Frighten me. Frighten me.

It was almost as though she could feel them reverberating, striking against the orc's bared form. Making his mouth convulse, his head ducking and angling sideways, while those black eyelashes fluttered against his grey cheek. Almost as though Rosa *had* struck him, somehow, and there was a strange, inexplicable regret, an impossible urge to take the words back—

And without at all meaning to, Rosa's shaky hand reached toward him, and slid against that scarred, heaving chest. Her fingers spreading wide, pressing flat against his warm skin, pulsing with the surprising power of his thundering heartbeat beneath.

"I mean," she whispered, "only if you want to. You don't have to."

There was a sudden, grating noise from the orc's throat—not quite a laugh—and a flex of that huge hand against her neck. "You say this, woman," he replied, oddly flat, "when I could so simply kill you, before you speak another word."

Rosa felt her fingers clutch against his chest, against the furious pounding of his heart. And instead of the fear she should have felt, there was only a strange, lurching awareness. Perhaps even—understanding.

"I know you won't kill me," she whispered. "You wouldn't."

The words came out sounding fervent, fierce—and even as the orc's mouth twitched into a brief, wry little smile, his blinking eyes on hers looked lost, bitter, almost bleak.

"You must tell me if I truly alarm you," his low voice said. "Or if you wish me to stop."

Rosa nodded, urgent and immediate, almost as though compelled—and that dark head nodded too, those dark eyelashes again fluttering against his cheek. And then he once again seemed to shake out his big body, quiet and fluid and graceful, as if settling it properly into place.

And then—Rosa shivered all over—those eyes lifted again, finding hers with deadly, breathtaking force. Eyes that were black, glittering, hungry.

The eyes of a monster.

They roved up and down her small frame, powerful and greedy and utterly disdainful, almost as though they were undressing her, exposing her—while that huge, looming bulk came a silent, purposeful step closer.

"Foolish woman," his voice said, hard, a threat. "Do you not know what orcs do to ripe little women like you?"

Rosa blinked, went to take an instinctive step backwards—but there was only the solid, sturdy lending desk behind her, holding her in place. Holding her here, alone in the library, only a hands-breadth away from a vicious, powerful, bare-chested orc.

"Do you not know?" he asked again, and this time he smiled, cold and bitter. And that huge, hand had come up, brandishing its black claws toward her eyes, before turning to trace those claws light, gentle, menacing, down the side of her cheek.

"We *mark* you," he hissed, the truth of that claim far too clear in those slowly tracing claw-tips, in those glinting black eyes. "With our claws, our teeth, our scent. We make you ours. *Forever.*"

Rosa shivered, her fingers gripping at the desk behind her, as the orc came another deadly, prowling step closer. Sliding that warm hand down her neck, now, over her collarbone, slipping purposely downwards. Until it finally found the slight swell beneath, and gently, fully enclosed it in that big, heated palm.

Rosa's breaths were already coming sharp and short, her body arching into the shocking, impossibly arousing feel of an orc's hand cupping her like that—when suddenly, oh gods, his other hand came up to do the same to the other side. Using more force now, long fingers rubbing and squeezing, hard palms pressing tight. While pointed claws scraped purposefully against the too-thin fabric of her dress, sinking straight through to the delicate skin beneath.

"And we *bare* you," he breathed. "We bare you not only for our eyes, but for all our kin. For all who wish to see."

Rosa heard her mouth give a strangled, inexplicable groan, and in reply the orc smiled again, curving and wicked. "You think you wish for this, foolish woman. Until it becomes truth."

And then, with a hurtling yank of his hand, he *tore* Rosa's *dress*. Straight down the middle, popping buttons and ripping apart seams with swift, easy efficiency, so that Rosa's whole front was entirely open to him, and his greedy staring eyes.

She couldn't help a startled gasp, her hands instinctively moving to cover herself—but the orc only gave another bitter smile, and in another rapid movement, he grasped both her wrists together, and dragged them up high above her head with a strong hand. Meaning that Rosa was entirely bared, exposed, trembling, while those eyes swept up, and down, and up again.

"Such a small, frail woman," he sneered, while his other hand came to tweak at her reddened nipple. "I shall be able to do whatever I wish with you."

Rosa's replying moan sounded more like a cry, especially when that hand began to caress further down her front, slow, teasing, merciless. Leaving faint red scratches on her pale bare skin, while gooseflesh scattered again and again, and those black orc eyes kept looking, assessing, judging.

"Nearly too small to fit an orc-son," that contemptuous voice continued, his fingers spreading flat against her waist, the claw of his thumb delving into her navel. "But mayhap"—his hand slid over to her hip, widening over the slight curve of it— "just enough, if you are very lucky. Do you wish to try this for me, woman?"

The first flare of true fear snaked down Rosa's spine—he'd said she wouldn't have his seed, right?—and the shake of her head was compulsive, immediate. Bringing a sudden, deep growl to the orc's throat, as that big hand rose back to her neck, circling close and powerful around it.

"You forget, woman," he said, mocking, "I am an orc. And thus"—something flashed across those eyes—"I shall have you. I shall plough you. I shall plant your empty womb with my sons, and fill you until you *burst*."

The words brought another choked, desperate cry to Rosa's mouth, her gaze searching his harsh face, bitter and cold and oddly, angrily triumphant. And for some bizarre, incomprehensible reason, she seemed to catch on that, on the look in his eyes, on the betraying, quiet gentleness in those fingers against her neck.

"Very well," she heard herself whisper, as her fluttering hand reached again for that warm chest, for the still-hammering heartbeat beneath it. "If it means that much to you."

She didn't miss the flare of true shock in those eyes, or the hard movement of his throat—and suddenly, somehow, the game was gone, the mask was gone, the orc's smooth face contorted with rage and pain and longing. And without warning those big hands grasped her, claws digging deep, and all but hurled her back onto the lending desk, straight onto her neat pile of sources. Sending paper and books sliding haphazardly, all under Rosa's back, but in this moment it was the least of her thoughts, what with the huge orc looming over her, his hands clenched tight to her bare knees, his chest heaving with ragged breaths.

"Foolish woman," he growled, as he roughly thrust her knees apart. "Do you not know what this could do to you?"

But there was no speaking, no rational thought remaining, because somehow, instead of trousers at the orc's groin, there was—*that*. A huge, bare, jutting grey orc-prick. Long, impossibly thick, slick all over. And leaking a viscous, white strand of shining, deadly orc-seed.

Rosa was frozen, staring, and far too late came the realization that she was on her back on the desk, with her legs spread wide and wanton. With every secret part exposed and opened for this orc's eyes—and for his taking. For this.

"Do you not know?" his voice said again, sounding almost pleading, as he leaned in further, thrust Rosa's thighs wider. Bringing that swollen, leaking hardness closer, so close it was just tickling at her coarse brown hair—and the sight of that, there, a huge, menacing *weapon*, waiting to impale her whole upon it, was wreaking wild, unthinkable havoc upon Rosa's screeching thoughts.

"I know," she heard her appalling voice whisper, bringing an immediate, tortured-sounding groan to the orc's mouth— and a sustained, shuddering twitch to that hard length, brushing ever closer against her. Almost as though it was seeking her of its own accord, seeking its way inside, and Rosa could feel her own body giving its frenzied, frantic reply. Her eager, greedy wetness opening and closing, fighting to reach for him, fighting for more—

"Foolish woman," the orc's voice rasped, but that hardness against her shuddered again, delving its smooth head just a shade deeper. Just beginning to spread her apart around it, and gods in *heaven* he felt good, he had to keep going, the hunger was churning flying *madness*—

Rosa's hands snapped up to clutch at his broad bare back, fighting to drag him deeper, deeper, please—but that big body over her stilled again, except for that hard cleft, still shuddering just inside her. "You cannot know," that voice hissed, or perhaps begged. "I may *break* you, woman."

The intensity of those words seemed to cut through the madness for an instant, and somehow Rosa's trembling hand had reached up to touch at his grey, angular face. "I know," she said again, with an inexplicable, urgent conviction. "But you'd help me, too. Take care of me. Wouldn't you?"

The orc's eyes stared down at her, through her, his big body held unnaturally still—but then his head bowed, his loose hair falling over his shoulder in a sheet of silken blackness. "Yes," he whispered, almost unbearably soft. "I will."

That was that, then. That was all Rosa needed, and her hand on his face had tilted it back up, bringing those eyes to hers. And she could see the hunger flashing, the madness surging against her own, he would have her, she would have him, and the hardness still jutting against her suddenly knew it, flaring and flexing and filling all at once—

And then, oh gods, there was pressure. That huge, delving head bearing down, shoving its way inside, parting her wet, pink, swollen body around it. It was hot and solid and exquisitely smooth, a slick merciless velvet invasion, and Rosa's hungry wetness was desperately clenching against it, dragging it in, deeper, more.

"Oh," her breath choked, her chest hollowing, her fingers clutching helpless at his face, his back. "Oh, gods. My *lord*."

A hoarse, guttural groan burned from the orc's throat, that thick hardness pushing further, faster, fuller. Truly impaling her now, trapping her bodily upon the heft of him, shocking, powerful, *alive*.

And the sight of it, flickering across Rosa's fluttering eyes, was just as shocking, just as powerful. This huge muscled orc leaning over her, his black hair hanging over his face, every hard line of him corded and taut and glistening. And at his groin, rather than just that jutting cock, there was also her own swollen body, flushed fuller and darker than she'd ever seen it. Wrapped tightly around that massive prick, taking him well over halfway inside her, and there was still so *much* of him left, surely this was impossible—

But he kept bearing down, impaling her ever deeper with deliberate, exquisite care. And she was taking it, she was drinking him deeper and deeper, stretching even wider, her nerves fraying, the world stuttering and tilting sideways—

And suddenly it was like the world had snapped away entirely. Her hands sparking and grabbing at him, her body thrashing, her legs wrapping tight around his back. "Fuck me," she gasped, not caring what that sounded like, what it meant. "Please, my lord, more, please!"

It was alive between them, her madness driving his madness, those dark eyes blazing on hers, those clawed hands powerfully thrusting her thighs even further apart. And with a single, furious snap of those hips, that massive cock drove the rest of the way inside, filling her, splitting her, breaking her in two.

Rosa screamed, her whole being flailing and arching, caught on him, trapped on him—and his replying, rumbling roar was more madness, more need, more punching flaring pleasure. And she had never needed anything so much in her life, had never made such sounds in her life, shrieks and groans and hysterical sobs, while those powerful hips finally began thrusting against her. Driving that massive orc-prick even deeper, tighter, too tight to draw out again, wedging them harder, wrapping her closer, spearing her upon his strength. She was part of him, one with him, fused forever, lost—

Until there was—euphoria. Screeching, shouting, mad euphoria, pulsing out wild and reckless, swarming Rosa's entire being. Convulsing again and again, quivering violently around the hot swollen pole inside her, while it seemed to swell fuller, deeper, taking everything—

And then he was the one shouting, his huge body arched, his head thrown back, his sharp claws sinking into Rosa's hips—and that power invading her locked, and *exploded*. Blasting out again and again inside her, flooding her with spurt after spurt of hot wicked orc-seed, too full to hold, too much to keep, Rosa's entire body stretched and used and on the edge of breaking—

There was a yanking jolt, a horrible wrenching, battering at Rosa's very soul—and then, somehow, the orc was away, separate, apart. And Rosa's used, gaping-open core was spraying out hot orc-seed, straight toward him, spattering that heaving, muscled body—and that slick, still-hard cock—with thick, dripping strings of glistening white.

Rosa's body was heaving too, her arms and legs tingling, the aftershocks radiating pleasure and discomfort and exhaustion all at once. While the orc still standing between her legs seemed to have gone instantly, unnervingly rigid, but for his blinking black eyes.

Rosa's hand reached for him on its own, caressing down that smooth muscled arm, but he didn't acknowledge it, didn't move. Only stood there and looked at her, his eyes flicking up and down her sprawled, sated form with something almost like shock.

"Ach," he breathed, and in a jerky twitch he'd pulled away from her, his hands on his grey face, his palms pressing into his eyes. "*Helvíti.*"

The word didn't make any sense—it was in the orcs' own primitive black-tongue, Rosa's sluggish brain supplied—and abruptly there was the awareness, powerful and almost breathtakingly painful, that he regretted this. He hadn't truly wanted what he'd just done. Perhaps he hadn't even truly wanted *her*. Had he?

Rosa couldn't breathe, suddenly, and she fought to sit up, to reach for him—but once again he twitched away from her, his hands dropping from his face, his eyes again trailing up and down her naked, debauched body.

"No," he said, his voice cracked, hoarse. "Lie down, woman. *Stay.*"

Rosa's trembling body could only seem to obey, nodding and lying back against the lending desk, while the world seemed to spin slowly all around. And while the orc grasped roughly at the last remnants of her tattered dress, tearing it off her pliant form, and then using it to mop up his own messy, sticky-white front, his fingers deft and familiar against that half-hard grey prick, and the hanging, soft-looking bollocks below.

"*Helvíti,*" he said again, more of a muttered curse this time, his eyes squeezing shut—but his hands kept moving, first tossing the tattered dress onto the desk beside Rosa, and then reaching down and dragging up his trousers, fastening them tight around his waist.

It was like he was hiding himself away from her, and even more so when he went for the tunic on the floor, roughly pulling it on, and then shoving his long hair back, his swift hands tying it up into some kind of loose knot on his head. And then he was standing there before her, tall and silent and fully dressed, the slight sheen of sweat on his cheek the only hint remaining of what they'd done.

Except, of course, for the fact that Rosa was still lying sprawled naked across the desk, her breaths still gulping, her tender, stretched body still steadily leaking hot orc-seed. And she needed him to touch her, so desperate she almost sobbed with it—and when that big hand finally, carefully came back to her knee again, she felt her breath choke in her throat, her whole body again needing to sit up, to reach for him, to put her hands to that silent, forbidding grey face.

But his hand snapped up, with surprising speed, to press flat against Rosa's chest. Holding her there, gentle but firm against the desk, while his other hand reached for her other knee, and spread it wider apart.

He was looking *there*, Rosa realized, with a sudden, mortified flush of heat. At the filled, stretched-open core of her, still leaking his thick hot orc-seed.

"Stay," he said again, quieter, and he released Rosa's chest, reaching again for her tattered dress. And then he very gently, very carefully, began wiping up the mess, with soft touches of the dress against her tender, inflamed skin.

Rosa couldn't help a gasp, stilling his hands against her, drawing his narrow eyes to her face. "Does this hurt you?" he demanded, but she shook her head, fighting to ignore the heat surging in her cheeks. Earning a flare in those eyes that looked almost relieved, before he returned his attention to what he was doing. Now accompanied, unexpectedly, by the thrilling touch of what felt like gentle bare *knuckles*, pulling her swollen crease a little apart, and then delving slightly *inside*.

His gaze was very intent on what he was doing, whatever the hell it was, and Rosa lay there and let him do it, while her thoughts spun strange, stunted circles in her head. She'd just—

done that. She'd been taken by an *orc*. She'd wanted him, asked for him, begged for him.

And it was supposed to have been research, it was supposed to have provided insight into what made these orcs weak—but right now, the only shocking insight was how desperately Rosa had wanted that, and how damned *good* it had been. How if this orc were to rise up this very moment, look into her eyes, and say, *again*, she would gasp, and nod, and pull him close.

But as it was, he'd seemed to finish whatever he'd been doing down there, because he tossed her ruined dress to the floor, and once again leaned over her. Not to kiss, or caress, or say something kind, as Rosa might have hoped—but instead to slide one strong arm under her shoulders, the other under her knees.

"W-what are you doing?" Rosa managed, her voice scratchy and thin, but already the orc had hoisted her easily up against his chest, and begun striding away. Toward the back room, her twirling thoughts pointed out, while her traitorous body seemed to curl closer against him, into that warm powerful chest, the still-hammering thud of his heartbeat.

"You must rest," his deep voice said, rumbling against her, before he carefully deposited her down onto something soft. Onto Lord Kaspar's cot, Rosa realized, as she blinked up at the orc with hazy eyes, and what in the gods' names would Lord Kaspar say if he knew she'd done such an appalling thing? If he knew she'd fucked an orc, and liked it? Liked *him*?

And even as that alarming thought studded breathlessly through her skull, her hand reached on its own, grasping at the orc's tunic. Holding him there, from where he'd been about to back away, and she searched those black eyes. Shuttered, distant, almost... afraid.

"Are you all right?" she whispered. "My lord?"

Those eyes seemed to shutter further, a twitch of the cool mockery returning to his mouth. "Foolish woman," he said, with only the slightest waver in his voice. "It should not be you asking this question, in this."

There was a stilted silence, the orc's face twisting in distaste, as though he'd just heard the obligation in his words—but then he took a breath, closed his eyes, opened them.

"Are you well," he said, very quiet. "Did I truly frighten you into accepting this. Did I truly"—his voice fell even lower—"*use* you."

But Rosa only felt a surging rising warmth, strong enough to bring a slow, genuine smile to her lips. "No," she breathed, soft. "I wanted it. I *loved* it, my lord."

The orc's eyes widened, his mouth clenching—and then a clawed finger snapped to her chin, tilting it up, the rest of his claws trailing sharp and menacing against her neck. "Foolish woman," he said again. "No falsehoods."

But Rosa only held those eyes, sinking into the odd, entirely unfathomable comfort of those claws, brushing so gently against her skin. "No," she whispered. "No falsehoods."

Something shifted again in his eyes, but before Rosa could follow it, he'd moved away, standing tall and powerful and breathtaking over her. "Sleep," he said, "and I shall stay."

And even as those words pulled at something, nagged at something, Rosa felt herself nodding, her eyes fluttering closed. She would sleep, he would stay, she would impress him, and be worthy. He would see.

8

When Rosa next awoke, she was lying naked and warm in Lord Kaspar's cot. Alone in the cot, which was odd—Lord Kaspar always slept late, always took up most of the cot, and always snored—and Rosa leisurely stretched and yawned and sat up, blinking about the room—

Until she found herself staring at an orc. *The* orc. *Him.*

The memories swarmed in a flood, the heat surging both to her face and deeper below, and it distantly occurred to her that she was rather sore down there, and quite noticeably wet. Not only that, but her entire body felt sore too—she'd been scratched, she realized, blinking down at the faint red marks on her arms and her chest—and her blonde waves were long and loose, and she was *naked*.

And the orc was openly, shamelessly staring at her. Studying her bare torso, his mouth pursed, his black eyes unreadable.

There was the compulsion, sudden and overpowering, to cover herself, to yank the blanket back up—but Rosa held herself still in the bed, letting him look. Thinking, oddly, of those quiet, intent moments before she'd fallen asleep. *Did I truly frighten you. No falsehoods.*

And whatever madness had overtaken Rosa last night—whatever utter *insanity* had compelled her to fuck an *orc*, all the way, for *research*—it was clearly still here, lingering close and breathless in her throat. Drawing her betraying eyes down the orc's clothed body—he was seated at the little table again, a new book open in front of him—and back up to that watching, waiting face.

"Good morning," she ventured, and she felt her mouth twitch up into a faint, careful smile. "Did you truly sit here and read *all night*?"

The orc gave a curt nod, his eyes still strangely watchful on hers, so Rosa took a breath, tried again. "You really can see well enough to read like that? In the dark?"

There was no nod this time, just more of that waiting, intent gaze, prickling against her skin. Looking almost suspicious, somehow, and Rosa's thoughts darted back to the pile—or rather, the mess—of sources on the lending desk. This was supposed to be research. This *was* research. And the orc could *not* know that, he couldn't even guess at that, not here, not now, not like this...

"Gods above, that sounds useful," she made herself say, with an attempt at another smile. "You must be so productive."

But his face didn't change, and here was the realization, far too late, that apart from the reading, Rosa had no idea whatsoever how this orc spent his time. Or what he liked, or why he'd come here, or even his damned *name*.

"We never did finish our introductions, did we?" she said, as brightly as she could. "What's your name?"

The orc's expression still didn't change, his mouth remaining tight and grim—and far too late there was another flare of comprehension, deep and certain and inexplicably hurtful. The orc didn't *want* to tell her his name. He didn't want to know who she was. And last night—Rosa felt her eyes squeeze shut—last night, he'd done all that for a reason. A *bargain*, upon his terms.

Give me leave to stay here, he'd said. *Tonight, and as many more nights as I should wish.*

Rosa's hands had been fisting into the blanket, and she belatedly pulled it up to her chin, as if it could protect her from this orc's watching, unnerving eyes. And instead of looking at him, she forced her attention up to the window, the grey sky outside it, and *wait*—

"Is it past *midday*?!" she demanded, her voice cracking, her gaze darting to the orc for an answer—and even though he still didn't speak, let alone move, the look on his face spoke clearly for him. Yes, it was past midday, and this should be obvious to anyone who looked at the window—and Rosa should have opened the library *hours* ago, and it was sheer dumb luck that Susan or Southall hadn't yet turned up for some reason or another. Good gods, how could she have been so *stupid*—

She leapt out of bed, without at all thinking, and looked round for her dress—Lord Kaspar usually left it on the floor somewhere—and then she felt her entire body go still, her breath coming out heavy and thick.

She had no dress. The orc had torn her dress, last night, and then used it to clean up his mess. And she didn't have any underclothes either, and she was sore all over, and especially down *there*. And she was standing naked in the middle of the room, and it was cold, and the actual orc she'd actually *fucked*—for a *bargain*—wouldn't even tell her his *name*.

Rosa bit her lip, blinking at the floor, fighting to swallow the inexplicable lump in her throat—when there was the sudden, solid feel of a warm hand closing around her wrist. *His* hand, drawing her toward his seated form on the stool, and then— she yelped—lifting her up easily by the waist, and then sitting her naked body on the table before him, her legs hanging off the side.

Rosa was shivering, blinking at those black eyes, and they didn't leave hers as his big hand reached over for the blanket from the bed, clenching it in his claws. And then twirling it up to settle down around her shoulders, his fingers deftly tying the two corners together, into a makeshift cloak.

"Stay," he said, the single word somehow pressing Rosa's shudders into stillness—and then his hand brushed against her throat, in a sign that could only mean approval. And Rosa felt her heart hammering, her breath catching, as that hand slipped down toward her bare breast. Not heated and sensual, like it had last night, but more... businesslike. Assessing.

And when Rosa blinked downwards, following his hands, it was indeed to the realization that he was—*inspecting* her. His fingers tracing carefully along the shallow scrapes he'd made the night before, his eyes glancing at her face, perhaps looking for signs of pain. But there could be no pain, not with his attention fully upon her again like this, and those warm, careful hands sliding down, and down, and down.

Rosa's cursed nipples had already hardened, and when those hands spread against her thighs, guiding them wide apart, she actually let out a harsh, choked moan, snapping his eyes back up to her face. But he *knew*, in a single critical glance he *knew*, and Rosa felt her cheeks burning, her gaze dropping again, watching him hold her thighs open, even as—she couldn't help another stifled, shameful groan—an astonishing quantity of that thick, viscous orc-seed oozed out from her, and pooled down onto the table below.

The orc's eyes on it looked almost arrested, and there was a sharp huff of breath from his mouth as he firmly, decisively thrust her legs closed again. As though he were—disapproving. Disgusted. Angry.

"It is a marvel," he said abruptly, his voice curt and flat, "that your womb is yet whole, woman. It is luck that this *patron* you have been fucking for your *work*"—his eyes narrowed unpleasantly toward her—"does not wield a small prick, or a gentle one."

What? Wait—he *knew* that? The shame surged through Rosa, from her face all the way downwards, because yes, it was true, damnably so. Behind Lord Kaspar's handsome, scholarly exterior, he *was* very well-endowed, with surprisingly rough tastes, and forceful, decisive demands.

And at first, that heady, deadly combination had seemed to draw upon all Rosa's secret, most shameful longings at once. Being taken firmly in hand, protected, guided, petted, *enjoyed*, by one who was strong and clever and powerful. One who thoroughly deserved one's subservience, and one's devotion, and one's trust.

But then, miserable and astonishingly painful, had come the rapid realization that it hadn't been just Rosa. It had been any number of convenient women, servants and courtesans and married ladies alike—and, of course, now the lovely Lady Scall. And even if Rosa was a particular favourite of Lord Kaspar's, and had been for years, her willing service was only part of a larger transaction. Another *bargain*. One that traded her steady job at this library for Lord Kaspar's unlimited, unfettered use of her body, her brain, her research. For his *war*.

Rosa's knees had drawn away from the orc's suddenly rough-feeling hands, pulling up to her chest, making her already-small form into something tiny and safe. She was doing what had to be done. She would do whatever it took to become a student. She *had* to. And this orc had shown himself all too willing to make similar compromises last night, which meant he could take his stupid sneering superiority, and shove it.

"I would thank you, sir," she said to the floor, her voice thin, "not to pass judgement upon me, when you have no comprehension of my circumstances. And particularly when you yourself made just such a bargain with me, just last night, with *great* enthusiasm!"

There was a faint, unmistakable growl in the orc's throat, snapping Rosa's gaze back toward him—and those eyes on hers were disapproving, contemptuous. "I only made this bargain," he said, his lip curling, "because you did so first. I knew you wished to trade your body to me, so I only turned this to my gain. I knew"—his eyes narrowed, cold and glittering—"that you are a foolish little woman."

The words felt like a slap, and it took Rosa far too long to answer, over the misery battering inside her chest. "*You* were the one who came back and offered it," she countered. "And *you* were the one who kept pushing it, after I refused!"

The orc's mouth was fully scoffing now, showing those sharp white teeth. "You did not refuse," he said coldly. "You dearly wished for this. You *begged* me for this. And when I gave you a half-hour of my play-acting, in return you threw at me your womb, and your priceless library, and mayhap even your *life!*"

His deep voice had risen to nearly a shout, echoing through the small room, and for an instant Rosa could only stare at him, and hug her knees closer to her chest. That wasn't true. He hadn't been play-acting. And she hadn't given him all that. She hadn't...

"You do not know me," he hissed at her, his voice soft again, deadly. "You cannot trust me. What if I had killed you. What if I had brought in my brothers to use you. What if I had thrown open this precious library and *burnt* it."

The fear jolted pure and powerful down Rosa's back, her eyes gaping at the orc's cruel, hateful face. "Don't say such things," she gasped at him, pleaded, before she could stop herself. "You wouldn't. I *know* you wouldn't."

But the orc shook his head, his gaze cold, glittering,

remorseless. "You do not know me," he said again. "But I know *you*, woman. You do not value your library. You do not do good work on its behalf. And you only have this *job* here because you have taught your tiny womb to take this rich man's fat prick!"

The pain felt like a physical thing, roaring to life deep inside Rosa's *soul*, and she could only seem to stare at the orc's face, while her vision began to swim, and the world seemed to tilt all around. *I know you. You do not value your library, you do not do good work, you only have this job because...*

And suddenly, for a horrible, terrible moment, it was like Rosa was back in the Charitable School for Girls again, standing small and shaky before Mr. Sullivan's desk. *Yes, sir. I know, sir. Please be gentle, sir...*

She scrabbled off the desk so fast she nearly fell, and she whirled around to face the orc on wobbly legs, clutching the blanket close over her hunched shoulders. No. No. *Gods* no. She had overcome that, she had used her brains and hard work to move beyond that, and never look back. She was a librarian, a researcher, and someday she would be a real student, a *real* scholar, and none of these awful, self-serving males would ever touch her *again*.

"Very well, orc," she spat, at those glaring black eyes. "If you're such a danger to me and my library, then get the hell out. *Now*."

But the infuriating orc only gazed at her, silent and far too still, until finally his mouth curved up, into a slow, cold, merciless mockery of a smile.

"I will," he said. "But thanks to your foolishness, woman"—he drew in a breath—"you must now come with me."

9

She must now go with him.

For a long, stuttering instant, Rosa could only stare at the orc, while all those grand claims about orcs stampeded through her thoughts. Orcs were violent, wicked, depraved. They lay in wait to thrust themselves upon their unsuspecting victims, to capture and ravish as they pleased...

Except. Except for how this particular orc was still looking at her, his body stiff, his big arms now crossed over his chest. And his harsh face all but dripping with disdain, and disapproval, and—yes, still, regret.

Rosa blinked at that for another endless moment, and then drew in a bracing breath, drew herself tall. "Of course I'm not going *anywhere* with you, orc," she said, her voice wavering. "You've been nothing but rude, and obnoxious, and judgemental, and now you have the temerity to cast full blame upon me for something *you* willingly proposed. So I would prefer"—she drew in more breath—"you to leave this library at once, and never return *again*."

The orc's eyes shuttered, but his body didn't move, and something twitched in his clenched jaw. "It matters naught what you *prefer*," he said flatly. "You shall yet come with me, woman. We leave for the mountain today."

Rosa was struck momentarily speechless, and she gripped the blanket tighter around her, and lifted her chin. "I shall not. I have no interest whatsoever in going *anywhere* with you, especially to a cold, dark, orc-infested *hovel*. And I have many important responsibilities here, and my patron has entrusted me with"—she caught herself, just in time—"with the library's responsible management."

There was an incredulous snort from the orc's mouth, a flare of something Rosa couldn't read in those shuttered eyes. "I should not call your work for this library *responsible*," he said, his voice chilly, menacing. "As for your *patron*, he shall soon find another to serve him in your stead. There is naught about you that another woman cannot easily replace."

Rosa flinched before she could stop it, the misery surging sharp inside. "Well, if I'm truly so useless," she gritted out, "then why will you not go away, and find another woman to kidnap, and leave me be!"

The orc's arms flexed against his chest, and the look in his eyes was pure, bitter loathing. "I cannot leave you be," he growled. "You bear my seed, foolish woman. And thus, should I not now address this, you shall also bear my *son*."

Oh. Oh, *hell*. And the memory of that, the vision of that, was suddenly so strong that Rosa felt faint. *I shall plant your empty womb with my sons,* he'd said, *and fill you until you burst.*

And Rosa had said—*yes.*

Gods, it had been sheer and utter madness, and Rosa stared at the orc with a rapidly rising horror. She bore his seed. And now she would bear his *son*?!

"You don't know that," she said, too quickly, too frantic. "It was only one time. It might be *fine*."

But there was a hard, brittle noise from the orc's throat, another contemptuous curl of his lip. "It shall not be *fine*, foolish woman," he said, clipped. "You have not of late released a seed, and thus, when it soon comes, my seed shall surely gain its end. Orc-seed does not fail, in this. It must not, to keep our kind alive, in these dark days."

Rosa's heart was pounding erratically, her gaze trapped on the orc's face. "So you mean," she breathed, "to—to take me away, to *kidnap* me, and force me to bear your *child*?"

The orc's glittering eyes briefly closed, those arms shifting against his chest. "No," he snapped. "Even if I wished to sire a son upon you, you are far too small a woman to risk this. More likely than not, my son should *kill* you."

Rosa felt her own eyes squeezing shut, the fear racing up her back in furious jolts, and she fought for air, for clarity. She was clever, she was a researcher, no matter what this orc said, surely there was some answer to this, some neat solution...

"There—there are people who help women with such things," she said, the words tumbling out in a rush of startling, sheer relief. "There are herbs. I'll go and deal with it that way."

But there was only another bitter, mocking sound from the orc, and when Rosa blinked at him again, he was shaking his head, slow and deliberate. "These herbs shall accomplish naught, against an orc-son. Orc-sons are far stronger than human babes."

Rosa should have argued that—how did he know, how *could* he know such things—but for some inexplicable reason, she didn't. "Well," she said instead, "there are people who address such quandaries—other ways. With tools, and implements, and such."

She couldn't help another unwilling shudder as she spoke, but she otherwise held herself still, held her eyes on the orc's impassive face. Surely not even a powerful orc-son could survive such a thing—she'd in fact just read multiple accounts of other orc-infested women managing similar predicaments thus—and that look in the orc's eyes confirmed it, distaste and disapproval and perhaps even unease.

"Indeed," he said, his voice very thin. "And even if these fools do not maim you or kill you with these *implements*, you must needs allow my son to grow large enough before you can be sure he will be reached thus. And what shall you tell your *patron*, when your little belly swells? Shall he believe it to be his own? Shall he be pleased with you?"

Rosa betrayed another convulsive wince, because despite his particular intimate preferences, and his vast swathe of conquests, Lord Kaspar was still outwardly a fastidious, proper man. A man who highly valued his scholarly and genteel reputation, and who therefore held a deep dislike of malignant rumour-mongering, and a particular aversion to illegitimate by-blows. And though Rosa knew for a fact that he had at least several of these running about the countryside, she also knew that Lord Kaspar had never once acknowledged them, let alone their unfortunate mothers.

"I—I'll deal with Lord Kaspar," Rosa said, though her voice sounded undeniably faint. "I'll figure something out."

"Shall you?" asked the orc, merciless, inexorable. "And shall your *patron* wish you to keep this job at this library, after this? Shall he wish the world to see the proof of what he does when he is alone with his silly little plaything?"

The words felt like a real physical blow, echoing Rosa's exact thoughts with cruel, devastating force. Because of course this awful orc was right, especially when Lord Kaspar was so close to finally gaining Lady Scall's fortune. If he discovered that Rosa was pregnant, he surely wouldn't hesitate to cast her out entirely, with no financial support, away from her beloved library, *forever*.

Rosa's breath was coming in shallow little gasps, her heart thundering madly in her ribcage, and she took a short, shaky step backwards. What had she done. Gods in heaven, what had she done.

"S-so what, then?" she managed, her voice badly wavering. "What am I to do?"

And why she had the slightest expectation that this horrible orc would provide the slightest assistance, she couldn't fathom—but she was staring at those forbidding black eyes, begging, pleading, needing. He had to do *something*. He *had* to.

There was an instant's stillness, and she could see the orc's throat convulsing, his eyes flicking away from her, to the wall beyond. "I swore, in this," he said, quieter now, "to care for you. So you shall come with me, and my brothers shall mend this for us."

Rosa's heartbeat kept clamouring, her thoughts skittering uselessly through her head. "Your brothers?" her voice echoed. "Other *orcs*?"

"Yes," he snapped back. "I have brothers with gifts of healing, who need no herbs, and no sharp tools. They shall help you."

"*Really*?" Rosa asked, the word coming out high-pitched, incredulous. "They would help me—deal with—one of their own *sons*, in such a way?"

Because in all Rosa's research, the orcs' fierce devotion to their sons had been one of the more credible-seeming claims of the lot. Hinting at the possibility of actual affection on the orcs' part, true paternal care for their own, and why would humans bother to create such an inconvenient falsehood?

"Yes," the orc said, his voice stubborn, his bottom lip jutting out. "They shall do this, if I tell them so."

And gods curse her, but looking at this orc, Rosa again, somehow, believed him. "And how long," she said faintly, "would such an endeavour take?"

"This, I do not know," came the orc's curt reply. "I should hope for only days, but it may be weeks. It hangs upon you, woman, and when your little womb brings forth its seed, to meet mine."

Oh. For some ridiculous reason, Rosa's cheeks heated at the words, and she belatedly dropped her eyes from his face, and fought for rational thought. "But I can't leave the library for weeks," she said helplessly. "Not now. I *can't.*"

"You can," growled the orc. "And you will, woman. It is this, or else your *life*. You cannot truly be so foolish as not to grasp this?!"

And Rosa wasn't, but Lord Kaspar, the war, her one chance to become a student, a scholar, someone worthy, someone who *mattered*—

"Foolish woman," the orc snarled, his face and voice scathing, and he rose to his feet, abruptly enough that the stool clattered sideways to the floor behind him. "I ought never to have touched you thus. Not only do you fail your priceless library, and sell your cheap favours to any who ask, but you wield no sense and no reason! I offer you *life*, and yet you dare to stand here, and refuse to welcome this?!"

There was no answering, no arguing with his tall bellowing form, and in two smooth, loping steps he closed the space between them, looming close and powerful over her. "My son," he hissed, "shall tear you in two, woman. He shall rip you apart, and you shall die screaming and in agony. And as much as I might welcome this fate for one so foolish as you, I have sworn to help you, so now I am bound to this, and to *you!*"

The terror and the revulsion swarmed all at once, choked and desperate and sickening, mashing wildly, mercilessly, against the visions of last night. His body driving into her, his claws so gentle on her neck, she was a fool, he would welcome this fate, he would truly rather she *died*, screaming, in agony—

"No," Rosa breathed. "I *will* die, you prick, before I'll be bound to *anything* with a cruel, violent, self-absorbed beast like you. You may consider your obligation complete, and our unfortunate acquaintance permanently ended. *Farewell.*"

10

Rosa rushed through the library, her face smarting and hot, her steps staggering and sideways. She bore an orc's seed, she might bear his son, and he wanted her to *die*.

She grasped at the front door, yanking hard upon it—but it only rattled in place, and remained firmly shut. And when her trembly fingers went to tug at the familiar latch, it was to the chilling, heart-stopping realization that it was—*changed*. The thick steel bent sharply sideways against the door, ensuring that no one could get in, or out.

Rosa stared at it for a long, pounding moment—the orc had done this, he'd *blocked* her *in*—and then backed her body away, shaking her head. No. No. There had to be another way, she would go out the back instead, and if he'd blocked that too she'd climb out a damned window—

But as she whirled around, her bare foot slipped on something—something flat and smooth, that hadn't been there before. And when her badly trembling fingers reached down to grasp for it, flipping it over, there was another jolt of chaos, surging up her spine.

It was a letter. From Lord Kaspar. To *her*.

Lord Kaspar had never before written Rosa in his life—gentlemen did not write letters to their library staff—but there was no mistaking the neat angled script, or the distinctive red wax seal, or the fact that Rosa had found it here, straight under the letter-slot. And after another instant's staring at it, she snatched it up, broke the seal, and snapped the letter open.

Dearest Rosa, it said. *You shall be gladdened to hear that my work on the project we discussed has reached the ear of the Citadel in Wolfen. My father and I shall soon present my findings to the Council itself, which has promised considerable resources toward fulfilling our plans, if they are deemed satisfactory.*

I am sure it does not need to be said that this project is now of prime importance, risking not only my reputation on a grand scale, but the resources and plans of the entire realm—many of which have already been set into motion, in preparation for my forthcoming revelations.

I shall expect your best work on my behalf, and I grant you my permission to take whatever measures are required to accomplish this, even should they result in the temporary closure of the library.

I shall return on the first day of the month to receive your report; if it meets my standards, I shall compensate you accordingly, as promised. And should your work truly impress, I shall also consider significant additional rewards, beyond any yet discussed, which are sure to be highly pleasing to you.

However, if you disappoint me, I shall be obliged to take drastic measures—including your immediate departure from the library without a reference, and the appointment of a replacement better suited to my needs.

Do not fail me.

The letter was signed not only with Lord Kaspar's familiar scrawl, but again with his seal as well. Suggesting the deep, dire importance of this appalling missive, and Rosa's frantic eyes read it again, and again. Until her hands holding it began shaking so badly that she could no longer follow the lines, and she let her hand fall back to her side, her eyes staring at nothing.

The Citadel. The Council. Considerable resources, prime importance. *Your best work. Do not disappoint me.*

And then, that teasing, tantalizing promise of significant additional rewards, weighed against that clear, shocking threat. A threat that Lord Kaspar had previously hinted at, of course—in truth, it had always underpinned their entire acquaintance—but he had never before spelled it out so boldly, or so cruelly. *Your immediate departure, without a reference.*

And that, Rosa knew, would destroy all her scholarly aspirations. It would ruin any chance she might have of finding work at another library or university. It would mean the sure, certain end of all she had ever cared for, or longed for. The end of her *life*.

But then, hanging so precariously on the opposite side, was that promise. *I shall compensate you. I shall consider significant additional rewards, beyond any yet discussed. Sure to be highly pleasing to you.*

And what the hell did *that* mean? Financial, no question, but highly pleasing as well? Hinting at something more intimate, more personal, and Rosa's thoughts tumbled backwards, to a day months before, when she and Lord Kaspar had spent an entire afternoon researching and discussing one of his projects, followed by a full evening in bed. And afterwards, holding her sated body close against his, he'd said, *You know, Rosa, were my situation different, I should rather enjoy having you for a wife. We should make clever children, don't you think?*

Rosa squeezed her eyes shut, but the vision only raced louder, faster through her brain. Lord Kaspar impressing the Council would surely come with money, favour, acclaim. And if the resulting war against the orcs was successful, even more so.

It would gain Lord Kaspar the kind of standing he'd always longed after, without any need whatsoever for Lady Scall.

Rosa's numb body finally, jerkily moved for the familiar lending desk, which—she stared blankly down toward it—had somehow been tidied again, all her orc resources stacked just as they had been. But she couldn't even find space to think about that at the moment, and she shoved the letter into the book on top of the pile, and put her aching head into her hands.

This was her chance. This was the *dream*. And all she had to do, to save her future, was to discover an impossible motive for an impossible war, in a useless pile of rubbish sources. Before Lord Kaspar returned, in *three fucking weeks*.

There was no way. None. Except...

Rosa twitched all over at the faint, purposeful noise from the back of the library—and then again at the distinctive sound of the wood floor creaking. And when she blinked up, through bleary, watery eyes, there was the orc. Striding straight toward her with purpose on his face, and a book still clenched in his clawed hand.

Rosa's body seemed to back away on its own, pressing flat against the wall behind her, while her breaths came shallow and thin, her hands clutching at the blanket still tied around her shoulders. This awful orc still had her trapped. He still wanted her *dead*. And maybe he'd realized just how easy that would be, how it could perhaps solve all his problems at once...

And truly, Rosa thought dully, maybe that would be the easiest solution for her, too. A quick, painless death, rather than a thoroughly ruined future, or an excruciating demise while birthing this bastard's *son*...

The orc's gaze swept up and down Rosa's trembling form, and he came to a halt before the lending desk. His big body gone unnervingly still all over, but for his fingers flexing against his book.

"Peace, woman," he said flatly, his mouth pursing. "I shall not harm you."

But even the sound of his voice was making Rosa flinch, and she backed closer against the wall behind her. "Y-you've locked me in," her quavery voice choked. "Y-you want to kidnap me. You said you want me to *die*."

The orc's face turned away, something jumping in his sharp jaw. "I do not wish you to die," he said, almost too quiet to be heard. "I ought not to have spoken thus."

Rosa blinked, and felt her eyes drop to the book in his hand, to his claws against it. "Well, you did," she replied, just as quiet. "That, and much else."

She could hear the orc's slow exhale, could see it in the slight movement of his tunic. "Ach," he said, oddly, and a furtive glance at his face showed him still not looking at her, and instead frowning down at the desk between them. "I indeed hold great anger this day at what I have done. But I ought not to have unleashed this upon you."

Rosa could only seem to stand there against the wall, clutching at her blanket, and the orc sighed again, and gave a jerky shake of his head. "I ought never to have made you this bargain last night," his voice said, harder now. "I did not understand the strength of what came upon me. I have heard my brothers speak of this, but I thought myself too wise to be swayed thus. I was foolish, and now we both must suffer."

Rosa's gaze had caught on his, searching those regretful black eyes. The words felt genuine, his voice felt genuine, but—

"You mean, you've never done that before?" she heard her wavering voice say, before she could clamp her fool mouth shut. "Truly?"

Because—her thoughts shifted back—he'd been so damn *good* at it, so instinctive, so assured. Even if it had been play-acting, he'd known just what to say, just where to touch, and even the memory of his sharp, gentle claws against her neck was sending a strange, hurtling shudder up her spine—

His mouth thinned, and he again looked away, his throat bobbing under his grey skin. "I have not," he said, "with a woman."

Rosa was briefly, momentarily stunned—that couldn't mean what it sounded like, could it?—but after another moment's searching his tense, taut profile, she was abruptly, inexplicably sure of it. This orc hadn't had a woman before. But he had had others, clearly other orcs, and likely easy and often. And that could not, *not*, be a flare of jealousy, curdling in Rosa's gut—

But suddenly it was entirely forgotten, trampled deep below, because that *was* a shocking new truth, wasn't it? And one that hadn't even been hinted at, in all Rosa's sources. Males taking other males, blatantly defying the firmly held laws of every province in the realm. And while that alone probably wasn't enough to start a war, it was—*something*.

Rosa's head was pounding, following the erratic pace of her heartbeat, and she gulped for breath, for a nonchalance she didn't at all feel. Maybe—maybe she could do this after all. If she could just focus. Plan. *Think*.

"Well, why *did* you offer that bargain to me, then?" she made herself ask. "If you knew it to be so risky, and you don't even *like* me?"

Her voice had come out sounding damnably plaintive, enough to draw the orc's frowning eyes back to her face, and away again. "I was only—curious," he said, clipped. "I wished to know the truth of this. I seek to study these things, and learn. I seek to help my brothers."

Oh. And in the chaotic mess that was currently drowning Rosa's brain, the most powerful wave of all was just more deep, dragging misery. He truly hadn't wanted her. He truly didn't like her. And perhaps it hadn't even been a bargain, after all, but something just as cold, just as calculating. Academic curiosity. Research.

And Rosa herself had done it for the exact same damned reason, hadn't she? So why the hell did she care, why did it matter, she needed to focus on her own research, her own plans. *Do not fail me...*

"I seek to help you also," the orc said, quieter now. "I do not wish you to die, for my folly."

Rosa could barely seem to breathe, blinking down at the lending desk, and there was another sigh from the orc, heavy and resigned. "No harm shall befall you in my care. Once this is done, I shall return you safely to this library, and this man."

This man. Lord Kaspar. And Rosa's breath only seemed to come shallower, her hands clammy, her eyes darting reflexively to her pile of sources, and that horrible letter hidden inside. *Take whatever measures are required. Even should they result in the temporary closure of the library... I shall return on the first day of the month...*

She had three weeks. And that could be—should be— enough time to learn what she needed to learn, while also dealing with her... predicament. It made perfect sense, it was the only logical solution, but...

"But," Rosa heard herself say, her voice strange, stilted. "I can't—*trust* you. You don't like me, you've been rude and cruel to me, you fully admit to using me for your own ends, and I don't even know your *name.*"

And gods, why was she harping on this, why wasn't she just saying, *yes, take me away,* doing whatever had to be done—but here was why. In the thundering, breath-catching truth of this huge deadly obnoxious orc, striding around the desk toward her, and sliding his hand against the back of her neck. Sinking those claws into her hair, tilting her face up to look at him.

Rosa's eyes were trapped to his black hooded ones, and her whole body felt suddenly taut, warm, waiting. Desperately needing this, somehow, this awful orc looking into her, seeing deep into her weak, broken, terrified *soul*.

"I am John of Clan Ka-esh," he said, quiet, the words sparking light and colour into his mesmerizing eyes. "And you, my little pet, shall come with me today to my mountain. Will you not?"

Rosa could only blink, and stare, while the words and the warmth and the hunger seemed to wash away all the screeching chaos at once. While the orc leaned slowly, purposefully closer, oh gods oh *hell*, and brushed a soft, gentle kiss to her parted, gasping lips.

"You will come with me, little rose," he said again, his voice all silken rising heat. "Yes?"

And curse her, curse Lord Kaspar, curse the entire damned *world*—because Rosa could only seem to swallow, and nod, and breathe. She would face this. She would be worthy. She *would*.

"Yes," she whispered. "I will."

11

His name was John.

Rosa's severely addled brain could only seem to marvel at that, again and again, even as the orc—his name was *John*—abruptly backed away from her, his eyes once more hidden, shuttered, distant. *John.*

And as the orc—*John*—began moving around the library, swift and silent and purposeful, Rosa only blinked, and stared. Watching with a strange, stilted bemusement as he piled up a precarious stack of books, plucked from various locations all over the stacks—and then beckoned Rosa over, with an imperious little flick of his fingers, as he carefully placed the stack upon the nearest table.

"Give me the blanket," he said, voice flat. "I have not brought a pack to haul these with, and there is naught else here that shall suffice to keep them safe on our journey."

Wait, what? Rosa's churning thoughts finally caught on this—he was planning to take away these books, to *Orc Mountain*?!—and she gave a wild, rather demented shake of her head. "You can't take books away from the library," she managed. "Unless you're a student at the university."

John fixed her with a hard, disapproving glare, at utter odds with the quiet, thrilling look in his eyes not a quarter-hour past. "But you come away with me, do you not?" he demanded. "Are not *you* able to take books from this library, so long as you return them safe?"

"No," Rosa shot back, more bitterly than she meant. "I can't. I'm not a student."

John only kept glaring at her, lips pursed, and then back at his pile of books. They appeared to be from an astonishing variety of subjects, anatomy and botany and history and geology and medicine, and his hand carefully came up, and traced down their spines. With almost the same reverence he'd used on Rosa's neck earlier, the very *thought* of it powerful enough to send a hard shiver down her form—a movement which, predictably, snapped his narrow, assessing gaze back to hers.

"I wish for these books, little woman," he said, his voice pitched lower, softer—and his eyes seemed to soften too, his thick lashes heavy against his cheek. "I swear to keep them safe, and to bring them back with us when I return you here. Will you not grant this small favour to me?"

"I *can't*," Rosa choked out. "I'm not a book thief. *Never.*"

John came a step closer, his hand reaching to slide familiar and wonderful against her neck. "But I wish for this for your joy also, little rose," he murmured, his voice all sweet melting pleasure. "Do you truly wish to be held in my mountain for days, or mayhap weeks, with naught of worth in your own tongue to read?"

The thought was thoroughly chilling, as this devious bastard well knew, his head tilting—and suddenly the warmth of his touch vanished, and he was striding smoothly toward the lending desk. Grasping out something from beneath it—*The Lady Bright*—before coming back, and placing it on top of his pile.

"You wish to read this tale, do you not?" he said, again bringing his hand up, curling close against her throat. "I know this shall please you, my little pet."

Rosa's eyes were trapped on the book, sitting so innocuous and yet so tempting on his pile, and she shuddered at the feel of those equally tempting claws, tracing light and gentle on her skin. "Come, let us take these," he whispered. "Should you grant this to me, mayhap I shall please you again, after. As I did last night."

The words sent a sharp, desperate thrill of heat to Rosa's groin—he would truly consider doing that *again*?!—and before she could stop herself, she felt her breath catch, her head giving a shaky, jerky nod. Saying—*yes*.

There was a flare of triumph in John's black eyes, an almost mocking noise in his throat—and before Rosa could digest that, react to that, his hand had already reached for her blanket, tugging out the knot he'd made, and dragging it off her shoulders. Leaving her standing there entirely naked before him, shivering with the sudden chill, while he completely ignored her, and wrapped up the pile of books into a neat, self-contained package.

"*Frábœrt*," he said, in the foreign-sounding black-tongue, and as Rosa watched, he yanked out the drawstring from his trousers, and tied it tightly around the package. Only then did he look back toward her, his eyes narrow and cold, lacking even the slightest trace of interest, let alone desire.

It was enough to finally set Rosa's brain churning again, the shame rising hard and hot to her cheeks. He'd been—play-acting, he'd called it. Pretending, just like before. Manipulating. Blatantly using her to get his way.

And Rosa could pretend too, she sternly told herself, as she bit against the inside of her cheek, and held her naked body straight and still. She was going along with this for a reason.

She was watching. Researching. She was going to use her three weeks to get Lord Kaspar his war, and save her future, and damn this awful orc to hell.

The awful orc—*John*—was now studying Rosa with his typical disapproval, his dispassionate eyes flicking up and down her shivering form. "Have you no more clothes, woman?"

She couldn't help a snort, earning in return an odd little flinch from John's mouth. "No," she snapped at him. "I don't. You ruined my dress, remember?"

John flinched again, as though even the memory of him doing such a thing was a deeply unpleasant one. "Do you not yet have a coat, or a cloak? It has rained here for nigh unto two days, and you have little meat upon your tiny bones to keep you warm."

Rosa tried for a dismissive shrug, but didn't quite accomplish it, what with still standing here naked and red-faced—and apparently too small and bony—in front of a huge, fully clothed, disapproving orc. "Good coats are expensive," she said finally. "I've been saving up, for a wool one."

She left out the crucial fact that Lord Kaspar was only willing to pay for frocks, the flimsier and frillier the better—but John seemed to follow that point regardless, his face gone even more disapproving than before. And in a jerky, unexpected movement, he reached for his own tunic, and yanked it off over his head. Leaving him broad and bare-chested, his plentiful scars looking even more frightful in the bright daylight, as he thrust his tunic toward her.

Rosa blinked down at it, and then up at his flat, forbidding eyes. Speaking all too clearly, without him speaking at all, and she *was* cold, and highly uncomfortable, so she finally nodded, and pulled on the tunic over her head.

It was huge, halfway down to her knees, and the laced neckline that had been entirely suitable for him plunged deep between her breasts, risking accidental exposure at any moment. But it was warm, and well made, and smelled of musk and sweetness, and Rosa drew it close, and flashed him a faint, reluctant smile. "Thanks."

He only looked away, his hand reaching for his carefully wrapped package of books. "Is there aught else that must be done here, before you come?"

Right, of course, and Rosa spent the next half-hour rushing about the library, tidying the back bedroom, searching for her ruined dress—it turned out that John had tossed it down the adjoining latrine—and writing cryptic letters to leave for Southall and Lord Kaspar. And finally, drawing up a large new "temporarily closed" sign for the door.

"And you'll fix the door?" she asked John, once she'd hung the sign—and he accordingly strode over and snapped the twisted metal back to its previous place, as easy as if it had been made of clay. And then he stood there staring at her, tall and impatient and imperious, looking for all the world as though Rosa had kept him waiting for weeks.

"I must needs carry you," he said, with a disapproving glance down toward Rosa's light, scuffed leather boots. "These silly shoes are worth naught, in this rain."

He himself was wearing a pair of large, sturdy-looking black boots, which Rosa couldn't even recall seeing before—where *did* orcs acquire footwear, anyway?—and she belatedly glanced back at his face. "Carry me?" she echoed. "All the way to your *mountain*?"

It had to be a full day's journey away, at minimum, over rough and dense terrain, but the expression on John's face didn't change in the slightest. "Yes. Now come."

There seemed to be nothing else for it, so Rosa moved tentatively toward him—and then found herself whisked bodily up with strong, sure arms, and pressed close against his bare chest. It was broad and warm, slowly expanding and collapsing with his breath, and for a brief, hurtling instant she wanted to touch it, stroke it, turn her face and taste it with her tongue—

John was looking down at her, his eyes entirely unreadable, though she could see the hard swallow of his throat. "You shall be still," he said, "and do not seek to speak, or distract me. I must stay aware, to ensure we are not seen."

With that, he shifted her to the side, supporting her entire weight with one damned *arm*, and nudged the door open, just a crack. Flattening himself, and her, close beside it, as he tilted his head toward the opening and inhaled, long and deep.

He was *smelling*, Rosa realized, clearly for the presence of other humans, even through this still-driving rain—and she watched in curious, bated silence as he did it again and again. His eyes distant, his body coiled and tense against her, his mouth frowning in concentration—

And in a juddering jolt of movement, he dodged outside, into the pouring rain. Shutting the library door decisively behind them, the latch clicking into place—and then he sprinted to a run. Tearing with astonishing speed away from the university grounds, across the road, into the open field beyond, his strides long and powerful, his clawed hands gripping almost painfully against Rosa's already-wet skin.

The forest was approaching, rushing up toward them—and Rosa couldn't help a shuddering twitch as they surged straight into the thick line of trees. But not into the close, constricting scrape of branches and leaves, like she'd perhaps expected—but instead only into hushed whispering darkness, tall tree-trunks flashing by as John dashed around and through and between, following some invisible, impossible path.

It was the strangest feeling, being barrelled through the forest in the strong, safe arms of a furiously sprinting orc—and even more so when those big arms shifted her more upright, spreading her legs so she was straddling his hip. Holding her the way a mother would hold a child, almost, so that her body was pressed up close against him, his arm circled tight beneath her arse.

He hadn't once looked at her in this, or even slightly broken stride, but Rosa could feel how this position would be easier, how her weight was spread more evenly against him. And how—she squirmed a little, and then, in a burst of daring, tightly wrapped her legs around his waist—she could make it even easier, working with his big body, rather than against it.

The hand against her arse lightly squeezed, almost as if in approval, and Rosa felt flushed all over as she leaned in closer, and inhaled the musky scent of his bare chest. It was slick and glistening now, drenched with both rain and sweat, his dark grey nipples pebbled, his muscles standing out stark beneath his scars. There were also tendrils of wet black hair stuck against it, coming out long and loose from his braid—and even worse, his hip was grinding unmercifully against Rosa's groin, every stride of his leg a torturous rhythmic stroke just *there*. And she realized, with a sputtering chagrin, that her tunic had worked its way upwards, so that her open, swollen bare heat was pressed directly against that glorious solid strength—

John stopped running so abruptly that the world seemed to stutter, and before Rosa quite knew what had happened, he'd deposited her down beneath a large tree, and backed swiftly away. His eyes distant, hooded as he gazed at her, and she blinked dazedly back, grasping at the tree for balance, trying to find purchase on her shaky legs.

"I must eat," he said, voice hard, as he thrust the wrapped package of books into her hands. "Stay here. And keep these dry."

Rosa nodded, clutching the books to her chest, while her eyes darted greedily up and down his drenched, bare-chested form. And then finding—her breath stilled—an undeniable, impossibly thick bulge, jutting out strong and hungry against the front of his trousers.

Gods. Rosa's betraying tongue had come out to lick her lips, and in reply there was a quiet, strangled noise from deep in John's throat—but without another word, he whirled away, and took off into the trees.

Rosa watched him go, her eyes lingering on his broad bare back, the hard curve of his arse—and then she sagged against the damp tree trunk behind her, and clutched the books to her chest, so tightly it hurt.

This was supposed to be research. This was supposed to get Lord Kaspar his war, and spare Rosa from an otherwise hellish fate. And she had to keep her wits about her, and pay attention, rather than being constantly befuddled by this alarming, appalling orc.

But the situation was not helped by John's inevitable return, perhaps a quarter-hour later. Now complete with a generous splatter of fresh blood across his glistening bare chest, and—Rosa nearly choked—also dripping red from the claws of his right hand, and from the corner of his mouth.

Gods, she was losing her *mind*, and Rosa squeezed her eyes shut, and fought to fill her brain with grisly images of whatever poor helpless animal he'd just devoured. "Better?" she managed. "Nice snack?"

His tongue darted out, long and black and sinuous, to lick the blood on his mouth, and curse her but Rosa nearly groaned aloud, her eyes arrested on the sight. While John's head tilted, his wet braid falling over his shoulder, as he raised his reddened claws to his mouth, and—Rosa nearly groaned again—slowly licked them off, one by one.

"Yes," he said, once he'd finished, in answer to her question. "I should have brought you a taste, but I know you humans only scoff at good fresh meat."

He was frowning at her again, as though this fact were some personal failing on her part, and then strode over toward her. Looming far too close, tall and bloody and breathtakingly powerful, as one hand grasped for the package of books she'd still been holding, and his other hand came to tug downwards at the too-low neck of her damp tunic.

Rosa froze all over, perhaps expecting him to expose her, or rip the tunic, the way he'd done with her dress—but he was only frowning, first at her collarbone, and then lower, to her sternum. "Yet," he said, almost more to himself than her, "you must hunger, woman. You weigh little more than a youngling, and your tiny bones ought not to be seen thus."

He again spoke with sharp disapproval, as if Rosa bore full responsibility for affronting his eyes in such a way—this, when he was literally still dripping with *blood*—and she belatedly yanked the tunic back together, hiding the objectionable sight of her bones from his critical gaze.

"Well, excuse me for offending your delicate sensibilities, orc," she snapped at him. "Maybe next time you can actually bring me some meat to eat, and you won't have to be quite so repulsed at the sight of me."

The orc's eyes flicked up to hers, something odd shifting within them, and he shook his head, whipping more loose black hair out of his straggling braid. "I am not *repulsed*," he said, his tongue sounding careful on the word. "I only do not follow this. Why does this rich man not feed you, as he should? Does he *wish* to keep his pet small and weak?"

Rosa had already opened her mouth, about to point out that feeding her wasn't Lord Kaspar's responsibility in the least—and more importantly, she was *not* Lord Kaspar's *pet*—but then she pressed her lips together, while the memories paraded behind her eyes. Her salary at the library was nominal, meant to be a small honorarium for an already-wealthy student employee, and Lord Kaspar had claimed an utter inability to order an increase to it, lest he be accused of favouritism amongst his lesser colleagues. And while he had on occasion given Rosa coin, when she'd been particularly desperate, it had always been grudging, annoyed, reluctant.

I've already gone above and beyond to give you this post, haven't I? he'd said once. *With my income being what it is, I cannot afford to have another mistress hanging on my purse-strings. You're better than that, Rosa darling. Aren't you?*

And while that mention of *another* mistress had been quite spectacularly lowering, at the same time, it had also placed Rosa in a different place, a different sphere, than the rest. Not simply another interchangeable pretty face paid for pleasure—but someone important, someone clever, someone worthy. *I should rather enjoy having you for a wife...*

"Lord Kaspar has—other priorities," Rosa said, belatedly, the words feeling thick in her mouth. "And principles, about such things."

The noise from John's throat was harsh and mocking, softened only by the sudden, warm touch of his hand against Rosa's neck. "This man is cheap," he said flatly, "and a fool. He should be far better pleased by a strong, warm, well-tended pet than one who is weak and hungry and cold. It is no wonder your work on his library's behalf has been so foolish."

Rosa's mouth opened again, about to attempt some kind of well-justified protest against the entirety of these absurd statements—but John's hand had slid up over her mouth, his claws pressing firm but gentle against her parted lips. "It shall be nightfall before we reach the mountain. You must eat."

Rosa managed a shrug—they'd packed no food, and in the still-drizzling rain there was no way to make a fire. And she wasn't about to eat raw meat—she wasn't that far gone, yet—and it was too early in the year for fruit or berries, so what the hell else was she supposed to do?

The orc almost seemed to follow her thoughts, his gaze

briefly casting over the wet forest around them, before settling back on hers again. And this time those eyes were flinty, determined, decisive, his mouth twitching with a clear, tight distaste.

"Very well," he said, the words a snap from his lips. "You shall kneel, woman. And then, you must suck your fill from my prick."

12

For what felt like the dozenth time since they'd met, Rosa was struck entirely speechless by this appalling, unfathomable orc.

"I will *what*?" she finally demanded, against those fingers, still held warm and close and fragrant against her lips. "Get down and suck you off? *Here*?! Also"—she glared at him, while the memory caught and flared—"don't you recall, just yesterday, how you mocked me for offering such a thing, and claimed to be too good for my weak little mouth?"

John's lip curled, showing a hint of a still-bloody white fang. "I claimed naught, and this is not *sucking me off*," he said, forming the words with visible care, and also deep disapproval. "This is only to sustain you. I shall not bring you to my mountain cold, with an empty belly, and muddled wits. You are liable to faint in fear, or catch a deathly chill, and thus break my vow to care for you, and earn me the scorn of all my brothers."

Rosa followed that with effort—clearly her brain *was* rather muddled, at the moment—and drew in a breath. "Why," she managed, "would your brothers scorn you? Don't you orcs steal away helpless women all the time? Surely there's plenty of fainting and chills and hysterics involved in that?"

John snorted, his fingers clenching slightly against Rosa's lips. "You ought not to heed all you read in these fool books," he snapped. "We orcs have not stolen any women for many, many moons. And we must well tend to those we have, to keep them safe and content, and gain their strength and fealty for our own. This, our wise captain has taught us."

Their captain. The orcs' current captain was named Grimarr, Rosa knew from her reading, and he was supposedly a coarse, vicious, cunning beast, who prior to the peace agreement was rumoured to have kidnapped and imprisoned an actual titled *lady*—but that highly horrifying thought was snatched away entirely, as John's sharp, tantalizing claws trailed downwards, curving against the damp skin of Rosa's neck.

"Kneel, woman," he said, softer, his eyes fluttering. "Drink my good seed."

But he was doing it again, his sweet-talking sweet-touching manipulating thing, and they were out in the open, the ground was cold and soaking wet, Rosa was *not* giving this damned orc *anything*—

"Nice try, orc," she said, her voice only slightly wavering. "But I'm afraid that sucking you off in a dripping-wet forest is *very* low on my list of priorities, at the moment."

John gazed at her for an instant too long, his eyes shuttered—but then he came a step closer, that warm hand spreading wider against her neck. "Do not play the fool with me, my silly little pet," he said, tilting her chin up with his sharp thumb. "Orc-seed is sweet and rich, as good as any meat. It is a gift, to weak frail women such as you."

Rosa swallowed hard against that claw, and gave a furtive shake of her head. "I refuse to countenance anything of the sort," she choked out. "It's utterly *ridiculous*."

"It is not *ridiculous*," John replied, those eyes narrowing on hers. "It is a truth known among orcs since the earliest tales. Not only shall our good seed fill women with our sons, but it also grows them fat and strong. It makes them into hearty, worthy mates, whole and hale enough to bear our sons."

Wait. He truly *believed* that, Rosa realized, blinking at his stubborn black eyes. And her own eyes unwillingly flicked down toward the package of books, which he still held carefully in his other hand, and this awful orc surely wasn't *this* stupid, was he?

"Hold these," he said, thrusting the books toward her—and then, without warning, without hesitation, his hands snapped to the front of his trousers, and yanked out his already-hard orc-prick.

Gods. It was long and thick and straight, jutting out from the mass of coarse dark hair beneath it. And in the brighter light Rosa could see every vein and ridge, and oddly enough, more faded, unmistakable scars, laddered up the length of him, even on the smooth, rounded head.

Rosa shot him a furtive, uneasy glance, but John only stared straight back, and then slowly, deliberately, curved his big hand familiar and easy around the base of it. And then slid up, with agonizing purpose, squeezing out a thick bead of white from that dark, glistening slit.

Fuck. Rosa could only seem to stare, dumbstruck, as he did it again, almost as if mocking her, taunting her, with such an audacious sight. And it was almost *working*, because Rosa's tongue had licked at her dry lips, the heat surging hot and powerful to her groin.

John didn't miss that, of course he didn't, and there was a hoarse, husky noise from his throat as his hand slid up again, even slower this time. "See?" he murmured. "This shall please you, pet."

Rosa kept staring, not breathing, as this shameless orc moved his other hand up to that deep slit, catching the bead of white just as it fell, pooling thick and viscous onto his clawed finger. And *then*, oh hell, he brought that finger up, and spread that thick whiteness, messy and slick, against Rosa's lips.

There was a jolting instant's shock—an orc had just wiped his *leavings* on her *mouth*?! But then it was too late, the trap set and sprung, because Rosa's traitorous tongue had slipped out, and *tasted* it.

The moan of pleasure from her throat was reflexive, guttural, utterly humiliating, and so was the way her tongue darted back out, licking desperately for the rest. Because gods, he tasted impossibly, appallingly good, almost like the sweet honey she had sneaked once at school, and had never, ever forgotten since—

Suddenly she was ravenous, her long-empty stomach audibly growling, and in return John actually laughed out loud, openly, perhaps for the very first time in their acquaintance. And though Rosa knew it was at her expense, she was brutally, bizarrely caught in the sight of it, the sound of it, deep and rich and rolling, his eyes crinkling, his lips curving up to show all those sharp teeth—

"Foolish little woman," his voice said, still silken and warm with his laughter. "Now kneel, and suck me."

He even reached for the books again as he spoke, plucking them out of Rosa's grip with a single flick of his claw, and bringing his other hand heavy to her head. "Now," he said, "before I think better of granting you such a gift."

Rosa's stomach was still grumbling, still flooding her with humiliation, but that last threat had done its work, because her trembling knees had fallen to the earth, seemingly on their own. And that huge, scarred, dripping hardness was *here*, directly in front of her face, and for a breathless instant there was a distant twinge of sanity, of rationality, what was she thinking, this was truly, breathtakingly *outrageous*—

But then John leaned forward, and his clawed hand nudged

that thick, slick cockhead between Rosa's panting, parted lips. Spreading them apart around him as he gently, inexorably bore down, more and more, as that glorious sweet taste charged through Rosa's thoughts, her consciousness, her very *self*—

She let out another dragging, wretched moan, earning another chuckle from above, low and succulent and mocking. And he was such an utter bastard, a lying manipulative *beast*—but there was scarcely room to follow that, to face that, when one was frantically and noisily sucking on a huge, liberally leaking, utterly delectable orc-prick.

He wasn't even thrusting, or moving, just standing there silent and scornful, without so much as a gasp. As though being publicly sucked off by a desperately ravenous woman was a thoroughly unremarkable occurrence—and Rosa's swift, shameful glance upwards proved it, his black eyes on hers cool, watchful, distant.

And maybe it was the fact that her stomach wasn't quite so hungry, now, her eager throat having already swallowed a considerable quantity of that thick sweetness—or maybe it was that cruel comment he'd made about her weak mouth, or even the sudden vision of the night before, of all his careful distance wrenched away, showing the truth hidden beneath. But whatever it was, Rosa was swarmed with a reckless, raging need to show him, to impress him, she was damn good at this, and this bastard was damn well going to admit it—

So she drew back slightly, sliding up the full length of him, learning him, exploring him. Delving and flicking her tongue all over the head of him, deep into that luscious slit, almost as if to drink him from the inside out—and then, after a thick, bracing breath through her nose, she sucked him deep again, as far as she could go, pressing him firm and powerful against her throat.

There had been just the faintest flutter of those eyelids, his face otherwise still distant and composed, so Rosa did it again, harder this time. Sliding up the length of him, licking and lavishing that smooth slick head, and then sucking him as deep as she could, her throat working and convulsing around him. She couldn't quite take him all the way, but circumstances had lain waste to her gag reflex years ago, and it was a very near thing, his coarse black hairs tickling at her nose—

There was a sound from John that might have been a gasp, even as his gaze remained remote, unmoved. So Rosa held her blinking eyes to his, daring him to ignore this, pleading with him not to ignore this—and then braced herself, and took him even deeper. Her throat flaring and twitching and silently shouting, jammed full of a huge invading orc-prick, while her fluttering hands came up and grasped for him, one to his warm hip, one to those heavy bollocks below...

That earned a hiss, a hollowing of his chest—and suddenly Rosa was driving her mouth onto him, with all the strength she could muster. Taking him urgent and powerful, sinking up and down his full length, her tongue twisting, her lips stretched and slurping, her throat screaming as she slammed his unrelenting heft against it again and again, and gods she needed this, she craved this more than *life*—

John's eyes still hadn't changed, not suggesting even the faintest interest in her efforts whatsoever, but that—*that*—was the unmistakable, thrilling feeling of his big hand, coming to rest against her head. His fingers skittering just slightly, those claws carding into her hair—

It was everything, *everything*, spurring Rosa on harder, faster, deeper. Her own hands trembling and clutching against him, her face burning, her eyes streaming water, that brutal demanding prick pummelling her throat again and again and again...

There was another gasp from his mouth, quiet, hushed, unmistakable. And those distant, dispassionate eyes finally flared, *finally* betraying him, and those powerful hips snapped forward, digging him so deep that she very nearly choked—

And then he poured out into her, flooding her, drowning her. Swarming her mouth and her throat with surge after surge of thick melting honey, so much that it blocked her throat, filled her cheeks, leaving her coughing and fighting to swallow—until he finally yanked himself out from between her lips, and the seed immediately surged after him, spewing out thick and humiliating and obscene from Rosa's gasping, swollen, reddened mouth.

She could feel his eyes watching, waiting until it subsided into a steady dribble, pooling messy and slick off her chin. And curse her, but even now her aching, shivery tongue had slipped out, licking at what she could, and swallowing it down her distinctly sore throat.

But John hadn't laughed, or mocked her, and when Rosa risked a furtive, shameful glance up toward him, his eyes weren't angry or regretful, like last time. Just watchful, intent, and that big hand in her hair slowly tilted her face up, showing him the utter mess he'd made of her, her chin still dripping with his thick sticky white.

"Foolish little pet," his voice said, so low she could barely hear it. "Ach, you *were* hungry."

Rosa couldn't seem to speak, only blinking up at him through oddly wet eyelashes, her heartbeat echoing erratic through her ears. And John's head tilted, those claws lightly scraping against her scalp, and he brought his other hand up, tracing the back of his finger into the mess on Rosa's chin.

"Here," he murmured, as he brushed that finger up against her parted lips—and there was only doing it, obeying it, licking and lapping at his skin. And again, when he went for more, and then again. Desperately drinking up whatever he would give her, as much as he would give her, until her face was mostly clean again, and she was sucking the last of his leavings from that gentle, careful finger, now sunk deep into her mouth.

"Do not put your tongue to my claw," he warned, still soft, when she perhaps went too close. "It shall cut you, should you not know just how to take this."

Rosa managed a nod, swirling her tongue more carefully, until his hand finally drew away. Reaching behind him, for where—Rosa's hazy eyes fought to focus—he'd at some point set down the package of books on a nearby rock. And now his other hand slipped away from her too, pulling out from her hair to carefully turn over the package, as if inspecting it for dampness or damage.

It left Rosa there gasping on her knees, cold and shaky and untouched, and suddenly flooded all over with shame. Why had she done such a thing, given this orc such a thing, when he clearly barely even cared? Certainly not as much as he cared about the books, based on how he was currently frowning darkly at a corner of the package, and then lifting it to his nose, inhaling deep.

Gods, it was all *madness*, and Rosa scrubbed at her still-sticky face with her clammy hands. She was here for a reason. She was here for research. She was getting Lord Kaspar his war, and saving herself from a hellish future, and that was all. Three weeks.

With effort, she staggered up to her wobbly feet, grasping onto the nearby tree for balance, while John continued to blatantly ignore her, in favour of untying the package, and then rewrapping it with deliberate care. Only sparing a brief glance back toward Rosa once he'd finished, his eyes again shuttered, somewhere else.

"Come, woman," he said, his voice clipped, utterly lacking the warmth of only moments before. "We have dallied long enough."

The hurt surged again, before Rosa's rational brain could

stop it—no, no, this was research, that was *all*—and she made herself nod, and walk her shaky body back toward him. Until she was close enough that he could again grip that powerful arm around her, and hoist her bodily up onto his hip.

"You must hold tight," he said, without looking at her. "Now that I have renewed my strength, I shall run with all speed."

Rosa mutely nodded, and that arm tightened against her—and then, with a forceful kick of his leg, they were off. Again tearing through the trees at a breathtaking pace, following some unknowable path, into terrain that became harsher and rockier with every passing moment.

But again, Rosa somehow seemed to sink into the curious, inexplicable safety of it. His big body shifting and striding, his chest close and bare and warm, his strong hand firm under her arse. His other hand even coming to touch her, sometimes, holding her steady against him as his graceful form leapt and dodged and climbed. Almost as though this were a frolic together, or a game, or maybe even a dance.

"I must drink," he said abruptly, perhaps in mid-afternoon, once they'd approached what appeared to be a cliff, with the distinct sound of a rushing stream below. "Stay."

He set Rosa down on the slippery rock, holding his big hands firmly to her waist as she caught her balance on her numb, tingly legs. And then—she blinked—he vanished, jumping down over the cliff, and when she carefully peered over, it was to the sight of his grey form scaling the steep, wet, rocky descent, as easily as if it were a grassy knoll.

She kept watching, bemused, as he knelt by the rushing stream below, first splashing his face with water, and then drinking deep. And then—her breath hitched—pulling out his messy braid with a jerk of his hand, and shaking out the long black hair around his head, sending droplets flying. Looking, for an instant, like a creature from another world, an elf, perhaps, or a dark fairy prince, tall and scarred and powerful, and dripping wet all over—

But the notion vanished as quickly as it came, as John's head spun to look up at her. His face sharp and increasingly disapproving, and his hand gave a curt, meaningful wave backwards. *I told you to stay*, it said, very clearly. *Get away from the edge, foolish woman.*

For some ridiculous reason, Rosa's mouth quirked up—this orc was already *so* damned predictable—but she obediently stepped back to where he'd first put her, and waited. And when he returned, it was indeed still with his typical disapproval, and his hair neatly braided again—but also, with his big hands cupped together, and carefully holding a clear, sparkling pool of water.

"You must drink," he ordered, thrusting his hands toward her. "I shall not have you collapse from thirst before we reach the mountain."

His voice was harsh, but his hands were steady, certain, waiting. And how had he possibly carried so much water up that cliff without spilling it, had he really managed this just for her?—and after a furtive glance at his forbidding eyes, Rosa carefully stepped forward, ducked her head, and drank.

It was the oddest thing, lapping up water out of an orc's outstretched hands, until she'd drunk all of it, and her tongue was lightly licking the last drops off his palms. And odder still that he let her do it, waiting with uncharacteristic patience— and then, once she'd finally finished, he brought up his damp hand to rub at her chin, at where it had still been sticky, from the afternoon's earlier events.

"Thank you, my lord," Rosa heard herself say, quiet, her gaze darting to his face—and then immediately away again, because *why* had she said that, especially the *my lord* bit?—but suddenly there was the soft, approving brush of a claw against her neck, making her breath catch in her throat. He'd—*liked* that. Being thanked, or being called my lord, or both, after tending to her in such a way. Almost as though she truly *were* his pet, ready and eager to follow his command, bend to his rule—

"We must go," his curt voice cut in, and Rosa silently nodded, and stepped toward him. And this time, she almost hopped a little up into him, his strong familiar arm catching easily around her arse, as if they'd done this hundreds of times before—and then he was off again, pelting through the trees, while Rosa clutched tightly against him, breathing in the delicious musky scent of his sweaty bare chest, and fighting valiantly to ignore the easy grace of his body, and with it, that constant, grinding pressure of his hard hip against her groin.

They had to stop several more times, usually to scale the increasingly forbidding terrain, with John's hand firmly holding Rosa's as she clambered up after him. And once, at a particularly tricky wall, he ordered her to climb onto his back, and hold on—which she did, clinging tightly to his bare shoulders and waist with all her strength, while his muscles shifted and rippled against her, his big body scaling the sheer cliff with swift, alarming ease.

It was nightfall when the mountain finally came close, towering tall and grey and craggy before them, and streaming smoke to the sky. And Rosa's body against John had gone very taut and still, because this was *Orc Mountain*. This orc was taking her to his dark, dangerous, infamous lair, deep under the earth, said to be full of mines and treachery and death. And there were likely *thousands* of orcs swarming inside, vicious and bloodthirsty, just waiting to ravish and kill—

John's running had finally slowed to a walk, his hip rolling smooth and easy against her, and he hoisted her up a little, tightening his hand beneath her. "Do not fear, woman," he said, though he wasn't looking at her, his gaze intent on the mountain ahead. "I have told you, you ought not to heed all these foolish things you read."

Rosa attempted a nod, but the fear was still rising and curdling, churning deep inside. And somehow John saw that, he *knew*, his eyes glancing toward her—and he halted altogether, before yet another solid, sheer cliff of stone.

"Foolish woman," he said, with a sigh. And then—Rosa couldn't help a sharp gasp—he shifted her up and over, so that she was directly facing him, with her arms still gripping his shoulders, her legs still tight around his waist. A position of undeniable intimacy, especially when—oh *gods*—she could suddenly feel that thick ridge at his groin, pressing hard and powerful and utterly devastating, straight between her spread legs.

"Heed this," he said firmly, and here was that hand, gliding warm and familiar around the back of her neck, tilting her head up. "You shall not come to harm here, woman. I shall keep you safe. I have brought you here to help you. And"—those black eyes narrowed on hers, quiet, thoughtful—"if you wish to show yourself a worthy woman before my brothers, you shall be brave, and watchful, and wise. You shall not be fearful and foolish, and thus shame me before them."

Rosa's heart was hammering, her body frozen, caught in the intensity of those words, and in the press of that huge hardness between her legs. Saying something he wasn't saying, or perhaps he was, his claws very gently scraping against her skin, his black tongue coming out to brush against his lips.

"And should you truly wish to please me," he said, his voice pitched even lower, "you shall obey me. You shall do all I ask of you, without question or complaint. You shall be"—those black lashes fluttered—"a good, brave, clever little pet, for your orc."

Gods, he could *not* be serious, he was using, manipulating, doing this again, whatever it was—but all the same, Rosa felt her stiff body relaxing against him, her hands slipping around to the back of his neck. A presumption that he didn't at all seem to mind, just hoisting her up a little harder, a little closer, oh *hell*.

"And if I do please you, my lord?" she heard her audacious voice whisper, against all sanity, all reason. "What then?"

His answer came in the slight, powerful, glorious roll of his hips, pressing that ridged hardness against her, dragging a helpless, choked moan from her throat. Surely he wouldn't, surely not now, surely this was just more manipulation, just this appalling orc wanting to get his way once again...

But the curdling fear had almost entirely vanished from Rosa's thoughts, shoved forcefully away by the feel of him, the sheer strength of him, the rampant trampling hunger. And for that, perhaps, for this, she could submit to this orc, and seek to please him. She could obey, impress him, be a good pet, a worthy woman...

And then, in three short weeks, she would take away everything she'd learned, and fulfill the dreams of a lifetime.

"Very well, my lord," she whispered, to those waiting black eyes. "Then please, take me to your home."

13

John's home was cool, pitch-dark, and abruptly, abjectly terrifying.

They'd entered it through what had seemed to be a solid stone wall—at least, until John had given it a complicated series of hard shoves with his hands, and a narrow opening had suddenly, miraculously appeared in the rock.

"Wait," Rosa said, frowning toward it, straining to follow whatever he'd just done. "How did you *do* that?"

But he only snatched her bodily up again, edging them both through the opening, before pressing a similar pattern into the stone on the other side. And then the wall crunched closed, leaving them in close, constricting, utter blackness.

Rosa's heart had begun pounding again, her body clinging close against John's solid warmth, but even a reassuring clench of his hand against her arse couldn't seem to shove away the fear—especially, oh gods, when she heard *voices*. Distant chattering voices, but rapidly rising, coming closer and closer—

The voices swarmed them in a flood, spilling all around and behind and even above, and with them was the distinctive feel of—*bodies*. Big, powerful bodies, shoving and jostling far too close, while the chaos of the voices grew so loud as to be almost deafening in the blackness. Speaking no words that Rosa understood, but only all guttural rumbling and growling, harsh and aggressive and deadly.

Rosa was desperately fighting to be brave, clutching to John with all her strength—but suddenly, something *touched* her. Brushing against her loose long hair, almost as though *carding through it*, and it wasn't John, and Rosa was quivering all over, and biting back a scream—

John's body instantly shifted beneath her, tossing her over to his other side, well away from whatever that touch had been—and then Rosa felt a hard coiled flare of his muscle, and an unfamiliar, replying yelp of pain. And then it was John's voice speaking in the black-tongue, the words snapping out cold and angry, vibrating deep and powerful through his chest.

The hubbub all around seemed to quiet somewhat, and then the voice spoke again, still in the black-tongue, but this time sounding almost contrite. Earning another curt reply from John, and then Rosa could feel his big body moving again, shoving its way through the crowd.

She couldn't seem to stop trembling, even as they finally left the chaos behind, the voices fading into a distant hum. And beneath her John's chest had sharply exhaled, and here was the feeling of his other hand, sliding firm and reassuring up and down her back.

"Fear not, little woman," his clipped voice said. "My foolish brother did not seek to take you, or frighten you. He has only never before seen a human bearing gold upon its head, as you do."

Oh. Rosa's shivers ebbed slightly, and that hand kept stroking against her, speaking silently of reassurance, safety. "I have told them to leave us be, until morning," he said. "But I yet wish you to meet my kin-brothers this night—one of them studies as a medic—and our mountain's Chief Healer. I wish to learn where we stand with your womb, and my seed."

Rosa's body twitched against him—how had she nearly forgotten about that, when it was the entire reason she'd come here—and she nodded, from where her head had somehow become buried in his warm, sweet-smelling neck.

John's hand gave a brief, approving clench on her arse, and he kept walking through the blackness, his steady steps seeming to angle ever downward. Turning left and then right and left again, taking her deep into some kind of unknowable maze, and it was only his hand's soothing strokes against her back that kept her silent, sane, breathing. She was in Orc Mountain. Dear gods, she was *in Orc Mountain*.

When John's steps finally slowed, after turning yet another corner, Rosa blinked up, and found—light. Not much, not bright, just a single lit candle—but after all the close dense blackness, it was utterly, shockingly wonderful.

And the light—Rosa blinked all around with sudden curiosity—was illuminating a room. An honest-to-gods actual *room*, with smooth grey stone walls, and a high, flat ceiling, rounding gently at the corners. There were no windows, of course, but the room was cool and clean and dry, with no mold or muck or dripping water to be seen.

And most intriguing of all, along several of the walls, the stone had been cut out to form what looked like long built-in *workbenches*. These were neatly stocked with a variety of mismatched opaque bottles, as well as a collection of shiny steel implements. There were several more stone tables rising from the floor in the middle of the room, and Rosa belatedly realized that she was looking at some kind of medical clinic. In *Orc Mountain*.

"How *fascinating*," she murmured, and when she wriggled downwards, John didn't resist, and carefully set her on the stone floor. Giving permission, she somehow knew, so she gladly took it, and trotted to the nearest workbench, tracing a careful hand against the smooth surface.

"This is incredible," she said, without at all meaning to, over her shoulder. "It's volcanic rock, isn't it? How in the gods' names did you carve it so smoothly, even against the grain of the stone? These walls and tables are *perfect*."

There was an odd flicker in John's eyes, but he followed her over to the bench. "Our fathers of ages long past learnt the secrets of this. They smelted an alloy strong enough to both cut it, and abrade it."

Rosa didn't miss the twinge of regret in his voice, and glanced back toward him. "And you don't still know the process for this now?"

"No," he replied, curt, his eyes narrowing. "We orcs have not oft had time or means to keep such truths safe for our sons. It is only sheer foolish luck that we even yet *live*."

Oh. Rosa's fingers kept sliding against the velvety stone, and she opened her mouth to answer—when behind them, there was a flare of movement, of more rough, unfamiliar voices. Of more *orcs*.

Rosa whirled around, her body twitching almost instinctively toward John's solid bulk, while her wide, darting eyes took in the sight before them. Three huge, powerful, grey-skinned orcs, two of them even larger than John, and one with a particularly scarred, hideous face.

They were all staring straight at Rosa, all with those glittering, pure black eyes, and she backed her trembly body closer against John, into the distant, tilting relief of his claws brushing against her back. He'd said he would keep her safe. He'd said he would help her. Hadn't he?

There was another moment's pounding stillness, while those three sets of orc eyes kept staring, and John's hand clenched against Rosa's back—until out of nowhere, one of them *laughed*. One of the taller ones, his face harsh and square but unmarked, except for a single thin scar above his eye.

"Finally went there, did you, brother?" he said, in common-tongue, his deep voice bearing an identical accent to John's. "Went well, looks like?"

John snapped something back in black-tongue, the words coming out gruff and tangled from his throat. But whatever it was, the orcs didn't quite seem to approve, because the big ugly one frowned, the smaller one looked pained, and the first one—the tall scar-eyed one—only laughed again, though it sounded more brittle than before.

John barked another reply, louder this time, complete with a distinctive, disapproving jab of his finger toward Rosa's flat waist. Surging a mortified, cringing heat to her face—he was clearly saying how small, how skinny, how unsuitable she was—and she felt herself shrink up even smaller, her arms crossing her chest, as if to protect herself from these orcs' mockery.

But to her vague surprise, they didn't look mocking. Only almost uneasy, their eyes glancing between her and John, until finally one of them—the big ugly one—stalked forward, and, to Rosa's genuine astonishment, gave her a curt little bow, his hand resting over his heart, his long black braid falling over his broad shoulder.

"Forgive our rudeness, woman," he said, in perfect common-tongue, lacking any trace of an accent whatsoever. "And welcome to our home. I'm Efterar of Clan Ash-Kai, this mountain's Chief Healer. And this is Salvi"—he nodded at the tall scar-eyed orc, and then the smaller one—"and Tristan. Both from Clan Ka-esh, like your John, here."

Clan Ka-esh. *Your* John. Rosa darted a brief look up at John's forbidding eyes—he had called himself Ka-esh, back at the library, hadn't he?—and then drew in a deep, fortifying breath, and attempted a smile at the orc's scarred face.

"Th-thank you," she said. "I'm Rosa Rolfe. From Dusbury."

The orc—Efterar—inclined his head, the very image of good manners, but for a swift, disapproving glance toward John beside her. "John tells us," he continued, "that you two have mated, but that neither of you wish for a son from this. Is this true, woman?"

Rosa felt herself flinch, her gaze following Efterar's up toward John's taut, narrow-eyed face. "Yes," she managed, her mouth dry. "That's true. I can't risk losing my job, and he doesn't want to be bound to a woman like me. And, I'm too small to survive it, anyway."

And why she was so freely speaking of such things to this hideous strange orc, she couldn't possibly fathom—but there was only a flicker of understanding, or even sympathy, across Efterar's watching black eyes. "Well, let's see about this, why don't we," he said, his voice conspicuously calm, reasonable. "Would you mind if I examine you, just to confirm a few things?"

Rosa risked another look up at John, who gave her a tiny, almost imperceptible nod. "But during this, Efterar shall allow Salvi's help," John said flatly. "*Ach*?"

John had glanced sharply between Efterar and Salvi as he spoke, hinting at some meaning Rosa couldn't follow—and in return Efterar sighed, and rolled his eyes. "Yes, fine," he snapped, in a tone that suggested it wasn't truly fine at all. "Now could you please lie down, Rosa?"

It didn't seem worth it to argue, so Rosa obediently clambered up to lie on the table, tugging down her loose tunic. Almost like the few times she'd visited a physician during her schooling, and the unexpected familiarity was strangely reassuring, despite the hard, unforgiving stone at her back, and the fact that four huge orcs were now looming tall and deadly over her.

"May I touch you?" Efterar asked, making Rosa twitch—but

John's hand had come to her shoulder, giving a slight squeeze. Saying, *yes, do this, be brave, please me*—and Rosa immediately, frantically nodded, bringing a look to Efterar's ugly face that might have almost been amused.

But the first touch of Efterar's hands—somehow, oddly enough, without claws—to Rosa's waist over her tunic was careful, distant, professional. Pressing very gently, and then moving lower, left, right.

"She's full of your seed all right, Ka-esh," he said, as his hands kept moving. "Did you fully empty yourself?"

John's fingers spasmed against Rosa's shoulder, and a glance at his face showed his jaw clenched, his eyes narrow, disapproving. "Ach," he said, voice flat. "Only once."

Efterar shrugged, as if that made no difference, and beside him Salvi visibly grimaced. "When were your last courses, woman?" Salvi interjected, curt but businesslike. "Are these constant, each moon?"

Rosa cast her memories backwards, counting days and weeks. "No, they haven't been regular for a while. Last was a few months ago, I think."

To Rosa's vague surprise, Salvi had pulled out a paper and charcoal from somewhere, and was making notes, while Efterar slowly moved his hands up to her collarbone, her neck. His ugly head tilting, eyes distant and thoughtful.

"So what, exactly," Rosa heard herself say, before she could shut her mouth, "are you doing, right now, Mr. Efterar? With this?"

John's fingers on her shoulder had clamped tight, but Efterar's face only looked amused again, his hand moving carefully to the side of her throat, where—Rosa fought to hold herself still—she could feel a distinctive twinge of pain, no doubt due to John's claws the night before.

"I was born with a certain kind of old power," Efterar said, now frowning toward her neck. "One that has been threaded throughout the history of my clan. And with this, I can see—or perhaps, more accurately, feel—into other living beings. I can feel what their bodies feel. I can most of all feel pain, or what does not belong."

That was truly fascinating, Rosa had to admit, especially since it was yet another point that hadn't been addressed in all her copious reading. The orcs had repeatedly been accused of dark magic, of course, but unsurprisingly, it had all been aimed toward the usual horrible ends, like maiming and ravishing and destroying. Not—*healing.*

"So you can feel another person's pain," Rosa said, "and then what? Can you make it better? Or worse?"

That seemed an excessively powerful—and dangerous—skill, but Efterar nodded again. "There are times when worse is what is wished for," he said steadily, though Rosa didn't miss the unmistakable distaste in his voice. "As John says you wish for now."

Right. Rosa felt herself draw in a heavy breath, her eyes again darting toward John—but he was currently glaring at Efterar, his bottom lip jutting out. "And what Efterar does not like to say," John snapped, "is that his Ash-Kai magic cannot predict, or understand, or explain. It can only feel, and act, in that moment, and not before, or beyond. It is *not enough.*"

Now that was an interesting point, Rosa rather felt, as she glanced toward Salvi, who was still writing intently on his paper, his mouth pursed. Efterar was looking at Salvi too, his eyes narrowed, and his hand abruptly dropped from Rosa's neck.

"And yet, all the charts and books in this mountain," he countered, "shall not show you or Salvi all the faint marks you have left on this woman, and the bruising deep in her throat, and between her thighs. It shall not show you the dregs of the *fear* that yet linger in her blood."

Rosa's face flushed red and hot—Efterar could *see* all

that?—and John leaned over her, his eyes flashing with anger, his claws gripping painfully on her skin. "This woman wished for this," he hissed. "She offered herself to me without prompt or question. She wished to be marked and bared and filled. She wished to choke herself on my prick, and gobble up my seed. She *wished* to be used and frightened by an *orc*."

He almost spat out the words, every one seeming to wrench the shame higher, tighter. And when his angry, glittering black eyes dropped down toward her, Rosa felt herself shiver all over, her breath choking in her throat. He was mocking her. Blaming her. Using her...

But the truth of that was blunted, somehow, in the way those eyes were looking at her, in his claws still pressing against her shoulder. In his other hand, abruptly coming up to trace, slow and gentle, down the side of her cheek.

"You wished to be taken," he said, his voice so smooth, so rational. "You wished to be forced and frightened by a fearsome orc, and used as a silly little plaything."

Rosa let out a sharp, humiliated gasp, her body twitching reflexively against the hard stone, and above her John's mouth spread into a dark, dangerous smile, showing all those teeth. "Speak this, woman," he murmured. "You wished for this. Yes?"

Those claws kept caressing against her cheek, breathtakingly soft, bringing out Rosa's breath faster, shallower. While his other hand was now sliding against her shoulder, his thumb circling. "And," he continued, "you yet wish for this now. Do you not?"

There was some kind of reply from Efterar, muttered in the growling black-tongue—but Rosa only had eyes for John, leaning close, safe, protective over her. His hooded gaze finally intent on hers, both those hands touching her with careful reverence, his lips parted, his scent warm and sweet...

"You wish for this," he purred, as the hand on her shoulder

circled downwards, moving ever closer to her heaving breast, and its already-aching nipple. "Yes?"

His eyes were like a flame in the dim candlelight, drawing her nearer, thrusting away at the unease and the shame. Rosa *did* wish for this, gods she wished for this, how did this cursed orc see so much, know so much, his hand finally, *finally* brushing over her hard nipple through the fabric of her tunic...

A choked, shuddering moan escaped from Rosa's gasping throat, and John *liked* that, John *wanted* that, his black tongue curling against his lips. "Yes?" he breathed. "Shall I show them just what you wish for, little pet?"

Little pet. And it was that, inexplicably, that seemed to whisk away the last of the orcs, the room, the shame. Leaving only this, him, she would be brave, a good little pet, a worthy woman for her orc...

Rosa's head nodded, desperate and frantic, and the responding flare of warmth in John's eyes, the approving scrape of his claws to her neck, felt as strong as a kiss, an embrace, a full-on declaration. She'd pleased him, and now he would please her, finally, he *had* to...

And when that big hand curved close over the slight swell of her breast through her tunic, covering it, there was only feeling it, gasping against it, silently pleading for more. And more, those claws gently flicking against her jutting nipple— and then more, as he reached for the too-low neck of the tunic. Tugging it over and sideways, so that—Rosa's breath juddered—her breast, with its pink, heaving, humiliatingly hard nipple, was entirely bare, and exposed to the room. To the strange, unfamiliar *orcs*.

There was a sudden choke of fear, catching tight in Rosa's throat—but John was here, solid and safe and powerful, leaning ever closer. Those eyes still speaking of his approval, his regard, while his big hand came to cover her breast, squeezing it in those long clawed fingers. *Mine*, it said, and Rosa felt her head nodding, her body arching up, pressing tighter into the proud warm wanting of that hand.

When his hand finally slipped away, leaving her bare breast open and jiggling to the air, there was no shame, no need to hide. She was his, he was pleased with her, and his tantalizing, wonderful fingers were stroking further downwards, dragging against fabric that suddenly felt too thick and hot and close.

And as John drew the tunic up, exposing her entire lower half bare to the watching room, Rosa's wild, whirling thoughts were almost, somehow, *grateful*. She was being such a good pet, showing her lord all that he wished, and when that warm, approving hand slid down over the mound of her, those claws carding into her coarse hair, there was only nodding, drinking up his touch, his approval, his command.

"Such a greedy little woman," he murmured, his eyes gleaming, his claws so sharp, so gentle, as they sank lower, lower. "You have wished for this all this long day, have you not?"

Gods curse her, but Rosa's head frantically nodded again, speaking only truth to her lord, those eyes, those tantalizing, breathtaking fingers. And when those claws pulled away just slightly, to press their pointed tips to the insides of her already-trembling thighs, Rosa willingly obeyed the silent command, and spread her legs apart.

There was an instant's quivering stillness, an approving flutter of those black eyelashes—and then another meaningful nudge of those claws, beneath her thighs this time. Guiding them upwards, wanting her to show *everything*—and again, Rosa eagerly obeyed. Bringing her feet flat up to the table, so that her knees were raised, high, apart.

It meant she was lying there, in the depths of Orc Mountain, on her back on a stone table, with her bare nipple red and exposed, her tunic thrust up above her waist, and her legs spread-eagled wide, showing these silent, watching orcs everything between them. How her hot, swollen pink heat was wildly quivering, still stretched from its last use, gripping again and again at nothing, pleading to be filled—

And then—a choked cry wrenched from Rosa's throat—her lord's hand was *here. There.* Those long, clawed fingers sliding slow and breathtaking down the dripping-wet crease of her, and then back up again. Not delving inside, not using those claws to pierce or to harm—but just rubbing flat and smooth, slipping ever deeper against her wetness, spreading it wider apart.

Fuck, it felt good. Like slow, devastating, beautiful torture, the pressure, the slick warmth, the very light tease of those claws. So deadly, yet so painfully gentle, exploring her most secret, shameful parts with breathtaking care. Opening her up for him, for his approval, and he *did* approve, his eyes half-lidded and hungry on hers, his other hand coming up to tug lightly at her still-heaving nipple.

The touch wrung another choked moan from Rosa's throat—and louder when he did it again, harder this time. Using her, playing her, showing her off like a gift, a rare jewel, a hard-won prize...

"Greedy little pet," John murmured, every word earning a reflexive jolt of Rosa's swollen heat against his still-sliding hand. "You shall now give me all that I wish, shall you not?"

Oh hell, he couldn't *mean* that, but Rosa was caught, staring, trembling, trapped, as that hand between her legs pressed deeper, all desperate grinding agony. "Shall you not?" he said again, his voice so smooth, those lashes so dark against his cheek. "Should I wish to wield my orc-prick against you, and plough your tight little womb as hard as I might wish, shall you welcome this?"

He couldn't mean it, he *couldn't*, but the promise was there in his eyes, the pressure rising and rising between her legs. His claws scraping, his fingers stroking, his lashes fluttering, while Rosa's helpless, frenzied body kept writhing and reaching reaching reaching—

"Shall you?" he demanded, with his hands, his voice, those glinting, hungry black eyes. "What do you say, little pet?"

Oh hell, oh fuck, Rosa's sanity whirling and screaming away, there was nothing else but this, but him, his pleasure and his rule, here for his command—

"Yes, my lord," she gasped, almost a wail. "Yes, my lord, please, yes!"

The pleasure flared across those eyes, bright and breathtaking, that hand grinding deep and forceful and utterly glorious—and then, oh, *oh*, the rapture was here, exploding, tearing her apart. Her entire body curling up with the power of it, her mouth releasing a broken, pent-up sound much like a scream. While the warm hand against her swiftly, roughly, spread her throbbing wet heat even wider, further open—just in time to show the thick, powerful spurts of seed, surging out white and obscene from deep between her legs.

It was *his* seed, from the night before, Rosa distantly noted, and how had it possibly still been there, still hidden inside her?—but she was suddenly too exhausted to care, and she felt her body sag back against the stone, used, spent, utterly debauched. She'd showed him, surely she'd proved herself to him, and perhaps now he would praise her, pet her, tell her she was worthy...

But instead, John only stood tall again, his gaze flicking purposefully away from hers. Away, toward—Rosa flinched, and froze all over—toward the three other orcs, who had been watching, all this time.

And they were still watching, oh gods. Efterar with a markedly disapproving frown, his eyes sweeping up and down

Rosa's sprawled body—while Tristan, the smaller orc, bore parted lips, and distinctly hazy eyes. And beside Tristan, Salvi had flung a long, muscular arm over his shoulders, and had bent his head to whisper something in black-tongue, even as his eyes remained firmly planted on the sight between Rosa's spread legs.

Far too late Rosa snapped her thighs shut, yanking down her too-short tunic with shaky hands—but none of the orcs even seemed to notice, and instead all just kept staring, as though she were still fully on display. And John, John had stopped touching her altogether, in favour of crossing his arms tightly over his bare chest, his claw-tips digging into his own skin.

"You see?" he snapped, toward the orcs. "I spoke only truth. This foolish woman wished for this, and for my taking."

Oh gods. Oh, *gods*. The shame was swarming Rosa again, battering against her in wave after wave, and her breaths were short, stunted, sparse. No. No. He was supposed to be kind, supposed to be gentle, the way he'd caressed her, the way he'd looked at her...

Efterar snapped some kind of answer toward John, but John shook his head, his braid flaring out behind him. "No," he shot back. "I did not. I asked her again and again. This one is so silly and useless and foolish, she would throw herself away upon my prick even if it were a sharpened *sword*."

The words seemed to crumple something inside Rosa, deep, powerful, merciless. He'd been—using her. Mocking her. Making a lewd, disgusting show of her, for his friends' judgement and amusement. For her humiliation.

And why had Rosa ever believed anything this awful orc had said. Why had she trusted him, clung to him, seen truth in those black eyes.

And now she was here, trapped in Orc Mountain, alone, helpless, unwanted, surrounded by mocking, powerful, lying beasts. Just like at school, just like the library, and what was she supposed to do, what was left, the panic rising and clanging all at once, she needed to escape to get out get away away away—

And with one deep, bracing breath, Rosa hurled her staggering, trembling body off the table, and sprinted for the door.

14

Rosa knew it was futile, before she even began—but even so, she couldn't seem to stop her frantically staggering legs, or the whirling, compulsive panic, screaming through her thoughts. She had to get away. She had to. She had to...

But she only made it a few steps down the pitch-black corridor until he caught her. *John* caught her, the distinct musky smell of him an instant assault on her already-choking breath—and even as she shoved and fought and flailed against him, he only yanked her closer in the blackness, his claws piercing sharp and shockingly painful against her waist.

"Stop this," he ordered, his voice deep and deafening over Rosa's wild, despairing wails. "Stop, woman!"

But he was hurting her, shouting at her, the pain and misery and shame howling all at once, breaking through her body her breath her skull. The black all around sparking with spots of white, she couldn't breathe she couldn't see she couldn't even *stand*—

Suddenly, somehow, she was falling. Falling into the darkness, straight into the familiar warm strength, while the white spots studded wide and powerful, and there were more talking voices, swirling faint and faraway, mashing all together. *You fool Ka-esh, what happened, she's having a panic attack, you stabbed her. No, she's not all right, when was the last time she ate or drank, from something other than your prick—*

The words were laced through with black-tongue, rumbling harsh through the heat against her, and finally Rosa was moving through space, being carried away in taut powerful arms. And while she should have fought it, fought him, her body could only seem to hang there, the white sparks still flaring behind her blank eyes.

She was trapped. Alone. Foolish. *Useless.*

Those rigid arms gently put her down, setting her limp body against something flat and soft, and there were more barked orders, the feel of a careful clawed hand lifting her head, and bringing something cool to her mouth. Water, Rosa's distant thoughts noted, so she drank and drank, until the white spots behind her eyes faded, and the world blinked away.

She didn't know how long she lay there, slipping in and out of consciousness, drinking whatever was given to her. Not only water, but something that tasted almost like broth, and something else that might have been goat milk. Always given by those same clawed familiar hands, and while part of Rosa wanted to revel in that, to sink into the reassurance of what that meant, there was something deeper, something stronger, that twisted tight and fearful inside. He'd used her. Mocked her. Humiliated her. *Useless.*

And when Rosa's eyes finally blinked fully open again, the first thing she saw was—*him*. Wearing a new grey tunic, and sitting tucked in here with her, leaning back against the stone behind him. In one hand he held a bulging waterskin, and the other held an open book—one of her library's books, Rosa noted with misgiving—but rather than reading it, he was gazing straight back toward her, his mouth a thin, disapproving line.

A hard chill raced up Rosa's spine, and her tired, aching body scrabbled itself backwards, away—only to find something solid and cold and utterly unforgiving behind her. Rock, she realized, darting a furtive, desperate glance all around. Rock, and more rock, she was trapped here, trapped in Orc Mountain, trapped with *him*—

Her heartbeat was dangerously rising, her breath lurching shallower—when John abruptly thrust the waterskin toward her. "Drink," his low voice said. "And do not fear. You shall not come to harm."

That was rather rich, coming from *him*—but the surge of irritation was enough, somehow, for Rosa to sit up, and to snatch for the waterskin. And then to drink, and drink, gulping the wonderful cool liquid down her throat.

When she'd finished, wiping at her mouth, she felt a little better, more like herself again. To the point where she could at least look around, and take stock of this—rock hole, or whatever it was, that he'd trapped her in.

And it was, indeed, a rock hole. But not a natural one, surely, again with the straight, smooth-cut walls, and gently curved corners. And it was deep and wide, with not even enough headroom above for Rosa to stand, and all along the longest side there was a perfectly flat stone shelf, which held a stack of unfamiliar books, and a single flickering candle. And the other long side was open to whatever lay beyond, perhaps—Rosa squinted in the dim light—a larger room, with two long, similar-looking holes in the wall opposite. Almost as if they were deep, carved-out *bunks*.

"W-where am I?" Rosa asked, her voice raspy and hoarse, and in reply John gave an imperious, telltale flick of his fingers toward the waterskin, still clutched in her hand. And for some fool reason, she actually obeyed, again drinking deep, feeling the cool water's relief on her dry throat. And when John flicked his hand again, saying, *give it back*, she obeyed that too, tossing the empty waterskin into his waiting fingers.

"You are in our mountain, in the Ka-esh wing," John said now, with particular slowness, as though he were talking to a child. "And, you are in my bed."

His bed. Rosa's heartbeat picked up again, her eyes searching around her, but yes, that made sense. It explained the flat silken softness beneath her—furs, she vaguely thought, rubbing a hand against one—and another one lay heavy and warm over her, like a blanket. And truly, this *would* be a lovely, marvellous bed to sleep in at nights, so cozy and private and safe—if not, of course, for the fact that it belonged to an *orc*. To *him*.

The memories surged again, dragging up the humiliation, the mockery, the shame. The image, far too strong, of herself spread-eagled on her back, his big hand curved powerful and proprietary against her dripping-wet heat...

She scrabbled back further, closer against the stone behind her, yanking the fur tight up to her neck. No. *No.* He was a cruel, manipulative beast. A *monster*.

"Y-you," she breathed, to those dispassionate black eyes, "have *one* chance to explain your actions, orc. *One*."

Those eyes blinked, once, but then that cold, familiar sneer curled across his mouth. "What must I *explain*," his flat voice said. "I have only done all I swore to do. I have brought you to my mountain. I have kept you safe. I have fed you and clothed you and tended you in my own *bed*."

Rosa's head was already beginning to ache, and she glared at his face, at his smug self-serving *rubbish*. "And in that room?" she demanded. "When you used me, and mocked me, and *humiliated* me?"

There was a flare of something new in those eyes, hinting at frustration, or disbelief. "I did not use you, or mock you, or *humiliate* you," he countered. "I only sated your hunger, and granted you the relief you craved. I gave you *joy*. You *wished* for this."

A brief, unwilling vision of that flared across Rosa's thoughts—him standing over her, warm and approving, while the pleasure flashed and soared—but she choked it back, shook her head. "You used it against me, to make a *point*," she gritted out. "And worse, you did it in front of your own *brothers*. Your own *family*."

Those eyes blinked again, and for an instant they looked almost—pained. "They are not my blood kin, in the way you humans think this," he snapped, his voice even harder than before. "I have none of these left. Tristan and Salvi are my—"

He broke off there, frowning mightily at the stone wall beside Rosa's head, and she frowned straight back at him, reluctantly following the pieces of that. He had no family either. And Tristan and Salvi were his—what? His friends? His *lovers*?

The thought of that curdled in Rosa's gut, and she pulled the fur up closer, covering where—she shot a brief glance downwards—she was still wearing the tunic, at least. "And you think," she managed, "that that somehow makes it *better*? That I would *want* to be mocked before them like that? Or that *they* would want to see such a thing?"

The curl was back on John's lip again, the frustration glittering across those eyes. "You think they have never before witnessed a woman's taking thus?" he asked, voice cold. "We orcs do not find shame in our pleasure, as humans do. When Salvi had a mate, he ploughed her before us each night, and made her beg and scream and spurt for our eyes. There was great joy in this."

Wait, what? Rosa's mouth dropped open, while her traitorous brain frantically dredged up appalling, absurdly compelling images of that—along with the compulsive, overpowering urge to ask what had happened to Salvi's mate. But instead, she clamped her mouth safely shut, and sucked back a series of deep, bracing breaths. No. John was trying to shock her. To distract her. To make his own horrible actions seem entirely forgettable.

"Well, what you did," Rosa countered, "had *nothing* to do with joy. And *everything* to do with you using me to make a point to Mr. Efterar! To continue whatever ongoing disagreement you two have going on between you. About—his Ash-Kai magic not being enough for Ka-esh like you."

The brief, betraying flare of surprise across John's face was surely unfeigned, so Rosa sat up a little straighter, and followed that where it led. "And you didn't like Mr. Efterar questioning you about me," she said. "So you *used* me, to show yourself justified. To make a point. To make it seem like *this*"—she gave a jerky wave between them—"is all due to me being stupid and foolish and useless, and nothing *whatsoever* to do with you!"

John's eyes had shuttered again, but he didn't speak, so Rosa drew in air, kept going. "When in truth, *you're* just as responsible for all this as I am, if not more. *You* made me that damned bargain, when you knew how dangerous it was. *You* offered to bring me here. *You* wanted me to suck you off in the woods. *You* filled me with your seed, and scratched me with your claws, and mocked me and exposed me to your friends, or your *lovers*, or whatever the hell they are. All because it pleased *you* to do so!"

There was nothing in John's eyes now, just a blank cold emptiness, and his mouth barked a brittle sound that might have been a laugh. "And I *told* you, woman," he said, his voice rising, "*I am an orc*. And this is what orcs do to silly little women like you. We mark you. We bare you for all to see. We make you *ours*. We do whatever we wish with you!"

The last came out as a growl, a condemnation, a threat. Leaving Rosa breathing hard, backed against the stone wall, and urgently, unaccountably, wanting to argue that. To say, *no, that isn't truly who you are, I know, I saw you, no falsehoods...*

But no. *No.* This awful orc kept telling her who he was, and why in all the gods' holy names should she not just believe him? Why should she justify his actions for him, make excuses for him, when he had repeatedly proven himself uncaring, distant, and cruel? Whatever had possessed her to trust a *monster?*

But suddenly, staring at this orc's empty, chilly black eyes, there was the inexplicable, incongruous vision of Lord Kaspar, and lurking behind him, the odious Mr. Sullivan. *We do whatever we wish with you. You will do this for me. You will learn to obey your betters. Do not disappoint me...*

The tightness was closing Rosa's throat, weighing against her shoulders, and she couldn't seem to help a brief, longing glance toward that neat little pile of books, sitting so innocuously on the shelf. Perhaps she could reach for one, lose herself in it for just a few moments. Escape long enough to forget, to pretend, to be wanted, to be *worthy...*

But they were the orc's books. She was in the orc's bed. The orc who cared nothing for her, not beyond whatever it was he wanted to take from her.

So Rosa numbly slid her aching body off the bed, wincing at the new flares of pain in her sides, and then stood to her shaky feet.

She would go.

15

This time, there was no frenzy, no running, no panic. Only a silent, blank certainty, filling the space behind Rosa's eyes, and swelling tight against her throat.

Her blinking eyes had already found the room's exit, a square of blackness in the wall to the left, and her feet seemed to turn toward it on their own. She would go. She would seek help however she could. Perhaps Mr. Efterar would be willing, perhaps she could offer certain favours as payment, perhaps he wouldn't care so much that she was too small, or too foolish or useless, so long as her mouth could do the job...

But when Rosa's silently padding feet stepped outside the door, she was abruptly faced with the sight of—John's friends. His *lovers*. Tristan and Salvi, one standing on each side of the corridor, entirely blocking her path.

They both looked huge and dangerous in the dim light, even Tristan, who—Rosa took an unwilling step backward—was actually *growling* at her, the noise low and threatening from his throat. And across from him, Salvi wasn't growling, but his black eyes were snapping with anger, his tall body looming taut and powerful over her.

Rosa stared blankly between them, while the distant, blunted fear marched closer and closer, and she gulped for breath, for courage. "Could you please," she choked out, "excuse me? Sirs?"

There was a swift, exchanged glance between the two of them that Rosa couldn't follow—but then, another glance behind her that was all too clear. And when her stiff body slowly turned to look, of course, there he was. John. Standing directly behind her in the open doorway, his huge, menacing form silhouetted by the faint candlelight, his hands hanging sharp and lethal by his sides.

"Where," he hissed, soft and deadly, "do you think to go, woman."

Rosa wanted to shrink backwards, but there was nowhere to hide, so she wrapped her arms around herself, gripping tight, holding herself still. "I want to leave," she whispered. "Please. I won't bother you any longer, I'll find my own means of travelling back home and dealing with my"—she had to fight for air—"my *predicament*, and you'll never need to spare a thought for me again. *Please*, my lord."

The last escaped before she could stop it, and she bit her lip, and blinked at the stone floor beneath her feet. Waiting for them to move, to let her go, please, *please*—but John's huge form only stepped closer, the distinct sweet smell of him swirling through the air. "No," he said, the word hard, flat, angry. "You agreed to come here, silly woman. You wished to please me."

Rosa's breath was coming in odd, hiccoughing gulps, and she forced her blinking eyes up, to his shadowed, unreadable face. "Yes," she said, her voice wavering. "I did. But you've just spoken the truth about yourself, and about me, as well. I *have* been silly, and foolish, and easily led. I should never have"— she gasped for breath, dragged it into her lungs—"sought to please you, or trust you, or follow you, as I did. I should have been wiser and cleverer. I should know, by now, that powerful men like you don't actually *help* women like me. You don't *care*. You only *use* us as you wish, for your own benefit, and throw us away when you're done."

Beside her, Tristan's growling had stopped, in place of a stilted, hanging silence, and that almost made it worse somehow, the fear and the truth and the darkness pressing in on all sides. And John had come even closer, the warmth of him almost tangible against her, and there was a harsh, twitchy shake of his head. "I am *not*," he said, cold, brittle, "a *man*."

But he was dismissing her again, throwing away the bulk of her argument without even *considering* it, and Rosa desperately fought to swallow back the rising, lurking sobs in her throat. "Yes, I'm aware, thank you," she managed. "But in your actions, orc, you have been just the same. You give me food and clothes and shelter, but in exchange, you use me, you manipulate me, you take your pleasure from me as you please. And not *once* do you deign to speak a single word of kindness to me afterwards, and instead you mock me, and scorn me, and call me skinny and foolish and stupid and *useless*, and I—"

Gods, she couldn't finish, not through the surge of gasping, shuddering breaths choking out her throat, and she had to press her hands to her face, spit the words against them. "I believe you, orc," she sobbed. "I *believe* you. You don't want me. You don't like me. So will you please, *please* just let me go!"

There was still only silence all around, no words, no movement. Only three huge orcs, trapping her there in a corridor, watching her weep, no doubt waiting to unleash even more mockery and derision upon her. And what would they do next, what would *he* do, surely it could only get worse from here—

"What in the hell," cut in a voice, a new voice, "is going *on* down here?!"

There was movement around Rosa again, the distinct feel of shifting bodies, and rising disapproving murmurs. And when Rosa blinked up to look, there was indeed someone new in the corridor. A—*woman*?!

But yes, yes, it was a real-life, flesh-and-blood, honest-to-gods *woman*, sporting close-fitting trousers, a head of long dark hair, a distinctively rounded belly, and a lantern. And she was striding toward them with unmistakable purpose, and also— Rosa blinked again—with genuine rage flashing in her dark eyes.

"You underhanded orcs," she snapped at them, at all three of them, and to Rosa's vague surprise, they all backed away, even John. "Is it true that you've had her stashed down here since *last night*? And no one saw the slightest need to even *mention* this fact to me?!"

There was a hiss from Salvi, close beside Rosa, his big body angling toward the new woman with obvious dislike. "Efterar saw her," he retorted. "*He* was the Ash-Kai in the room."

"Yes, and then he and Grimarr were called away when Eyarl was attacked by those damned masked hooligans last night, and then almost *died,* on our own damned *land!*" the woman spat back, and then took in a deep, clenched-looking breath, as if to calm herself again. "And they *did* tell me just now, as soon as they returned, thinking that surely I would have already known, because *surely* one of *you* would be clever enough to think of such a thing!"

There was only silence from the three orcs around them, and more uncomfortable shifting, and finally the woman ran an irritated hand through her hair, and turned to face Rosa. And then she seemed to go still, the colour fading from her reddened cheeks, and she carefully lowered the lantern to the floor at her feet, and then reached out both hands toward Rosa.

"Oh, *sweetheart*," she said, her voice dropping. "Are you all right?"

And looking at this strange woman, with her strange trousers and her creased brow and sympathetic eyes, seemed to swerve something, break something, in Rosa's thoughts. And somehow, she found herself clutched into the woman's surprisingly strong arms, and desperately weeping into her shoulder.

"No," Rosa gasped, through broken, ragged breaths, as a firm hand stroked up and down her back. "I'm not all right. I want to go. *Please.*"

There was an instant's stillness of the woman's body against her, but that reassuring, stroking hand didn't stop. "You're sure? Right now?"

"Yes," Rosa begged, her eyes squeezed shut. "*Please.* Will you help me?"

There was an odd, familiar growl, rumbling the air close behind them—but the strange woman entirely ignored it. And instead, Rosa could feel her head nodding, her shoulders squaring, her capable determination seeming to shove away all the world's obstacles, all at once.

"Of course I will," she said firmly. "Now come along, love. Let's take you home."

16

Escaping Orc Mountain, it turned out, wasn't nearly as difficult a task as Rosa had anticipated—at least, not when one had a woman like this managing the job.

"Ezog, I need you to bring Baldr to me," she said, toward the first shadowy figure they met in the corridor, which proved to be—Rosa couldn't help shrinking backwards—quite possibly the most hideous, ruined face she'd ever seen in her life. But the creature only nodded and flashed the woman a ghastly smile, which the woman returned with a warm, approving clap of her hand to its huge shoulder before it loped away into the darkness.

"What," Rosa managed, once they'd started moving again, "was *that*?"

"Who, Ezog?" the woman said, with an astonishing degree of unconcern. "Oh, you mean his *appearance*. He's from Clan Bautul, you see, and they've always had to deal with the worst of the fighting, and that does wreak its havoc on one's face, you know? He's really a lovely orc."

She flashed Rosa what she clearly meant to be a reassuring

smile over her shoulder, but Rosa could only seem to stare. "And who," she croaked out, "are *you*?"

The woman skidded to a halt, so unexpectedly that Rosa nearly crashed into her. "Dear *gods*," she said, turning to fix Rosa with a sheepish, apologetic grin. "Only six months here and my manners are already laid to utter waste. I'm Jule, of Clan Ash-Kai, mate to the orcs' captain, Grimarr. You'd perhaps know me as Lady Norr, of Yarwood."

"Lady *Norr*?!" Rosa's shrill voice echoed. "The one the orc captain *kidnapped* and *imprisoned*? And then—"

Her eyes darted down to the woman's telltale rounded waist, but the woman only laughed, and caressed a hand almost affectionately against it. "Indeed," she said dryly. "And then I vanished from the realm, or perished in childbirth, or was killed and eaten by the orcs—depending upon whom you ask. I need to make more public appearances, but it puts Grimarr in such a state, I don't like to push it."

She shot Rosa another wry, meaningful grin, as if Rosa were sure to understand ornery overprotective orcs, and there was an instant's odd, twitching realization that Rosa somehow, perhaps, *did*. "Right," she said, with some confusion. "Um, I'm Rosa Rolfe, by the way. Of Dusbury."

"It's so lovely to meet you, Rosa," the woman replied, as she turned and kept walking. "And I'm so sorry I didn't know you were here earlier, as I'd have come at once. This mountain can be quite terrifying at first, and some of these orcs are utterly clueless about women. And, they're *outrageous* exhibitionists, which really is a shock—until they've properly accustomed you, at least."

That last bit was said with a wink over her shoulder, as if she herself had been—*properly accustomed*—and maybe even *enjoyed* it. And Rosa's mouth was opening and closing uselessly, but nothing else would seem to come out, so she kept trotting along behind Lady Norr—or *Jule*, she'd said—

who had taken a sudden, sharp right, through another square hole in the wall.

It was another room, with those same smooth stone walls, and gently rounded corners. But rather than bunks, or workbenches, this room prominently featured rows of shelves, fronted by a long stone counter, which currently had another hulking, hideous, scar-faced orc standing behind it.

"Morning, Hanarr," Jule said pleasantly, with a warm smile toward the orc, again not even seeming the slightest bit unnerved by his fearsome face. "I'm here on behalf of our Ka-esh guest here, Rosa. She'll need some food and supplies for an upcoming two-day journey. Your best, and most human-adjacent, if you don't mind, please."

Rosa was barely following at this point, but the strange orc took one look at her, and then immediately nodded, and went off to rummage through the densely stocked rows of shelves behind his counter. Shelves which—Rosa couldn't deny a distant flare of interest—seemed to include a few actual *books*.

"What is that book?" Rosa's voice piped up, before she could stop it. "The small one, on the end there?"

It was a little leather-covered volume, bound with an odd type of braiding that Rosa had never before encountered—and to her surprise, the orc immediately went to pluck it from the shelf, and brought it back to her. "Here you are, woman," he said, in a heavily accented voice. "Do you wish me to pack it with the rest of your goods?"

"Oh, no, I couldn't," Rosa said, reflexively—but then, gods curse her, she opened the book. And this book wasn't written in common-tongue, or any language she had ever before seen— but instead in an utterly beautiful, curling, handwritten script that almost seemed to flow across the page.

The script was studded with block letters and small illuminations, some of them breathtakingly intricate, and one of which—Rosa brought the book closer, squinting in the dim lantern-light—contained an exquisitely drawn, hard-featured face, with delicate pointed ears.

This book had been written by *orcs*. In their supposedly primitive, supposedly barbaric *black-tongue*.

And in all Rosa's endless reading about orcs, there hadn't been a single mention of black-tongue ever being a written language, let alone one so complex as this, and she watched her shaky finger trace along the page, feeling the imprints of the script in the thin vellum. A real language, entirely unknown to humans. *Here*, under her fingers.

"Here you are, Lady Captain, Lady Rosa-Ka," interrupted the orc. "Shall I not pack this book for you? I am sure John-Ka should wish for this, for his mate's comfort on her journey."

He was giving Rosa a broad, sharp-toothed smile, which was so thoroughly alarming that it took a moment for the rest of his words to burrow into her thoughts. "*John-Ka* would wish this?" she echoed, her voice faint, "for his *mate*?"

"Ach, yes," the orc replied, with another eager, terrifying smile. "John-Ka always takes good care for his own. A lucky woman, you are. You shall be kept safe, and fat, and content."

His eye did something toward Rosa that might have been meant as a wink, but she could only seem to stare, dumb-founded, as her hands fluttered down to grip at the counter between them. "Um," she said, "I shall?"

"Ach, yes," the orc insisted, as though this were entirely obvious. "John-Ka shall wish to take special care of his mate. He is the last of the Ka, so he shall wish for a strong son. Or many, should the gods be so kind."

That was said with a meaningful, lingering glance at Rosa's waist, drawing her faltering hand toward it, while her other hand kept gripping at the counter. "I think you're—misinformed," she said. "I am not John's *mate*. We are only—unfortunate acquaintances."

The surprise in the orc's eyes wasn't at all put-upon, and

gave way to confusion as he slid a neatly wrapped package across the counter toward her. "Do you yet wait for him to speak vows?" he asked, his head tilting. "We Ka-esh do not oft offer these. One's mouth may speak any number of empty words, but one's acts speak only truth."

His hand waved up and down Rosa's form, as if to say, *look, here is the proof of this*—and Rosa glanced down, following his hand, to find—oh. She was still wearing John's *tunic*.

"But that's just," she stammered, and looked to Jule for help. "It was just a *loan*. Because he tore my *dress*."

But the orc only appeared even more confused than before, and beside Rosa Jule made a face that was half-wincing, half-amused. "Thank you so much, Hanarr," she said, as she reached to take the wrapped package, leaving the beautiful little book on the counter. "And please, put all this to John's account, will you?"

The orc nodded, and Jule ushered Rosa out of the room, and back into the corridor. And as they began walking again, Rosa fought to drag her attention away from Hanarr's baffling claims, and instead to the truly fascinating mountain all around her. The smooth carved walls, the surprisingly high ceiling, the twists and turns that actually seemed to follow the grain of the mountain's rock, perhaps to ensure its structural integrity...

But despite all her efforts, Rosa's thoughts kept escaping her, and whirling back to where she least wanted them to go. To *John*. The last of the Ka, whatever that meant. His warm hands, his watching eyes, the unnerving stiff menace of his big body looming in the doorway. *I have kept you safe, I have tended you, one's acts speak only truth...*

But no, no, *no*. Rosa had given him a chance to explain. She'd given him chances again and again, she'd believed him, she'd trusted him with her entire *future*—and in return he'd mocked and scorned her, called her a silly little woman, *we do whatever we wish with you…*

There was wetness welling again in Rosa's eyes, threatening to spill down her cheeks, and she impatiently dashed it away with a shaky hand. She had to suck it up, and move on. She had to find a way. She had to deal with his—his *son*, and then…

She reeled backwards, her heart pummelling her ribs—because somehow, suddenly, John was *here*. His huge form whirling to life in the corridor before Rosa and Jule, blocking their path, that sweet smell of him unfurling through the air.

"This woman cannot yet leave here," John hissed, his angry eyes flicking between Rosa and Jule. "She yet bears my seed, and is liable to *perish* if she is allowed to birth my son. She is far too small to bear this."

Rosa's eyes were blankly blinking at his shadowed face, the fear lurching high and wide—yes, yes, this was true, this was why she had come to this damned mountain in the first place—but beside her, Jule only snorted and kept walking, steering her around John's stiff, looming form.

"Well, John, maybe you should have thought of that before you touched her," Jule snapped back, over her shoulder. "Aren't you supposed to be the clever orc around here?"

Rosa felt herself wince, darting a foolish, furtive glance back to where John was still standing there in the middle of the corridor. Looking undeniably enraged, his eyes glittering, his hands clenched to fists at his sides.

"This woman *wished* for this," he snapped, and he lunged to catch up again, his huge body almost vibrating with tension as he began striding close beside Rosa. "Do not deny this, woman. You wished to come here. You wished for an *orc.*"

The last came out with a vindictive bitterness, clenching something deep and painful in Rosa's belly, but on her other side Jule rolled her eyes, and kept walking. "And now she doesn't," she shot back. "Shocking, John, truly. Better luck next time."

A low, sustained growl burned from John's throat, which Jule entirely disregarded, in favour of enthusiastically waving at something down the corridor. "Baldr!" she called. "Come, and meet Rosa."

Rosa twitched all over, because yes, it was yet another huge, hulking orc, jogging toward them—but upon closer inspection, this one wasn't quite as alarming as some of the others had been. His scars were shallower, his greenish face a bit younger-looking, and as he approached he smiled at Rosa, warm and genuine, setting his dark eyes sparkling.

"Greetings, new Ka-esh woman," he said, with a fluid little bow. "Welcome to our mountain. I am Baldr of Clan Grisk, Left Hand to our captain. How may I serve you?"

His eyes had cast a telltale glance between John and Jule, betraying more awareness than his affable exterior suggested, and Jule grimaced, and jerked her head toward Rosa. "Rosa is travelling back to Dusbury today," she said, "and she'll require an escort. I'm currently not in a position to leave the mountain"—she waved down at her swollen waist—"especially with those horrid men lurking about, so would you mind accompanying her, Baldr? You and Drafli, perhaps?"

John's growl was steadily rising, but Baldr didn't seem to notice, his eyes unflinching on Jule's. "Ach, woman, I am happy to go. I shall fetch Drafli, and return at once."

With that, he gave another polite little bow, before turning and jogging back down the corridor. While beside Rosa, John's big body seemed to loom even larger, closer, his rage and agitation almost shuddering into her skin.

"My woman shall *not*," he spat at Jule, "go away alone, with a *Skai!*"

His woman. An odd jolt rippled up Rosa's spine, but Jule only whirled to frown mightily at John, her eyes flashing.

"What has gotten *into* you, John?" she demanded. "Aren't you supposed to be the cleverest orc in this mountain? Drafli wouldn't *touch* her, and you *know* that. And they won't be alone, Baldr will be there, and I trust him with my *life!*"

The sound from John's throat was nearly a bark, deep and hoarse and anguished. And in an abrupt, twitchy movement, he spun to face Rosa again, his hand reaching out for her—but then snapping away, clenching against his side, as if he'd had to force it there.

"You cannot truly wish to leave here thus, woman," he said, his voice almost pleading. "You are not yet well. You must rest, and fully heal first."

Jule entirely ignored him, pulling Rosa back to a walk—but John immediately kept pace again, his glittering eyes intent on Rosa's. "You must rest," he insisted. "For even one more day. I swore to care for you."

Rosa swallowed hard, her thoughts flicking back to that awful moment in his bed. To his face, his voice, his words. *This is what orcs do to silly little women like you. We do whatever we wish with you...*

"But you—you *don't* care for me," Rosa finally said, her voice cracking. "You don't even *like* me. You think I'm silly and stupid and useless. You only want to *use* me, for your own gain."

John blinked at her, and then shook his head, whipping his braid behind him. "I do not wish to *use* you," he countered, the frustration heavy on his voice. "I shall keep you safe. I shall tend to you, until you are well. And"—his eyes frantically darted about, settling on the pack in Jule's hand—"I shall—read to you, whilst you rest. I shall read this tale we have brought with us, from your library. *The Lady Bright.* You cannot leave without this book."

Rosa's steps faltered, because damn it, the books, she couldn't possibly leave those precious books here in *Orc*

Mountain—but beside her Jule scoffed, and kept walking. "Oh, give it up, John," she snapped. "Rosa's not going to tolerate more of this rubbish for a stupid *book*."

Jule was right, of course, that would be utter foolishness—or would it, because John's blinking eyes on Jule's face were equal parts disbelieving and enraged. Saying, *how dare you dismiss and denigrate a book's power thus*—and the commiseration suddenly seemed to flare, catching deep in Rosa's gut. And clenching even tighter when John's furious gaze snapped back to hers, his black eyebrows raised high, as if to ask, *can you believe she just said that?*

And curse her, but Rosa felt it, acknowledged it, *appreciated* it—and this damned orc saw it, he *knew*. And his hand had jerked out toward her again, this time brushing soft and almost compulsive against her arm before yanking away again, too late.

"You cannot leave here, without your books," he said firmly, triumphantly, his eyes steady on hers. "You should *never* wish to be a book thief. And should you stay, woman, I shall show you *my* books. I shall show you my *library*."

Wait, he had a *library*? Rosa's still-walking feet faltered again, her eyes darting helplessly toward Jule's face. Orcs didn't have *libraries*. Did they?

"Don't let him get your hopes up, Rosa," Jule replied flatly. "It's barely even a library, more like an empty old room. And half the books are falling apart anyway."

But Rosa felt utterly trapped in place, her brain leaping back to that beautiful little book Hanarr had shown her. Did John truly have more books like that? And they couldn't truly be *falling apart*? Surely John wouldn't allow such a travesty in his own *library*?

"How many holdings," Rosa heard her traitorous voice say, her eyes narrow on John's. "And what kinds? How old? Sourced from where?"

John's eyes narrowed back at her, and for an instant, she was sure she almost saw—*suspicion*, whispering within them. Almost as though he *knew*. About Lord Kaspar, the letter, the three weeks. But he couldn't know, *surely* he couldn't know...

"I have more than two hundred volumes," John finally replied, slow. "Some are archives, many are guides and treatises. Some are tales and sacred texts. Some, I know not what they are. Many of them have been kept safe by my clan since the days of old."

Oh. Oh, *gods*. He *couldn't*. Archives, sacred texts, some he didn't know, *falling apart*. Kept safe by his clan, since the days of old... *hundreds* of years, maybe even older...

The longing swarmed Rosa in a flood, so powerfully she had to gulp for air, for rational thought. This orc had an *ancient library,* of *genuine orc sources*, he was offering to *show it to her*, it was like he was holding out a silver platter of sweet-cakes, frosted with cream and honey...

"And you would," she gulped, "allow me to access them? And read them?"

The suspicion flared again across his eyes, accompanied by a telltale tightness on his mouth. "Most of these are in my own tongue," he said. "Thus, you could not read them."

Oh. Of course. Rosa felt her hopefulness fall again, plummeting deep, her eyes dropping to the floor. Of course he didn't really want her to know, to learn, to discover more about his people. Offering up the library was surely just another empty gesture, another manipulation. And that was all.

So Rosa bit her lip and kept walking, only distantly noticing the floor beneath her feet gradually tilting upwards, the faint but distinctive whiff of freshness in the air. Until before her, John's still-hovering body jerked to a halt again, looming over her, blocking her path.

"I shall," Rosa heard him say, tight, as if through gritted

teeth, "read these books to you. I shall even answer your questions of them. If you stay."

He would *read* them to her. It was enough to snap Rosa's watery eyes up to his, searching for the truth of that—and here, whirling to life in her stunted-feeling brain, was the realization that this—this was indeed *exactly* what she needed. Access to the orcs' own works. Answers to her questions. Real primary sources, true and bare and powerful. And this was her once-in-a-lifetime chance to become a student, to save her future...

But instead of agreeing, saying yes, like she surely should have, Rosa felt her hands pressing to her face, shutting him away, shaking her head so hard it hurt. "But you don't *want* me to stay here, John," her thin voice choked. "You don't even *like* me. You're only trying to manipulate me again. To get your way again. You already swore to keep me safe, and tell me no falsehoods"—her voice wavered—"and just look how that's gone for me. You don't *care*. I can't *trust* you."

And that was truth, enough truth to set the temptation stark against the reality. John was still only in this for himself. An *orc*. A cruel, manipulative beast. A *monster*.

Rosa forced herself to start moving again, slipping sideways past John's rigid, immobile form, and for a hanging, silent moment, it was done. Finished. She'd made the right decision, she would never see this horrible orc again.

And, she thought blankly, even if she did end up destroying her future, at least she wouldn't need to be responsible for a *war*, after all. For the ruination of this surprising mountain. For the bloody, premature deaths of these surprising orcs, who again didn't seem at *all* what her sources had claimed them to be...

"Wait," came John's voice, cracking on the word. "Little rose. Please."

Rosa felt his hand before she saw it, the familiar warmth suddenly circling close and deadly against her bare neck—and it was enough to shock her into stillness again, sending the rest of the world scattering away. Leaving only this huge, vicious orc, lurching once more to stand before her, and—trembling.

And yes, he was actually *trembling*, his eyes blinking, his fingers quivering against her skin. And as Rosa blinked back up toward him, his other hand skittered up to echo the first, cupping her bare neck between them, in something that ought to have been thoroughly frightening—but instead felt deeply intimate, almost like reverence.

"I did not," he said, his voice thick, "truly wish to frighten you, or harm you, or speak false to you. I did not wish to—*use* you. I only"—he grimaced, those eyes squeezing shut, opening again—"I have never before—known aught, such as this, between us. I do not—*understand*."

Rosa could only keep blinking, watching him draw in another rasping breath. "You vex me, woman, and confound me, and—and *call* me, even when I seek to push you away. This *weakens* me, but"—his chest hollowed—"I ought not to unleash my anger toward you. It ought to be toward me. It is because I do not understand. I must needs—*learn*."

As he spoke, those shuddering hands gave Rosa's neck a little shake, almost a threat—but there was no menace in it, no fear. Only the urgent wild brightness in those black orc eyes, held so powerfully to hers, finally speaking his truth.

"I shall never forgive myself, should you come to harm, for my folly," he breathed. "I wish you to be safe. I wish to care well for my"—his throat convulsed—"my *pet*. I wish to rule you with kindness, and gain your trust, and bring you joy. And mayhap even frighten you—but only in the way that you wish."

The words had dropped to a whisper, quiet and deeply ashamed, soft enough that Jule—still standing beside them, surveying all this with her hands on her hips—might not have heard. But Rosa heard, and the cursed responding heat fired straight to her groin, and dragged a hoarse, broken gasp from her throat. His *pet*. He wanted to *rule* her. *Frighten* her.

John's eyes spoke the truth of it, his lashes fluttering dark and regretful against his cheek as his gaze blinked away, toward the wall behind her. But his hands were still circling her neck, with such careful stilted reverence, his claws so gently scraping against her skin. And in this moment, there was only this, him, his scent, his warmth, his truth.

"This shall please you, my sweet rose," he breathed, his eyes again bare, ashamed on hers. "To stay here until you are free of my son, and until then, to be my fat, happy little pet. To see my library. To read my books. To learn more of my kin. To—to take your joy with me. Yes?"

Somewhere, far inside Rosa's thoughts, was the realization that there were more orcs approaching, and that Jule was speaking again, saying something that surely echoed Rosa's own rational brain, shouting deep within. But the longing was too strong, the ache almost overwhelmingly powerful, the bare, shameful compulsion to nod, to feel her throat move against the strength of his huge warm hands...

"No falsehoods?" she breathed, to those blinking black eyes, and he slowly shook his head, his fingers squeezing just a shade tighter. Still here, still safe, everything she'd ever wanted, a student, a pet, fear, *truth*, dangling, waiting...

She had three weeks. And she had to know. She *had* to.

"Then you need to prove this to me, orc," she whispered. "Teach me. Starting *now*."

17

For an instant, all else pooled away, but for the echo of Rosa's words, pinging against the stone walls all around.

Prove this, orc. Teach me. Now.

John's dark eyes blinked at her, once, twice—and then, in a quick, breathless movement, Rosa was jolted up off the ground, and into his arms. Back in her place on his hip, his strong hand holding her easily against him.

He strode down the corridor with swift, firm steps, and without so much as a backwards nod toward Jule. But Rosa's furtive, searching glance over his shoulder showed Jule looking almost satisfied as she stood there, a small smile twitching up her mouth.

"Just holler if you need help, Rosa," she called after them, her voice carrying down the corridor. "And we'll be *watching* you, John."

John entirely ignored this, and hoisted Rosa closer as he stalked around a corner, blocking Jule from view. It was completely dark here, without so much as a flicker of candle-light, and despite herself, despite everything, Rosa felt her face angling into his skin, breathing in his musky, sweet scent. And in return, she felt a slow, approving slide of his other hand up her shoulder, curving against her neck.

Gods. Rosa shouldn't have shivered, but she did anyway, her eyes fluttering—and she didn't miss John's replying huff of grim satisfaction. But his hand was still there, still so warm and safe, his claws scraping soft against her skin as he walked.

He stopped within short order—perhaps sooner than Rosa's traitorous clinging body might have liked—and he carefully eased her down onto the floor, before moving slightly away. And suddenly, there was light. Flickering to life from a steel lantern, set upon a solid wooden table.

And in the light, Rosa saw—a *library*.

It was a tall, spacious, rounded room, carved from the already-familiar grey stone. And the walls had actual *shelves* cut into them, circling all the way around the room, from the floor up to the high, vaulted stone ceiling.

And upon these shelves, there were *books*. Manuscripts. Papers. Scrolls. Not many, as Jule had said, not compared to what one might expect in a human collection—but they were neatly organized, and even a single initial glance already proved them highly intriguing. Unfamiliar bindings, unfamiliar materials, some fascinating-looking slabs of *wood* that looked distinctly like tablets...

Rosa had already drifted toward the nearest shelf, reaching to carefully pull down a thick, elaborately bound book. And as she opened it, she gasped aloud, her eyes widening at the sight.

It was—*beautiful*. A work not unlike the little book she'd seen earlier, but this one was far grander in scale, full of intricate illuminations accented with gold leaf, and that same lovely, elegant script. Script that—Rosa gingerly turned one thick vellum page, and then another—had many repeated forms, and was studded through with charming little flourishes and embellishments.

"What is it?" Rosa heard herself ask, her voice hushed. "A devotional book?"

The breathtaking illuminations had already suggested as much, full of detailed, fantastical images of humans and orcs— and Rosa wasn't at all surprised when John nodded. "It holds the ancient wisdom of our Ka-esh forefathers," he said. "We study this from our earliest days."

That was deeply fascinating, and so was the fact that there were a number of similar volumes shelved together. And once Rosa had carefully put the book back, and plucked out another, and another, she understood that the book Hanarr had shown her had been one of these, too. Each one slightly different, though they all seemed to begin with the same text, likely a prayer, or an incantation.

"Could you recite it to me?" she asked John, eagerly brandishing the page toward him. "This prayer? Surely you know it?"

John had been standing immobile behind her, his watching gaze entirely unreadable, but he finally nodded, and began to speak. The words rolling from his mouth in the orcs' unfamiliar black-tongue, the sounds rumbling from deep within his throat.

It was utterly foreign, and also inexplicably beautiful, and the sound of it, the sight of John speaking it with such ease, seemed to clutch something tight in Rosa's belly. Distracting enough that she nearly forgot to follow along, but she belatedly did so, her eyes narrowing as she fought to match the words to the text.

"Your language is letter-based, and *phonetic*," she said, once he'd finished. "Just like our common-tongue, and how *intriguing*, John. What is your name for it?"

He was still watching her warily, his gaze flicking down to the open book in her hands, and back to her face. "*Aelakesh*," he said, and Rosa repeated the word aloud, feeling its unfamiliar weight on her tongue. *Aelakesh*. Not a primitive, illiterate black-tongue at *all*. Those damned sources had been wrong, unsurprisingly, *again*.

"And what does this prayer mean?" she asked, eyeing him, remembering that promise of his about answering her questions. And though she didn't miss the tightness on his mouth, he sighed, and nodded.

"It asks for wisdom," he said. "It begs for light, and learning, and truth. It calls for a wise Priest to rise up, and lead us with knowledge into the dark days to come."

Oh. Rosa's first thought, random and disjointed, was that she rather approved of this Ka-esh take on worshipping—but already the next thought was here, spilling from her mouth. "And who is your Priest? An eschatological figure? I mean"—she winced, catching the unmistakable confusion on John's face—"a mystical future saviour, of sorts? A demigod, perhaps?"

John blinked, and then loudly scoffed, as though even the idea were thoroughly absurd. "Ach, no. The Priest is one of us. He is a wise Ka-esh orc, with the will and the strength to lead our kin into the light."

Rosa considered that, her eyes studying that telltale blankness on his face. "And do you have a Priest now?"

"We do not," John replied, voice curt. "Not since the death of my elder brother Fror, this winter past."

There was a very faint inflection on this Fror's name, as though he'd perhaps meant more than John wanted to allow, and Rosa's gaze dropped back to her book. "Was Fror a good Priest? Did he fulfill the terms of this prayer?"

There was an instant's stillness, and when Rosa glanced up again, John's eyes were distant, a furrow between them. "He sought to. But he sought also to please, and to forsake change. To keep peace among his kin."

Of course this damnably predictable orc would see that as a

weakness, and Rosa felt her head tilt, her eyebrows rising. "And you wouldn't? If you were in his place?"

"No," John snapped back. "We orcs cannot afford not to learn and grow and change. We now face the dawning end of our kind. We must do all within our power to stave off our *death*, before—"

He broke off with a grimace, clearly not meaning to betray so much, and Rosa's churning thoughts flailed backwards, to Lord Kaspar, to that letter. *We need to wipe out those bastards once and for all. Risking the resources and plans of the entire realm. Do not fail me...*

Rosa swallowed, and abruptly turned away from him, back to the reassuring shelves of books. The next section seemed to be mostly records and archives, made up of carefully organized sheets of paper and vellum, and loose quires of varying sizes. They were all again written in this Aelakesh, but Rosa recognized enough to determine that many were birth and death records. Others looked more legal in nature, while still others were clearly technical, focused on what appeared to be mathematical and geographical content, much of it based around mining.

And next, to Rosa's deepening fascination, were practical books. Cookbooks, and hunting books, and even books on warfare, with vivid illustrations of gruesome battle scenes, depicting both orcs and humans. And next was a large collection of medical volumes, anatomies and herbals and remedies, many of them with little annotations in the margins.

And then, surprisingly, was a small, eclectic collection of books in *common-tongue.* Mostly more medical volumes, but also a variety of scientific and historical works, and even a few popular sagas.

"You said you didn't have any human books here!" Rosa snapped over her shoulder toward John—though it felt difficult to muster up true anger, when one was faced with such delightful reading possibilities. "You *lied* to me, so I would permit your *book-thieving* from my library!"

"I did not lie, or *thieve*," John replied, with damnable coolness. "I said there was naught of *worth* here to read in common-tongue. I did not say I had no books at all."

Rosa made a face at him, but still felt far too diverted to argue, and eagerly turned toward the next shelf, which was set slightly apart from the others. And when she carefully opened a little book with a badly broken binding, she heard herself gasp with pleasure, because this one was another orc book—but this time, instead of the already-familiar Aelakesh, it was written in *Osadan*. The language of the realm's far west, and the lands past the ocean beyond.

And Rosa hadn't at *all* considered that orcs might know how to speak other languages, let alone write an entire *book* in Osadan. Or rather—she glanced at the shelf again, and tugged over a loose folio to peer at the script on the front—an entire *shelf* of it?!

And how *wonderful* to finally be able to read one of the orcs' own books—even if this one was only another cookbook. And as Rosa scanned through the pages of recipes, she felt her mouth twitching up, the delight bubbling in her throat.

"Pan-fried eel?" she read aloud, glancing at John's dangerously blank face. "And dried moose-antlers? And squirrel-stew! Complete with boiled eyeball garnish! Truly, John?!"

She couldn't help laughing, especially at the unmistakably perturbed look that had begun stealing across John's face. "*Garnish*?" he repeated, his voice careful on the word. "What is this?"

Rosa explained, between lingering chuckles, showing him that particular line on the page—and as John blinked at it, his thick brows furrowing together in concentration, Rosa suddenly understood that he couldn't *read* it. Not well, at least, so she promptly read aloud the entire recipe to him, translating into common-tongue as she went.

"... And, finally, season with much salt," she read, "and eat this very good dish with great gusto, before your brother steals it from you."

She shot John another amused smile, and for an odd, hanging moment, he didn't reply, only blinked down at the page, and then at Rosa's face. And then he glanced intently away, but not before she caught a very faint twitch at the corner of his mouth.

"This indeed seems a good meal," he said. "I ken most orcs should eat it with gusto, before it is stolen. Most of all this—*garnish.*"

Rosa's heart quivered—was John making a *joke*?—and she felt herself laugh again, grinning up at his deceptively blank face. "I *need* to see this meal, John. You need to let me write this recipe out, and take it to your kitchen. *Please.*"

She was only half-teasing, but John's mouth twitched up again, drawing Rosa's eyes to the inexplicably compelling sight. "Mayhap," he said, "should you copy out the whole of this book into common-tongue, I shall then take it to the kitchen."

Oh. And suddenly he wasn't joking at all, not really— because he truly *couldn't* read this book, is what he meant. And he didn't want to admit it, he was perhaps ashamed to admit it—especially when there was an entire shelf of books in this language, here in his own library. And there was another rush of understanding, or maybe even commiseration, deep in Rosa's belly.

"Well, do you have any vellum, or paper, and a quill and ink I can use?" she asked, glancing around the room. "And if you have any thread and wax, and a curved needle, I could fix this binding while I'm at it."

John had again gone unnervingly still, blinking at Rosa's face—but then he gave a quick, jerky nod. "I shall find these, and bring them," he said. "Is there aught else you should need?"

Aught else. His eyes had briefly swept over his little collection, lingering on several similarly worn bindings, and then on a neat stack of folios that likely ought to have been bound at one point, but weren't. And then, faint but unmistakable, he shot a dark, frustrated glance at that whole shelf of books he couldn't read. No doubt taunting him day after day, long-lost hidden truths of his own ancestors, sitting there forgotten and forlorn, waiting in vain to be discovered again.

"Well," Rosa said slowly, "if you had some lead, for ruling, that would be helpful. And a sharp knife, for pricking and trimming. And if you want any new bindings, you'll want properly sized boards for the covers, and possibly leather to wrap them with, too."

Even as the words came out her mouth, she realized that they were no doubt a grave mistake, committing her to days of work, if not entire weeks, and for what? So this orc could have a few more books to read? This awful, selfish orc, who'd been unspeakably rude and cruel to her, and who was currently supposed to be proving to her why she should stay? And failing miserably in the task, clearly, because somehow Rosa was the one accommodating *him*, yet again?!

But perhaps John had followed that, his shoulders rising and falling as his eyes settled on hers. Speaking of determination, of resolve, of regret...

His big body jerked toward Rosa's, his hands settling strong against her waist. And in a swift heave of movement, he lifted her up and deposited her on the nearby wooden table, her legs dangling off the side.

"What are you—" Rosa began, but then the words spasmed in her throat, because John had sunk to his knees on the floor in front of her, and was currently *spreading her knees apart.*

The world stuttered to stillness, Rosa's entire body caught, her heart pummelling against her chest—and before her, John's kneeling form hesitated, his black eyes blinking up at her, his hands halfway up her thighs, where he'd already been sliding up her tunic. *His* tunic.

"I seek to prove to you why you should stay," he said, slowly, as though Rosa were a particularly dense child. "This is what you wish for from me, is it not?"

What she wished for. And sitting here, spread-eagled on a library table with an *orc* kneeling between her legs, Rosa could almost taste the sudden surge of longing, smooth and desperate and shockingly powerful. What she wished for, from him.

As if to prove his point, John lowered his lashes, looked up at her through hooded eyes—and then he *growled*. The sound deep, threatening, frightening, rising in his throat as he bared his sharp white teeth toward her...

Rosa gasped, loud and betraying, her spread-apart legs stuttering against his strong hands. And in reply, flickering behind those half-lidded eyes, there was triumph, maybe even mockery—but also bitterness. Bleakness. *This is what you wish for, from me.*

Rosa swallowed hard, and her shaky hand skittered toward his, holding it against her thigh. "It's not all I wish for," she heard herself say, her voice thick. "I also wish"—she cast a helpless look at the shelves all around—"to learn more about your library. Your culture. Your home. *And*, I want you to teach me Aelakesh."

The last came out in a rush, her pronunciation badly mangled, but John had clearly followed, his brows drawing close together. "Why."

The answer lurched without hesitation, without even the slightest guile. "I *love* learning, John. And I especially love studying languages, and discovering how they work. And yours is so *intriguing*. It would be such an *honour* to learn more about it. Real scholars *dream* of rare opportunities like this."

There was a distinctly disbelieving look in John's eyes, and too late Rosa glanced away, and bit her lip. Good gods, she shouldn't be betraying so much to this orc, she wasn't even supposed to *care*. She was supposed to be here for research, she was supposed to want to learn his language so that she could better find those damned atrocities, save her damned future, and become a damned scholar. And what if John mocked her again, what if he said, *I would never teach such a foolish, useless human my own tongue...*

But the look in his eyes wasn't critical, or mocking. Only steady, considering, and Rosa twitched at the heady, jolting feel of his big hands moving again. Sliding gentle and inexorable up her thighs, sliding up her tunic as he went, further and further and further—

Rosa choked, but he didn't stop. Not until his warm, purposeful hands had stroked all the way to her waist, revealing *everything* beneath. All her most secret, most shameful places, bared and spread apart, on a level with his blinking, watching eyes.

Rosa's face felt painfully hot, and flushed even hotter when she felt her wet body clenching, gripping at nothing, the humiliating sound actually audible in the hushed stillness. And even worse still—she cast a fearful, mortified glance downwards—when that thick, telltale whiteness again began seeping from inside her, pooling on the solid wood below.

Fuck. Far too late, Rosa sought to shut her legs, to shield herself from those too-close eyes—but John's hands on her thighs were much too strong, and his glance up at her face was hard, perhaps even disapproving. And as Rosa stared, trapped, frozen, he slowly, carefully leaned his dark head forward, slipped out his long black tongue, and—*licked* her.

Rosa yelped, scrabbling at him, shoving him away—even as

the foreign, unfamiliar sensation of what he'd just done seemed to linger, reverberating, lighting up every nerve under her skin. He'd *licked* her, *John* had done that shockingly delicious thing, and she couldn't think, could only shiver, breathe, stare at the rising confusion in his blinking eyes—

"What vexes you, woman," he said, as that sinuous black tongue flicked out, oh *hell*, to brush at his lips. "Is this not what you wish for?"

Rosa had to gulp for air, for reason, even as her stunned, shameful body had begun pulsing again, clenching at him, dripping out more of that mortifying white. Betraying her with brutal, deadly immediacy, while John only dropped his eyes to look at it, his gaze clinical, dispassionate.

"You wish for this," he said again, and this time his hand slipped downwards, the pad of his thumb tracing against Rosa's dripping, swollen heat with an ease that felt almost proprietary. Sparking even more shocks of impossible pleasure up her spine, her entire body wriggling on the table before him.

"So why," he continued, frowning up at her face again, "do you protest? No falsehoods, woman."

Rosa was still shivering with pleasure, her mouth opening and closing, the words bubbling up on their own accord. "I've just never," she managed, "no man's ever, I mean—"

Her badly trembling hand waved at him, at her, at *this*— and she could see the understanding flare across his eyes, chased by an almost immediate disapproval. "None of these men have tasted you?" he demanded. "Even this foolish rich man did not taste his own *pet*?"

It was a clear condemnation, and Rosa shivered again, her gaze angling away from him, toward the safety of his books. "No," she whispered, quiet, ashamed. "Never."

She could almost feel John's eyes boring into her, hard and unsettling. "But you showed some skill with your mouth, when you drank from me," he said flatly. "Surely you learnt this from these men?"

Even as a shameful part of Rosa inwardly preened at the praise—she'd shown some skill, he'd *liked* it—far stronger was the uncomfortable urge to curl up. Cover herself. Hide away...

But John was still too close, too powerful, both hands back on her thighs, shoving her further apart. Exposing, demanding, waiting. Expecting an answer.

"Yes," she whispered, to his hands, rather than his face. "But I told you. Men don't give. They only take."

There was a harsh, hanging stillness, fraught with heaviness, discomfort, perhaps even blame. While Rosa's helpless, spread-apart body only clenched again, exposing her with brazen, appalling flagrancy, and her face flushed even hotter, flooding her with shame. She shouldn't want such things, she didn't deserve such things, she was foolish and skinny and *useless...*

But rising between her legs, low and steady, was a sound. Not from her, but from John, and when her gaze darted furtively to his face, he was again—*growling*. His teeth bared, his dark eyes narrowed and glittering, his claws black and dangerous as they pressed gently against her bare thigh.

"And I told *you*, woman," he said, deep, menacing, "I am not a man. I am an *orc*. And when an orc gains a woman"—he dropped a hand back between her spread legs, traced his thumb slow, taunting, utterly thrilling up between—"he bares her. He covers all her parts with his scent. He drinks his fill of her whenever he pleases."

A helpless, heaving groan escaped Rosa's throat—he couldn't mean this, he couldn't *possibly* be doing this—but then all else blinked away, because he *was*. His head leaning in closer, his growl rising as he inhaled, his chest filling with the scent of her—and then he again slid out his tongue, with slow, deliberate purpose, and *licked* her.

Rosa instantly squealed and flailed, the impossible sensation whirling and shuddering. And in return, John only laughed, dark and mocking, and did it *again*. Running that long, sinuous black tongue up her swollen parted crease, lingering upon where he'd filled her, on where more of his own thick white was already oozing onto his delving tongue...

Rosa moaned again, blinking, dazed, wondering—to which John gave that dark laugh again, and then used the pads of both clawed thumbs to draw her dripping heat even wider apart. And gods, the vision of that, the *truth* of that, an orc's deadly claws nudging so gently against her most vulnerable, secret place, doing with her as he wished, using her as his own...

"More, pet," he growled, hoarse and heated, and he couldn't mean he wanted to see more, taste more of his own *leavings*— but Rosa's audacious, appalling body was already obeying his command with shocking abandon, pulsing and clenching and pushing, squeezing out more of that betraying white, from where it had been hidden inside, perhaps waiting for just this moment...

John watched it with arrested, fluttering eyes, his claws clamping with approval against her thigh—and then he again leaned forward, and caught its pooling warmth with his tongue. Lapping it up with astonishing eagerness, and now delving deeper, following it to its source—

Rosa's breaths were juddering, her eyes glued to the sight, the slick slurping sounds, the impossible unreality of it. This cold, distant, angry orc, with his head thrust between her parted thighs, his long slippery tongue flicking and twisting with such deliberate intent, sinking deeper and deeper...

And *fuck*, his tongue was huge, it felt *alive*, it felt like a godsdamned *snake* was writhing within her. A snake that was unspooling its delicious poison deep inside, setting her jolting and convulsing around it, her back arching, her hands grasping at his silken black head, she couldn't possibly bear any more, she *couldn't*—

But he only chuckled again, cool and mocking and desperately thrilling, vibrating into her through his huge, thrusting tongue. And it *was* thrusting, this orc was actually *fucking* her with his mouth, his lips now pressed close and hot against her, in almost an obscene, open-mouthed kiss. And she could feel his sharp teeth, threatening to sink into delicate skin, while his tongue kept punching her, claiming her, splitting her flailing body upon its writhing furious power—

Rosa screamed as the release tore at her, exploding from his still-driving tongue, consuming the whole of her in its shouting, hurtling wake. Wracking her again and again around him, upon him, her body no longer her own, but an *orc's*.

And the orc's tongue was still there, but licking and lingering gently now, giving her shameless, quivering heat something to rub against, to clench against, to perhaps even kiss at. Until the aftershocks gradually subsided, and that slick tongue gave one final, deliberate lick—or maybe a kiss back—before he slowly pulled away, wiping at his face with the back of his hand.

And it was the sight of that, inexplicably, that seemed to snap Rosa back into herself again. Into the vivid, unimaginable truth of this moment, with her debauched, gasping body sprawled and spread-eagled on a library table, generously dripping its excesses onto it. While the fully clothed orc before her coolly stood tall, smoothed back his still-neat braid, and looked down at her with carefully blank eyes.

Oh. Oh, *gods*. Rosa heard herself whimper before she felt it—what had she just *done*—and she frantically pulled herself back in, snapping her legs together, wrapping her arms tight around her chest. He was going to mock her again. He was going to blame her again. He was going to walk away...

The sobs were lurking, threatening, about to escape—how

had she possibly been so foolish, *again*—when a low, sustained growl jerked her head up. *He* was growling, and his warm hand circled around her neck, strong and menacing and deadly.

"I told you, pet," he said, slow, a threat. "Whilst you are here, you shall please me. And thus, you shall not hide yourself, or your joy, away from me. You shall show all I wish to see, and all I have done to you. You shall be bared, both before me and before my kin, and you shall *not* be ashamed. Do you understand?"

Rosa blinked at him, at the cold command in his eyes, at the danger in his voice—and for some bizarre, unaccountable reason, she felt her curled-up body relaxing, her throat swallowing hard against that press of his palm. A touch that felt almost soothing, suddenly, even as his other hand snaked back down to her thigh, and unceremoniously shoved her leg apart.

"Good," he murmured, soft. "Should you hide thus from me again, little rose, I may need to punish you, until you learn to obey."

Rosa's gasp of shock was instinctive, appalled—but there was heat in it, too, and hunger, and perhaps even *relief*. And when those claws slipped up her bare thigh, coming to card gently into her secret patch of dark hair, she felt herself shiver, warm, alive.

"I understand," she heard her shameful voice whisper, to those waiting black eyes. "I shall seek to learn, my lord."

Those eyes fluttered, once, his lips slightly parted—but the nod of his head was brusque, businesslike, satisfied. *Pleased.*

"Good," he said firmly. "Now you shall come, little pet. I shall teach you the truth of my home."

18

To Rosa's surprise, John's tour of Orc Mountain began not with mines, or forges, or chaotic scenes of vicious orcs battling together—but with a stop back in that same trading-room with Hanarr.

"We need food and drink," John announced to Hanarr, without so much as a hello. "Aught fresh that you have, brother."

Hanarr seemed inordinately pleased by the request, scuttling at once around his rows of shelves, while also casting furtive, bright-eyed glances over his shoulder toward Rosa. "Ach, this shall please you, John-Ka," he called, from behind a shelf. "And you, Lady Rosa-Ka."

John visibly winced at that, but otherwise only stood there, his claws impatiently tapping on the counter, until Hanarr returned bearing a basket that appeared to be overflowing with food. "Here, John-Ka," he said proudly. "Berries, and nuts, and dried meat, for Lady Rosa-Ka!"

John winced again, but curtly thanked Hanarr for his efforts. And then, rather than taking Rosa elsewhere to eat—a dining room, perhaps, or even his bedroom—he bodily plopped her up onto the counter before him, and thrust the basket into her hands.

"Eat," he ordered. "Slowly, so you are not ill."

Rosa likely should have protested the manhandling, or the ordering, but her eyes were already roving over the basket's contents, her stomach audibly grumbling. The food mostly seemed edible, if rather unusual—the nuts weren't anything she'd seen before—and after another impatient wave of John's hand, she carefully began to eat.

John's eyes didn't leave her the entire time, even as he and Hanarr launched into some kind of discussion about supply lines and product sourcing, studded through with occasional words of black-tongue—or, rather, Aelakesh. Rosa listened with interest as she ate, particularly noting the assumed authority in John's voice and manner, and the surprising way Hanarr deferred to all he said.

"Um, do you *command* Hanarr?" she asked John, once she'd finished eating, and he was once again leading her through the dark corridor, lantern in hand. "And your mountain's *supply chains*?"

"This is only the Ka-esh *supply chain*," John replied vaguely, without quite looking at her. "Now come. Next I wish to take you to my medics."

His medics? That odd statement was accompanied by a sharp turn into another room, which—Rosa blinked—she *recognized*. It was the medical clinic John had brought her to the other night, when he'd made an *example* of her to Efterar and his friends. Or his *lovers*, or whatever the hell they were.

And one of those lovers was *here*. The tall, scar-eyed one named Salvi, leaning over a workbench, and mixing something in a bottle. While across the room another slim, smooth-faced orc was bent over an open book, and writing inside it.

Rosa's feet had begun dragging, her eyes lingering first on that table in the middle of the room, and next on this Salvi, who was currently flashing her a wary, sharp-toothed smile. As if he hadn't recently seen her naked and exposed in this very room, and then tried to bodily prevent her from *leaving*.

"This is Eben, one of my medics," John said, gesturing toward the new orc, who was giving Rosa a careful nod. "And Salvi you have met."

Rosa mutely nodded toward both Eben and Salvi, though she felt her feet edging sideways, back toward the door. A movement that Salvi seemed to notice, and he abruptly strode forward, clutching his bottle in a hand that somehow, suddenly, bore no claws.

"Ach, woman," Salvi said, still with that hesitant smile. "I know we haven't met on the best of terms, and for this, I ask your forgiveness. We Ka-esh aren't yet at ease with women in our home, and"—he glanced at John—"of all our brothers, we didn't expect *John* to be the first to bring a woman here."

He offered Rosa another smile, quick and hopeful, and she felt her resistance thawing—at least, until she grasped one of the possible implications of that last statement. "And was that because," she said, before she could seem to stop it, "because John already had, er, *obligations*, to *you*? Or, um"—she cleared her throat—"to Tristan?"

Salvi blinked at her, once, and then shot John a look that Rosa couldn't at all read. "Ach, John and I know better than to seek such now, with each other," he replied, his voice not quite light. "I ken I would tear his head off, and he my prick."

But he hadn't said anything about Tristan, Rosa noted, as her cursed brain darted back to what John had said about Salvi and his mate. *He ploughed her before us each night. There was great joy in this...*

Salvi loudly cleared his throat, and then thrust out the bottle he'd been holding toward Rosa. "A gift for you, woman," he said, with a joviality that felt slightly forced. "Drink up."

Rosa eyed the bottle with misgiving—it was dark brown, so

the contents were anyone's guess—and John nudged it purposefully toward her. "It is a kind of milk we have made, that shall help you grow stronger," he said. "You have already drunk this, in my bed, and welcomed it. It shall not sicken you."

Rosa tentatively took the bottle, and gave a careful sniff. "What's in it?"

"Milk from the Ash-Kai's new goats, mostly," Salvi said promptly, with a wink. "And a bit more. Naught that'll harm you."

John was guiding it toward her again, now with that telltale stubbornness in his eyes. "This is a proven remedy for weakness, pet," he said firmly. "We have studied this at length with both orclings and women. Salvi has marked all this in his books, should you wish to read these later."

Oh. Well. Rosa's resolve was again faltering—especially if they'd actually *researched* it, and documented it properly—so she carefully brought the bottle to her lips, and tasted it. It was indeed the same thing she vaguely remembered drinking in John's bed, and it actually *wasn't* terrible, and once she'd finished it, she was rewarded with a satisfied rub of John's hand against her back.

"Good little pet," he said, low and approving, sending an unexpected jolt of goosebumps up Rosa's spine. "Now, Salvi shall survey you."

Being *surveyed*, it turned out, apparently meant the same thing as being measured and weighed. Rosa meekly obliged this time, earning more pats and murmured praise from John in reward, and she was almost disappointed when Salvi finished, turning away to write a long list of numbers on a sheet of paper, and then breaking them into some kind of mathematical equation.

"Well?" John asked, clipped, to Salvi's back. "Salvi?"

Salvi turned and held out the paper toward John, who snatched it away with surprising force, his narrow eyes scanning down the page. "As we thought," John said, his voice curiously flat, his hand thrusting the paper back. "Thank you, brother."

Salvi shrugged with seeming carelessness, and tossed the paper onto the counter. "You might again ask Efterar," he said offhandedly, though his eyes were intent on John's. "Or even Sken. They might see aught that we cannot."

John answered with a snort, and swiftly ushered Rosa back out of the room, and into the corridor again. Leaving her to blink up at his grim face in the light of his lamp, her thoughts whirling, unsettled. "What was that all about?" she asked. "And who's Sken? And is there—is something *wrong* with me?"

She couldn't hide the tremor in her voice, and perhaps John heard it too, hesitating in the corridor to face her. "Sken is another of my brothers with an old, powerful gift," he said flatly. "But I should never trust his cryptic sight against the clear truth of Salvi's survey, when this has again proven what we yet knew. Should you bear my son, you are likely too small to survive it."

Right. Rosa winced, eyeing him, digesting all that. "And me having your son was still—a possibility, to you?" she asked. "You didn't actually—*want* that, right? With me?"

John didn't reply, and instead kept walking, his eyes straight ahead, his mouth tight. His non-answer speaking just as much as an actual answer would have, and the understanding seemed to crash against Rosa all at once, powerful enough that she felt faint.

John *did* want a son. Even if it was with her.

But no, no, *all* orcs wanted sons. It had been a constant theme in Rosa's research, hadn't it? Orcs wanted sons, orcs went to great lengths to gain sons, an orc would steal and pillage and *kill*, to gain a son. And Rosa was here to see what else these orcs could do, what other atrocities they hid in this mountain, three weeks...

She felt oddly frantic, suddenly, her eyes darting about the corridor—and thankfully relief came, in the form of another opening in the wall. This one emanating a sharp, acrid smell, and a dim flickering light, which—Rosa's steps slowed, her eyes peering inside—was due to several tiny, controlled fires, above which several unfamiliar orcs were holding more of the glass *bottles.*

"Wait," Rosa said, her voice unaccountably shrill. "John, is that a *laboratory*?"

She'd read about laboratories, of course, though as a woman, and therefore not a student or a scholar, she'd never been permitted to enter one—and she fully expected John to ignore her, and keep walking. But his eyes had closed, briefly— and then he actually *nodded,* and ushered her toward the door.

Rosa stared up at him, entirely dumbfounded—and even more so when John said something loudly in Aelakesh to the three orcs inside, and they all stopped their work at once. They were again all relatively slim and smooth-faced, and they all gave purposeful little bows toward John, before seeming to fix their collective attention upon Rosa.

"Ach, brothers," John said beside her, nudging her forward. "This is Rosa. She wishes to see your work."

Rosa again gaped at John with genuine astonishment, but he only gazed back at her, his eyebrows rising. *Is this not what you wished for,* his face asked, without him needing to speak at all. *You said you wished to learn.*

Rosa couldn't help a delighted smile, and even an apprecia- tive squeeze of his arm. And before he could change his mind, she took a few careful steps toward the nearest orc, who had a set of small vials arrayed on a tray before him.

"Thank you for having me," she said, with a tentative, hopeful smile. "What's your name? What are you working on?"

The orc's black eyes on hers were undeniably wary, darting again toward John—but at the telltale impatient wave of John's hand, Rosa could see the orc's throat swallow, his head nodding. "I am Aaron, of Clan Ka-esh," he said, his voice faintly accented. "I study blood, and which kinds of blood best suit other kinds."

Aaron, who studied *blood compatibility*? Rosa was already highly intrigued, and proceeded to spend the next half-hour peppering Aaron and the other two researchers—Brandr and Marcus—with as many questions as she could think of. They replied with creditable patience, even going so far as allowing her to try using one of their small flames herself—they turned out to be clever little *burners*—to help create some kind of distilled disinfectant. And by the time John ushered her out again, Rosa was flushed with pleasure, and a surprising, twitching gratefulness.

"*Thank* you, John," she said, with a genuine grin up at his carefully neutral face. "I've always wanted to properly see inside a laboratory, you have no *idea* what a thrill that was. Also, I can't say I ever imagined orcs studying *blood compatibility*—that's a really experimental science, you know, I've heard they're doing a lot of research on it at the Dusbury University right now. How did *you* ever get involved in it?"

John's answer was an overly casual shrug, a slight tension on his mouth. "We lose many lives to blood loss," he said, his voice carefully flat. "It is only wise that we study this."

We, almost as though he were again a crucial part of that, and Rosa tilted her head, considering him—at least, until they'd passed another door. This one with a bright, blinding light emanating from within it, along with a rhythmic, deafening clanging sound.

"What's in this one?" Rosa asked, as she stopped to peer inside. "Oooh, is this your *forge*?"

She was surely testing John's patience at this point, but again, he only sighed, and ushered her toward the door. Where he silently signalled at the four masked, pounding orcs inside, who, just like the researchers, stopped their work at once, setting aside their tools. These orcs were all larger, sweaty, and bare-chested, and as they raised their masks to look at John, Rosa realized that they were also older and rougher-looking than he was, their faces marked with lines and scars. But again, they all gave deferential bows toward him, and then focused their attention on Rosa.

John made another round of introductions—the orcs were apparently named Asger, Soren, Harald, and *Gary*—and they explained that the Ka-esh forge ran night and day, with multiple shifts working on a range of projects. "We forge and smith all goods here," said Gary, with unmistakable pride, "but now that the war is over, we Ka-esh have turned most of all to tools, and lamps, and jewels."

Rosa's eager request for elaboration soon led to a tour of a small adjoining room, which housed a variety of their work. There were still some weapons, most of all the orcs' distinctive curved scimitars, but also things like pickaxes, shovels, and chisels. Along another wall were smaller tools, knives and pliers and tongs, which, Gary explained, were used by the Ka-esh medic teams in their work. And next was even a set of lovely wrought-iron lamps, which, Gary continued, would eventually be installed in corridors throughout the mountain, to provide light so guests like her would be able to see.

"And here," Gary added, leading Rosa toward a smaller shelf, "are the jewels. I have finished this *kraga* just today, after ten days of work upon it."

His chest had puffed out as he spoke, his claw nudging against one of the multiple glittering pieces lying on the shelf. And when Rosa stepped closer to look, this *kraga* proved to be a solid, circular piece of beaten gold and silver, with an elaborate clasp on one side. Rather like a necklace, or maybe a torc, but made of tiny little ropes all wrapped together, making a beautiful, cleverly intricate whole.

"It's lovely, Gary," Rosa said, with a sincere smile up toward him. "You're a true master."

Gary seemed surprisingly affected by the praise, his grey cheeks turning a bright shade of red. To which John gave an unmistakable snort, and then curtly thanked the orcs before ushering Rosa back out into the corridor.

The next room Rosa glimpsed appeared to be a meeting-room, with abstract-looking artwork carved into the walls, and next was what appeared to be a shrine, currently empty, but featuring a collection of skilfully carved stone figures. And then a room that held several more orcs, studiously bent over angled-top desks, with quills gripped in their hands.

"One more quick tour?" Rosa asked John, with a hopeful little grin. "Please?"

John answered with a low, irritated groan, but once again, he obliged. And this time, Rosa was treated to an enlightening—if rather incomprehensible—explanation of Orc Mountain's geological environment, and all the planning and engineering and mathematics that apparently went into sustaining such a complex underground home.

The three orcs—Tvalli, Orval, and Ronan—willingly included John in their explanations, and once Rosa's questions had faded, the discussion morphed into a detailed analysis of a new passage dig they were directing, and how to address some unexpected geological problem that had arisen. And though Rosa scarcely understood half of what was said, by the end, she was eyeing John with a rising, unsettling appreciation.

"How have you learned all this, John?" she asked cautiously, once they were again walking down the corridor. "And are you—*in charge*, of all these orcs?"

John's shrug was definitely too casual this time, his gaze steady on the corridor ahead. "I have learnt such things since I was an orcling," he said. "It is the duty of the Ka."

Rosa pondered that, frowning up toward him. So he *did* mean he was in charge of all this. Didn't he?

"And who are the Ka?" she asked. "Hanarr told me you were the last one. And these orcs keep calling you *John-Ka*."

She could see John's jaw clenching, but he again answered the question, his voice brisk. "We orcs are split into five clans— Ash-Kai, Bautul, Skai, Grisk, and Ka-esh. From the days of old, the Ka-esh have borne two sides—Ka and Esh. The Ka have been winnowed for many years, and now that Fror is dead, I am the last of these."

He spoke matter-of-factly, as if this were a minor detail of little import, rather than the unnerving suggestion of war and grief and devastation that it was. The Ka have *been* winnowed.

"Did you know your parents?" Rosa asked, her voice quiet. "Before they died?"

John didn't answer, and instead sharply turned a corner, and strode down another long corridor. This one tilting slightly upward beneath their feet, and Rosa caught the surprising scent of what seemed to be *fresh air*.

"Where are we going now?" she asked, inhaling the sweet freshness deep. "Outside?"

Her voice actually wavered at the thought—gods, it felt like *days* since she'd seen the sky—and John cast her a sidelong look as he halted against a solid stone wall, and gave it several purposeful shoves with his hands.

"Do not hope too much, pet," he said. "It is not *outside*, as you might think."

The wall crunched to the side as he spoke, moving on what Rosa now saw was a steel track beneath it, which had previously been entirely hidden by the stone. "How *marvellous*," she gasped, bending over it—but then there was a blast of light and wind, and all else vanished as she stood there, and felt it, and breathed.

It was, somehow, another—room. A room that seemed on the very edge of the mountain, and which had part of the ceiling cut away, revealing the clear blue sky above. There were similar cracks in the thick stone walls, showing bright bands of rock and trees, and when Rosa darted over to look closer, she realized that she was gazing out onto a rocky plain at the base of the mountain. And from the outside, this cleverly engineered little room would likely look just like another part of the rock, and not like a room at all.

"What a *marvel* this is," Rosa said to John, who was still lingering back by the door, with his hand over his eyes. Shielding against the bright light of the sun, she realized, with a twitch of surprise. "Is it for surveillance?"

He shrugged, and waved his other hand toward a few stone benches Rosa hadn't yet registered, which were set directly under the opening to the sky. "It has been used thus," he said. "But it was built for Ka-esh women, who yet need sun, when we do not."

Oh. Another more careful glance around the room showed that it indeed seemed meant for comfort—there was more abstract white artwork carved into the walls, and the floor was tiled with a clever stone pattern. And there were more benches along the walls, and even what looked to be a few empty *flower-pots* studded about.

"It's lovely," Rosa said, and she meant it. "It would be a perfect place to come and read, and also keep an eye on any outside goings-on, as well. Like that orc, John. What's *he* doing?"

Her eyes had caught on a moving figure a short distance away, striding down the nearby rocky descent. He was a truly massive orc, by far the largest Rosa had seen yet—and even at this distance he was profoundly scarred, his huge sloped shoulders covered with deep lines and gouges. He was wearing only a dark kilt, his long hair tightly pulled back into a thick black braid, and in his hand was one of those distinctive curved scimitars, glinting silvery-white in the bright light.

John had bolted over to stand beside Rosa, glowering out at the orc through his fingers. "*Helvíti*," he hissed, his voice surprisingly angry, his body coiled tight. "That fool, *fool* Skai. He shall not, he *cannot*—"

Rosa blinked at him, and then at the strange orc, who had just settled his massive bulk down upon a large rock, and grasped for a smaller rock with his huge fist. And then, resting his sword against his knee, he began to sharpen the blade's edge, the shirring sound whistling high-pitched through the open air.

"What do you mean?" Rosa asked, frowning at the visible displeasure on John's form, which was almost vibrating beside her. "He's not doing anything, he's just sitting there—"

But John was shaking his head, spitting out what sounded like another Aelakesh curse. "He risks all we have done," he growled. "He calls down *war* upon our heads."

What? Rosa kept blinking at John, not at all understanding, because while he'd occasionally seemed irrational before, he'd never been entirely unhinged, surely? And surely there was no way an orc sitting on a *rock* could be calling down *war*?

She opened her mouth to speak, to ask—but before a word came out, John's hand clasped over her face, and he dragged her bodily backwards from the opening in the wall. While Rosa belatedly kicked and shoved at him, shouting muffled into his hot palm—and suddenly his other hand was on her neck, and *squeezing.*

It wasn't hard, not really, but still enough to snap a true jolt of terror up Rosa's spine, her eyes wildly searching his, which were now glittering with rage and perhaps even—*fear.*

"Silence," he gasped, harsh, in her ear. "Or you shall *suffer,* woman."

It was a threat, John was *threatening* her, he'd promised to be kind, he'd *promised*—but the shout that had been rising in Rosa's throat seemed to break at the look in his blinking eyes, at the way they kept darting toward the light. Toward the—men?

Yes, good gods, toward the *men*. The strange, silent men who were creeping around the seated orc, emerging out from behind rocks and trees. The man who was currently prowling in front of their *wall*, so close Rosa could have reached out through the crack, and touched his black-clad *sleeve*.

They were all dressed in black, they all had weapons gripped in their gloved hands, and they all wore masks on their faces, covering their noses and mouths. Leaving only their eyes, glancing back and forth between one another, organizing, communicating, as they moved closer and closer to the seated orc. Planning an *attack*.

And before them, the huge orc just kept sitting there. Not moving, not looking up, not showing any sign of having noticed the encroaching men. Just scraping his stone again and again, the sound loud and unnerving in the otherwise taut silence.

Rosa's heart was thundering, her head shaking, her body straining against John's grip. Someone had to warn the unsuspecting orc, the men were about to *kill* him, surely John would do *something*—

But John's claws were digging in, his powerful form dragging Rosa further back, away. "No, pet," he hissed in her ear. "Please. He knows what he does. He *knows*."

And before Rosa could think, react, resist—the men lowered their swords toward the orc, and charged.

19

There was an instant's jangling stillness, Rosa's heart screaming in her throat, John's hand clamped over her mouth. While running men swarmed the seated orc, shouts finally rising as the first man swung, his flashing blade arcing straight toward the orc's exposed neck—

When in a breath, the orc *leapt*. Flying up off the rock with astonishing force and speed, his massive body spinning in midair, his scimitar whirling out in a bright ring of light. Knocking several of the men backwards, blood spraying from one of their arms, while more men scrambled forward, swords swinging—

The huge orc knocked them away with another spinning whirl of his sword, and then grasped for the next man's flashing blade with his bare hand, and hurled it point over hilt through the air. Striking another man straight in the head, and sending him staggering backwards until he fell, his own sword clattering away on the stone.

That left six men still standing, and they were approaching the huge orc with more care now, creeping around from all sides. While the orc held his form very still, watching, waiting—

The men surged in a swarm of black, blades stabbing and swinging with force, precision, sure and certain death—and from deep within the mass of writhing bodies and clanging swords, an inhuman howl rent the air, broken, bitter, bloodcurdling. Painful enough to squeeze Rosa's eyes shut, her head dizzy and pounding, that orc was going to *die*, she couldn't bear to watch him die, please, gods, *please*—

But then, abrupt and cloying, was more silence. Ringing thick and horrible in Rosa's ears, thundering in her chest. Silence that was broken, finally, by an exasperated-sounding sigh from John's breath against her ear.

And when Rosa risked opening her eyes, blinking toward the light, it was to the astounding, impossible sight of the *orc*. Standing tall, whole, and blood-soaked, while a mass of wounded men groaned and twitched at his feet.

"*Helvíti*," John hissed again, but his hard grip on Rosa's face and neck had finally loosened, and he rubbed at his still-squinting eyes. "Come, woman. There is no time to waste."

Rosa couldn't find the wherewithal to argue—her body had begun convulsively shivering—and she allowed John to pull her away from the light, away from the sight of that unmoving, blood-covered orc. Back into the depths of the mountain, suddenly so dark that even John's lamp didn't seem to penetrate it.

John rushed through the corridors, dragging Rosa's staggering body close behind him, until he burst into the medical clinic, where Salvi and Eben were still working. "There are ten wounded men," John told them, clipped. "On the scree, north side. Do all you can, at once."

Salvi and Eben immediately leapt into motion, before John had even finished speaking. Eben rushing out the door, sprinting away at a full run, while Salvi grasped for a huge pack

Rosa hadn't seen before, strapping it onto his back. "Any deaths?" he demanded at John, his gaze searching, sharp. "Or deserters?"

"Not yet," John said back. "I shall call for a search."

Salvi nodded, and snapped some kind of visor over his eyes before also darting past them, and out of the room. Leaving John and Rosa entirely alone again, and for an instant John only stood there, his palms pressed to his face, his shoulders rising and falling with the weight of his breaths.

"Are you all right?" Rosa asked him, tentative, putting a careful hand to his arm. "John?"

She could again feel the tension, vibrating through his form, clenching at his jaw. "I only," he began, and dropped his hands, meeting her eyes. "I must now address this, at once. It shall be best, mayhap"—he drew in a thick breath—"if I take you elsewhere to wait, whilst I work."

What? Rosa's head was already shaking, her fingers clutching at his sleeve. "No," she said. "I want to stay with you. Please. You promised to teach me."

John shot her a look of unmistakable, unnerving frustration before again rubbing at his face. "I cannot teach you aught, in this," he snapped. "I also shall not have time to calm you, and all this has made you truly afraid, ach?"

Right. Rosa felt her resolve hardening, and she attempted a shrug, a tremulous smile at his eyes. "I was only surprised, is all," she said. "I've never seen an actual *battle* before, and of course it was highly stimulating. And of course I'll try to stay out of your way, because of course you need to focus on your— your *work* right now. Because you *are* in charge, John. Of the Ka-esh. Aren't you?"

A noise much like a growl rumbled from John's throat—but then he abruptly reached down, and snatched Rosa up. Settling her close against his hip, back in her same familiar place, as he turned and kicked off into a run, sprinting down the black corridor.

He'd left his lantern behind, which meant that Rosa couldn't see where they went next, or who he was speaking to in his gruff Aelakesh. But his hands stayed firm on her all the while, his body warm and close. And whenever he became particularly stiff, his claws digging into Rosa's skin, she felt herself stroke at his back, leaning closer into him, until she could feel him slightly relax again.

She didn't know how long he spent rushing around the mountain in the dark, clutching her in his arms. But when finally there was light again, and he set her gently down to her feet, Rosa couldn't deny a distant disappointment, even as she glanced with interest around this new, unfamiliar room.

It was large and open, with a little fire crackling at the opposite end, and multiple metal-framed beds scattered about. Looking not unlike another clinic, or even a small hospital, and Rosa recognized Efterar, standing over a bed across the room.

And in that bed—Rosa twitched, her eyes widening—was the orc. *That* orc. The one who'd fought off ten men at once. And up close, he looked even larger and more alarming than he had before—especially since his huge, broad-shouldered body was indeed covered all over with fresh, vicious-looking wounds, several of which were still dripping *blood.*

But there was no sympathy in John's glinting gaze on the bloody orc, only contempt, or perhaps even rage. "*Helvítis hálfviti,*" he growled, as he stalked across the room toward the bed, dragging Rosa close behind him. "You cursed *fool,* Simon. Do you not *know* what you have *done*?!"

The wounded orc was gazing at John with wary, narrow eyes, his bottom lip jutting out. "I fight ten men," he said, his deep voice heavily accented. "I *win.*"

It was a fair point, Rosa rather felt, but John's answering snarl was immediate, surprisingly vehement. "You have risked our entire *treaty*, Simon," he hissed. "Leave it to a Skai to throw away *years* of work and planning, so you could enjoy an aimless and reckless brawl with *bandits!*"

"They attack first," Simon said stubbornly. "And I no kill."

John's bark was sheer frustration, his hand yanking against his hair. "Only because I have six medics out there fighting to keep them alive!" he shouted. "Do you not know how much this shall cost us? Do you not know what tales these men shall tell, when they run back to Preia to report to their war-hungry masters?!"

To Preia. To Lord Kaspar's home. His father *Duke Warmisham's* home.

And wait, those men had truly come from *Preia*? And they were lurking around Orc Mountain, lying in wait for whatever hapless orcs they might find? This couldn't be a thing that was actually *happening* here, could it? Especially if it was the *men* breaking their own treaty?

"*Men* break treaty," Simon rumbled back, in an unnerving echo of Rosa's own thoughts. "Men attack eight lone orcs this moon. Eyarl almost *killed*, two nights past. Now, men have fear. Men no attack again. Weaker orcs *safe*."

He waved his huge hand at John, as if to suggest that John was one of these weaker orcs—a sentiment John clearly disagreed with, his entire body thrumming with anger. "And this plan was made with care, with all five clans, was it? With those who now must address the fallout from your deeds? Or, mayhap"—his lip curled—"you sought leave from the captain to do this?"

As he spoke, he shot an angry glance over his shoulder, to where two more people were striding into the room. One of them was Jule, flashing Rosa a tired-looking smile—and behind her was yet another massive orc. Not quite as big as this Simon, but still shockingly large, with huge sloped shoulders, and a grim, scarred face.

"Simon did not seek leave from me," the new orc said to John, his powerful voice heavily tinged with danger. "But neither have you gained leave to condemn him in my place, brother."

John betrayed a very faint wince, a dark glance toward Simon. "And shall *you* now condemn him, Captain?" he asked coldly. "Shall you keep from him the help and the tools his clan needs to do their work? Shall you set upon him the same checks you set upon me?"

This captain strode across the room toward them, reaching a huge hand to clap against John's shoulder. "We have spoken of this at length, brother," he said firmly. "When it comes to women, we must tread with great care. Ach, new Ka-esh woman?"

His dark eyes settled upon Rosa's as he spoke, his mouth drawing into something that might have been intended as a smile, but still made Rosa flinch, all the same. And behind this new orc, thankfully, Jule stalked over too, and gave an exasperated roll of her eyes as she drew him back to a slightly less intimidating distance away.

"Didn't I tell you, Rosa, manners are a lost cause around here," she said. "Rosa, this is my mate Grimarr, of Clan Ash-Kai, the orcs' captain. *Right*, Grimarr?"

"Ach, ach," said this Grimarr, with a sideways glance at Jule that seemed almost affectionate, or amused. "We welcome you to our mountain, new woman. Now, brother"—his gaze slid to John—"shall it please you to stay and gloat, whilst I condemn Simon for what he has done? Or shall your time be better spent caring for your new woman, and seeking means to help us through this?"

He was *criticizing* John, Rosa realized, when John had already been working on this situation for what felt like *hours*—and John visibly stiffened, his face blanching, his mouth thin and tight. "I shall go," he said, very smoothly.

"But first I wish to see Efterar, for a short time, when he is free."

Efterar's head snapped to look at John, his eyebrows rising—and after a brief exchange with Simon, he strode over toward them. And at John's clipped request, Rosa soon found herself the subject of yet another examination, while John silently stood and watched, his arms crossed, his eyes still glinting with anger.

"You're doing better, Rosa," Efterar said to her, once he'd carefully rested his hands first to her head, and then down to her belly. "But you're still severely underfed, and fatigued. After this, you should get plenty of rest, eat at least three times a day, get regular sun and activity, and drink as much of John's seed as you can. You'll want more fresh seed in your womb, too, especially if you've come around on the son, because this is"—he frowned down at Rosa's waist—"two days old, now?"

Wait, what? Rosa's severely overwhelmed brain was struggling to follow this, and she drew up her tattered thoughts, made herself speak. "Um, what does that have to do with anything? Not that I don't want—I mean—I'm not already *pregnant*, am I?!"

She shot John a chagrined, fearful look, but he only kept glaring at Efterar, who in turn was still intently focused on Rosa's belly. "No, not yet," Efterar replied vaguely. "But fresh seed makes a stronger son, and helps ready a woman for his growth and birthing. Just ask John, he and his *medics* claim to be the experts around here."

The word *medics* was spoken with unmistakable scorn, and Rosa wasn't surprised when John growled back, low and harsh in his throat. "And thus I and my *medics* know, Ash-Kai, when you do not," he snapped, "that this woman is too small to birth an orc-son. As we have told you. Do *you* wish her to join the twenty dead women we orcs have already made this past twelvemonth?"

Rosa's head jerked toward John, her beleaguered brain again wildly whirling, but Efterar seemed wholly unconcerned. "You should not put so much weight on this," he countered. "You are a small orc, and you Ka-esh have the most successful births of us all, once you actually get to business. It's not like you're Simon, here."

Rosa shot an uneasy glance toward Simon, who was now deep in an unpleasant-seeming conversation with Grimarr and Jule. The actual words drowned out by another growl from John beside Rosa, sounding choked, frustrated, aggrieved.

"Our survey, which is founded in *research*," he said, clipped, "has given this woman a fifty percent likelihood of birthing my son alive. Do you have aught of worth to say to that, Ash-Kai, beyond this deep insight that I am Ka-esh, and *not Simon*?"

Efterar shrugged, his eyes still frowning at Rosa's belly. "No," he said. "But her body does seem to like your seed. She wants more. I can just—*feel* it."

Rosa's face flooded with heat, and thankfully John seemed just as provoked as she felt, another harsh bark vibrating from his throat. "Ach, that changes *all*," he growled back. "Let us wager her *life* on what you *feel*, Ash-Kai. When you are done here, mayhap you shall go see how you *feel* about all the Preian men Simon has almost killed on our behalf today. Men who only now *live* thanks to my *medics*!"

With that, John spun on his heel, and stomped out of the room. Dragging Rosa close behind him, back out into the pitch-black of the corridor. His strides long, fast, furious.

And though Rosa could no longer see his face, the strength of his anger seemed to crackle into the darkness all around them. Anger at Simon, who'd apparently risked an entire *peace-treaty* with what he'd done. At Efterar, who'd ignored John's legitimate-seeming points, in favour of his own thoroughly unfounded *feelings*. And anger, even, toward this captain, who'd censured John in front of his brothers, and put *checks* upon him, whatever that meant.

And in the whirling chaos of Rosa's brain, strongest of all was the need, compulsive and irrational, to reach her free hand toward John. To stroke him, smooth and purposeful, just like she'd done earlier today. To feel the tension dissipate, just slightly, under her touch.

"On a scale of the kinds of days you usually have," she heard herself venture, soft, into the spiralling darkness, "how bad was today?"

Beside her John grunted, the sound bitter, mocking. "Ach, bad enough," his voice snapped. "These men have been seeking just such a brawl for many moons now. And now that they have gained this, they shall run back to Preia, flaunt their wounds that we have staunched, and claim we attacked with no cause. We must hope that Lord Otto is yet fat and content enough to once again come to our aid, and keep us from yet more war, and more—"

He broke off sharply, as though he'd just remembered who he was talking to, and Rosa felt her throat swallow, her heart beating jaggedly in the darkness. The men would run back to Preia. To Duke Warmisham. Lord Kaspar's father, who'd apparently set them up to this.

But wasn't the Duke waiting on Lord Kaspar's research? Rosa's research? Hadn't he said full-on war was undesirable... at least, until the peasants could be induced into fighting it for them?

Rosa's heartbeat clanged louder, and she fought to keep her steps steady, one after the other. "But surely the realm's lords don't actually *want* another war with orcs now?" she made her hollow voice say, lying, *lying*. "I can't imagine why Duke Warmisham would be ordering his men to secretly break your treaty. I mean, he and Lord Otto are supposedly allies, and *Otto* has publicly defended your treaty, again and again, and denounced this kind of behaviour."

John's laugh was cold, brittle, incredulous. "Foolish woman," he said. "Lord Otto shall only *denounce* this as long as we keep him rolling in wealth, and even then, he does *naught* of true substance against his fellow lords. Even now, Lord Culthen of Tlaxca seeks to stir up strife in this realm's capital Citadel, urging these lords to war. Lord Anton of Dunburg seeks to block our trade, and sets attacks upon any loads of goods we hire. And Duke Warmisham of Preia"—John spat the name as if it were a curse—"not only sends men to prod us into attacks such as this, but he also seeks to stir the fear and fury of the common people. He sends paid men to taverns and markets to spread word of our wickedness. He spreads books and signs and treatises full of tales of the deadly, filthy Orc Mountain, and the black armies and beaten women within it."

Oh. Rosa felt dangerously dizzy, suddenly, blinking at where she knew John's face to be, while the undeniable reality behind his words slowly streamed through her skull. *This project is now of prime importance,* Lord Kaspar's letter had said. *Risking the resources and plans of the entire realm...*

And while Rosa had of course known, intellectually, what that might mean, hearing John actually say it all out loud, here in this bitter darkness, seemed to twist tight and painful into the mess already swirling through her head.

Of course Duke Warmisham had a broader plan. Of course he would be seeking to goad orcs into foolish actions that could then be used against them. Of course he would be seeking to stir up swathes of anti-orc sentiment, in advance of announcing the newly discovered and deeply shocking atrocities of Orc Mountain. While his fellow lords prepared to support just such an announcement, by preventing the orcs from gaining supplies, and drumming up support in the realm's capital...

And worst of all, Duke Warmisham had clearly fobbed off

the job of researching the orcs' atrocities to his so-called clever son. Who'd then, of course, turned and dumped the whole job onto *Rosa*. Who was now here, in the orcs' own mountain, spying, watching, *lying*.

Rosa's hard swallow was audible in the silence, and she heard John laugh again, the sound even colder, more bitter than before. "Ach, foolish woman," he said, his voice almost taunting. "Duke Warmisham, whose second son is your *patron* at this library. The man whose scent yet fills your mouth and your womb. The cheap, selfish fool who starves his own *pet*, whilst she eagerly toils on his behalf."

Damn it. *Damn* it. John did *not* know about Rosa's research, could *not* know why she was here—but she couldn't see his face, couldn't stop her own face from flooding with heat. And John could see that, oh gods what would he say, he couldn't know Rosa would ever do such a thing, he *couldn't*—

"I *hate* Lord Kaspar," she blurted out, before she could stop it, before she could think. "I *hate* him, John. You're right, he's cheap, and foolish, and because he's marginally intelligent, he gets away with foisting the actual effort off onto everyone else, and being praised as a rare genius. He's never gone without, he's never had to suffer, he's *never* had to fight or work for something he believes in. He uses people—*especially* women— and throws them away without a second thought. I *hate* him, John. I *hate* that you can still smell him on me."

Her voice had gone hard and fervent, her hand gripping against John's solid bare arm, and she felt her other hand grasp for his face, feeling the sharp line of his jaw in his darkness. "I *hate* him," she said again, thick and hoarse. "You *have* to believe me, John."

It made no sense, none of this made sense, not Rosa's words, not the way her hands were suddenly clutching at him, not the abrupt stillness of his solid body against her. And surely not the shouting whirling mess in Rosa's head, not panic but just sheer desperate need, she needed to prove it, to hide it, John needed to know, he could never, *never* know…

She shoved at John's immobile form, pushing him back against the corridor's stone wall, and he didn't resist. Not even when her shaking, tingling hands fumbled for the front of his trousers, where they somehow knew they'd find his long, thick hardness, swollen and hungry, pulsing against her fingers through the fabric.

"Please, my lord," she heard herself whisper, the words deeply shameful, even as she reached inside and drew him out, felt the thick velvet strength of him bobbing bare and alive under her touch. Fuck, he was big, and he was swelling even larger in her fingers, his smooth rounded head already streaking wetness against her palm. And curse her, but Rosa's hand had snapped up to her mouth, all of its own accord, so her eager tongue could lick her palm clean, moaning aloud as the sweet honey of him exploded across her consciousness—

She could hear a short, strangled moan, could feel it in her bones—and in a jerky, staggering movement, she dropped to her bare knees on the stone floor. Wincing at the flare of pain, clutching at John's strong thighs for balance in the dark—and then breathing in deep, turning her face up. Licking her lips, parting them wide, waiting in the sudden watching stillness…

The feel of John's hard, silken cleft on her tongue was an offering, a revelation, and Rosa nearly sobbed as she sucked on it, lurid, deep. Earning a swarm of liquid in return, all sweet slippery honey, and she gulped it deeper, sucking him all the way inside. Until her lips were spread as wide apart as they could go, and he was nestled thick and powerful against her frantically convulsing throat, dripping his rich bounty straight down into it.

Fuck, Rosa had never felt so hungry in her life, and the urge to keep sucking, keep drinking, was towering over all else, trampling the world in its wake. And when she felt John draw out, taking this gift away from her, she actually moaned her protest, grabbed uselessly at his taut, unyielding arse—

But then he sank back in again, fluid and easy, settling his dripping head back into its place in her throat. Its honey seemed thicker now, more plentiful, and comprehension dipped and soared as Rosa nodded around him, and slowly drew back, just as he'd done. Feeling his thick length slide out between her wet lips, running her hungry tongue along every scar and vein and ridge, until she was flicking at his oozing slit, tasting and teasing, drawing that delectable honey from its source...

He sank deep with astonishing power this time, thrusting that leaking head hard into her throat, and Rosa shuddered with relief at the taste of it, the truth of it. John wanted her. He wanted a hungry, willing pet, who could swallow him deep, who could milk out his seed, who would suck him off in a pitch-black corridor. A pet who would take his side against his own brothers, and against these awful men, who only wanted more war, more death...

So Rosa lavished him, worshipped him, sucking him deeper and harder than she'd ever taken anyone before, her throat working and convulsing, learning to accept his strength. Until she felt the frenzied, whirling exultation of her lips settling around the actual *base* of him, her face crushed against his thick musky hair, she had an orc's entire prick in her mouth and she had to be worthy, he had to be pleased, he *had* to be...

His release sprayed out with no warning, only the sheer, shocking thrill of that huge, all-consuming cock in Rosa's mouth spewing itself straight down her spasming throat, and pooling into her belly. While his thick shaft in her mouth strove and shuddered, his hairy groin pressing even harder against Rosa's stretched-out lips. His breath coming out in a harsh, rasping moan, setting the dark aflame with the deep, violent truth of his joy.

Rosa didn't stop sucking until he'd fully finished emptying himself, his hardness softening in her mouth, his big body sagging against the wall behind him. Only then did she finally draw back from him, careful, reverent, feeling the slick slide of his spent length slipping between her parted lips.

She lingered at the end, nudging her tongue against that softly open slit, and it occurred to her, distant and blunted, that she didn't want this to be over yet. She didn't want to be separated from him. And what if she were to start again, coax him back to hardness, and...

His groan was low, almost pained, and for the first time in this she felt his hands, warm, guiding her face away, drawing himself out. Leaving her empty, lightheaded, on the verge of whimpering, while she felt him moving before her, perhaps tucking himself away again.

"Hungry little pet," he murmured, the words soft enough that Rosa nearly didn't hear them—but she had, and she tilted her head up to him, licking her lips, almost as if in supplication. *Please, my lord, please...*

Her prayer was answered not with a touch, or a caress, as she might have wished—but instead with the glorious, head-swarming truth of strong arms circling close around her, and snatching her up. Tucking her tight against his solid, comforting strength as he once again began striding back down the corridor, as if nothing at all had changed.

But something *had* changed. Something in the relaxed ease of his body against Rosa's, in the slow steadiness of his breath, the easy thump of his heartbeat under her spread fingers. In how Rosa's nuzzle into his neck was met by an almost-tolerant tilt of his head toward her, his hair tickling at her forehead.

"You must never tell Efterar that you did this, so soon after he told you to," he said, without warning, his voice soft. "I know seed helps you, but I should not wish him to know that I should ever follow his fool *feelings*."

Rosa could have easily argued several of these statements, but instead she found herself laughing into John's neck, the sound husky, unfeigned. "Of course not," she murmured back. "Efterar seems a bit of a self-righteous arse sometimes anyway, doesn't he?"

John actually chuckled, and hoisted her up closer against him. "Shhh, woman," he said. "He and his Ash-Kai magic are oft seen as the saviour of our mountain."

But Rosa's head had lifted to search John's face, even as she couldn't see it, while her surprisingly calm brain belatedly pulled together all the seemingly disparate bits and pieces. Drawing together a little pool of clarity, out of all the day's unimaginable chaos.

The books John had taken from her library. The books in *his* library. The medics. The milk, the survey, the mathematical probability, the medical tools, perhaps even the blood compatibility. The twenty dead women. *He's supposed to be the expert. Shall you ban him from his work. When it comes to women, we must tread with great care...*

His Ash-Kai magic cannot predict, or understand, or explain. It is not enough.

"You're trying to help women like me, aren't you?" Rosa heard herself say, quiet. "You're trying to learn how to keep us safe, as we bear your sons. *That's* what you want to focus on right now, rather than this foolish, endless war."

She could feel John's astonishment, prickling the air around them, clenching his claws against her. But then, to her distant surprise, he nodded, his hair brushing at her cheek.

"Ach," he replied finally. "There is much else I must do, much other work to be done—but this alone is my highest calling. My true life's aim."

Rosa nodded too, closing her eyes, sliding up a careful hand to stroke against the hard lines of his face. "Then *you* are the true saviour of your mountain, John," she whispered. "*You're* the one who will rescue your people. *Without* magic, but with *knowledge.* Even better than magic, because as long as you write it down, and put it in a library, knowledge can be shared with *anyone. Forever.*"

She could hear the fervency on her voice, could feel it in her touch against his skin. And though John didn't answer, there was a soft, telltale trace of his claws, curving against the back of Rosa's neck. Speaking his approval, without speaking at all.

The warmth unfurled sharp and powerful, enough to set Rosa's eyes fluttering, her breath catching in her throat. She'd pleased him. She could be worthy, maybe, after all, as long as he never, ever found out. Even after this was over in three weeks, even when she returned to Lord Kaspar, and...

Rosa forcibly shoved that unsettling thought away, and snuggled closer against John's strength, as a massive yawn escaped her mouth. And in return, she felt rather than heard him chuckle, his chest vibrating warm and tolerant against hers.

"Sleepy little rose," he whispered. "Rest now. I shall care for you."

It was like Rosa was filled to the brim, suddenly, so quiet and easy and safe, wrapped in her clever lord's arms. So she settled her head on his shoulder, drew in a deep, contented breath, and slept.

20

When Rosa awoke the next morning, she half expected to find a mountain at war. Full of armed and furious orcs, ready to battle against the dukes and lords—including, perhaps, Lord Kaspar—who were beating with swords and catapults upon the orcs' doorstep.

But instead, there was only a surprisingly calm-looking John, sitting fully dressed at the opposite end of the bed, and gripping another basket full of food and milk. "Yes, those fool men yet live, and shall likely leave today," he said curtly, in answer to Rosa's careful question, as he passed over the basket. "We shall now have a few days' peace before what next shall come. Now eat, pet, and drink, whilst I read to you."

Rosa blinked owlishly toward his face, and then down to his other hand. Which, incredibly, was indeed holding a book. And not just any book, but—her heart gave an off-kilter patter—*her* book. *The Lady Bright*.

"Truly?" she asked, her voice high-pitched, and she belatedly stuffed a piece of cheese into her mouth. "Would you, then—maybe—consider starting it over? So you know what's happening?"

John's claw had already opened the book to the middle, to the exact place Rosa had stopped reading. But at her suggestion, he actually shrugged, and obligingly flipped back to the first page.

His voice was low and smooth as he began to read, telling of the wronged lady trapped in the vile prison, and Rosa felt herself sigh with deep, undeniable contentment as the words washed into her. Who would ever have thought that an *orc* could read so beautifully, his voice easy and expressive, the tale rising to colourful, vivid life with every page he turned...

Rosa was truly sorry when he stopped, her little basket of breakfast entirely empty—but then was the equally exciting discovery that John had actually arranged for her to have a *bath*. And that a shadowy door on the back wall of his bedroom was actually a full *latrine*, complete with some kind of remarkable piping contraption to bring in hot water.

"Good *gods*, John," Rosa gasped, as she eased her suddenly filthy-feeling body into the steel basin he'd filled, and into the powerful, fundamental thrill of warm, liquid pleasure all over. "This is an absolute *marvel*."

John didn't reply, but instead only handed her what appeared to be a bar of genuine, strong-smelling soap. It was an order, clearly, but one that Rosa couldn't even pretend to resist, and she immediately set to scrubbing herself all over. While John—her hand froze, mid-scrub—moved around to kneel behind her, and began combing her hair *with his claws*.

It led to an orc silently *washing Rosa's hair*, in a dark, stone-walled, surprisingly cozy latrine. And in that moment, with her head willingly tilted back, and John's claws softly scraping at her scalp, Rosa couldn't help the rising, nagging suspicion that in another world, another life, becoming an orc's pet might be an occupation worth serious exploration.

"Thank you, my lord," she murmured, once John drew her out of the tub again, her bare body squeaky clean, her damp hair now plaited down her back in a neat new braid. "This was—excessively kind of you."

John led her naked form back out of the latrine, and into the dim warmth of the larger, lamplit bedroom. "I swore to care for you," he said, as he came to a halt beside a stone shelf Rosa hadn't noticed before, and pulled off what appeared to be a clean grey tunic. "Now, I shall dress you."

Rosa blinked, but willingly complied as he drew the tunic over her head. It was just as large as his last one had been, hanging down to her thighs, fitting far more like a voluminous dress—but this time, John also reached for a long black strip of leather, and tied it loosely around her waist. Creating an effect almost indeed like a dress, if not for the shorter length of it, or the dangerously deep slit at the neck.

"Good," John said, casting an assessing gaze up and down Rosa's form. "Now come."

Again, there was no thought of refusing. Only slipping her hand into his warm one, and allowing him to lead her out the door, and into the corridor. He'd again brought a lamp, illuminating the stone walls with a flickering orange glow, and Rosa felt her hopefulness rising as they walked, the corridor tilting steadily upward under her padding bare feet.

"Where are you taking me?" she asked. "The library?"

John shot her a sidelong look, a curt nod. "You said you wished to work in my library, and learn Aelakesh. Yes?"

Rosa's gasp of delight bubbled up on its own, and she couldn't help a bright, eager grin toward his blank face. "Truly, John?" she said, clasping her hand to her heart. "I would *love* that."

John nodded again, as if he'd expected no less, and then sharply turned a corner. And here, again, was his library, spacious and high-ceilinged and lovely.

But this time—Rosa's steps hesitated behind John—there were *other orcs* in it. Two orcs, in fact, rather disparate in size, sitting side by side at the room's large wooden table. And when one of the orcs turned to look at them, blinking with long-lashed eyes, Rosa's breath choked off in her throat, her belly twisting tight.

It was Tristan. John's *lover*. The orc who, along with Salvi, had tried to prevent her from leaving the other day, and who'd growled at her with such ferocity. And who, Rosa noted with deep misgiving, looked even more handsome than she remembered. His skin a silvery grey, his eyes large and expressive, his mouth sensuous and full.

"You shall work and study here with Tristan today," John announced toward Rosa, the words slicing through the whirl of jealousy currently clouding her brain. "He is our best scribe, and shall teach you well. I have also brought these tools you wished for."

He waved a hand at the empty side of the table, which indeed boasted an impressive variety of writing and binding tools. But that meant—Rosa twitched—John truly meant her to work here, across a table from his *lover*. Who happened to be sitting beside—she twitched again, and then openly stared— the massive, deadly orc who'd single-handedly fought all those men yesterday. Simon, of Clan Skai.

He was wearing a tunic today, and appeared in surprisingly good health compared to his bloody state in the sick-room. But the parts of him that Rosa could see—his craggy face, his neck, his huge veined forearms and hands—were still heavily marked by cuts and scars, some still fresh and angry-looking. And his glittering eyes were staring straight back at Rosa, with a look that could only be suspicion, or perhaps even dislike.

Rosa couldn't help a reflexive shudder, and a fearful, uneasy glance up at John's face. "Um," she said. "And you'll stay too, John, won't you? And help teach me? And read to me, like you said?"

John's brows furrowed together, his head giving a decisive shake. "There is much I must now address today," he said flatly. "Thanks to our wise, foresighted Skai"—his mouth thinned, his eyes narrowing toward Simon's hulking form—"I must now spend these next days mired in plans and meetings, staving off the new war-plots of men."

Oh. Rosa fought to hide her disappointment, but likely failed miserably. "And I can't—come with you? Like yesterday? And learn?"

"You shall better learn here," John replied, his voice firm. "This is what you wished for, pet."

Rosa felt herself grimace, her eyes darting toward Tristan— who was looking back toward them, his brow delicately furrowed. "And mayhap, John-Ka," he said, soft, "you shall return to us at noontide, and review our work."

John shot Tristan a look that was heavy with unspoken meaning, sparking another unnerving flare of jealousy deep in Rosa's gut. "Ach, I shall seek to do this," John snapped. "Does this appease you, woman?"

Appease you. As if Rosa were suddenly pelting him with insatiable demands, and she felt herself shrink back slightly, her arms crossing against her chest. "Very well," she heard herself say. "I suppose."

John's eyes briefly closed, and she could see his shoulders rise, and fall—and then he purposefully stepped closer to her, and circled his hand gently around the back of her neck. To where it was familiar, steady, safe—and even more when that hand tilted her head up, drawing her eyes to his.

"You shall stay here, little pet, whilst I do what must be done," he said, his voice smooth, reassuring. "You shall do good work, and seek to please me upon my return. Whilst I am gone, you shall ask your questions of Tristan, and know that he shall help you on my behalf, and keep you safe."

Keep you safe. Rosa's eyes darted again to the table, this time lingering on Simon's giant, watching form—but a purposeful little shake of John's fingers snapped her gaze back to his again.

"And you shall not fear Simon," he continued. "He has sworn only to work here today, and not frighten you, lest he risk the captain's wrath. Ach?"

Rosa could only swallow and nod, wholly caught in the glittering power of those eyes. "Very well," she heard her voice say, quiet, shameful. "I shall seek to please you, my lord."

John gave a satisfied-sounding grunt, a triumphant pat to Rosa's hot cheek—and then, without another word, he spun on his heel, and stalked out of the room.

Rosa watched him go, her arms still wrapped tight to her middle, while the contented-feeling warmth that had filled her all morning seemed to seep away a little, vanishing into the stone all around. Because that, just there, had been John—*manipulating* her. Again. Hadn't it?

And as much as Rosa couldn't deny that she'd fallen for it, again—or that she'd perhaps even *liked* it, in the moment—it was still a chilly, unsettling reminder of what he really was. What all *this* really was. The food, the bath, the reading.

John wanted to prove this to her. He wanted her to stay. Not because he liked her, or valued her—but because he didn't want her *blood* on his hands.

And now that Rosa knew about John's goals—helping women like her was his *life's true aim*, he'd said—it all made far more sense than it had before. This was personal, for John. And it wasn't about her. It was about his *work*.

And if Rosa had learned anything from yesterday's chaos, it was just how much John cared about his work, and his responsibilities. And letting a woman like Rosa die—or even letting her run away from him—would surely call into question his competence, his integrity. It would weaken his standing as a leader before his people.

John didn't truly care. Rosa wasn't truly his pet. He *needed* her to stay. And it didn't matter, it *didn't*, Rosa was only here to save her own future, three weeks, and that was all...

Rosa felt herself swallow, her eyes fixed unseeing to the floor—until she jumped at the sound of a cough, coming from the table. "Should you wish to join us, Rosa," said a soft voice— Tristan's voice—"I could teach you and Simon our letter-forms together."

Rosa couldn't help a suspicious, miserable glance toward him, and his infuriatingly handsome, symmetrical orc-face. Which blinked back at her for an instant, his eyes wide and dark, before he ducked his head, his pointed ear-tips turning a faint shade of pink.

"Or not," he said, even softer than before. "As you wish."

Rosa grimaced, her gaze inexplicably darting to the huge Simon orc—who, as it turned out, was glaring straight back at her with a fierce, ghastly frown. "Fool woman too proud to learn," he said, in tones of deep conviction. "Or too stupid. Forget her, little Ka-esh."

Rosa's incredulity rose in a furious swarm—she was certainly *not* too proud or too stupid to learn another language—and she felt her weak-kneed body stalk to the table, and drop down onto the chair across from them.

"Of course I want to learn," she snapped. "What do I need?"

Tristan still wasn't meeting her eyes, but gingerly slid over a few sheets of rough-looking paper, as well as another sheet covered in carefully written letter forms. A kind of explanatory chart, Rosa realized, and she noticed that across the table, Simon had one also.

"You remember how to prepare the quill, ach?" Tristan

asked quietly, in a question clearly meant for Simon, rather than her. "Once this is done, mayhap we shall begin with writing each form, and reviewing its sound."

Simon was carefully scraping off the end of his quill with a sharp black claw, frowning in intense concentration, and Rosa fought to ignore him as she prepared her own quill and ink, and made a few experimental strokes on the paper. It was a decent quill, surprisingly, and she wrote out a few lines just to test it, to feel the familiar, reassuring certainty of pen and ink in her fingers.

"Braggart woman," came Simon's voice from across the table, heavy with dislike. "Tiny hand make easy."

He was glowering thunderously at Rosa's paper, and Rosa ignored the unpleasant stutter in her chest as she glared straight back. "I've been doing this for most of my life," she snapped at him, without thinking. "Unlike some people, apparently, who enjoy starting *wars* for fun instead."

Simon's sudden, menacing growl made the hair on Rosa's neck stand up, and beside him Tristan's hands were fluttering, from his paper to his quill and back again. "Form one," he said, his voice higher-pitched than before, "is called *sa*. It makes a hissing sound, and is drawn from bottom to top, thus."

His trembly hand drew a surprisingly elegant letter, and Rosa swallowed down an unhappy twinge of what felt almost like guilt as she mimicked it on her own paper, and made a few annotations about the sound, and the way of drawing it.

It took Simon much longer to make his form, his big hand gripping the quill with visible care, the resulting letter large and childlike. But Tristan rewarded him with a quick, quietly stunning smile, and then moved on to the next letter, and the next.

Tristan was a good teacher, Rosa could admit, patient and thorough, without the superiority or condescension she'd always disliked in her own schoolteachers. And Aelakesh truly was a fascinating language, and also quite enjoyable to write, and as they worked, Rosa felt her own prickly unease fading beneath the strength of her rising, nagging curiosity.

"Why *are* you learning to write now?" she heard herself ask Simon, before she'd even noticed her mouth opening. "You didn't learn your own language as a child?"

Simon's vicious glare was enough to make Rosa drop her quill, to which Tristan's hand snapped across the table, and passed it back to her. "Our written language was almost lost in all the warring," Tristan's quiet voice replied. "Thus, many of our kin have never had a chance to learn it. Simon learns now at the captain's behest, to better help he and our Priest John-Ka face these new threats that have now arisen."

There was quite a lot to unpack in that, and Rosa tilted her head, considering it. "You mean to say that your captain's *making* Simon learn to read, to compensate for that unsanctioned brawl yesterday?" she said, half-smiling despite herself at the baleful answering glower on Simon's face. "And did you just call John your *Priest*? He told me there hasn't been a Priest in Orc Mountain since Fror died."

Tristan betrayed an unmistakable grimace, and beside him Simon snorted, his glower shifting into satisfaction. "Only Ka-esh think John Priest," he said. "All other orcs know better. Even *John* know."

Tristan's eyes had sharply narrowed, in the first sign of unpleasantness Rosa had seen from him today. But he didn't speak, which again left Rosa to ask the question, because of course it had to be asked, quite desperately, after a cryptic comment like *that*.

"What's wrong with John?" she demanded, the words sounding unaccountably defensive. "Why *can't* he be your mountain's Priest? He's been raised to do it, he's very clever, and he obviously cares deeply about you lot, even if you make a habit of doing incomprehensibly foolish things. Like goading men into brawling with you, when you're supposed to be bound under a *peace-treaty*!"

It was a clinching argument, really, and Rosa was briefly mollified by Tristan's glance of bare, warm-eyed appreciation toward her. But beside him Simon snorted again, and jabbed his huge black claw down into the wooden table, deep enough to leave a mark.

"John sway you to say this, foolish woman," he snapped. "I know you see. I smell you in hidden Ka-esh den. You know I no *goad*. I *sit*. I hone own blade, on own *mountain*. This is *all*."

Right. Rosa felt herself wince, without meaning to, and Simon surely saw it, jabbing at the table again. "John sway you," he continued flatly. "He *use* you. He is hard orc. Cold orc. *Selfish*. He rail on Skai for our ways, when his own sins are cruel and grave. When"—he shot a dark look at Tristan beside him—"he *kill* own clan brother's *son*."

Wait, what? Rosa blinked, wholly taken aback—but there was truth in Simon's glittering gaze, and she didn't miss the telltale wince on Tristan's mouth. Pained, regretful, and perhaps even... *guilty*.

"John *killed* his own brother's *son*?" Rosa echoed, blank, her eyes held not on Simon, but on Tristan. "Not *your* son, Tristan?"

It was appalling, really, how unsettling that thought was, and how powerfully the relief flared when Tristan gave a chagrined shake of his head.

"Not mine," he said, quiet. "Salvi's. And"—his eyes flicked back toward Simon, almost stubborn now—"the orcling had not yet been born, and thus it was yet his mother's choice to make. John only helped her gain her own wishes. He was"—his throat visibly swallowed—"a good Priest, in this."

Simon growled again, furious and menacing, his claw again gouging into the table. "No," he hissed back, though his eyes were on Rosa, rather than Tristan. "John turn against his own kind, for what *he* think best. He do this to me, this day past, when I only keep safe my kin. And now John scheme with new mate"—he jerked his hand toward Rosa—"to do this to *own son*. Not *fit* to be Priest."

Wait. Simon—*knew* about that? Rosa was trapped, suddenly, in the vehemence of his glare upon her, and it took far too much effort to find a response in the mess shouting in her brain. "I'm not John's—er—*mate*," she said, her voice oddly distant. "And he's concerned for my *survival*, and that's hardly a bad Priest, is it? Didn't you know that twenty women *died* last year, giving birth to *your* sons?"

Simon's answering laugh was immediate, grating. "And how many orcs dead from human swords this year?" he demanded. "Many twenties. This no different."

"It *is* different," Rosa shot back, inexplicably enraged. "Women like me are on *your side*. We *care*. We want to *help* you."

Even as she blinked at those baffling words coming out her mouth, and the surprisingly fervent earnestness behind them, Simon's laugh sent another hard chill up her spine. "Women care not for orcs," he said flatly. "Some want thrill of orc fuck. Some bored or alone or harmed by men. Some wish for coin or shelter. Almost all caught in bond, as you. There is no *care*."

Rosa couldn't deny a strange, hurtling commiseration as Simon spoke, almost as if she had felt his pain, *lived* it—at least, until that last bit. *Caught in bond. As—you?*

Beside Simon, Tristan was visibly wincing again, and Rosa could feel her heartbeat rising, pulsing louder in her ears. "Caught in bond," she repeated, carefully. "What—what does that mean?"

Simon laughed again, almost amused this time, but not quite. "Ach, this *good* Priest not speak this to own *mate*?" he said. "Bond come with all orcs. Orc fuck woman, put scent upon her, fill with seed. Woman then hunger, and follow, and *obey.*"

He was smirking at Rosa, and as she stared with slowly rising horror, he brought up his huge hand, and circled it around his own neck, claws digging deep into his own grey skin.

"Woman wish to serve orc," he said, in a taunting voice that scraped at Rosa's bones. "Wish to say, *ach, my lord, I shall please you.* Wish to believe all orc speaks, even if he *lie.* Even if words betray woman's own *eyes.*"

Rosa's gaze was fixed to Simon's claws against his neck, and her breath was coming very shallow, her heart jolting wild spikes under her skin. That wasn't true. It couldn't be true. John couldn't have done such a thing to her. Made a—a *bond.* Could he?

"Woman wish even to *kill,*" Simon continued, his taunting voice gone lower, thoroughly frightening. "Wish to kill own *son,* if orc command. If this gain his end. Make seem like selfless, noble Priest. Ach?"

That couldn't be true, it *couldn't*—but Rosa's thoughts had instantly swarmed with the images of it, the feel of John's claws against her skin, his smooth, steadying voice. His constant—*manipulations.* Even that one not just an hour ago, the way he'd put his hand around her neck, held her eyes in his...

And Rosa had known, she *did* know, John was in this for himself, wasn't he? For his own work, his own goals. And surely he would use any resource at his command, even if it was... a bond. *Magic.* A *lie.*

The fear had begun trickling, raw and intensely painful, while Rosa's brain skipped back, back. Finding, all too easily, all the moments where she shouldn't have obeyed John, shouldn't have agreed—but she had. Gods curse her, she *had.*

"That is not," Tristan's voice cut in, sounding very far away, "the whole truth, Simon, and you know this. This bond between orcs and women exists, ach, but it does not *control*. Women leave orcs all the time. Salvi's mate left him. The captain lost two mates before this one. And tell me, when was the last time a Skai kept a mate for longer than a twelvemonth?"

Tristan had risen to his feet, his eyes flinty on Simon's—but then Simon rose too, deliberate and deadly. His huge body towering over Tristan, making Tristan—who would have been a tall man—appear like little more than a *child*, and Rosa didn't miss the very slight quiver in Tristan's form, even as he stubbornly kept his gaze on Simon's furious face.

"Do not taunt me, little Ka-esh," growled Simon, deep and deadly. "You no ken what you speak."

Tristan's shiver felt visceral this time, his throat bobbing, but he didn't drop his eyes from Simon's face. "Ach, I know," he said, his voice almost devastatingly quiet. "We have seen what some of you Skai do in secret, to these women you cannot keep."

The tension rippled across Simon's huge form, his hands curled in massive fists at his sides. "You no understand, little Ka-esh," he hissed, "so you wrong to *blame*. Skai clan *dying*."

"Ach, because your *women* are dying," replied Tristan, though his voice wavered, and he took a jerky step backward. "And yet, you will not allow us to—"

"*No*," Simon cut in, so deep it almost vibrated the room. "We no show our women no false, pretty, smooth-speaking Ka-esh. So you no steal, and *kill* Skai sons!"

"We do not wish to *kill* your sons," Tristan's voice countered, though it was badly trembling now. "We wish to *help* them. And their mothers. *Your* mates."

But Simon only laughed, the sound cold, deafening, terrifying. "You lie," he hissed, as he took a menacing step toward Tristan. "Ka-esh *always* have secret plan. Secret from orcs.

Secret from *humans*. You wish me to *make* you tell true, pretty little Ka-esh? You wish to speak loud of newest plan, from good *Priest*, for *all* to learn?"

Simon had shot a dark, mocking glance toward—toward *Rosa*, and before him Tristan's grey face was looking deathly ill, his clawed hands groping for the wall behind him, his throat convulsing. "Please," he said, his voice cracking. "Do not. I—misspoke. Please, I—"

Rosa's gut was churning, sparks of true, genuine terror firing up her spine—when suddenly, thank the gods, another orc strode in. It was Salvi, and Rosa couldn't have ever imagined being so relieved to see his tall, scar-eyed, capable-looking form, as he took one look at Tristan and Simon, and hurled himself across the room to hover snarling and furious between them.

"What the *fuck*," Salvi growled, his gaze searching Tristan's hunted, wide-eyed face—and then he whirled around to glare at Simon, his claws out, his teeth bared. "He was *teaching* you, Skai, at the *captain's* behest, so you could help dig yourself out of the hole you've gotten us all into. And this is how you repay him? I could taste his fear halfway across the *mountain*!"

Both Tristan and Simon grimaced, and thankfully Simon took a half-step backwards, even though he was still a good head taller than Salvi, and likely twice as wide. "Go away, false healer *djöfull*," he hissed. "I never harm weak Ka-esh. Even when Ka-esh bait me. Taunt me. Speak *lies* of Skai."

"They're not lies if they're *true*," Salvi shot back. "And John was off his fucking *rocker* to even allow a Skai like you in his library in the first place, let alone with *them*. Now, why don't you kindly waddle your oversized arse the *fuck* out of here, before I go take all this to the *captain*, and call you out for breaking your vows to the rest of us, for the *second time* in *two damned days*!"

Simon's lips curled back, baring a mouth full of sharp white teeth. "I break naught. I keep safe. I *enforce*. I no stray from vows, as false healer Ka-esh, who no mine or forge, as Ka-esh ought. Instead play-act as medic, and heal *naught!*"

"Oh, fuck *off*," Salvi snarled, his voice deep with loathing. "If John's not Priest of this mountain, then you're sure as *hell* not our Enforcer. And if I'm not a medic, then tell me why the hell none of those men you fought yesterday are burning to ash in a *pyre*, despite your best fucking efforts!"

Simon's eyes dangerously flashed, his fists rising, and for a moment, Rosa thought he was going to smash Salvi straight in the face—but then he abruptly spun toward the door, his huge body held very stiff. "I thank you for teaching, little Ka-esh," he said, to the corridor, without looking back—and then he lumbered off, leaving a stony, crackling silence behind.

"Jumped-up ignorant *fuck*," Salvi hissed, viciously, into the silence, before turning back to Tristan again—and then his body seemed to still, and his hands snapped to Tristan's face, tilting it up to look at him. "Hey," he breathed, quiet. "Hey, *sæti*. You're all right. Ach?"

It seemed an unbearably private scene, suddenly, and Rosa made herself look away as she heard Tristan sniff, heard the shifting of clothes and skin. "Ach, you're all right," Salvi said, so soft Rosa almost couldn't hear it. "I'm here. No one's touching you but me. Ach?"

There was another sniff, followed by silence, and when Rosa risked a glance over toward it, Tristan was tucked close into Salvi's chest, Salvi's clawed hand stroking again and again at his hair. While Salvi himself glared at the wall, his jaw set and grim.

But then Tristan purposefully shoved away, ducking out of Salvi's embrace entirely, and wiping at his eyes with his palms. "I should," he said, his voice thick, "find John-Ka."

Salvi immediately stiffened, his shoulders hunching, his

hands clenched at his sides. "Why?" he demanded. "Whatever do you need *him*—"

But Tristan had darted a pointed glance toward Rosa, who was now caught blatantly staring at the two of them, and indeed wishing, disjointed, that John would appear, just how Salvi had. That he would draw her into his arms, and pet her, and tell her that everything would be all right...

But no. *No.* John had lied to her, again. He hadn't told her about this—*magic bond.* And the more Rosa stood here and considered it, the more it all made a kind of sick, devastating sense. John had manipulated her, again and again. He'd intentionally, systematically used that bond against her. Women *wish* to serve, to obey, to believe...

And in the slowly, dangerously rising horror, there was the awful, fundamental realization that maybe all her research had been right about this, after all. The orcs truly *did* wield dark magic. Not just healing magic, like Efterar's. But magic that could trap. Coerce. *Control.*

It was a cruelty. An atrocity. Perhaps even enough to start a *war.*

Rosa's arms clutched around her waist, her heartbeat punching painfully against her ribs, and she only distantly noticed Salvi cursing, and then stalking back out the door. Leaving her alone with Tristan again, but Rosa couldn't even look at him, could only stand there, and blink at the floor. Waiting, waiting, for—

Him. John. Striding into the room, snapping Rosa's gaze up toward his, almost as if by silent command. As if by a secret, illicit *control-bond,* and the bitter, prickling certainty of it only sparked higher as he approached, his eyes flat, his steps quick on the stone floor. And as his brisk, businesslike hand clasped to the back of her neck, Rosa grasped for resistance, for courage. The orcs seduced, controlled, *magic*...

"Woman," John's voice snapped, not kindly. "Speak to me."

Rosa was truly, desperately shivering, blinking at his harsh, narrow-eyed face. He was a hard orc. A cold orc. He lied. And she'd found what she'd come for, she would tell Lord Kaspar and save her future, and she didn't care, she *didn't*…

"I've changed my mind," she heard herself say, shaky, resigned, dead inside. "I want you to take me home."

21

Rosa expected her grand announcement to be met with anger, or disbelief, or perhaps more exhortations or promises or pleading. What she did *not* expect was for John to give a short, exasperated sigh, and clasp her hand, and yank her toward the door.

"Wait," she said, glancing helplessly back at Tristan's equally confused-looking face. "Are you actually—you're just going to—*agree*?"

John just kept on walking, dragging Rosa down the pitch-black corridor, so fast she had to jog to keep up. But he hadn't yet spoken, and she glowered in vain in the darkness, and jerked at her arm in his grip. "John," she said, uneasy, exasperated. "What are you *doing*?"

He came to an abrupt halt in the corridor, and Rosa heard an odd, out-of-place click—and then his hand dragged her again, until there was the unmistakable, incongruous sound of a *door* slamming shut behind them. And then—Rosa blinked, and shielded her eyes—there was light, sparking to life from a lamp on a small wooden table.

And the table was in—a new room. A—*human* room.

Strangely but unmistakably so, with its closed, tightly fitted wooden door, and its lack of any stark, carved-out features. Instead, this room was small and cozy, with a lower ceiling than most of the other rooms Rosa had seen so far, and bright white-washed walls. And placed within it was a set of sturdy, but undeniably human-made, wooden furniture. Including a four-poster bed, complete with a *quilt*, and beside it, a small, empty *cradle*.

Rosa stared at the cradle for an instant too long, her stomach uncomfortably lurching—and she belatedly whirled around to gape at John's smooth, blank-eyed face. Which still betrayed every single trace of his *rubbish*, and *manipulation,* and *lies*.

"You're—*trapping* me in here?" she demanded at him, her voice shrill. "You're not going to let me leave?"

"No," John replied, cold, implacable. "I shall not. You have become vexed, and afraid, and overset. I swore to care for you, and I shall not allow you to run away, and risk your own *life*, on a baseless, fearful whim. Most of all one that has been sparked by a fool Skai, who has surely done this to provoke me, even after he swore to the captain that he would not!"

The first flare of anger had flashed across John's eyes, and Rosa felt her own anger kindling to match, her arms crossing tightly over her chest. "It's not a baseless whim," she shot back. "It's you lying to me, *again*. You keeping secrets from me. You *manipulating* me, with your smooth-talking Ka-esh *rubbish!*"

"Ach, now you *do* sound like a Skai," John replied, clipped. "What shall you claim of me next. I steal my brothers' women, and next murder their sons, whilst I scribble in my dastardly book and cackle with glee?"

The words caught Rosa up short, and for a sudden, hurtling instant, there was a wild, ridiculous, *appalling* urge to laugh— but she shook it off, and glared straight back at him.

"You didn't tell me," she hissed, "about this *bond*, between us. The *control-bond*. The one that apparently makes me want to please you, and obey you, and even kill our *son*, as long as it helps your campaign to become *Priest*!"

Something stuttered in John's eyes, so fleeting Rosa almost missed it, before he gave a hard shake of his head, whipping his black braid behind him. "My campaign to become Priest is *dead*," he snapped back. "And this bond is not fate, or a rule. It is only a truth of nature, one which exists in all creatures, and between women and men also. Do not tell me"—his lip curled—"that you did not wish to please your cheap rich lord? You did not wish to obey him, and suckle the seed from his fat prick?"

His voice had gone chilly, mocking, and thank the gods there was only more anger, shoving away that curdling, unpleasantly unnerving image. "No," Rosa shot back, her teeth gritted together. "I already told you, you smug arse, that I can't stand Lord Kaspar, and I only did it for the *library*. For my *education*, and my ongoing *existence*. I never wanted him to fuck my throat in a soggy forest, or in a gods-damned public hallway. And I *sure* as hell didn't want him to growl at me, or frighten me, or put his *claws* around my neck!"

John was gazing at her again, his eyes almost painfully cold, his mouth thin and tight. "I have done *naught* you did not wish for. I seek to please you, and *help* you."

"Help me?" Rosa shouted back. "*Help* me?! No, you seek to lie to me, and *manipulate* me, and *silence* me into being your *pet*! You seek to cover up the bald, disgusting truth that you've cast some kind of vile orc *spell* on me!"

John's throat made a noise that might have been a groan, or a snort. "Do not flatter yourself, woman," he snapped. "Had I truly wished to cast some absurd magic upon a woman, you may be sure I should not have chosen you! A bony, vexing, fickle little *strumpet*, who thinks herself clever, yet is thrown into a foolish raging *fit* over a few words from a *Skai*!"

Rosa's mouth was uselessly opening and closing—had John just called her a *strumpet*?!—but before she could speak, he came a swift, dangerous step closer, claws bared, a low growl burring from his throat.

"I should have chosen," he hissed, "a tall, hale, hearty, and serene woman. One who does not sell herself to the highest bidder, or prattle constant questions with every breath, or play-act as wiser than she truly is!"

The words seemed to strike at Rosa one by one, catching and reverberating at something deep and fundamental within. Hard enough to make her stagger backwards, her hands clutching against her flailing heartbeat, and it felt like there was ice, suddenly, crackling inside, breaking apart.

A strumpet, who sells herself. Prattles questions. Pretends to be clever...

Rosa's breath was coming in thin, high-pitched gulps, the sound far too loud in this lovely little room, and her gulping swallow was audible too, striking at her ears. Good gods, what was wrong with her, what did it matter, she was a *spy*, she'd come to help start a *war*, John was cold and hard, he *was*, she would get out of here and run back to Lord Kaspar and *she did not care...*

She could hear John's heavy sigh over her choking breaths, could feel him stepping closer—and then the abrupt, juddering warmth of his hand on her neck. His hand, gentle, tilting her head up to meet his shifting eyes, and he was opening his mouth, he was about to speak—

"Please don't," Rosa heard herself gasp, her wet eyes blinking at his. "Don't say anything. Not like that, not now. Please."

John's eyes briefly closed—but then he nodded, quick and furtive, his throat convulsing. And as Rosa stood there, looked at him, it was almost as though she could see his regret, his resolve, rising, shuddering across his face...

The movement swarmed in a rush, the room swirling wide and sideways, rushing up to Rosa's back—and when it settled again, she was lying on the four-poster bed, her limbs sprawled against the soft quilt. And John, John was looming over her, dark and huge and menacing, and she twitched at the feel of him yanking off the black leather belt he'd given her, pooling her tunic-dress up loose against her waist. And then—Rosa yelped aloud—he grasped both her arms with one clawed hand, dragged them up over her head, and used the belt to lash them to the bedpost with a graceful, devastating ease.

It left Rosa sprawled and tied on a bed, with her chest helplessly heaving, her entire bottom half exposed and entirely naked to the room. And to the orc, the odious, vicious, *lying* orc, who was kneeling between her spread legs, and looking down at her with glinting, dangerous eyes.

"What the *fuck*," Rosa gasped, "are you *doing*."

John's expression didn't change, his huge body close, coiled, deadly. "I swore I should care for you," he hissed. "Thus, I shall be a kind lord, and grant you what you sorely need, in your distress. What you *wish* for."

Rosa spluttered at him, fully about to say that this was the very *last* thing she wished for, of all the things to wish for upon the entire *earth*—but then, gods curse him, John growled at her, and *touched* her *bare thigh*.

The touch was gentle, careful, perhaps almost hesitant, at total odds with that rasping, terrifying sound from his throat—but together, it was warm, and primal, and *wonderful*. Dragging Rosa's hissing breath out through her teeth, her eyelashes furiously fluttering, and above her John actually laughed, not quite as mocking this time.

"Foolish woman," he said. "You wish for this also, ach? You wish for me? Even if you yet think I have cast some cruel spell upon you?"

His hand had begun sliding up Rosa's thigh, slow, glorious,

setting her skin sparking in its wake. And she was squirming despite herself, sucking in air, feeling the strength of his soft leather against her bound wrists—and fighting back the almost overpowering urge to nod. To say, *keep going, don't stop, please...*

"You *had* to have done *something*," Rosa replied, though her voice sounded breathless to her ears. "It's the only thing that makes *sense*."

"Is it?" John countered, eyebrows rising, as that hand kept sliding. Not slipping down between Rosa's parted legs, as her traitorous thoughts might have hoped, but instead gently scraping its claws up over her hipbone, curving against her waist. Drawing the loose tunic up with it, and Rosa couldn't *think*, especially when—her mouth gave a strangled moan—he exposed her bare breast, and then tugged at her nipple, gentle, purposeful, *proprietary*.

"Is it?" he asked again, his eyes cool, demanding on hers, as that warm hand slid over to the other side, and did the same there, tugging, twisting, teasing. "Or might it be, mayhap, that I swore to care for you, and I have done so? I saw the danger we foolishly courted, so I have brought you to my mountain, I have given you good food and milk, I have nursed you in my own bed, I have washed you in my own *bath*. I have shown you my home and answered your questions and given you leave to work in my library. Ach, I have *tasted* you, when no man has done so, and granted you the thrill of fear you crave. Even now I pet you, and soothe you, even after you have sought to endanger yourself by leaving, and blamed me for what I have not done. Ach?"

The utter *prick*, and Rosa tried for a glare, which proved surprisingly challenging as he brought up his other hand, now playing with both her hardened, peaked nipples at once.

"You yelled at me too, orc," she choked out. "And, you've also tied me to a *bed*, and called me stupid, and prattling, and bony, and a *harlot*!"

John's head tilted, his eyes flicking up to hers, even as his hands settled closer against the slight swell of her breasts, cupping them soft against his palms. "You *are* bony, and prattling," he said, with damnable coolness. "But I did not call you *stupid*, or a *harlot*. I said you think yourself cleverer than you are, which is truth, if you find yourself taken in by a Skai. And you *have* sold yourself to the highest bidder, and now"—his mouth quirked, smug—"this is me, pet."

He punctuated the words with an insolent pinch to both nipples, drawing a heated moan to Rosa's mouth, and something that might have almost been a smile—which she bit back, hard, as his hands smoothed back down her bare waist.

"You—you called me a strumpet," Rosa managed, her voice sounding abominably warm. "A *strumpet!*"

John's mouth actually twitched up, brief but true—and with a cocked eyebrow, he finally, finally skated his hand downward, and lightly traced it between Rosa's parted legs. Earning a frantic, desperate choke from her throat, and an equally desperate clench of her swollen-feeling wetness against his gently delving finger.

It was humiliating, and highly betraying, and John actually laughed out loud, real and genuine, for only the second time in their entire acquaintance. His face lighting up, his dark eyes crinkling at the corners, his gaze warm and amused and perhaps almost—*affectionate*.

"You *are* a strumpet, pet," he said, with no small satisfaction. "You spurn the rich, powerful, titled man who claims you, so that you may be trapped and taken by his enemy. By an *orc*."

And as he spoke, it was almost like the dark, bitter truth of that had stolen back into the room, into his eyes. Shuttering the warmth back behind it, locking it away into cool distance again, and suddenly Rosa needed it again, craved it again. This rare, hidden version of John that teased and laughed, and argued over technicalities, and—*wanted* her. *Cared* for her.

The strange, thundering certainty of that seemed to worm its way inside, wriggling deep—and deeper still when she saw his shoulders rise and fall, his eyes closing again. And when they opened this time, they were dark, dangerous, deadly.

His harsh, fundamental growl seemed to light up every nerve under Rosa's skin at once, choking off her throat, clutching the hunger tight in her belly. Her eyes fluttering, her body squirming, tugging in vain at its restraints, trapped under the sheer, ravaging power of a fierce, fiendish orc.

His stroking claws were sharper this time, scraping red lines against her skin, but Rosa only bucked and gasped, moaned at the exquisite, teasing agony. And when those claws thrust her legs wide apart, and trailed so gently against her quivering, dripping heat, there was only a rippling jolt up her back, a sound from her throat that might have been a cry.

"Oh," she breathed, as he did it again, his eyes hot, dark, hungry for blood. "Oh gods, John, please, please!"

She had no idea what she was begging for—or did she, as those clawed fingers trailed again, circling, circling. So sharp, so lethal, so heavy with the promise of pain, of real harm. So heavy, suddenly, with a question of—*trust*.

"Please," Rosa whispered, to those crackling eyes. "Please, my lord."

John saw it, he *knew*, the awareness swift but sure, shuddering with truth. With the impossible, shouting thrill of one of those clawed hands, slipping up to press gently against Rosa's neck—while the other spread her thighs wider, nudged her swollen, clenching heat apart.

"You shall not move, once I breach you," he whispered, soft. "And you shall speak at the first sign of pain. You shall swear this to me. No falsehoods."

Rosa was fervently nodding, her throat spasming against his pressing hand, and her legs had widened even further, seemingly on their own. "I swear, John," she whispered, pleaded, to those eyes. "No falsehoods."

His answering nod was rapid, jerky—but his deadly finger below, moving slow and gentle, was anything but. Tracing against her with impossible care, that pointed claw smoothly, quietly, sweetly, nudging her swollen heat apart.

Rosa could feel the wetness dripping—whether still his, or hers, she didn't know—but in this moment there was no shame, no need to hide. John wouldn't allow it anyway, her distant thoughts reassured her, he wanted her bared and eager—but more than that, she'd promised him she wouldn't move, and she needed to please him, prove she was worthy...

And she was, she *had* to be, because that single, sharp-tipped finger was slowly, surely, slipping inside her. An orc's actual deadly *claw*, sinking into Rosa's softest, weakest, most vulnerable place, and she held her body very still as she felt it opening her, invading her, the bare pleasure and hunger and longing crashing beneath her skin.

But there was no pain, at least not yet, even as Rosa felt herself clenching and flaring tight around his deadly invasion. Wanting him deeper, fighting to drag him deeper, and John huffed another laugh as his other hand flexed on her neck, his gaze flicking up to her face.

"You swore not to move," he whispered, though he didn't sound entirely displeased. "Foolish woman."

Rosa swallowed hard, her eyelashes fluttering at the feel of her throat moving against the gentle pressure of his hand. "I c-can't help it," she breathed. "Forgive me, my lord."

His eyes almost seemed to darken in the lamplight, flaring bare and hungry, and Rosa felt that single finger sink a little deeper. Drawing up another sustained, convulsive clench of her wet heat around it, and *gods* he felt good, he always felt good, even when he had his actual *claw* sunk halfway up inside her—

"More," she gasped. "All the way. Please, my lord."

His answering glance at her face looked almost dazed this time, but his head nodded, his eyes dropping back to what he was doing between her parted legs. And Rosa's gaze had dropped too, and was fatally caught on it, her most vulnerable parts wide open and unashamed, while an orc's huge grey hand pressed close, his long, clawed middle finger vanished, sucked up, deep inside...

Rosa's body was clamping, dripping, gripping tight, her mouth choking out a constant stream of gasps and groans as he sank deeper, deeper. Still no pain, not yet, though for the first time, there was the shocking, spine-melting feel of sharpness inside, so deep, oh *hell*.

"Is it pain," John gasped, his eyes bright with alarm, and when Rosa frantically shook her head, he immediately relaxed, his throat bobbing. "I have reached the head of your womb," he murmured, "but I seek to slide up behind it. As I did with my prick, when I fucked you thus."

Good gods, that admission, those words, slipping so heated and easy from his mouth. This damnable orc had been thinking of *anatomy* when he'd fucked her, he was thinking of it *now*—and the thought was so wildly, thoroughly compelling that Rosa betrayed a hoarse, gasping cry, her eyes immediately darting to his groin. His tented, delicious groin, with an incriminating spot of wetness on his trousers, at just the head of his massive length...

"Fuck me again?" she croaked at him, and though she'd sworn not to move she was breaking it, trying to yank her arms from their restraints, the need to reach him, to touch him, suddenly so strong she felt faint. "Please?"

John's answering bark of laughter was breathless, amused, even as his eyes seemed to darken further, his head shaking. "Ach, no," he breathed. "You wish not for my son, you ken I have cast a *spell* upon you. You have almost *left* me today, over this."

Almost left him. Spoken with no small trace of bitterness, and Rosa was caught blinking at him, gasping for air, her invaded body still throbbing and convulsing around him. And for a hammering, hanging moment, she felt her mouth open, fully about to say, *I don't care, I wouldn't truly leave yet, please, just do it anyway, I need to feel that again, please—*

But she gulped it back, just in time, and she fought for breath, for coherent thought. "Then—show me. Need to see you. *Please*, my lord."

She was sure he would refuse, abruptly, absolutely certain of it—but then, without warning, his hand dropped to the front of his trousers, quick and lurching, and yanked himself out.

And. The *sight* of this again. The way his claws gripped it so easily, so casually. The long, powerful strength of it, the dripping string of thick white from the slit, the lines of those scars across the length of it. And Rosa was again squirming against her restraints, desperately needing to touch it, to feel that silken soft-ness under her fingers, to taste that sweet honey on her lips...

"Be still, pet," John ordered, though his voice sounded just as frayed as she felt. "Or I shall hide it away again."

Oh gods, he *couldn't*, and Rosa's body immediately froze in place, clamping even tighter around that finger—that *claw*—still nearly all the way inside her. And in return John actually laughed again, his head tilting back, the sound warm, husky, so beautiful she might break—

"Please, my lord," she begged, against all thought, all better judgement. "Please. Show me."

His answering laugh was deeper this time, harder, rough with promise—and then, as Rosa stared, caught, yearning, he slid his clawed fingers up his own length, slow. Leaning forward onto his knees as he did so, so that—Rosa choked—

the resulting, thickening string of liquid dropped down to pool on her bare belly, glistening against her shivering skin.

It was one of the most thrilling sights of Rosa's entire *life*, up there with when this huge cock had been jutted up inside her, and her moan was loud, long, entirely unfettered. Earning another short laugh from John's mouth, another thick, visible splutter of white from his deep, delicious slit.

"Fuck," Rosa's voice groaned, all on its own. "Don't stop, my lord. *Please.*"

His answering groan meant he wouldn't, he couldn't, and his fingers on his scarred, veined length slowly slid up again— this time, while his finger between Rosa's legs sank a shade deeper. As if he were fucking both of them at the same fucking time, and Rosa heaved and shuddered at the truth of it, moving but not caring, even as she felt the sharpness nudge again, deep inside, oh *hell*.

"More," she begged him, searching his face, drinking up his fluttering eyes. "Please."

He did, he obeyed, his head nodding as the claw between her legs nudged even deeper, as his other hand stroked up his length again, milking out more of that spluttering white, pooling it thicker on Rosa's bare skin. Marking her, even if he wasn't fucking her, and she felt her body arching, swerving, driving onto that invading finger, needing it, *more*—

"Be still," he hissed, a flash of anger sparking across his eyes, but that only made it worse, made Rosa's body writhe harder, flaunting her, defying her. Needing only to hurl herself onto an orc's claw, to ram herself deeper, to feel the impossible, mind-bending truth of an orc's *knuckles*, pressed up against her pulsing, dripping-wet heat—

"Can't," she choked at him, the sparks flaring brighter, the room flickering all around, narrowing to this, only this, hunger and craving and mad, screaming sensation. "Please my lord, please John-Ka, *please!*"

And oh, he was with her, suddenly, he was here, that long clawed finger finally, finally gliding in and out a little, matching the hard strokes of his hand on his swelling, dripping cock. Looking like a dark avenging god, a furious beautiful monster, his eyes rolling back, his lips parting, his entire body jerking into his hand—

"Open your mouth," he hissed, barely audible, but Rosa obeyed, immediate, powerless—and then, fucking hell, that cock in his hand visibly stilled, the huge bollocks beneath it pulling up tight—and then he fired. Spraying out streams of thick, milky white, all over Rosa's breasts and belly and even her face, spattering into her open mouth, sparking bright and warm on her tongue.

And the sight of it, the reality of it—an orc's huge prick spraying her with his seed while he drove into her with his claw—finally, *finally* set free Rosa's desperate, devastating relief. The pleasure furiously screaming, throbbing around the tight invasion of his finger, while her body writhed and flailed, and the white heat flared across her eyes, battered against her heart. Consuming her clean and whole and pure, while the orc's claw, and still-sputtering cock, marked her, brutalized her, claimed her for their own.

The aftershocks kept convulsing, even as the pleasure gradually faded, as that deep slit's spray tapered to a trickling ooze, again pooling on Rosa's belly. As that invading finger slowly, gingerly drew out of her, and then raised to his own slightly trembling lips, and slipped itself deep inside.

It meant Rosa was left lashed to a bed, her legs sprawled wide, her bared body coated in a thick, messy sheen of orc-seed. While her traitorous tongue kept darting out, almost on its own, to lap at the mess, and her eyes were caught, arrested, on the sight of this gorgeous, enraging orc, flushed and undone, his own finger—that had just been *inside her*—sucked deep and greedy into his own mouth.

His eyes blinked, once, long-lashed and almost surprised—and then his finger yanked out from between his lips, fast enough that Rosa expected to see blood in its wake. But there was nothing, only a tightening of his mouth as his gaze flicked up and down her debauched, dripping body.

"Are you in pain," he said, stiffly, through still-pursed lips, and Rosa considered that, and then shook her head. Even as her own cursed tongue swept out again, licking helplessly at more of the damned delicious mess, and she could see John's eyes following the sight, the faintest flare of warmth flicking behind them.

"Foolish pet," he murmured, but his long arm had reached up, easily, to wipe at some of the slick on Rosa's cheek. And then he slipped it between her lips, the taste bursting bright on her tongue—but mixed, this time, with something sharper, less familiar. And as her tongue tentatively nudged at his claw, there was the jolting, heat-swarming realization that this was *that* finger. The one that had been *inside* her, and filled her with such furious, forbidden pleasure.

"Thank you, my lord," she whispered, and John acknowledged it with a silent nod as he did it again, again. Wiping up the mess he'd sprayed on her face, feeding it to her, with a quiet, intense care that seemed at sudden, utter odds with the version of him that had made the mess in the first place.

Or was it, because another flick of heat had crossed his eyes as she sucked harder at his finger—and then even more as she lightly bit on it, holding it in place, carefully curling her tongue against his claw.

"Do you yet wish to leave?" he asked now, his voice cool, as he obligingly delved his finger deeper, that claw nudging very gently against the back of her throat. "Or shall you stay, and be grateful for my care for you?"

It was him being a dominant arrogant arse again, Rosa's rational brain noted, from somewhere very far away—but at the same time, it also—wasn't. Because he was still—asking. Still, perhaps, offering. And even if he'd tied her to a bed and covered her with orc-seed, even if this had all been some kind of evil distraction ploy—Rosa did, in fact, feel surprisingly calm again. Collected again. Cared for.

"You know I didn't really want to go," she heard her appalling voice murmur, once he'd drawn that finger free again. "Though I truly would appreciate it if you told me things like that, John. I can't *trust* you, if you keep secrets from me."

John's eyebrows lifted, betraying a smugness that was clearly borne of the shameful fact that she'd just trusted him enough to take his *claw* inside her. But then his gaze slid away, and he reached down beside the bed, where his hand produced, to Rosa's vague surprise, what appeared to be a rag—and which he brought up to her face, wiping her cheeks clean.

"I have answered *scores* of your prattling questions, pet," he said, his eyes intent on his work. "What more can you wish to know?"

Rosa stuck her tongue out at him, purely for that *prattling* point—and in return he promptly nipped at her tongue with his rag, dragging a bubbling, reluctant laugh from her throat. "Well," she said, watching him, working up the nerve. "Why don't you ever retract your claws, like the other orcs do? Is it that you don't want to?"

It was something she'd been wanting to ask, ever since she'd noticed Efterar's claws retract her first night here—but this was why she hadn't, the way John's eyes closed off at once, all chilly guarded distance. But she waited, watching him, as he finished wiping her face, and moved the rag down to stroke, gentle, at her neck.

"I lived, for many years, with orcs who were not—kind," he said slowly. "I sought to keep safe those I cared for, and foolishly thought that if I never drew in my claws, I should always be ready to defend them. Until one day, I found that I could not draw my claws in again."

Rosa's heart seemed to wrench, her eyes caught on his distant, dispassionate face. And before she'd quite realized it, her arms had yanked on her restraints again, trying to break free, to touch him, to wipe away that look, to bring the warmth back to his eyes...

"And you couldn't try to fix it?" she asked, wincing even as she heard the words, because of course he would have tried, he was *John*. "Nothing worked?"

He shook his head, a twitch of bitterness drawing at his mouth. "I fused the bone," he said, his voice deceptively steady. "By the time I came here, even Efterar's vaunted magic could not alter this."

Oh. Rosa winced, even as she followed that suggestion backwards, to the implication that he hadn't always lived here, after all. "And where did you live before this? With whom?"

John visibly grimaced this time, his rag slipping down to her shoulder, moving with perhaps less gentleness than before. "The Ka-esh oft house their mates and sons away from the mountain, in camps deep under the earth," he said. "My father raised me in one of these, mayhap for eight summers, until he was killed. Then I was moved between other camps, oft with Tristan and Salvi, who had also lost their blood kin."

He said it all with a curt, distant matter-of-factness, as though it meant nothing to him, this horrible tale of devastation and loss. "And you didn't know your mother?" Rosa whispered, though it almost hurt to ask the question. "You couldn't have gone to live with her?"

John barked a laugh, bleak, bitter. "I killed my mother, with my birth," he said. "As have so many of my kind."

But the misery only wrenched tighter, cruel, scraping, even as John's rag dropped to Rosa's breasts, cleaning them off with agonizing gentleness. "I—" she began, a croak. "I killed mine, too."

John's hand abruptly stilled, his eyes blinking unseeing toward it—and then darting up, brief, to her face. Searching her, brows furrowing, almost as if she might be lying, as if she had to be lying—but she felt herself attempt a smile at him, not a smile at all.

"My father only made it a few years after that," she heard her hollow voice say. "Some kind of disease, I never could find out what. But he was a scholar, you know, at the Dusbury University, he specialized in languages, and before his death he arranged for me"—she dragged for air—"to go to boarding school. Until the money ran out, at least, but after that, I learned—"

John's eyes were very intent on hers, his hands very still, waiting, listening, *safe*—so Rosa somehow found more air, the rest of the words. "I learned that there were—other ways to pay," she whispered. "With men. Like Lord Kaspar. And before him, my schoolmaster. Mr. Sullivan. They took care of me, gave me an education, as long as I"—she swallowed hard—"obeyed."

She could feel her heartbeat pattering, her breath locked in her throat, her eyes fixed, trapped, helpless upon John's. Almost as if to tell him, *now you know, I really am a woman who sells herself, a strumpet.* And what would he do now, would the revulsion flare across his eyes, would he call her foolish and stupid and useless...

But instead, to her vague surprise, John only kept wiping. Moving the rag down to her waist, gently mopping up his mess. Frowning as he seemed to hit upon a stubborn spot—where he'd first dripped on her, perhaps—and then he actually *spat* on her skin, a harsh straight hiss of water, before scrubbing at it again. And then clamping the sopping rag between his teeth while he caressed both hands up and down Rosa's front and sides, smooth, lingering, as if to make sure he'd done his work well, and gotten every spot.

Next he spat the rag away too, sideways onto the floor, and finally reached up to where Rosa's wrists were still tied to the bedpost. And with a few jerks of the leather she was free again, her fingers only slightly tingly, and he was carefully holding her hands, and turning them over, as if inspecting them for any sign of damage.

"This binding calmed you, ach?" he said, more to her hands than to her face. "Should it further help if I tie your legs also, next time you are vexed?"

The heat and the hunger surged bare and unbidden, escaping in a helpless groan from Rosa's mouth. Making John's lips twitch up, his eyes flicking to hers—and then holding there, an instant too long, before looking away again.

But it had spoken something, revealed something, all the same. Calling up that memory of Hanarr speaking, saying, *we Ka-esh do not oft speak vows. One's actions speak only truth.*

And John's actions said, very clearly, that he didn't want Rosa to leave. But also, perhaps, that he didn't care about her past, about the men. That perhaps this wasn't all about his work, or his reputation. Perhaps he did care about—*her.*

That thought was suddenly, inexplicably alarming, and so was the shocking, brazen part of Rosa that grabbed for his broad shoulders—he was still *clothed*, the bastard—and dragged him down onto the bed beside her. He came willingly enough, his big body settling heavy on the quilt, and Rosa took the liberty of tucking herself up long against him, her head on his shoulder, her arm and leg creeping across him to hold him close.

"If I'm a strumpet," she murmured, into his neck, "you're a—a *scoundrel*, John-Ka. A merciless, devious *reprobate.*"

"A *reprobate*," he repeated, slow, as though testing the word on his tongue. "Why is this? Because I just gave you all that you wished for?"

Rosa nipped at his neck, and was rewarded with a full-body shudder beneath her, a hissing growl from his throat. "You did *not*," she countered. "I threatened to leave you, so you railed at me, and tied me to a bed, and—and *ravished* me. With your *claw*."

John sighed, and there was the delicious, thrilling touch of his hand, coming to rest against her back. "I ought not to have *railed* at you, as I did," he said, quiet. "This was wrong. I ought to have better calmed you from the start. It did not please me"—his throat swallowed, audible—"to see you so vexed, pet."

Oh. It was—an *apology*. Hurtling another jolt of warmth up Rosa's back, and before she'd quite caught herself, she pressed a soft little kiss into his scented neck. "Thank you," she whispered. "John-Ka. My lord."

And it made no sense, Rosa was here as a spy, she was here to help start a *war*, this orc might very well have still cast some kind of awful *spell* upon her—but somehow, all that seemed to matter was the answering clench of his powerful body, the heat of his exhale.

"So I have proven this to you," he said, his claws gently stroking at her back. "And you shall yet stay, little rose, and be my pet, until all this is done. Ach?"

And in this moment, curled safe and content against a deadly, smooth-talking orc, there was no refusing, no listening to that distant shouting voice. Too far away, too far gone, three weeks, or rather, nineteen more days...

"Yes, my lord," she breathed. "I'll stay. Until it's done."

22

When Rosa left that small, wooden-doored room again, hand in hand with a tall, silent orc, it was like something, again, had changed. Something that had swept away all her uncertainty, and replaced it with a bright, buzzing curiosity.

"Why *do* you have a human room here, John?" she asked, as they began walking down the corridor again. "For guests?"

John's face had, predictably, gone blank and unreadable in the lamplight, blocking Rosa out. Denying that this room meant anything, pretending he didn't care at all... and that, combined with that highly conspicuous cradle, was answer enough.

"Oh, I see," Rosa said, quieter than before. "It truly is a lovely room, and I'm sure any woman would be delighted to come and stay there. Has it housed other Ka-esh mates before? Salvi's, perhaps?"

She was probably pushing it with that question, but John answered anyway, despite the still-blank look on his face. "Salvi's mate never came here. She did not wish to live with orcs."

Oh. Rosa filed that away, studying John's expression, the slight inflection of his words. "And she didn't wish to have an orc's son, either?" she asked carefully. "Was that true, what Simon said you did?"

John muttered something in Aelakesh that included the word *Skai*, and sounded suspiciously like a curse—but then he sighed as he led Rosa around a corner. "That is truth," he said, voice flat. "Salvi's mate needed my help, so I gave it. Efterar gave his help also, when I pushed for this"—he frowned at the wall—"but no one yet blames *him*."

Without quite meaning to, Rosa bumped against John's arm with her shoulder, flashing him a quick, rueful smile. "Of course not," she said. "They all know you're the brains behind this entire mountain operation, John, even if they don't want to admit it. I mean, I've only been here for a few days, and I can already tell that without you Ka-esh, your people would have gone extinct several millennia ago."

She truly did mean that, and felt a reflexive ripple of delight at the twinge of approval on John's mouth. "There are foolish Ka-esh also, foolish woman," he said. "But along with all this blame I bear, I at least now wield the power among my clan brothers to foist the fools away."

"Small mercies," Rosa replied, with a genuine grin. "What do you do, pack them off mining? Set them to digging tunnels for a few weeks, or months?"

The look on John's face suggested that he did exactly that, and Rosa couldn't help a peal of laughter, another bump at him with her shoulder. "Devious orc," she said. "So why *aren't* you Priest of Orc Mountain, anyway?"

Her voice was light, but the meaning behind it wasn't—and she could almost feel the heaviness settling again, weighing on John's shoulders. "The Priest wields much power," he said slowly. "He walks before the captain in the darkness, and guides our kind into the unknown. He commands funds, and labour, and resources. And thus, all five clans must agree upon this choice. I have not"—he grimaced—"gained this blessing, from the Skai. And thus, from the others also."

Oh. Ohhhhh. That explained a *lot*, actually, including John's clear animosity against the Skai, and the way it seemed almost personal for him. A twinge of irrationality, even, a crack in all his outward composure, and Rosa was still considering that as he led her back into the library. Which, thankfully, was now only occupied by Tristan, who was bent over the table, writing on a sheet of paper in clean, elegant-looking common-tongue.

"There is more I must do away from here today," John said, as he turned toward Rosa, and rested both hands heavy on her shoulders. "Shall you stay calmly here without me, or shall I return to find you caught in another ill-founded frenzy?"

Rosa tried to glare at him, but couldn't quite pull it off. "It was *not* ill-founded," she countered. "It was entirely logical and empirically sound, based on the information I possessed at the time."

John's eyebrows went up, but so did the corner of his mouth, twitching with unmistakable amusement. "Foolish pet," he said. "I shall return."

With that, he leaned forward, the scent of him flaring deep into Rosa's lungs, and then, oh gods, he—*kissed* her. Kissed her full on the lips, for only the second time in their *entire acquaintance*, and even as Rosa was simultaneously calculating and lamenting that truth, she felt herself immediately sinking into it, drowning in the wonder of it. An orc's soft, heated, delicious-tasting mouth, all clever lips and long tongue and sharp teeth, kissing with careful, calculated thoroughness, just as he did everything else. And the hunger was already surging again, Rosa's mouth eager and moaning, maybe he would put her on the table again, kneel again, and then—

He drew away far too soon, leaving Rosa open-mouthed and gasping, her lips feeling swollen and reddened, her face very hot. While John, the raging *reprobate*, only looked coolly, smugly satisfied, and lightly patted her cheek before turning and striding out the door again.

"Devious bastard," Rosa muttered, once she'd found the breath to speak again. "Has he always been so—"

She snapped her mouth shut, glancing guiltily toward Tristan—but Tristan was smiling back, warm and surprisingly stunning, his ear-tips again turned a faint shade of pink. "Ach, John-Ka has always been thus," he said. "I find it is easier to yield from the start."

Rosa looked at him for an instant, while her brain resumed its wild frantic shouting, spewing out what could only be more abominably unnerving jealousy. "Um," she said, while her eyes desperately searched the room, and settled on Tristan's sheet of paper. "Right. Um, what are you working on?"

Tristan's long-lashed eyes blinked, once, but he accordingly looked down at his paper, and smoothed out the edge with his hand. "I write letters to the humans, on our captain's behalf," he said. "With these, we seek to express our regrets at what our errant brother has done, and reassure them that he has been confined to our mountain, and forced to hard labour."

Hard labour? Despite everything, Rosa felt her mouth curve up, her eyes glancing at Tristan's neat letter-charts on the table. "Learning to read is hard labour?"

"Ach, for an orc like Simon, it is," Tristan replied, with a half-smile of his own. "Most Skai are taught only to fight from birth, at the cost of all else. This has been to our gain, but mayhap not"—his smile twisted—"to theirs."

Oh. That was another intriguing piece to the puzzle—a hint, perhaps, that Tristan might not share John's views on the Skai—and Rosa mentally filed it away with all the rest. "And do you think these letters will actually help?" she asked next, as casually as she could. "Will they stave off more war?"

She was thinking again of her three-week deadline, of Lord

Kaspar. Of the fact that she was supposed to be *helping* with this damned war. Learning all she could, searching for more atrocities, saving her future...

Rosa rubbed hard at her prickling cheeks, but thankfully Tristan didn't seem to notice, his eyes still fixed to his letter. "Letters have helped us, in the past," he said. "Many humans do not think orcs capable of reason, so our letters stand against this. With these, we also ask to meet, and oft make offers, and send gifts. Aught we can do"—he again smoothed at the letter's edge—"to remind the humans that we are not monsters. That we cannot *bear* more war, and more death."

Oh. There was a sudden, glinting vehemence in his eyes, draining the warmth from Rosa's face. And any kind of appropriate response seemed stuck in her throat, *of course you aren't monsters, of course we don't want more war...*

"Rosa!" interrupted a voice, and Rosa spun gratefully toward it. It was Jule, tall and pregnant and smiling, striding into the room, and giving Tristan a companionable clap on the shoulder before dropping herself into the chair beside him. "It's so good to see you still up and about. Tell me, how are you faring? Has John been behaving himself?"

Rosa's tongue still felt thoroughly tangled, but she somehow managed an answer that didn't give too much away—did she want to divulge that John had tied her to a bed, or worse, that she'd *enjoyed* it?—and then directed the conversation to the fascinating things John had shown her around the mountain so far, and her current studies of Aelakesh.

Jule seemed intrigued by that—her own Aelakesh was extremely rudimentary, she confessed, gleaned mostly from listening to Grimarr and the other orcs speak. A fact that was truly lamentable, Rosa rather felt, and she eagerly launched into a detailed explanation of Aelakesh's many virtues. Earning a warm, approving smile from Tristan, who quietly offered his help however it was needed—and soon they'd passed a highly enjoyable hour practicing phrases and pronunciations together, and laughing at their many mistakes.

"One other thing, Rosa," Jule said, once she'd reluctantly stood to leave again. "If you don't mind me asking—what's the situation with you and Lord Kaspar Sippola? I heard"—her dark head tilted—"you work for him?"

Her voice was careful, with a slight inflection on the word *work*, and Rosa's heart abruptly began thudding, her eyes dropping to the table. Good gods, Jule probably *knew* Lord Kaspar, from her previous life as Lady Norr, and she could not guess, she could not know, John could never, *ever* find out...

"I don't actually work *for* Lord Kaspar," Rosa blurted out, without thinking. "He's the patron of the library where I work. And he's"—she squared her shoulders—"a real swine, actually. Thinks he's a brilliant gentleman scholar, when he's really just marginally clever, with enough power to wring the real work out of everyone else around him, and then take the credit for it. While he fucks his way through their wives and *chambermaids*."

Her voice had turned chilly, strangely bitter, and she was distantly surprised to see Jule give a terse, knowing nod, her arms crossing firmly over her chest.

"Kaspar forced himself on one of my youngest serving-maids," she said, voice flat. "When he came to Norr Manor with his father on a diplomatic visit, a few years back. And when she became pregnant, Kaspar refused to help her, or acknowledge the child as his. I'm glad you're away from him, Rosa. Quite frankly"—she grimaced—"poor Louisa deserves better, too. She's already had to tolerate *way* too much from scum like him."

Louisa. *Lady Scall*, she meant. And as Rosa was still digesting that, Jule turned and strode off, leaving only a sickening, uncomfortable churning in Rosa's belly. It truly hadn't occurred to her that Lord Kaspar might be hurting Lady Scall, too—and while Rosa hadn't before heard that particular tale of the serving-maid, it sounded very like many of the other whispers and warnings she'd heard about Lord Kaspar over the years.

And suddenly Rosa couldn't bear to think of it, of *him*, and she lurched up out of her chair, and toward the nearest shelf. The shelf, it turned out, with all those books written in Osadan, and Rosa gently, gratefully traced her fingers along their bindings. Dragging in the faint, familiar scent of paper and dust, while willing her jumpy heartbeat to slow. Lord Kaspar wasn't here. She still had nineteen days...

She spent the next half-hour plucking out the books one by one, and after some direction from Tristan, translating their titles into John's well-organized master catalogue. Next she pulled out that book of recipes, frowning down at the page with its delightful squirrel stew—and then she deliberately put it back, and drew out another one instead.

It led to her working quietly and companionably at the table across from Tristan, making thorough use of all the writing and binding supplies John had acquired for her. Some of them were clearly rather makeshift, and not to the standards she was accustomed, but she persevered, and soon was in possession of a half-dozen pricked, ruled, and folded quires, clean and ready for copying.

The translating itself was the fun part, especially given the many curious—and often highly amusing—expressions the orc author had used. Rosa frequently had to ask Tristan for guidance, but he didn't seem to mind, and as the afternoon slipped by, it occurred to Rosa that again, she was actually *enjoying* herself. Enjoying being trapped in Orc Mountain's library, doing intensive labour on the orcs' behalf, while trading genial comments back and forth with a kind, handsome, soft-spoken orc who may or may not have also been receiving John's—*attentions.*

But Rosa successfully managed to shove that thought away

too, along with multiple other equally uncomfortable misgivings. And by the time John returned, several hours later, it was almost easy to smile up at him, and even to reach a hand to slide against his waist.

"You're back!" she said. "Did you have a productive afternoon? What have you been up to?"

John's eyes bore a decidedly wolfish cast, flicking up and down Rosa's form. "Ach, much," he said absently, as his hand came to rest on her shoulder, his claws drumming lightly against her skin. "What work have you done, pet?"

His gaze dropped to the table, his brow furrowing, and Rosa accordingly brandished one of her new quires at him, feeling her cheeks inexplicably heating. "Well," she began, "I know you wanted the recipe book, and those repairs to your broken bindings, but Tristan helped me catalogue all the Osadan books"—she shot him a swift smile across the table—"and after that, I thought you might rather have a translation of this one, to begin."

John had carefully taken her quire into his hands, blinking down at the title she'd neatly written at the top. *A Treatise on the Gainful Birthing of Orclings.*

"It's a midwifery manual," Rosa said brightly, "with a variety of case studies. It discusses a variety of manual techniques and herbal remedies to reduce the maternal mortality rate, though of course"—she grimaced—"that's mostly with the aim of getting more children out of a single woman. Typical males, right? However, it does talk about one poor woman in Osada who apparently birthed *seven* total orclings, can you imagine? I haven't actually translated that part yet—it'll likely take me another few days to get that far—but I thought it was relevant, don't you?"

She belatedly realized she was babbling, and decisively clamped her mouth shut, while an unaccountable anxiety marched through her brain. What if John would have preferred the repairs, or the book of recipes. What if this had been over-stepping, or foolish, or useless...

Tristan gave a faint cough from across the table, a sound that snapped John's gaze up toward him, eyes narrowed—but then Rosa could see his throat convulse, his eyes darting back to her face. Looking almost—stunned. Bewildered. Wondering.

"I did not," he began, and he visibly swallowed again, "know that this book was here. In my library."

Something warm was bubbling up in Rosa's belly, and she flashed him another quick smile. "Of course not," she said. "How would you, if you hadn't been taught Osadan? I mean, it's an awfully tricky language even with an accomplished teacher, it probably took me three years to get the verb conjugations right, and even now I still really need to think about it."

John was still looking at her, his eyes almost painfully intent—but then he dropped his gaze back to her quire, and carefully flipped through it with his claw. Scanning Rosa's lines of neat, flawless script, covering page after page.

"How many languages," he asked, his voice very even, "have you learnt, pet?"

Rosa shrugged, though her face still felt hot. "Only three, really," she said. "The common-tongue, and Osadan, and Alba-jan. I can read a fair bit of Kraitish, but not well. And, I suppose"—she rifled through the papers on the table, and snatched up her sheet of writing from earlier that day—"now I'm learning Aelakesh, aren't I, Tristan?"

Tristan answered with a gratifying smile, which John didn't see, as he was too busy frowning at Rosa's new sheet of neat Aelakesh script. "Ach," he said, the sound deep in his throat. "This is all—yours?"

He shot a look at Tristan that might have been accusing, but Tristan was nodding back, a single eyebrow slightly arched. To which John visibly swallowed again, and squared his shoul-ders, and fixed his eyes back on Rosa.

"This is good, pet," he said. "Your work pleases me."

The warmth seemed to lick all the way up Rosa's body, from her feet to her face, and she couldn't help another quick, sheepish grin toward him. "It really hurt you to say that, didn't it?" she said lightly. "Don't deny it, John, you look like you've just eaten rotten squirrel."

There was a choked sound from Tristan at the table, and an unmistakable, deeply satisfying quirk at the corner of John's mouth. "Rude little pest," he said, even as his hand rose to cup at her cheek, brief, approving. "Next time, you shall bow your pretty head, and say, *thank you, my lord.*"

Rosa couldn't help a peal of laughter, another flush of warmth at that thrilling word *pretty*. "I shall *not*, you devious reprobate. I know *exactly* where this leads."

"Ach, do you?" he asked, his brows rising. "Then I ken you shall welcome this, my hungry little pet, and beg me for more."

Rosa's clever retort was swallowed in the surge of sheer, breathtaking craving—and of course John knew it, flashing her a smug, dazzling smile. "Now come," he said firmly, as he reached for the lamp on the table. "You must eat. I shall show you the kitchen, and if you behave, after this I may reward you."

Rosa did her best to behave—how could she not, with an incentive like *that*—and she accordingly stayed close to John's side, asking her questions of him quietly, and smiling politely as he introduced her to any number of strange and alarming new orcs. She even met another actual *woman*, by the name of Stella, who seemed perfectly content to be publicly manhandled by her mate—a massive Bautul orc called Silfast who, Rosa decided, was quite possibly the most hideous living being she had ever seen, and who she still managed to greet with a smile.

"Was I good enough?" she asked John, once they were finally back on his bed, and she was running her hands up and down his delicious form. Even taking the liberty of tugging off his tunic, a presumption that he didn't seem to mind, only raising his arms above his head, and watching her with hungry, half-lidded eyes.

"Ach, you were fair, pet," he said, all cool imperious command. "And you asked me only sixteen questions through all this. As your reward"—he waved an insolent hand toward his tented groin—"you may suckle me."

Rosa protested and elbowed at him, laughing, and despite her best attempts at resistance, she soon found herself indeed kneeling over him, frantically suckling his bounty while he moaned and bucked up into her throat.

"Good pet," he breathed afterwards, without prompting, his lashes fluttering at the ceiling. "Ach, your throat is so sweet, little rose."

The resulting warmth seemed to envelop Rosa all over, lasting not only that night, but all throughout the next day. A day where she purposely refused to think about wars or Lord Kaspar at all, and instead focused only on learning.

She learned Aelakesh with Tristan and Simon, practicing the new sounds and letter-forms until they were embedded into her brain. She learned more about John's library—not only continuing to translate the midwifery book, but also taking breaks to further update his catalogue, clean and organize his shelves, and repair several of his most tattered bindings. And she even learned more about orcs, asking Tristan and Simon as many innocuous-seeming questions as she dared, ignoring Simon's snarky non-answers, and finding herself deeply appreciating Tristan's thorough, thoughtful replies.

And while some of what she learned was unsurprising— orcs would eat almost anything, they needed less sleep than humans, they had a similar lifespan—other revelations were truly intriguing. Orcs took vows very seriously. They often sought to mate for life, whether to another orc, or a human.

Their sense of smell was very highly developed, to the point where they could even smell certain *emotions*. And each clan had its own unique culture and role within the mountain, though much of their collective history and skills had been lost in the constant wars.

More than once, Rosa felt a compulsive longing to seek John's opinion—but John stayed away for most of the day this time. A fact that began to drag slightly at Rosa's lingering warmth—at least, until he finally did return, and immediately strode straight across the room toward her. Fully ignoring Tristan and Simon, in favour of bending his head into her neck, and inhaling slow and deep.

"Ach, little pet," he breathed. "Have you done good work for me today?"

His body felt oddly taut, and Rosa slid her arms around him, fingers spreading wide, instinctively rubbing the tension away. "I think so," she murmured back. "Would you like to see?"

It led to her shyly showing off all that she'd done that day, rather like a hopeful pupil seeking to please an exacting schoolmaster—but John did seem pleased, and again, perhaps even surprised. And when he abruptly bent down, and gave Rosa one of those thorough, delicious kisses, she actually staggered with relief and pleasure, and had to clutch at him to stay upright.

"Can I come with you now?" she asked him, damnably hopeful. "Surely I deserve some kind of reward for all my hard work, John-Ka?"

He answered with a surprisingly tolerant half-smile, a gentle scrape of his claws against her neck. "Ach, you do, pet. What should please you?"

"I'd like to see more of your mountain," Rosa replied promptly. "And visit the laboratory again. And, maybe you can tell me what *you* did today."

John's eyes had instantly shuttered, but he flicked his claw at her cheek, and accordingly guided her toward the door. "I did much work," he said vaguely. "And many meetings. Now, do you ken you might find the laboratory from here, without my leading you?"

The challenge had the desired effect, of course, tearing Rosa's attention away from his continued non-disclosures, and toward the splendid opportunity to explore Orc Mountain, with her indulgent lord close by her side. It took some time to find the laboratory, but it was entirely worth it—especially when John even did a little experiment with her, comparing two separate disinfecting solutions Marcus had been working on, and discussing their observations together.

Next John tasked her with finding the shrine, which took significantly more effort, and next, his bedroom. Which proved surprisingly impossible, and led to Rosa darting wildly from room to room with the lamp while John followed, clearly trying not to laugh. "You're enjoying your pet's *suffering*, you *reprobate*," Rosa gasped over her shoulder, though she was laughing, too. "Just tell me where it is, you—"

But then the pleasure stilled all at once, shuddering into silence, because Rosa had darted to another door which *should* have been John's bedroom. But it wasn't, it was something else entirely—and Rosa stood frozen in place, her eyes gaping, unblinking, while the sights in the room seemed to flash into her vision, one after the other, imprinting with staggering force.

It was a room of—*debauchery*. Of perhaps a dozen orcs, all in varying stages of undress, all taking their pleasure with one another. Or, rather, some were taking pleasure— like that one, sprawled on a bench with his trousers pulled down, while another orc knelt between his legs, his head bobbing over his groin. Or the naked orc on his hands and knees, head bowed, while another orc knelt behind him, his hips snapping loudly against the first orc's bare arse.

But. Close behind them, there was another naked orc, standing *shackled,* face-first, to the stone wall. There were huge, vicious-looking metal cuffs around his wrists and ankles, and behind him was another orc—in fact, *Gary*, the helpful orc from the Ka-esh *forge*—delivering hard slaps to his bared arse with a clawed hand. Another orc was similarly shackled across the room, but behind him another orc was driving his hips against his arse, while two more orcs hungrily watched, their trousers visibly tented. Almost as though—*waiting their turns.*

And most shocking—or compelling—of all was the naked orc on his knees before the small crackling fire, his streaming eyes held on the light. His hands were bound behind him, and there appeared to be some kind of gag in his mouth, and something else protruding out of his bare arse. And around his neck was a thick metal ring, which—the comprehension slammed into Rosa's screeching thoughts—looked very like the piece Gary had shown her in the Ka-esh forge. The one he'd called a *kraga,* the one she'd thought was a lovely, innocuous *necklace.* And attached to the kneeling orc's *kraga* was a heavy chain, and holding that chain was—*Aaron*, from the *laboratory*. Standing calmly and fully clothed behind the kneeling orc, with a slim wooden *switch* in his hand.

And as Rosa stared, her heart threatening to leap out of her chest, Aaron slapped the switch against the orc's bared arse, making him jerk and moan, struggling against his restraints— and then a sustained spray of white shot from his groin, spattering wide into the fire before him.

Good *gods.* Rosa had spent half a lifetime learning the hidden depths of men's desires—but even so, there was only pure disbelief, reverberating sharp and powerful through the entirety of her being. Orcs did such things? *Enjoyed* such things? And surely—surely John *knew*?!

She somehow shot a frantic, accusing glance over her shoulder toward John—and found him looking just as frozen as she felt. His eyes and his body caught, trapped, and—Rosa's wide eyes darted downwards, to his visibly tented groin—*betrayed*. John *wanted* these things. He—*liked* these things?!

The memories were roiling now, punching into Rosa's churning, shouting gut. "Y-you," she stammered, as she lurched a few staggering steps away, deeper into the corridor. "You *like* this. Don't you? Gods, John, you—yesterday you *tied* me to a *bed*. You—you've threatened to *p-punish* me. You want me to *obey* you."

And suddenly the game was gone, this cheerful, innocent charade they'd been playing of a lord and his pet. And it had been a charade, of course it had, Rosa was a *spy*, she had eighteen days left to find an atrocity worth starting a *war* over, and wait, *wait*—

"You know I should never do aught that might truly harm you, woman," John's harsh voice cut in, flat, cold. "Humans cannot heal or bear pain as orcs do. And most humans have not been raised to blend pain and fear and power and pleasure, as we have."

As we have. As *he* had? Rosa's horror was surging again, and she gaped at his face, at the bitterness glinting in his eyes. "All of you?" she managed. "All the orcs in this *mountain*?!"

And yes, yes, maybe *this* was the war-worthy scandal, the atrocity she needed to shout from the rooftops. The orcs force each other, they beat each other, they tie each other to walls and then *take turns*—

"Not all orcs seek this, or find pleasure in this," John countered, his voice noticeably strained. "It mayhap runs deeper among the Ka-esh than the other clans, but even among us, many do not welcome this. Ach, Tristan will weep if I even—"

Rosa's heart plummeted with shattering strength, her legs

badly wobbling, and John's hands shot out to steady her, even as his face visibly grimaced, his eyes squeezing shut. Clearly not meaning to have shared such a gods-damned crucial fact, and between Rosa's swarming shock and rage, there was a powerful, gut-wrenching *hurt*.

"So *that's* why you're not mated to Tristan, then," she said, brittle. "Because he doesn't share your—*proclivities*. Because you would be otherwise, wouldn't you?"

John's eyes fluttered open again, his brows furrowing, but he didn't deny it—so Rosa kept ploughing on, every word a biting, miserable truth. "You don't have to pretend, John. I mean, of course you like him, how couldn't you, he's really very lovely, and—"

She couldn't seem to finish, her voice caught in her closed-off throat—at least, until another realization, even worse than the first, seemed to slap her in the face. "And—and when you said," she choked out, "that you wanted a tall, hale, hearty woman—*this* is why, isn't it? So she can handle all these things you want to do to her?!"

John's hands were still gripping at Rosa's arms, tight enough to be almost painful, and he barked a growl, deep in his throat. "Heed this, woman," he hissed. "I care for Tristan, mayhap more than any other orc yet alive. But I shall never seek to take him as a mate, and I have not touched him in many moons. Not only because we do not seek the same pleasures, but"—he grimaced again—"also because he and Salvi have not yet settled matters between them."

Oh. Rosa's beleaguered brain twitched back to Salvi comforting Tristan, Tristan pushing him away—until John growled again, looming huge and menacing over her. "And my wish for a hale, hearty woman comes only from my lifelong wish to have a son. And my wish not to *murder* my son's own mother with his birth!"

Oh. John—John was finally admitting this, now. A *lifelong*

wish. And as Rosa blinked at him, digesting that, his hand snapped up to grip at her chin, giving it a little shake, while a hard, mocking laugh scraped from his throat.

"Ach, and you truly ken, little *pet*," he said, taunting, "that you could not bear what else I might wish to do to you? You have already taken me full into your little throat, and your little womb. You have already given me leave to bind you, and pierce you with my *claw*. You could not next bear a little punishment when you displease me? You could not wear a pretty little *kraga* on your little neck? You could not suck me before my kin, and flaunt to them your deep little throat? You could not"—he stepped closer, his eyes scornful, wicked—"welcome me into the one place within you I have not yet taken? The place where I yet smell *that man* upon you?"

Oh, *fuck.* John had not just said all that, he had *not,* and Rosa's belly could not be heating this way, her breath coming in even shorter, more desperate little gulps. *A little punishment. A pretty little* kraga. *Suck me before my kin. Welcome me into the one place, where I yet smell that man...*

Rosa's heart was thundering, her gaze affixed to his face, to that bitter, sneering anger in his glittering eyes. He was challenging her, goading her, maybe still mocking her. He was a hard orc, a cold orc, selfish, cruel, he'd lied to her about that damned bond, and now about his seemingly civilized and intellectual Ka-esh brothers also having a secret den of *debauchery.* About him apparently wanting to punish her, and mark her, and flaunt her, and...

Rosa's mouth had gone bone-dry, her throat swallowing, and curse him, he *saw*, he *knew*. He was stepping closer, the heated sweet scent of him unfurling through the air, and the hunger on his face was so strong, so vicious, so breathtakingly compelling...

"Do not play-act with me, little pet," he purred. "You wish for naught more, this night, than for me to carry you to my bed, punish you as you deserve, and then fuck your pretty, red little rump. Ach?"

Rosa's answering gasp was loud, frayed, shocking even to her own ears, and in return John only laughed, the merriment flaring brief but true in his eyes. "Ach, my little pet is just as depraved as her orc," he hissed, with cool satisfaction. "You only do not like to admit such things, ach? You wish for me to be the one to command you, and frighten you, and thus it is not your truth to bear?"

And damn him, because Rosa couldn't muster a single word to deny it, astute bastard that he was. And when he tilted her face further up, his claws dancing against her throat, it was like he was playing her, beguiling her, leading her astray from all the things she was supposed to be focusing on. She wasn't here to learn his language, or help him in his library, or fulfill his depraved, audacious demands. She was here to search for atrocities. She was supposed to help start a war. She was a *spy*...

And yet, Rosa swallowed. Took a breath. Held those dangerous, glittering eyes with a reckless, compulsive, desperate driving hunger...

"Very well, my lord," she whispered. "Please, command me."

23

Rosa's words were a betrayal. Another betrayal, in an increasingly long line of them, wrung out one after another by this damned devious *degenerate* orc.

But she didn't take it back. Didn't look away. And John wasn't looking away either, his gaze dark and intent, his body huge and aggressive, his black tongue darting out to lick, slow, at his lips...

But then his head twisted sideways, his eyes squeezing shut, and Rosa could see the tension snapping into his shoulders, his face. Blocking her away, saying that he might not truly do any of that, after all, and Rosa's disappointment flared with irrational, inexplicable force.

"What," she gasped, breathless, even as her hand slipped toward him, caressed up his hard front against his tunic. "Why not, my lord."

John's mouth grimaced, his chest filling and emptying, heavy against her hand. "I am," he said, between breaths, "an *orc*. I can yet"—he drew in more air—"taste your *fear*, at this."

His eyes had flicked toward the nearby pleasure-den, from which was currently emanating a variety of telltale slapping sounds, as well as a harsh, strangled cry. And while Rosa's shock was still there, somewhere, pinging around inside her skull, stronger still was the rising driving hunger. John wanted to *punish* her, he wanted to take her and...

And it was madness, it was sheer foolhardy self-*immolation*, but rather than pleading, arguing, or even attempting to sway him, Rosa—somehow—stuck out her *tongue* at him. And then, for good measure, jabbed him in the chest with her finger.

"Because *you*, you horrid reprobate," she snapped, her voice not quite even, "once again, didn't *warn* me. You didn't think to mention, by the way, silly pet, we Ka-esh like it *very* rough, and you might see some things around here"—she jabbed him again—"that could make your hair curl. But noooo, you only show me medics and scholars and *libraries*, because as usual, you're a calculating manipulative *brute*, who wants to *seem* perfectly tame and rational and enlightened, when you're *not!*"

And oh, there was the anger, kindling faint but sure in those blinking eyes, chasing away something that might have almost been relief. "Next to you, foolish pet," he said, his voice chilly, "I am both *rational* and *enlightened*. My choice not to speak of such things to you is only shown wise, when you squall and flail and swat at me thus, like a sulky, ill-raised orcling."

Squall and flail? Like a sulky *orcling*?! Rosa's brief, overpowering urge to laugh was flattened by a genuine outrage, and she again jabbed at his chest. "I do *not*," she said, "*squall*. Or *flail*. Or *swat*."

But here, making Rosa's heart stutter, was the grin. Spreading sharp-toothed, mischievous, *ruthless* across his delicious curling lips. "You *do*, foolish pet," he replied, "and you *shall*."

With that, he lurched forward, so fast Rosa scarcely saw him move—and then she was being forcibly grasped, manhandled, and tossed over John's broad *shoulder*. Her head hanging down his back, her legs belatedly kicking against his front, against the hard, powerful clamp of his arm against her thighs.

"Flailing," he said, impossibly cool, as he strode down the corridor with the lamp still in hand, entirely ignoring Rosa's kicks and shrieks of protest. "Squalling. Swatting. You are too easy, pet."

"I am not," Rosa shot back, her voice oddly nasal due to being hung upside-down, "*easy!*"

John laughed out loud at that, deep and rich, and in retaliation she tried swatting for his arse, which was damnably close to her face—but that only sparked him to yank her closer, grasping at her own arse over her too-short tunic.

"Foolish pet," he said, as that hand purposefully palmed at her, and then—oh gods—began sliding her tunic upwards. "Do you wish me to begin your punishment now? While any of my kin who pass shall see?"

"No!" Rosa wailed, as she kept flailing at him, redoubling her efforts to escape. "No, please, my lord!"

She felt rather than heard him laugh this time, his shoulders shaking beneath her, the warmth tangling with the indignation and the humiliation and the damned frenzied craving. And when John strode into another room—his room, *finally*—Rosa's relief thudded all through her, tingling in her hands and feet. Even as John dragged her into his bed, and then—she yelped—shoved her downwards, onto her hands and knees on the soft furs, while he knelt close and strong and menacing behind her.

"When you fight me, pet," he said, his voice deadly smooth, "you shall be taught your place. You shall be trained"—his hand slowly, deliberately pulled up her tunic—"to yield to your lord. To please me."

Oh hell, he'd exposed Rosa's bare arse, and was now

plucking off her tunic altogether, his fingers quick, adept. And then trailing their way down her back, until his claws were lightly teasing at her arse-cheek, flaring out wild arcs of sparking, spattering pleasure.

"I won't," Rosa gasped at him, *goaded* him, the words taking almost every fragment of her resolve. "You utter prick."

John's low, triumphant laugh sent more heat scattering, anticipation prickling rampant under her exposed, vulnerable skin. And that hand gently drew away, leaving her shivering, panting, untouched, waiting, *please*—

His slap was gentle, careful, intent—but still a shouting firing mayhem, obliterating all else in its sheer, mind-melting strength. Hurling a full-body shudder down the whole of Rosa's kneeling form, so powerful she could barely hear his laugh, husky, hot.

"You wish to be taught, pet," he purred, as his still-lingering hand gently trailed away again—and then landed in another earth-spinning slap, just a shade harder this time. "You wish to be taken in hand by your lord. By an *orc*."

Rosa's shuddering form curled up slightly, almost as if to hide itself from the humiliating power in that claim—but suddenly both those hands gripped to her arse, tilting it back up and out, and then—Rosa moaned aloud—thrusting her bare thighs apart. Showing him far more than before, exposing the entire line of her crease, all her most hidden places bared and opened for an orc's punishment—

It made his next slap even more powerful, more dangerous, even as it was still gentle, careful. Even as—Rosa arched and keened—that hand lingered this time, tracing its claw all the way down her crease, before drawing back, slapping again, oh *hell*.

"Do you learn your lesson, pet?" his voice asked, mocked, as he again traced that humiliating line of her, so smooth, so proprietary. "Shall you better seek to please your lord?"

That, at least, dragged up a jolt of genuine fury, though it was distant, stunted, beneath the still-flaring pleasure of that single, deliberately tracing claw. "I *have* sought to please you," she gasped, glancing over her shoulder toward him—which was a grave mistake, because the way he *looked*, his eyes both dark and deadly bright, his lips parted, his cheeks unmistakably flushed.

"I, um"—she had to haul in air, but she couldn't look away, even as his eyes became mocking again, challenging. "I've worked for *days* for you. I've tolerated a variety of unwarranted *outrageousness* from you. And"—where were the words, the air—"*ég er að læra Aelakesh*, John-Ka."

It was one of a few stupid phrases she'd asked Tristan to teach her—*I'm learning Aelakesh*—but gods, it had been entirely worth it, based on the look in John's eyes alone. True astonishment, and then disbelief, and then—*hunger*. Pure, potent, blazing with bare, powerful longing.

And then he swatted her *again*. His face gone fully blank again, fully revealing that she'd drawn out too much—but if she was being exposed like this, if she was provoking a damned devious orc into swatting her like a sulky orcling, he could surely damned well admit that he was getting off on her speaking his damned language.

"*Ég fíla Aelakesh*," Rosa gasped, forming the unfamiliar words as carefully as she could. "*Ég fíla—John-Ka.*"

I like Aelakesh. I like—John.

His eyes had widened, his nostrils flaring, and Rosa did not miss the heady, mouthwatering sight of his free hand, coming to briefly brush against his massively tented trousers. Which also—Rosa swallowed hard—betrayed a visible, growing streak of wetness down the front.

"*Ég fíla á þér typpið*," John breathed, his eyes burning on hers, his lips barely moving. "You like my prick. Speak this."

Rosa had to lick her lips, suck in breath, her gaze

desperately darting between his eyes and his groin. "*Ég fíla,*" she said, as clearly as she could, "*á þér typpið, John-Ka.*"

John's moan was reflexive, guttural, the very sound making Rosa's bared body frantically clench and flare. To the point where—she had to force her trembling limbs to stay in place—she could feel a streak of wetness, oozing from her swollen groin, stealing down her thigh.

"*Ég er,*" John's strangled voice said, his glittering eyes dropping, fixed to the sight, "*svo blaut.* So wet."

Rosa fought for air, for conscious *thought*, over the blaring shout of her heartbeat. "*Ég er svo blaut, John-Ka.*"

His groan sounded dangerously close to a cry this time, his eyes squeezing shut. "*Refsaðu mér,*" he hissed, and his hand on Rosa's arse drew back—and then slapped her again, hard enough to sting this time. "*Refsaðu mér.*"

The understanding ricocheted through Rosa, clamouring against the furious hurtling pleasure. "*Refsaðu mér,* John-Ka," she breathed, as her bare arse seemed to thrust itself toward him, brandishing itself for him, begging him. "*Refsaðu mér!*"

His answering slap was almost painful, but it was everything, *everything,* even the way it skittered as it landed, and then slipped down to skate against her swollen, clenching, spread-open heat. Making her choke and gasp and keen, and even more, oh hell, when he brought his shaking fingers to his nose, and *inhaled.*

"Gods," Rosa gasped, without at all meaning to, her eyelashes madly fluttering, her body again pushing back toward him. "Fuck. *Ég er svo blaut,* John-Ka."

His whole form visibly, viscerally stilled, his hand hovering against his mouth, his eyes blacker than Rosa had ever seen them—and suddenly his hands dropped to his tented, wet-stained groin, and yanked out his cock. Huge, veined, glistening, and dripping a thick stream of shiny, succulent white.

Rosa nearly sobbed at the truth of it, its massive heft

vibrating hard against his clawed fingertips—and then again when his hand snapped up to catch the thick white in his palm. And then he slicked himself all over in it, coating himself with its slippery sheen, the sight almost too powerfully primal for Rosa's blinking, staring eyes. And then—she cried out, long, loud—he brought his still-dripping hand up, and rubbed that wetness deep and purposeful between her spread arse-cheeks.

And gods, he'd said he wanted this, and now that it was happening—was it happening?—the trepidation and anticipation and sheer *yearning* were raging and shouting all at once. Needing this, craving this, how could she possibly do this, oh hell she had to do this—

"How do I say," she gasped at him, "fuck me."

And fuck the bastard, because he actually laughed, hoarse, genuine, frayed. "*Ríddu mér*," he breathed, as he rose up to kneel behind her. His body so hot, so close, and Rosa let out a raw, high-pitched howl as that slick, smooth hardness slipped between her parted cheeks, just nudging at where it was—it wasn't—supposed to be. And it was *huge*, and Rosa was not, and she kept hauling in air, fighting back the swirling seething panic—

"Breathe, my pet," came John's rasping voice, his hand running up and down her flank. "*Andaðu, hjartað mitt.* You have been fucked thus before. Ach?"

Even the words sent a hard, wringing thrill up Rosa's back, and she jerked a vehement nod. "Ach," she choked out. "I mean, yes, but you're so much *bigger*, John-Ka."

It came out sounding like a plea, but both John's hands were stroking her shivering sides now, big, warm, capable. "I shall also be gentler," he said, soft, "and wetter. And I shall stop, at the first sign of real pain. You shall speak this to your lord, pet. Ach?"

Rosa nodded again, yes, *yes*, and those stroking hands slid down to her arse-cheeks, gently spreading them apart.

Opening her up more for him, for the smooth slick head of him, and she could feel more of that hot liquid pooling out of him, coating her, perhaps even seeping inside…

"And *you* shall be the one to first take *me*," he murmured. "Just as we have done with your throat. You shall ease me into you, until you are full. Ach?"

It was both impossibly thrilling, and deeply reassuring, and Rosa's thoroughly scrambled brain held to that, clung to that, as she heaved in choking breaths, and sought to relax herself against his quietly pressing heft. To just feel it there, not pushing yet, only vibrating against her, shuddering out more of that slick, viscous heat into her tight, resisting entrance.

Fuck, it felt good, even just like this. An orc's huge, dripping-wet cockhead nudging against her, kissing at her, seeking to open her up around it. To explore her darkest, most secret parts, to fully make her his own, and as Rosa settled herself a little closer, she could feel him flaring back, speaking his pleasure…

"Will you," she heard her voice whisper, as she shifted still closer, felt it open her a little further, "speak to me, my lord? Please?"

The hardness against her shuddered again, and it felt so *good*, and Rosa felt her resisting body open a little more, welcoming his invasion—and then, oh gods, John began to speak.

"*Þú ert svo falleg, hjartað mitt,*" he gasped. "*Ég elska hvernig þú lætur mér líða.*"

The words rolled so easily from his mouth, smooth and low and surely full of filth, and Rosa felt herself arch and moan with longing, with hunger, with the shouting craving need to have this orc, to take this orc, to feel the strength of him inside her. To earn her lord's approval, to gain his trust, to open herself for him, show him how much she needed him…

"*Ég fíla á þér typpið, John-Ka,*" she breathed, as she felt herself relax a little more, easing back further. Beginning to feel the full heft of him now, meaning that he was actually sinking *inside* her, and their moans seemed to rise together, John's hands tight on her arse, his harsh breath skittering against her skin.

"Again," he whispered, his voice breaking. "More, pet."

So Rosa said it again, and sank back further, swallowing him deeper inside, feeling the very slight burn of pain this time. But the steady pulse of silken liquid did seem to help, and so did his patience with this, with the way he wasn't moving, only stroking her with those hands, waiting. And a furtive glance back showed him watching, too, his dark head bent, his braid falling over his shoulder, his glittering eyes intent upon the sight of his huge cock, which was somehow buried halfway inside her—

Rosa's groan snapped his gaze up to hers, his lips parted, his tongue brushing slow against them. Saying he liked this, he liked *her*, and as she watched, he slid his hand back up her side, claws scraping soft, until he'd reached the back of her neck, and circled quiet, tender, approving around it.

"Good little pet," he said, his voice hitching as she pushed back a little further, took him still deeper. "This pleases me."

And oh, it was good, that truth in his voice, the accompanying shudder of his cock so deep inside her. Making Rosa's body shudder around him in return, a skin-tight rhythmic clenching that made his eyes roll back, his hardness within her swelling even fuller, deeper, *fuck*—

And Rosa was doing this, she was impaling herself on an orc, she needed all of him, *now*—and she thrust back, hard, all the way. Shouting as he sank full and whole inside her, his groin pressed flush and tight to her arse-cheeks, his bulging bollocks nestled up close against her dipping-wet heat. While behind her he'd actually *roared*, his hips already circling, moving Rosa's entire body with him. Meaning she was truly trapped, now, skewered, pinioned whole upon an orc, and the entire world was thundering with it, screaming all around her, fraying white and wild behind her eyes.

"*Ríddu mér*," she gasped at him. "*Ríddu mér*, my lord, please!"

His moan was thick, cracked, as desperate as she felt, and those hips circled again, deathly strong, moving her whole with them. Punching home the sharp, swirling realization that he wasn't actually going to thrust, it was too tight, too dangerous— but in this moment Rosa didn't care, didn't want his damned calculated gentleness, and she fought to yank herself away from him, to feel the delicious agony of her lord pulling her apart, remaking her with the violent slam of that cock—

John's growl felt visceral this time, his huge body almost vibrating as he pinned Rosa even harder to him—and then, without warning, he rolled back. Flat onto his own back, dragging Rosa down on top of him, grasping her close into his tight embrace, leaving her scarcely able to move. And her only possible recourse was to grind her arse down against him, meeting him as his hips ground up, his huge cock just slightly circling inside. He was keeping her safe, making her his, gasping groaning Aelakesh into her ear as his hand slid down and stroked, once, against her dripping wet heat—

Rosa's release ripped out of her with a scream, with the furious firing euphoria of her trapped body wrenching again and again on her lord's beautiful heft, worshipping its strength, wringing out its pleasure. Needing more, craving more so much it hurt, feeling the ecstasy jolt and crack and flare—

And then, inside her, John *exploded*. His invading force spraying out so hard Rosa could feel it juddering against her, flooding her, bathing her with stream after stream of hot, swarming orc-seed. While beneath her his hot, powerful body arched them both to the sky, his mouth howling, his claws on her belly scraping sharp and deep and utterly, thoroughly lost.

When he finally relaxed again, sagging onto the bed, it was like all the tension pooled out of Rosa's body too, leaving her limp and trembly and sticky all over. Still trapped on an orc, lying on her back on top of him, and with a low groan John rolled them both to the side, his big body tucked up close behind her far smaller one, his slowly softening hardness still hidden deep inside.

"Foolish woman," he whispered, his voice thick, scratchy. "I told you to keep this gentle. You might have drawn your *blood*, with all your flailing."

Rosa elbowed back at him, but otherwise felt too sated, too full of unspooling warmth, to mount a proper argument. "I suppose I probably did get a little too"—she gulped in a breath—"involved."

John's hand was skimming down her side, over the curve of her hip to her thigh, and back up again. "Ach, *ég fíla þetta*," he said, the words deliberate enough that Rosa could follow his meaning. *He liked that.* "But we must take care with your little body."

His hand kept stroking, warm, soothing, so thoroughly and utterly delicious that Rosa's next question seemed to escape all on its own, without any conscious thought. "Will you ever take me again the—the *regular* way? Like we did the first time?"

And she surely should not have asked that, based on the sudden stiffening of John's body against her, the clench of his hand as it stilled on her hip. "I ken it is best," he said, very evenly, "if I do not."

Oh. Right. Because this was still only a short-term thing, an extended exercise in deadly offspring avoidance. And this—an orc's body curled warm and protective and safe behind hers— was still just him luring her into staying, until all that was done. Taking care of her, like he'd promised.

And if an orc's idea of taking care of a woman also involved tying her up, or punishing her, or cuddling her after he'd just plundered her arse, what did that matter? Why did Rosa care? She was here to learn, to spy, eighteen days...

"How will I know if I'm pregnant, from that time?" she made herself ask, her eyes blinking toward the stone wall. "Will Efterar be able to tell?"

"Ach," came John's quiet answer behind her. "But I shall also be able to smell our son upon you, when he comes."

Our son. When he comes. As if he were already on his way. An *inevitability.*

An unbidden quiver rippled up Rosa's back, and John's hand abruptly began moving again, sliding up and down her side with purposeful reassurance. "Do not fear, little rose," he said, though his voice sounded oddly thick. "I shall keep you safe."

And in this moment, with an orc's body so close against hers, his hand smoothing so intent on her skin, it occurred to Rosa that—she *believed* him. She trusted that he meant this. He would keep her safe. Gods, he'd even done so just now, hadn't he? Ensuring she hadn't injured herself, taking their pleasure this way, rather than *that* way. Even right now, just here, stroking her, soothing her, staying with her.

It was the kind of thing Lord Kaspar would never have done—his casual disregard of Rosa's discomfort had always been total and absolute—and something seemed to be swelling in Rosa's chest, kicking unsteadily at her heart. She trusted John. She—*liked* John. He was controlling, secretive, devious, dangerous—and curse her, she *liked* him. An *orc.*

"I think you might have a twisted perception of *safe*, John-Ka," she said, attempting to keep her voice light. "I mean, over just the past few days, I've been tied to a bed, and *punished*, and impaled upon something that might better resemble a *lamp-post.*"

John's chuckle behind her was warmth, ease, solace. "Ach,

and I ken you have yet never been so content as you are this night, foolish pet."

He was right, damn him, and Rosa huffed out a breath that wasn't quite offended. "*And*," she continued, louder, as though he hadn't spoken, "I was subjected to the appalling sight of your—your secret Ka-esh pleasure-den. A *pleasure-den*, John! Just down the hall from your *bedroom*!"

The shake of John's body behind her was longer, sustained, and his hand dropped down her front, to gently pinch at her damnably peaked nipple. "Squalling again, little pet," he purred, his voice alight with mischief. "Do not play-act with me. I know you are curious of this. You mayhap even wish to go back to watch, and learn more. Ach?"

Watch. Learn *more*. Another hard shiver chased down Rosa's back, not even close to afraid this time, and John chuckled again as he scraped at her nipple with a single sharp claw. "I ken you do not like to admit this, pet," he murmured. "You are ashamed of your hunger for such things. But why?"

Rosa swallowed, loud enough that he surely heard it. Why. And why did she want to say it, why did she want to tell this abominable orc, of all people...

"Because it *is* shameful," she whispered. "To want to be used and overpowered. To want to be—afraid."

John's scoff behind her was hoarse, immediate. "Who says this?" he demanded. "This harms no one, pet. It does not harm me, it does not harm you. You were *content* today, to work for me, and be fully my pet. You are at *peace*. I can taste this upon you. Even now."

Rosa swallowed again, and she could feel his hand, again stroking up and down her side, sure, safe. "The only harm lies," he said, quieter, "with these *men*. The men who have harmed you, to steal your gifts for their own. The men who have *taught* you to be ashamed, so you shall keep their dark secrets safe."

Rosa's breath had gone still, the whole world shuddered

still, but for that warm hand, caressing up and down her side. "There are orcs who do this also," he continued, his voice a whisper. "There are orcs who did such to me. But I ought not to feel shame for the deeds of others. My deeds, and my wishes, are my own."

Rosa's brain shouted, rebelled—orcs had done *what* to him?—but then it stuttered, catching, finding something to cling to in the suddenly screeching chaos.

"But you *are* ashamed sometimes, John," she countered. "Of being an orc. Of doing things, or liking things, that make you an orc. As if orcs are all violent, aggressive *monsters*."

Now it was John swallowing, John's silence, John's hand gone still against her skin. And Rosa heard herself let out a laugh, bitter, broken, perhaps even angry, because it was so painful, and so gods-damned *foolish*—

"I knew that was rubbish before I ever *met* one of you," she said, her voice rising, wavering. "And I know it so much more now. You orcs are so much more interesting, and unique, and *alive*, than I ever could have imagined. And you're my favourite one, John, you're so clever, you work so hard, you're so committed and consistent and—and *noble*. You should be *proud* of who you are."

There was another choked stillness, broken not even by the sound of a breath—until behind her John shifted, raising himself up onto his elbow, tilting her head up so their eyes locked. Held. Spoke. No falsehoods.

"You're *marvellous*, John," Rosa whispered. "Any woman would *love* to be your pet."

There was more stillness, his black lashes blinking, his throat convulsing. "Ach, well," he said, finally, his voice sounding less certain than Rosa had ever heard him. "It is luck, then, mayhap, that *you* have gained this honour."

Rosa elbowed back at him, watching the warmth spill across his eyes, feeling it spill deep inside her belly. "It is not *luck*," she countered. "It's the gods wreaking their cruel revenge on me, and giving me a lord who thinks I'm prattling, and bony, and a *strumpet!*"

But John's laugh was almost unbearably gentle, and he lowered his mouth, kissed softly at her cheek. "Ach," he breathed, "and yet, you are also a worthy pet for your lord, little rose. Just what an orc should wish for."

The warmth shimmered deeper, brighter, flickering up Rosa's spine, enveloping her heart. Just what an orc should wish for. Worthy. *Worthy.*

She couldn't seem to stop smiling, suddenly, beaming delightedly up at his watching eyes, and a bright giggle escaped her lips. "You're just saying sweet things, you reprobate," she murmured, "so I'll forget all about your secret pleasure-den."

"Ach, no," John said back, his mouth slyly curving up, all devious delicious danger. "I say such things so you shall *remember* it, pet."

Rosa ignored the immediate surge of heat in favour of sticking her tongue out at him—an action he returned with a teasing little snap of his teeth toward it, sending another full-body shiver deep into her bones.

"I wish you to leave all this shame, pet," he said, soft, but firm. "You shall obey me, in this."

"Only if you leave it too," Rosa countered, bumping his nose with hers. "And be the devious, calculating, *deviant* orc that you truly are. Complete with claws, and teeth, and a *lamp-post* between your legs."

John's growl wasn't angry, but pleased, warm, *hungry.* "You shall watch your words, pet," he breathed. "Else this *lamp-post* may teach you to do so."

And Rosa was a good pet, such a good pet, because she only gasped, and smiled sweetly, and kissed him. "I am here to learn, my lord," she said. "Do your worst."

24

Over the next few days, Rosa threw herself headlong into her strange, surreal new existence. She wasn't a spy, or a university librarian, or a lord's secret mistress. She wasn't, for now, even an orc's mistake. Instead, she was a Ka-esh pet, coddled and protected and obedient, living only to serve her lord, and to meet his every whim with a smile.

Surely, it helped that John's whims weren't particularly onerous, and that they consistently seemed to accommodate Rosa's own preferences. If John wished to provide lavish breakfasts each morning, and then read *The Lady Bright* to her in bed while she ate, what fault was there to find in that? If he insisted she study Aelakesh with Tristan and Simon until noon each day, and then spend her afternoons reading, puttering around the library, and working on her own book projects as she wished, how could she complain about that, either? And if he took her in bed each night—carefully avoiding that one particular kind of pleasure, but making thorough, glorious, repeated use of everything else—surely that wasn't worth protesting over, either?

The only thing there was to complain about—beyond the

constant churning mess shoved deep into Rosa's brain, and which had begun to reek distinctly of guilt—was John's work. Work which he'd continued to keep Rosa carefully separate from, speaking only in the vaguest of terms of meetings, and deadlines, and various ongoing projects. Making it quite clear to Rosa, without clearly speaking of it at all, that no matter what a good, obedient, worthy pet she was, he still didn't want her involved in his day-to-day activities. Especially when it had anything to do with the men, and the looming threat of war.

Even Tristan and Simon had become surprisingly tight-lipped about the situation with the men, to the point where Tristan had told Rosa, in stilted tones, that it might be best to ask her questions of John-Ka. And when she had tried asking Jule—who continued to stop by the library almost daily to chat—Jule only rolled her eyes, and muttered darkly about damned fool lords who couldn't leave well enough alone, and who would be better off spending their limited time and money on their neglected wives and children, or lacking that, their horses.

"Do you really need to work *again*, my lord?" Rosa tried asking John again, late one night in his bed. "What could possibly be so important?"

Her voice had come out low and lazy, her hands stroking his bare shoulders with contented, familiar ease. She'd just spent a good half-hour sucking him off, during which he'd dragged her lower half fully around on top of him, so that he could take her with his tongue at the same time. It had been utterly *spectacular*, and at this moment, Rosa just wanted to revel in the loose-limbed satisfaction of it, of her lord looking at her with such easy, tolerant eyes.

"Ach, I must," he said, but there was true reluctance in his voice, in the wry twist on his mouth. "There is much I must yet address today."

Rosa was getting better at gauging days and nights in the

perpetual dark of the mountain—the orcs kept consistent schedules in many ways, from mealtimes to the hours fires stayed lit, and John had continued to take her to his Ka-esh sunroom on a regular basis—and Rosa halfheartedly jabbed at his bare chest with a finger. "It's not today, it's *tonight*," she corrected him. "And there's *always* something you need to address. Even orcs need to sleep *sometime*, John-Ka."

John dismissed that entirely reasonable point with a careless shrug, though his eyes darted a telling glance across the room toward where Tristan had, indeed, just strolled in, giving them a brief wave before slipping into the bunk opposite. Tristan, Rosa now knew, slept similar hours to her own, though he'd made a habit of waiting until she and John had finished their regular evening activities before coming to bed. And while Rosa still felt the urge to cover up whenever he appeared, John, of course, held little patience for such prudery, especially in his own bed.

"I shall be here when you wake, pet," he said firmly, with a satisfied pat at her bare breast, and then a pinch to her still-peaked nipple. "I have heard that Bautul's hunters brought in some honey today. I shall trade for this, and bring some for your breakfast tomorrow."

Rosa couldn't deny the spark of eagerness at that—John had already deduced, and taken full advantage of, her partiality for sweet treats—but when he again made to leave the bunk, she clutched at him, pulled him back against her. He didn't resist, gazing down at her with eyebrows raised, and she swallowed, stroked a careful finger down the hard line of his jaw.

"Is your work really so important," she ventured, "that you can't stay even just a little longer? If you truly don't need the sleep, maybe you could even just read with me for a while?"

She nodded toward his own small stack of books on the nearby shelf—for someone who loved books as much as he did, he certainly seemed to spend very little time reading them—and his sidelong glance at the books indeed looked almost regretful. "I cannot, pet," he said. "I must first meet with the captain, and next Eben, and next survey the new northern tunnel. We have also just learnt of two more women carrying Skai orc-sons, and this must be dealt with at once. And the men—"

He halted there, grimacing, but it was still more detail than he'd given her in days, and Rosa clung to that, to him. She was only a pet, curious and interested, she didn't need to learn any information, or return to Dusbury, ever, and especially not in ten short days...

"Have the lords answered any of your letters yet?" she asked, as lightly as she could. "Have you heard any news from Preia? Has there been any response to Simon's attack, and the injured men?"

John's face betrayed a faint twitch, and he drew away from Rosa, easing his fully naked form out of the bed entirely. Bending to grasp his trousers from the floor, showing a brief but impressive view of his bare backside before yanking them on.

"No," he said curtly, as he pulled his tunic on over his head. "We have been sent no return letters."

Oh. Rosa silently watched him, something twisting deep in her belly. "Do you think the lords are still pushing for war? Even despite all your efforts to prevent it?"

But John only dismissed the questions with a jerky shrug, and took a step toward the door, as if to leave. But then he reached back, abruptly, and rustled his hand in Rosa's already-mussed hair.

"Do not fret," he said. "We shall take care of all this. *You* must sleep, little pet. You need this rest."

With that, he turned and strode off, leaving Rosa alone in his bed, blinking after him in the light of her candle. Thinking, with a surprisingly fervent misery, of Lord Kaspar, and the ten measly days she had left. And after that, war would surely come...

And despite John's ongoing reluctance to discuss this looming war with her—or perhaps because of it—Rosa hadn't missed the rising hints of preparations all around her. The fully armed, scary-looking bands of orcs in the corridors. The constant clangs and shouts from what she now knew was a sparring-room, only one level up from the library. The murmurs in the kitchen and the corridors about men, and skirmishes, and strategies. All spoken in quick, clipped Aelakesh, and while Rosa's understanding of Aelakesh was still extremely rudimentary, she'd begun listening very carefully, and asking Tristan to translate words and phrases that she often heard. Things like *armed*, *bands of men*, *no attacking yet*. Suggesting that, perhaps, war was even closer than John wanted to allow...

But maybe it was just paranoia. Maybe it was just Rosa brooding, thinking too much. Lord Kaspar had told her there was no money, hadn't he? He'd said they were waiting on her revelations. So maybe the situation with Simon hadn't truly changed anything. Maybe everything really was *fine*, at least until she...

Rosa forcibly bit off that thought, and glanced toward Tristan's dark silhouette in the bunk opposite—perhaps if he were very tired, he might let something slip?—but that hope was dashed by the sudden appearance of Salvi, striding tall and silent into the room, and making straight for Tristan's bed. Something he did most nights, Rosa had noticed, though so far she'd only ever seen them speak to each other for a few minutes, the words quiet and clipped, before Salvi went over to his own bunk to sleep.

But this time, there was no speaking. No sleeping. Only Salvi first shucking his tunic and trousers onto the floor, exposing his tall, grey-skinned, fully naked form to Rosa's blinking eyes—and then hurling himself into the bed with

Tristan. Pinning Tristan's smaller, still-clothed body close beneath him, and cutting off Tristan's obvious noise of protest with a deep, powerful kiss.

Rosa stared at this new development, unexpectedly intrigued, as Tristan seemed to melt into Salvi, his eyes fluttering shut, his mouth kissing back with fluid, familiar eagerness—but then he suddenly, visibly stiffened, and shoved Salvi away. And Rosa could hear Salvi's growl of disapproval, or maybe frustration, and when Tristan spoke a few breathless words of Aelakesh, Salvi frowned, and then—looked straight across at *Rosa*. His eyes dark, irritated, dissatisfied.

"You won't be vexed, woman," he said, curt, "if I have Tristan here, ach? Will this frighten you, or aught else?"

Rosa's face swarmed with heat, but she was already frantically shaking her head, waving the question away. "No, no, of course not," she replied, too quickly. "My apologies, I don't wish to be rude—"

She belatedly fumbled to blow out her candle, plunging the room into utter darkness. To which there was a satisfied chuckle from the bunk opposite, a sound of quiet movement. "Ach, you could have watched," came Salvi's voice, husky, smug. "Now, any other fool excuses, *sæti*?"

There was no audible reply, but Rosa could hear more movement, the sounds of skin and furs sliding, of more fabric being thrown to the floor. And then a harsh, strangled moan from Tristan, and Salvi's low, triumphant laugh in return.

"*Guðir*," Salvi breathed. "*Þú ert svo fallegur, sæti.*"

Rosa now knew enough Aelakesh to recognize that for what it was—*you are so beautiful, my sweet*—and Tristan's soft answer was just as heated, earning a half-laugh, half-groan from Salvi. And then it was only breathless moans and Salvi's rasping praises, the sounds of skin stroking and slapping, rising harder and louder until Tristan's voice arched into a howl, and Salvi's into a deep, guttural snarl.

Then it slowly settled into just their breaths, heaving together, almost as one. Leaving Rosa oddly breathless herself, blinking up into the darkness, and again feeling that inexplicable, compulsive twist in her belly. John would return, in the morning. He had work to do. She was only a pet, and that was all...

It took Rosa too long to fall asleep again, even with the soft furs over her, with both her hands crossed protectively over her waist. John would return. He wanted her just as much as Salvi wanted Tristan. And of course he wouldn't tell her everything about his work, about a *war*, she was only a...

Rosa's dreams were tense, uncomfortable, full of libraries, students, a certain handsome lord—but when she finally jerked awake the next morning, John was indeed waiting there, just as he'd promised. Sitting at the opposite end of the bed, and holding his usual bottle of milk, alongside a full bowl of what appeared to be fruit and seeds, drizzled all over with thick, golden-brown honey.

Rosa snatched it from him with genuine delight, and it soon proved to be the single most delicious meal she'd ever eaten in her entire *life*. And once she'd demolished it all, and John had finished the latest chapter of *The Lady Bright*, she thanked him by shoving him back onto the bed, kneeling between his legs, and enthusiastically dragging out an entirely different kind of sweetness. Swallowing it all down without missing a drop, until her stomach felt very near to bursting.

"Hungry little pet," John said, as he drew her up again, and ran both hands over her slightly rounded waist. "It pleases me to see your little belly so full. You shall drink more of me tonight, ach?"

The heated promise of that stayed with Rosa throughout the rest of the morning, even as John once again went off to his mysterious work, leaving her to study in the library with Tristan and Simon. Tristan was sporting a new set of angry-looking teeth-marks on his neck, but beyond his flushed ear-tips, he didn't make any reference to the night before, and instead meekly informed Rosa that he and Simon would be working on a letter for the next while, and perhaps she would prefer to continue on her own projects instead?

Rosa would, of course, and she worked with fierce concentration throughout the morning, enough that she scarcely noticed the abrupt appearance of Salvi, several hours later, coming in to watch over Tristan's shoulder. At least, until Salvi bent his head to Tristan's wounded neck, gently kissing it with lips and tongue—and Tristan actually growled at him, loud enough that Rosa jumped, and Simon's head jerked up to glare over at Salvi with a surprising vehemence.

"Go away, *djöfull*," Simon hissed. "Little teacher no want you. No want Ka-esh *liar*. *Vow*-breaker. *Son*-killer."

Salvi immediately growled back, his body snapping tall and rigid behind Tristan. "He's Ka-esh too, you giant lout," he shot back. "And if he doesn't want me, why does he *reek* of my scent today?"

The last bit came out with a vicious satisfaction, but across from Rosa Tristan winced, while Simon snorted, loud and derisive. "All orcs need fuck," he snapped. "It no mean he *trust* you. It no mean he want you bothering *work*."

Something cold prickled in Rosa's belly—was that true of *all* orcs?—and her eyes searched Salvi's taut, pale-looking face, the unmistakable unease on his mouth.

"Of course Tristan trusts me," he said, with a joviality that didn't at all match his expression. "We've been together since we were orclings. Kin-brothers for life. Ach, *sæti*?"

His hand dropped to squeeze companionably against Tristan's shoulder, and in return Tristan gave a quick, jerky nod, his eyes intent on his paper. To which Simon only snorted again, crossing his arms over his huge chest.

"*He* lie," he said, pointing a claw at Tristan. "And *you* lie, *djöfull.* As all Ka-esh. I hear what you do to kind little teacher. I hear how you make him your mate, how he spurn all others for you, even your false Priest. And how you next cast him away, for *woman*. For *son*. And next"—he leaned forward, lunging his finger toward Salvi's chest—"you and false Priest *kill* son! Betray little teacher, for *naught*!"

Rosa couldn't seem to stop staring between the three of them, while the chill in her belly wrenched colder, deeper. "Wait," she said, without meaning to. "You two used to be *mated*? And then you"—she frowned up at Salvi—"you *left* Tristan? *Him*? For a *woman*?"

There was a collective grimace from both Tristan and Salvi, and a visible swallow in Salvi's throat. "We had not," Salvi said thinly, "spoken vows."

"But I thought Ka-esh *didn't* often speak vows," Rosa countered, her voice flat. "Aren't you supposed to show your affection through your—actions?"

Her traitorous brain had darted to earlier that morning, to John bringing honey on her breakfast—but that secretly thrilling thought was immediately thrust away by Simon's loud, bitter laugh. "Ach," he hissed. "No speak vows, these liar Ka-esh, so naught to break. But this still *done*. He still *lie*. He play at love for kind little teacher, until he find *woman* to fuck! And when she swell with son, he *kill it*!"

Good gods. Tristan was looking almost deathly ill, blinking rapidly down at his paper, and behind him Salvi bobbed on his feet, his claws out, his mouth nearly spitting with rage. "You gigantic bumbling *arse*," he snarled. "You have no idea what you're talking about. We Ka-esh need sons just as much as the Skai do, and you fucking know it. At least we *contribute* to this mountain, and our people's continued existence, rather than running around like senseless *barbarians*, starting unnecessary conflicts, and leaving scores of *dead women* in our wake!"

Simon's growl was steadily deepening, his huge body rising

to loom over Salvi's, his teeth bared and deadly. "Skai fight and *die* to save *you*. Skai keep weak Ka-esh *safe!*"

"Well, maybe we don't need you anymore," Salvi shot back. "For once, thank the gods, the brains are finally running the show!"

Simon made a deep, gravelly sound much like a bark, terrifying enough to make the hair on Rosa's neck stand up. "Liars," he growled. "Thieves. Hard orcs. Blame Skai, but break own *vows*, and kill own *sons*. Fail even with these great *brains* to keep many more *men* away from mountain! Men who not just roam. Men who now *stay*. Men who make an *army!*"

Many more men. Who now *stay*. An *army*. Rosa's body had wrenched very tight and still, her eyes locked on Simon's face, and she scarcely caught Salvi's snarled reply, something about Simon being half the cause for this mess in the first place. Because her heart was pounding, her gut lurching, more men, maybe more of *Duke Warmisham's* men, *here*, and wait, hadn't John said, just last night...

"How many more men?" Rosa heard her voice cut in, curiously hollow. "How long have they been here?"

Tristan was speaking, suddenly, but Simon's laugh was louder, scraping, grim. "Many, many days," he said. "And soon, should these *brains* not find a way through this, we shall have *war*."

25

They would have war.

Rosa couldn't follow, couldn't move. Could only stare at Simon, at Salvi—and then at Tristan. Tristan, whose face was written all over with chagrin, and misery, and *guilt*.

He'd *known*.

"But John," Rosa gulped, staring. "John said—he told me—you hadn't heard anything. From the men."

And Lord Kaspar told me they had no money, she wanted to shout. *They're waiting on my research, in nine days—*

But even as the thought rose and rebelled, Rosa felt its naivety, its laughable foolishness. What did it matter, what Lord Kaspar had told his librarian weeks ago? Clearly, much had changed since then. Simon had fought and injured *ten men*, she'd seen it with her own eyes, and then she'd seen the preparations all over this mountain, and just how much John had worked these past days. Of *course* there had been a response from the men, why had she ever hoped there wouldn't be...

"I have spoken this to you, woman," came Simon's voice,

grating, triumphant. "Again and again. Ka-esh *liars*. Even *Skai* see how much this false Priest no tell his own mate. I ken you yet know *naught* of his deep plans. You know *naught* of his secret ploys. You know *naught* of how he—"

"Stop!" interrupted Tristan's voice, echoing high-pitched through the room. "And leave. Both of you. Please!"

There was an instant's twitching stillness, in which both Simon and Salvi jerked to look at Tristan. Who was biting his trembling lip with a sharp white tooth, his eyes blinking hard, his hand gripping at the quill he'd still been holding.

"*Please*," Tristan repeated, and after another instant's frowning down at his bowed head, Salvi spun on his heel and stalked out, with Simon's huge body lurching close behind him. Leaving Rosa alone with Tristan, and staring dully across the table at his drawn, ashen face.

He had *lied* to her. *John* had lied.

And Rosa wanted to yell at Tristan, demand how he could hide such a thing from her—but the words wouldn't come, and she wrapped her arms around her waist, squeezing tight. It shouldn't matter. She didn't care. She didn't.

"I am sorry, Rosa," came Tristan's hollow voice. "I told John-Ka to speak of this to you. I *told* him."

He sounded on the verge of weeping, Rosa realized, and she dropped her own blinking eyes to the table. "I knew he was hiding something," she made herself say, through her own trembling mouth. "It's the Ka-esh way, apparently."

The silence between them felt thick, suddenly, heavy with accusation. Hinting, perhaps, at Salvi's lies to Tristan, too—and a glance upwards showed Tristan's throat convulsing, his clawed fingers flexing against his quill.

"Ka-esh are not always thus," he said, very quiet. "Salvi has never spoken false to me. He did not truly betray me, as Simon said. I"—his shoulders squared—"I granted him leave to do all he did."

Rosa kept staring blankly toward him, while her skittering brain called up a memory from what felt like weeks ago, a lifetime ago. *When Salvi had a mate*, John had said, *he ploughed her before us each night. There was great joy in this...*

"What, so you just ran back into *John's* arms instead," she said, colder than she meant, "and then you two sat back and watched the show together?"

Tristan's wan face didn't change, his eyes intent on his quill. "Ach, we did," he replied, his voice wooden. "John-Ka showed me much kindness, in this. And if I could not have Salvi for my own, I could yet draw joy from seeing him take such pleasure in his mate, and in filling her with his seed, and sparking his son inside her. He is"—his throat convulsed—"stunning, in his joy."

Rosa's stomach roiled, hard enough that she had to clamp a hand to her mouth. "Good gods, Tristan," she said, muffled. "If I ever saw—someone I cared about—do all that with someone else, especially after he *left* me, I would *never* be able to see the good in it, let alone forgive him for it. *Ever.*"

Tristan's shoulders rose and fell, his eyes blinking at where he was now gripping his quill between both hands. "I have not forgiven Salvi," he whispered, so quiet it was almost inaudible. "But I ought to. He wanted a woman and a son. We all want this. We *must.*"

But the quill in his hands suddenly snapped in two, the noise unnervingly loud in the hushed stillness. And it had gotten ink all over Tristan's fingers, and he scrubbed at them, forceful, as he lurched unsteadily to his feet.

"I ought to," he said, without looking at her, scrubbing again, "go. I must—"

He didn't finish, and turned and stumbled away, out into the darkness. Leaving Rosa entirely alone in the library, for the first time since she'd arrived at this mountain, and she looked blankly around at its already familiar shelves, and then down at the papers on the table. Her Aelakesh notes, and then set carefully on top, her translation of *A Treatise on the Gainful Birthing of Orclings*.

She'd just finished it earlier that morning, and she'd been unaccountably excited to show it to John—but now she could only seem to blink at it, at the glossy leather-wrapped cover, the neat stitches of her binding. John had lied to her. He'd known the men were here, he'd been working on addressing this war perhaps this *entire time*, and he'd intentionally kept her an ignorant, oblivious pet. Foolish. *Useless.*

Rosa didn't look up when she heard him come into the library, some time later. Just kept staring at her book, her heart painfully floundering, as he sighed, and walked over to stand beside her.

"I hear Simon has vexed you again," his clipped voice said. "You ought to know, pet, not to allow a Skai to provoke you thus."

Rosa's head jerked up, her eyes narrowing at John's disapproving, stupidly attractive face. "Are you going to tell me again that Simon was lying, then?" she asked, her voice thin. "Are you going to keep pretending that he and the Skai are the whole problem here, rather than the army of *men* that's apparently camped on your doorstep?!"

John didn't move or speak, didn't betray a single twitch— but Rosa *knew* him, *knew* it was true, and she gripped her hands to the chair beneath her. "You *lied* to me, John," she snapped. "You pretended as though nothing was happening with the men. You let me believe that you've been spending your days doing scientific research and digging tunnels, rather than planning for a *war!*"

John's face still hadn't changed, his eyes unnervingly steady on Rosa's. "And why, woman," he said, his voice very careful, "do you wish to know so much of this war."

There was a pulse of sudden panic, hurtling deep and hidden inside, but thank the gods Rosa's mouth was already speaking, rescuing her with surprising vehemence. "Because I'm *trying* to *trust* you, John! I'm trying to serve you, and please you, and forget the shame, and accept myself as your"—she had to take a breath, shaky—"your *pet*. And how am I supposed to do that, how am I supposed to feel safe with you, when you keep *lying* to me!"

John only kept looking at her, not speaking, and Rosa bit her lip, blinking at the stone floor. "And I *hate* being ignorant, John," she whispered. "I *hate* not knowing things. I thought you *knew* that."

She could hear John's heavy exhale, the slight shift of his form. And when she glanced up again, her eyes unaccountably wet, he was leaning back against the table before her, his gaze fixed unseeing on the shelf beyond.

"These men marched from Preia two days after Simon's attack," he said, the words very even. "It is not a full army— Duke Warmisham does not yet have the funds to rouse a full army—but two regiments. Two hundred armed men. They have set up camp at the base of the mountain, but they have not yet mounted an attack, or sought to break their way in."

Rosa stared wide-eyed at him, her heart skipping. Two hundred men. Not yet attacked. Not yet...

"Lords Otto, Anton, and Culthen have not yet sent their own men to join them," John's steady voice continued. "But neither did Otto stop these regiments from crossing his lands. We know these lords—Duke Warmisham and Lord Kaspar among them—still meet in their Citadel to urge for war, and they hire yet more men to attack our trade. They spread yet more tales and treatises across the land of our great wickedness, and these travel with great speed."

Oh. Rosa sat very straight and still in her chair, her hands now gripping together on her lap, her fingers cold and clammy.

"So what are you doing in return?" she said, through her oddly dry mouth. "What comes next?"

John shrugged, his lips thinning. "We work, and we wait. We have sent many scouts, we send letters and call for councils. We file grievances at each attack upon our trade wagons. We have again forbidden any orc from stepping above ground, or meeting any man in battle. We have blocked all upper exits to our mountain. But"—he ran a hand against his hair, his eyes still glowering at the bookshelf—"the men yet stay. They wait, also."

It felt hard to speak, suddenly, Rosa's gaze now fixed to her hands. "And what," she croaked out, "are they waiting for?"

The silence settled thick, oppressive, tainted—and Rosa's quick, furtive glance upward showed John finally looking back at her, his eyes so distant, so cold. So... *guarded.*

"We know they seek more men," he said, very smooth. "But we know not from where these men will come. Of these lords who push most against us, Lord Otto alone has the wealth to fund an army large enough to truly threaten us. But he has not done so. Yet."

Something had begun rattling in Rosa's thoughts, lunging wild and panicked for escape. *They're waiting for the peasants,* it wanted to shout. *They're waiting to spread the word of your new atrocities, and spark a public rebellion. And surely, surely they've sent these trained men here to prepare, to set up plans and supply lines, to direct and reinforce any attack when it comes...*

"Thus, I wish to ask you, pet," came John's voice, velvety soft, setting off more clanging panic in Rosa's skull. "Do you know aught of this? You have worked for Lord Kaspar, and shared his bed, for many years. Did he speak to you of their plans? Did he seek your help?"

Oh gods. Oh, *gods.* Rosa was staring at John's face, his blank, blank face, and she felt bolted to her chair, her breath locked in her lungs. John couldn't know. He couldn't. He could never, *ever* find out.

But maybe, she realized, with a slowly creeping horror, he *suspected*. And maybe—maybe *that* was why he'd lied to her all this time. That was why he'd kept the war plans so secret. He didn't trust her, and he couldn't, nine days, he *couldn't*...

And what could she say, to an orc, who thought his pet was lying to him, spying on him, selling him out to his enemies. An orc who—Rosa couldn't help a painful, full-body shudder—knew what she'd been reading, that day in the library. An orc she'd tried to bribe, that first day, into telling her the truth about his people...

"Lord Kaspar asked me to research you," she blurted out, before she could stop it. "He gave me a list of sources to read. So I read them, and I thought they were total rubbish, so that's why I tried to learn more from you at the library. That's all. I haven't even"—she heaved in a breath—"seen Lord Kaspar, since then."

John was gazing at her, his eyes almost painfully intent on her face, and Rosa felt her chest hollowing, her cheeks hot and smarting. He couldn't know. He couldn't...

"I don't want to see him, either," she continued, quieter, the words sounding thankfully, abominably true. "Gods, it's been such a *relief*, being away from him, all this time. Doing something—worthwhile."

And wait, she didn't mean that, did she? Her work in the Dusbury Library had surely been worthwhile, even if half of it had involved accommodating Lord Kaspar's lordly urges—but Rosa's gaze had seemed to catch, and hold, on her new book on the table. And then at her stacks of Aelakesh notes and exercises, and then—she swallowed—at the library all around her. Not significantly changed from when she'd first arrived, but the differences were still there. It was neater, cleaner, brighter.

Easier to use, to appreciate, to enjoy. It had been—taken care of.

Just like she had been, something whispered, deep and forceful inside, as her stomach badly twisted and churned, her gaze fixed again to John's watching, weighing eyes. Bearing perhaps not as much suspicion as before, but more... thoughtfulness. Deliberation.

"You now know where we stand, with this war," he said finally. "Is there aught more you might wish to ask of me, upon this? Or tell me?"

He was offering to answer more questions, Rosa realized, blinking at his too-remote face—and he was also giving her one more chance. One more out. One more opportunity to say, *Lord Kaspar's bribed me to spy on you, and help him start this war...*

But John couldn't know. Ever. And Rosa gulped back the blockage in her throat, and made her head shake back and forth. Saying, *no, no, nothing, never...*

And maybe she was imagining it, the faint flare of something new in John's eyes, the added grimness on his mouth. But he nodded, once, his eyes fixing back to the shelf behind her, his arms crossing over his chest.

"Then tell me, mayhap," he said, so smooth, "of what you have done today."

Yes, yes, *gods* yes, *anything* else, and the relief spasmed in Rosa's belly as she frantically nodded, her gaze dropping to the table. To her neat, brand-new translation of the *Treatise*.

"Well," she said, her voice too high-pitched. "I did finish your book, John. And do you know, at first I wasn't sure about it—at least some of it *has* to be exaggerated—but the more I've read it, the more I truly think it could help you. *All* of you."

John glanced down at the book, his eyebrows raised, but he didn't otherwise speak. Waiting for Rosa to keep going—*listening* to her, her thoughts whispered, while her gut spasmed again—so she took a bracing breath, let it out.

"This author claims to have studied *hundreds* of women, with a seemingly rigorous methodology," she said. "And he's developed comprehensive lists of which foods and herbs proved most beneficial, and detailed descriptions of stretching and massage that helped prepare women for birth. And this part"—she reached to open her book with a shaky hand—"makes a credible case for inducing birth at least two full months early, if you have an orc like Efterar to help you. It also has a section on birthing in water, and this part is about how to make sure you properly detach and weigh the placenta. Apparently orc placentas are larger and more metabolically active than humans', which is quite fascinating, don't you think?"

She was babbling, most definitely, but John didn't look annoyed—in fact, his eyes had narrowed with his telltale deliberate focus—so Rosa just kept talking, flipping to another part of the book. "And most importantly, according to his research, women whose orcs stay with them throughout their pregnancies apparently have a *much* higher rate of survival. He attributes this to immunological therapy—essentially acclimatizing the woman's body over time to the orc's particular genetic makeup, and teaching it to therefore welcome his offspring. And, also, he claims increased maternal nutrition. From. Er. All the"—she couldn't help a weak, shamefaced smile—"seed drinking. It's healthy, apparently. Like you keep saying."

John didn't smile back, though his eyes had taken on a distinctly disbelieving cast. Almost as if he couldn't possibly believe Rosa was saying such preposterous things, but she kept going, digging deeper. "And I actually think," she said, "the implications of that are huge, don't you? The fact that successful orc-women *relationships* might be the key to your survival, rather than just successful *births*. So maybe you need to shift some focus to there. Maybe you need to give your orcs better tools to communicate. Maybe instead of all your foolish feuding with the Skai, you need to actually teach them how to treat women, or how to speak common-tongue, or even how to write. And not just as *punishment*."

John still wasn't speaking, just looking at her with those disbelieving eyes, and Rosa swallowed, gave an uneasy shrug. "If you read to the end," she continued, quieter, "the author ultimately claims to have an eighty-five percent success rate birthing orcs, if all measures are followed. Even with small women. Like me."

The room around them had suddenly gone very quiet, very still, and Rosa could feel John's slow exhale, the way it caught in his throat. The way his eyes were now glittering, his hands clenched at his side, his jaw taut and square.

"And you," he said finally, so soft, so close to mocking, "truly *trust* all this, woman. A strange book, by a strange, long-lost orc from ages past. A book I did not even know I *had*."

Rosa fought to objectively consider the question, even as her heart was erratically pattering, her mouth gone entirely dry. "Maybe?" she heard herself say. "I mean, almost everything I know, I've learned from books. From reading. It's how we communicate with people we can't see, to the people who come after us. It's *knowledge*, John, and knowledge informs new choices, new actions. Knowledge changes us, if we'll accept it. Knowledge changes *everything*."

Her voice had gone low, fervent, perhaps almost pleading, and her heartbeat kept thundering, her breaths coming shallow and quick. And John just kept gazing at her, his eyes hooded, dark eyelashes blinking—and then, oh thank the *gods*, there was his tongue, brief, black, slipping against his lips. Betraying him.

Rosa scarcely felt herself rising to her feet, reaching toward him—even as she watched her hands grasp at his shoulders, and shove him down into the chair she'd been sitting in. His body sprawling heavy but easy into it, *willing*, and that was a betrayal too. And even more when Rosa's tingly fingers fumbled for her tunic, and yanked it off, threw it to the floor.

John's dark, blinking eyes roved up and down, drinking in the sight of her naked form, and Rosa stepped closer, between his parted thighs. Tilting his face up with a trembling hand, catching and holding those blinking, *betraying* eyes with her own.

Rosa couldn't speak, couldn't bear to break it, but she somehow nudged a hand down to his groin, felt the familiar swollen heft through his trousers. Gripping it, waiting for it, and when his own hands came, obeyed, pulling his thick, dripping hardness out into the air, it felt like a promise. A revelation.

And it didn't need to be spoken, only taken. Only made truth in Rosa's stepping closer, climbing up onto those powerful thighs. Spreading herself open over him, over that hard, dripping, very real danger—and then lowering herself upon it, slow, steady. Finding the thick, slick, shuddering head of it, learning it, tasting it, kissing the glory of it with swollen wet lips. Feeling it speak back, swell back, flaring and spurting, sinking deeper and deeper into her, into *there*, breath by breath. For the very first time, since that fateful night in another library, another life...

Fuck, it felt good, felt like *everything*, felt like nothing else Rosa had ever known. Like this orc's bared, blinking eyes on her were just as strong as the huge, bared orc-prick driving its way inside her, stretching her, splitting her in two around it. And it took all Rosa's breath, all her courage, to keep looking, keep sinking, taking more and more, so tight and full she felt she might break—until her groin sank flush against his, his huge hardness fully buried inside. While her starved, stretched-out body shivered and clutched at him, craving, impaled, trapped. Where he belonged, where *she* belonged. *Home.*

"Oh, my lord," she whispered, without knowing it, following it. "*Ríddu mér*. Please."

The words sparked in John's eyes, in the sustained flare of his invading heft locked inside her—and he rolled his hips, gentle, but enough to wedge himself just a little fuller, a little deeper. Tilting at just the right edge of pain, and *oh* it was good, and when he did it again, Rosa rocked herself back, meeting him. Feeling her body arch and heave, clamping around the massive, irreconcilable truth of him, of this. Her orc, her lord, within her, taking her, there, like this, until—

"No falsehoods?" she whispered at him, soft, shaken, and she felt the swallow of his throat, drowned in the flutter of his eyes.

"No," he whispered back. "*Ríddu mér*, my brave little rose."

And it was everything, the whole of the world crushed down to this, to an orc's praise and eyes and prick, his heated voice saying in his own tongue, *fuck me*. And Rosa's body was writhing and rocking on its own, arching and moaning, driving, impaling, revelling. Needing this more than life, needing to be trapped and skewered whole on her lord's strong driving cock, more more *more*—

Her hands were clutching at his face, her eyes dazed and frantic on his, her breath skittering at the sight of his tongue, curling against sharp teeth. Flashing to life images of him in the forest, his teeth dripping red, and then Tristan's neck that morning, and—

And it was unthinkable, unconscionable, but Rosa was fucking an orc where it mattered, she was his, she would please him, show him, be worthy. Her hands gripping at the back of his head, dragging him downwards, thrilling all over at the shocking feel of his tongue on her neck, distantly realizing that he'd never done this before, never so much as *kissed* her there. And maybe this was why, the way his teeth were already scraping, seeking, his breath coming out harsh, anguished—

John yanked back, dazed, but still licking his lips, again, again, matching each smooth, heart-swarming roll of his hips against her. "You are," he gasped, with effort, "weak. Small. This may—break you."

But they'd already been over this, Rosa had no patience for this, not anymore. "You're a good lord," she breathed, between moans. "Take care of me. Trust you."

And he didn't believe that, or did he, his eyes again going somewhere she couldn't follow. Thinking, maybe, back to where they'd been just before this, *is there aught more you might wish to tell me...*

And suddenly, Rosa couldn't bear the sight of it, the very thought of it. Not like this. Not with her core, her very self, filled with him, bared wide open for him...

"Please, John-Ka," she choked out. "*Ég vil þig.*"

I want you. I want you, I need you, I adore you—and she could see his capitulation, could feel it, the invading pole inside her swelling even fuller, barring any escape. And his head bent, slow, reverent, his soft mouth skating against delicate skin, tongue tasting and teeth scraping, savouring, seeking—

And then he *bit* her. Swift, deft, ruthless, his sharp teeth sunk deep into Rosa's actual *neck*, and she could feel her blood warming to meet him, answering him, filling him. Drowning in his hard, hungry swallows, the sweet salve of his sliding tongue. The hoarse, steady moan from his throat, the buck of his hips up beneath her, his hard cock punching deeper, swelling wider, shuddering and straining, while his bollocks below rose, bulged, caught, tilting on the edge—

His blast inside her was vicious, merciless, glorious. Spraying out spurt after spurt of hot, thick, deadly orc-seed, flooding Rosa's belly with him, pouring her full. While his throat kept swallowing, filling him with her in turn, and it was right and it was good—and as Rosa's own release shot and screamed into pulsing fire, she *understood*. The entire world thrust into utter clarity, perfect relief. John was hers, she was his, matched, worthy, wise, *whole.*

John trembled as he slowly drew his head back, his eyes dazed and blinking, his mouth stained with red. *Rosa's* red, but there wasn't even shock at that, not anymore. His seed, for her blood. The trade women made with these orcs, perhaps entirely inequitable on its face, but not feeling that way, not in this moment. Not with him.

"Are you all right, my lord?" Rosa whispered. "John-Ka?"

He blinked again, his big body jerking beneath her—and it was almost like his awareness had jerked back too, the presence snapping across his eyes. His hand lifting to his mouth, wiping at the blood—and then his eyes blinking at his hand, seized, arrested.

"*Helvíti,*" he breathed, still staring, almost as if compelled—and then dropping his wide eyes to Rosa's wounded neck, and then further down. Down to the sight of *that,* Rosa's groin spread wide and flush against his, still trapped, split open, with him buried all the way inside.

"Ach," he said, shaking his head, squeezing his eyes shut, hiding himself away. Sinking into his own shame, of being an *orc.* And he couldn't, not now, not like this. Not again. Not after that.

"You know, I should like to understand," Rosa's voice said, almost steady but not quite, "whether this biting you orcs seem to instinctively pursue could also provide some kind of immunological benefit in the woman's subsequent childbirth. It could be a fascinating hypothesis, don't you think?"

John was blinking at her again, sufficiently caught off guard for the moment at least, so Rosa kept talking, letting the words unspool as they wished. "I imagine we probably even exchanged a similar quantity of body fluids, wouldn't you say? I mean, I don't even feel *slightly* dizzy, so you couldn't have drunk too much, right? And also"—she jabbed at his still-clothed chest, while more understanding swarmed—"were you ever going to tell me that this was something you wanted to do? I thought you were supposed to be embracing your true orc nature, John-Ka. It was part of the *deal*."

Her voice had risen with unmistakable triumph, her mouth twitching into an inexplicable smile, and John only gazed at her, still blinking, still with her *blood* on his lips. And the sight was so thoroughly, powerfully breathtaking, so impossibly enthralling, that Rosa had to look away, gulp for breath.

"And here I thought," she continued, "I'd heard all of it, with your secret pleasure-den, and all that business with the chains, and punishments, and public copulation, and such. You are such a scheming *reprobate*, John-Ka."

And he *was*, the calculating bastard, so why was Rosa still smiling at him, drinking up the still-dazed languor in his still-blinking eyes. "What else do you want with me, John," she demanded. "Tell me."

He didn't immediately answer, but his hooded gaze had dropped, brief, to where their bodies were still joined together. To the still-impossible reality of that, his orc-prick jutted all the way inside her, and the warmth swarmed again as Rosa realized what he meant. He *had* wanted this. He'd wanted this, and, maybe, all else that came with it...

"I want all you should wish to give me, pet," he said finally, slow, his voice all smooth liquid heat. "But I yet do not wish to truly frighten you, or bring you shame, or grief. And"—his eyes shifted—"I do not wish to further entangle you in a war against your own *kind*."

Oh. *Wait.* The comprehension flared, vivid and forceful, as Rosa blinked at him, absorbing the weight of those words. Had all his secrecy on this just been, perhaps, another ill-guided attempt to protect her? To keep his pet *safe*?

All at once the entire world felt bright, alive, and it was suddenly easy, so easy, for Rosa to roll her eyes at him, and give a haughty toss of her head. "I *like* being frightened in the bedroom, and you know it," she replied primly. "And I think *I* should get to decide how entangled I wish to be in any armed conflicts, thank you very much. As for the shame and grief"—her voice lowered—"we've been dealing with the shame point already, haven't we? And so far, most of my grief about you stems from all these secrets you keep from me. Secret bonds, secret pleasure-dens, secret *bloodthirstiness*. Secret *armies*."

John just kept looking at her with those gorgeous blinking eyes, and Rosa drew up breath, truth. "Why do you hide all these things, John?" she whispered. "I've been a loyal and obedient pet to you, haven't I? Why can't you tell me?"

Because he didn't trust her, was still the answer, taunting deep inside, but Rosa thrust it firmly, fiercely away. "Give me a chance," she continued, holding her gaze to his. "Let me show you how I can be an even better pet to you. How I can please you, and *help* you. I mean, haven't I just made the orcling-birthing discovery of the *century*, while slaving away free of charge, locked inside your library?"

John's gaze didn't falter, though his throat visibly convulsed. "Mayhap," he said, and that was an allowance, a true concession, wasn't it? "But I thought it pleased you, to work in my library, and learn Aelakesh."

"It does," Rosa said fervently, putting both hands flat to his chest, feeling the powerful thuds of his heartbeat beneath it. "I *love* it, John. I just want—*more*."

It was true, damnably so, spilling out so fervent and easy from Rosa's lips. She was sitting impaled on a lying, devious orc, who'd just *bitten* her—and she *did* still want more, so much more. Not secrets and atrocities, but just—knowledge. Truth. To be part of not only John's library, and his bed—but his *life*.

"I *know* you, John," she whispered, as her hands fluttered back to his face, stroking against the familiar lines of it. So severe and forbidding at first glance, but hiding surprising warmth, unfathomable depth. "I can help you. I can please you. If you'll let me, I can be the pet you've always *dreamed* of."

To prove her point, she wriggled upon him again, squeezing at that slightly softened heft inside her—and when it shuddered, thickened, she couldn't help a harsh moan, a full-body shiver. Gods, it felt good, he felt good, and his eyes were watching her with almost painful intent. He was considering it. He was...

"What do you say, my lord," she whispered. "Please? Teach me? Everything?"

She'd rocked on him again as she spoke, feeling the answering flare deep inside—but even stronger was his eyes, his truth, his soul.

"*Ríddu mér*," he said, a curse, a command, a vow. "I shall try."

26

True to his word, John promptly began Rosa's expanded education that very evening. Not, as she might have expected, with meetings and war councils—but rather with an impromptu visit to the Ka-esh *pleasure-den*.

"Should you truly wish to know all the hidden longings of orcs," John said as he led her toward it, "this is where you shall best learn, pet."

The room was indeed just as shocking as it had been last time, full of orcs taking their pleasures together in the most astonishing of ways. But John seemed entirely unconcerned— about both the alarming goings-on, and the number of wary glances they were getting—and led Rosa over to sit on an empty bench against the opposite wall.

"Now, pet," he murmured, as he tugged her close onto his lap. "We shall watch together, and I shall answer your questions. And if you are vexed, you shall speak."

There was no arguing that, especially once his low, heated voice indeed began answering Rosa's questions with easy, unashamed steadiness. *Ach, yes, Marcus wishes for this. No, cane-*

strokes such as this, for an orc, shall wholly heal within a day. Ach, Brandr is mated to Benjamin, this is why no other touches him.

"Have you actually—*done* all these things, John?" Rosa finally asked, breathless, perhaps almost afraid of the answer. "And would you, um, want to do all of them? With—me?"

Her heart was suddenly, wildly beating, her gaze fastened to where several orcs were brutally taking their pleasure with a single moaning, kneeling orc. John's eyes had followed hers, narrowing at the sight, and then he tugged her closer against him, his hands spreading wide against her belly.

"I have done much of this, ach," he replied, with remarkable coolness. "But it has never pleased me to be at another's mercy. And it should never please me to share my pet with another, or cause true or lasting harm. You are too small and precious for this."

The words wriggled and fizzled deep inside—*precious*, he'd said—and combined with the all-too-fascinating sights before them, Rosa had begun to feel dry-mouthed and shuddery all over. And when John slipped his warm hand under her short tunic, and carefully eased his clawed finger up into her swollen heat—which was still dripping wet, thanks to their own thrilling activities earlier in the library—Rosa felt only pleasure, hunger, *more.*

"Does that please you, pet?" John murmured, as he nodded toward the orcs Rosa was blatantly staring at—a bound, kneeling Ka-esh named Abjorn, who currently had another orc kneeling close behind him, thrusting into his bared backside while several other orcs watched. "Should you wish to do this with me?"

Rosa gasped and squirmed in response, earning a light pinch of disapproval from John's free hand—no squirming with his finger like this, it meant—and she drew in air, deep. "I—maybe?" she whispered, tentative, exposed, deplorably truthful. "Maybe just—with someone watching, to start?"

She was too aroused to be ashamed, her thoughts lingering on all the thrilling possible visions of it, and John's finger sank a little deeper, his voice a heated purr in her ear. "*Gott*," he murmured. "We shall."

That promise whirled and sang all night, even as Rosa again rode John in his bed, his cock buried deep, where it mattered, where it belonged. Even as she somehow fell asleep pinioned on his hot, sweaty form, his claws gently scraping her back—and then awoke again, hours later, with him *still there*. With him actually *sleeping*, his chest rhythmically rising and falling beneath her.

It was surely morning, so Rosa carefully reached to light the candle—and then studied him with a tilting, rising affection. Drinking in his faintly fluttering lashes, the slight twitches of his limbs, the surprising softness of his features in sleep. Gods, he was a beautiful orc, all sharp angles and smooth skin, and he felt beautiful, too. Still hidden soft and safe inside her, until—Rosa gasped—his eyes abruptly snapped open. Blinking up toward her first with visible confusion, and then with increasing, undeniable hunger.

"*Ríddu mér*," he ordered, without so much as a good morning, but Rosa couldn't even protest, not with that hardness swelling within her like that, filling her with his life, his warmth. So she again rode him, rocking atop his hips while he gouged and circled deep inside. Keeping his arms folded behind his head the entire time, the prick, even as his mouth curved up, and his hooded eyes swept up and down her body with lazy, insolent appreciation.

It wasn't until they'd again found their pleasure together, his hips arching up as he poured himself out inside her, that Rosa heard a sound from the bed opposite. And when her head jerked toward it, she realized, with true shock, that Tristan was still there, lying on his side, facing toward them, wide awake. And he wasn't alone, Salvi was curled close behind him, and both of them were blatantly staring across at John and Rosa. And—Rosa swallowed—Salvi's hand was buried in Tristan's trousers, sliding up and down with fluent, familiar purpose.

A clawed pinch at Rosa's nipple snapped her attention back to John, who was watching her with raised, skeptical brows. Silently saying, clearly, *isn't this what you wanted? What I promised you?*

And Rosa couldn't muck this up already, no matter how much of a devious reprobate he was—so she stuck out her tongue at him, and then gave another hard, pointed rock against his hips. As if to say, *what are you waiting for, then?*

The heat inside her—which had again considerably softened—flared with delicious, immediate, deadly force. And in a sudden, stunning jolt, John's strong hands yanked her down, close against his bare chest—and then flipped her bodily over, easy and powerful. So that she was on her back, blinking up at him, while he leaned on his forearms over her, boxing her in, covering her with warmth and hunger and *safety.*

"*Horfðu á mig,*" he breathed. *Look at me.* But there was no looking away, it was an utter impossibility, and Rosa's reverent hands slid up around his back, caressing him, adoring him, as he slowly, deliberately, fucked her into his bed. Every stroke a smooth, thrilling, impossibly powerful jolt of sensation, of sparking heat, of sheer, crackling ecstasy.

He finished with a howl, his upper body rearing up as his hips ground against her, his cock again firing out inside. Flooding her full of him, *again*, and Rosa could feel the liquid swelling, stretching her, until there was pain, and she was about to burst—

The awareness flashed across John's eyes, and he wrenched himself out of her, away. So swift Rosa cried out, clinging back toward him—but it was too late, he was gone, and in his place there was—a *flood*. Surging out from between her legs with astonishing force, spurting onto him, spraying all over his bed, and—her fluttering hands snapped down to the furs, too late, too late—even pooling off the bed, and onto the *floor*.

"*Damn* it," she breathed, casting a mortified glance across the room, to where Tristan and Salvi were most definitely still watching—but here was John's hand, gripping at her face, and twisting it back toward him.

"You wish to learn, pet," he breathed, so soft she scarcely heard him. "And you wish me to be an orc. Thus, I shall take pride in my helpless little pet's messing upon my bed. And should you show *aught* more shame of this"—his eyes flicked toward Tristan and Salvi—"I shall make you lick it clean again, naked, whilst we all watch you."

Fucking hell. Rosa's swallow could surely be heard throughout the room, but she nodded, her face burning, ignoring Salvi's low laugh from the bed opposite. And John, John was thoroughly enjoying this, and his smile was truly breathtaking, showing his sharp teeth, crinkling his eyes at the corners.

"Now you shall stand, pet," he purred. "And show me how you look, after you have been fucked five times in a night. And mayhap"—those eyes sparked with wickedness—"you shall thank me, also."

Gods curse the reprobate, but Rosa was doing this, he was testing her, he'd taken her like that *five times*, when until now he'd repeatedly refused to do so—so she nodded, and obeyed. Shoving herself off the side of the bed, standing on shaky legs, naked, holding her eyes to John's. While valiantly fighting to ignore the worsening mess, streaming down her thighs, as three orcs watched. And as John's finger made a little twirling gesture that clearly meant, turn around.

Rosa did, despite the still-surging heat in her cheeks, and she even managed a smile at John once their gazes locked again. "Thank you, my lord," she breathed, her voice wavering.

"For taking me like this, five whole times. And"—she drew in breath—"staying with me, as you did, this night."

The approval flared in those eyes, bright and breathtaking, and finally John took pity on her, rising from the bed too, and reaching down for one of the rags he kept on hand. "Good pet," he murmured, as he began wiping her clean. "This pleased me."

The warmth bubbled higher as he dressed her, and brushed out her hair with his claws, and neatly braided it again. As he led her out of the room, waving a casual farewell to Tristan and Salvi, who were still together in the bed, though Salvi's face was now buried in Tristan's shoulder, and Tristan's eyes gazed unseeing up at the ceiling.

"You know, my lord," Rosa said, giving his arm a companionable bump with hers, once they were a good distance down the corridor. "You also neglected to tell me the truth about Tristan and Salvi. That they were actually *mated*, before. Until Salvi betrayed Tristan, for a *woman*."

John glanced vaguely down toward her, his brows furrowing. "Ach, I did tell you there were unfinished matters between them, did I not?" he said. "This woman wished for Salvi, and few orcs would scorn this chance for a son. Sons are the future of our kind. They are"—his eyes angled away, to the corridor—"what many of us most long for, from this life."

Right. Rosa couldn't seem to find an answer to that, at the moment, or even a question. Perhaps because—her gaze slid to his sharp profile, and held there—there'd been a new kind of honesty in it. A frankness she hadn't heard before. The same kind of openness, perhaps, that he'd shown her in his pleasure-den, and even in the way he'd taken her, and made her show it off to him afterwards. *Five times.*

Almost as though John truly *had* decided to trust her. Almost as though he'd decided to make her fully his pet.

And in doing so, he'd also decided to make her *more*.

The certainty of that stuttered, slightly, as Rosa realized John had led her into the library—he wasn't going to just leave her again?—but no, no, he only strode to the table, plucked up her new book, and thrust it into her hands before drawing her back to the door.

"I meet with the captain and his mate each morning," he said, without Rosa even asking. "Today, I wish you to speak to them of this *discovery* that you have made."

There was no refusing, of course, especially once John had led Rosa up through the Ash-Kai wing, pointing out various rooms of interest along the way. And soon she found herself ushered into a cozy, firelit meeting-room, which—Rosa twitched—contained not only Jule and Grimarr, but also Baldr and Drafli, two orcs Rosa didn't recognize, and *Simon*.

They were all sitting around a low table, and John made a rapid round of introductions—the scarred but warm-eyed orc beside Baldr was named Nattfarr, of Clan Grisk, and the hulking, hideous orc beside Simon was called Olarr, of Clan Bautul. They greeted Rosa with surprising politeness—Nattfarr even flashed her a quick, genuine smile—but Rosa also didn't miss the exchanged glances around the room, the clear hints of uncertainty, or perhaps even wariness, at her unexpected presence.

"My woman has made a *discovery*, in my library," John announced to them, once he and Rosa were seated at the table. "I wish her to speak of this to you."

Rosa froze—John wanted her to do *what*?—but the bland look in his eyes clearly said, again, *This is what you wanted, isn't it? You wanted to be part of my life. Show me what a good pet you can be.*

And the challenge in that, the command in it, somehow made it easier. Made it possible for Rosa to open the book, and begin speaking, with a voice that only slightly wavered. Making an actual, if ad hoc, scholarly *presentation* to a room full of huge, intimidating, terrifying orcs.

But they listened. And asked questions. And then, to Rosa's ongoing astonishment, they even launched into a lively, surprisingly intelligent *discussion*. Debating first the author's credibility—Olarr's father's father had lived in Osada, apparently, and had spoken of an orcling specialist there—and then whether any of the findings had since been replicated, to anyone's knowledge. And then which findings were worth seeking to replicate, and which actions, if any, should be next pursued.

John actively participated in the conversation, making points with impressive rapidity and eloquence, and showing himself entirely unafraid to call out his fellow orcs—or even to throw around the potentially incendiary point of Jule's current pregnancy. He also included Rosa in his arguments, giving her openings, almost as if testing her—and after her initial shock, Rosa took the bait with gusto. Expanding upon his points with as much coherency as she could muster, often calling on particular passages in the book for added reinforcement.

By the end of it, not only was Rosa thoroughly enjoying herself, but John had managed to gain Grimarr's permission to further research several of the book's key assertions, while also commandeering new resources—more rooms, certain orcs from other clans, more time from Efterar, and something called trading-credits. To Rosa's astonishment, John even pitched her idea of teaching classes on common-tongue to improve orc-women relationships, which seemed to come as a genuine surprise to everyone at the table.

"You Ka-esh would truly offer this?" Grimarr asked John, the suspicion all too clear in his assessing eyes. "To *all* clans? Not only Ka-esh?"

His gaze had flicked, with purpose, to Simon, who together with Drafli had remained the quietest orc in the room, and whose eyes were now narrow and suspicious on John's face. "Ka-esh no wish to teach Skai," Simon said, with a distinct air of finality. "Ka-esh wish Skai to stay stupid and alone, and *die*."

Rosa didn't miss John's sudden stiffening beside her, his lip curling. "We wish for no such thing," he snapped, his voice chilly. "If you Skai truly wish to learn, we should be pleased to teach you. Has not Tristan well served you thus, these past days?"

Of course no one could argue against Tristan, not even Simon—and soon John had been tasked with creating an additional proposal on the subject to present the following week. An order that he accepted with just as much nonchalance as the rest, though Rosa didn't miss the telltale glint of satisfaction in his eyes.

"That went well, didn't it?" she asked him, once they'd said their farewells, and were again walking through the corridor. "You're pleased, right?"

John's sidelong look at her was indeed pleased, and perhaps even proud. "Ach," he replied. "This is more than I have gained for my work in many months. It helped, I ken, to have a woman's own voice in this."

Rosa fought to ignore the surge of answering warmth, and tilted her head, eyeing him in the lamplight. "But surely Jule has supported your work, until now? She's a clever woman. And also *pregnant*. With an orc's *child*."

But John shrugged, steering Rosa around the corner with a brush of his hand. "The captain keeps her safe here, where Efterar can care for her each day," he said. "And thus, she does not fear for her life, as most women do in her state. And she is most loyal to the captain, whose most pressing matters are the men, and peace between the clans. And"—John shrugged again—"she is not a scholar, as you are."

As you are. He really meant that, Rosa realized, blinking up at his impassive face. He'd said that, he didn't look concerned or even uncomfortable, in fact he barely seemed to notice he'd said it at all…

"You really," Rosa said, breathless, "think I'm a *scholar*?"

"Ach, are you not?" John said, absently guiding her around another corner. "You have studied five languages, you have read legions of books, you are quick and curious. You find the hidden heft within what you see and read, and then speak it with clearness and ease. Even one of the most powerful humans in the *realm* stole you for his own, so he may gain from your insights."

No one had ever said anything so lovely to Rosa in quite possibly her entire *life*—and without thinking, she launched herself bodily toward John, clutching her arms around his waist, burying her face in his warm chest. "Thank you, my lord," she breathed. "*Thank* you."

He'd momentarily stiffened, clearly startled—but then she felt him relaxing again, one hand stroking at her back, the other coming to tilt up her face toward him. To where he was looking bemused, but maybe even affectionate, too.

"Foolish pet," he said. "You shall not be so thankful, mayhap, when I command you to plan this fool Skai-teaching scheme you have now bound me to. And then you shall propose your plan in a week, just as the captain has asked, in my stead."

Rosa jabbed at his side with her elbow, but she couldn't seem to stop grinning at him, or even standing on tiptoes to press a quick, furtive kiss to his neck. He wanted her to write a *proposal*. He wanted her to *present it*. As not his work, but her *own*.

"And," John continued, lower, though his head had tilted away, almost as if to better expose his neck to her mouth, "you ken these lessons shall need teachers, woman. More than only Tristan."

His voice seemed casual this time, but surely, *surely*

wasn't—and Rosa felt her body lock against his, her heart madly, wildly beating. What was he saying. What, good gods, was he *saying*.

But a fleeting, wide-eyed glance at John's carefully blank face said everything for him. He was saying the same thing he'd said last night in the library. And when he'd taken her like that, five times. When he'd slept the whole night through with her in his bed, and showed her his pleasure-den, and asked her to present her findings to a room full of orcs.

And the same thing Rosa had said, perhaps, when she'd *agreed* to all that. When she'd finally discovered all this devious orc's secrets, all the hidden depths of his depravity, and still said, *Thank you, my lord.*

His eyes were so wary, so gods-damned distant. So—*afraid.* And Rosa should have been afraid too. Of the war, the future, her library, Lord Kaspar, that deadline that had somehow dwindled to eight short days...

But instead, she was—nodding. Bobbing her head, holding those eyes, and saying—*yes.* Yes, to a question he'd scarcely even asked, but suddenly she knew he *had* been asking. With every single action today. Every answered question. Every touch, every look from his eyes.

I shall try, he'd said last night, and he'd meant it. No falsehoods.

"Yes, my lord," Rosa whispered, and it was as strong as a bond, a vow, a word written in ink on a fresh new page. "I will."

27

The next day passed in a whirl of delightful activity, taking Rosa and John all over Orc Mountain.

Their first stop was to meet with Salvi and Eben in the Ka-esh medical clinic, talking over the terms of their new research project. Next was a meeting with an exacting Grisk orc named Ymir, who was apparently in charge of the mountain's trading-credits. And then was a consultation with Hanarr about needed supplies, while Rosa ate the overflowing basket of food Hanarr had procured for her.

"Next, pet, we shall meet with Efterar," John said, with relish, once they'd left Hanarr's storage-room. "He shall not be pleased, I ken."

Efterar was indeed not pleased to learn that he'd apparently been commandeered for John's research. "The captain's offered my *support* to your latest mad scheme?" he snapped, fixing John with an almighty glare. "Because of some old *book* you found mouldering in your *library*?"

John's expression had begun to straddle something between incredulity and sheer malice, but before he could bark back an equally acerbic reply, Rosa thrust herself between them, and launched into what she hoped was a convincing argument in favour of the plan. Calling up several of the book's points Efterar had previously seemed to agree with, including the bit about fresh orc-seed making for a stronger son, and adding extra nutrition, as well.

"And perhaps," Rosa continued firmly, "you could allow Salvi and Eben to work with you on this, just in the short term? That way, you can delegate as you need to them, and they can report to John on your behalf?"

Efterar's irritable expression had shifted—not to agreement, but instead to something more considering, as his gaze flicked up and down Rosa's form. "Impressive," he said, to Rosa's confusion, as he reached his big hand to tilt her chin up, frowning down into her eyes. "How long have you been here again? A week?"

"Fourteen days," Rosa answered automatically, with a slight wince. "Why?"

Efterar was still frowning, his eyes dropping to her breasts, and then her belly. "Your gains are considerable," he said, almost more to himself than to her. "You've added more weight than I could have expected in such a short time, your muscle mass is increased, and your eyes and skin have cleared almost entirely. Well, except for the bite and scratches, but"—his eyes fixed to Rosa's neck, before glancing down to linger on her groin through her tunic—"it looks like your mate's been careful elsewhere, and nothing's infected, so good enough. Do you feel more mentally alert, too?"

It was taking Rosa a moment to digest all this—John still wasn't her *mate*, surely—but perhaps she *had* felt more mentally alert of late? And when she shot an uncertain glance downwards at her own wrists, there was the surprising realization that perhaps they *didn't* look quite as thin as they had previously?

"Ach, she is much improved," John said finally, into the

silence, when Rosa still couldn't seem to speak. "We have followed all your counsel with care, brother. She drinks fresh seed and milk each day, and eats all I bring her. She also sleeps well at nights, oft sees the sun, and stays busy with her work. It was she who found this book, and then wrote it into common-tongue, so we all may gain from this."

The look on Efterar's face echoed just how Rosa felt—had John truly paid *that* much attention to implementing Efterar's advice? But the stubborn set of John's jaw suggested that, despite all his apparent animosity toward Efterar and his unsci-entific magic, he had.

"Oh," Efterar said finally, still with visible bewilderment. "Well. All right, then, I suppose. Send Salvi and Eben, if you must."

Now it was John's turn to look surprised, his eyes briefly widening before he nodded, curt, and looked intently away. "Good," he said. "This shall help, brother. I—value your work, and your guidance."

With that, John turned and stalked out, leaving Rosa to give Efterar an apologetic smile, and then chase to catch up. And rather than teasing John about the extremely difficult conces-sion that clearly had been, she bumped him with her shoulder, and shot him a quick, jaunty grin. "How long will it take, do you think," she said lightly, "before he and Salvi murder each other?"

She could see the relaxation in John's form, could almost preen at the flare of bare, genuine gratefulness in his eyes. "Three days at most, I ken," he said, as he drew her close, and pressed a soft, spine-tingling kiss to the top of her head. "Now come, pet. There is much more to address today."

Rosa complied, of course, her body still warm all over as John took her to the forge, reviewing the day's priorities with his orcs, and then the laboratory. And then, to another meet-ing, this one again with Grimarr, Nattfarr, Baldr, Drafli, and

Olarr, and a few others. Though this time, the orcs spoke mostly in Aelakesh, and the main point of discussion seemed to be the men currently camped at the mountain. The *war*.

Rosa listened as carefully as she could, picking up bits and pieces here and there, and fighting to ignore the thrilling distraction of John's claws absently caressing at the nape of her neck. The men had apparently camped on the mountain's south side, they had enough supplies to last them at least ten more days, they had still shown no sign of actually attacking. Yet.

Something had begun gnawing in Rosa's chest as she listened, her eyes casting searching glances toward John beside her. He was again actively involved in the discussion, his Aelakesh clipped and self-assured, his opinions clearly respected by all at the table. And by meeting's end, he again seemed satisfied with its conclusions, a grim smile playing on his mouth.

"Do not fret over these men, pet," John said, once they were back in the corridor again. "I have told you, my brothers and I shall take care of all this. We shall not be beaten by a mere two hundred men. And you shall never need to again bear this cheap cruel lord, who has so carelessly harmed you. I shall keep you safe."

Oh. Rosa's belly lurched at that, her breaths coming shorter, shallower. John would keep her safe. She would never need to bear Lord Kaspar again. And as deeply, powerfully compelling as that thought suddenly was, Rosa still only had seven days left. Seven days before Lord Kaspar expected her back at the library, armed with explosive revelations.

And what if she didn't return at all? What then? Because that *was* what John was saying, wasn't it?

It was, she realized, with another lurch deep in her belly. Again. He truly wanted her to—*stay*.

"You are safe here, pet," he repeated, his eyes angling toward Rosa's face. "Come. I ken what may calm you."

Rosa gratefully nodded, and accompanied him into another room—the Ka-esh medical clinic. Where Salvi and Eben were currently working, as well as Aaron and Brandr and Marcus. All of them hesitating at the sight of Rosa and John, particularly as John ushered Rosa across the room, and lifted her up onto the examination table.

"My medics have been seeking my leave to study you for many days now," he said to Rosa, entirely ignoring the watching orcs around them. "Most orcs mated to women balk at this, so it is rare that we have a woman to survey. I have not wished to frighten you with this, but"—his fingers tilted Rosa's chin up, locking her eyes to his—"I ken you shall now accept this for me, ach?"

Rosa's throat swallowed—he was offering her up for his medics' *study*?—and she couldn't help a quick, uneasy glance around at the five watching orcs. All of whom had been nothing but kind and respectful to her these past days, but—

"Will they need to—touch me?" she asked John, her voice not quite even. "Or, um, *do* things, to me?"

The uncertainty had begun flaring, her body curling in on itself—until John gave her chin a gentle but purposeful shake, dragging her eyes back to his. "They shall not touch you," he said firmly. "Only I shall do this, whilst they watch and learn. And if you wish to stop the lesson, you shall only speak this. Ach?"

There was a low, whispering burn in Rosa's belly—John was going to *use* her to teach his medics a *lesson*—and somehow, the unease blinked entirely away, replaced by something that almost felt like eagerness. She would help John, in this. She would be a good pet for her lord. She was safe, cared for, *worthy*.

It was a strange certainty, perhaps, especially once she'd

given a sharp little nod, and John promptly drew her tunic off over her head. Leaving her sitting there completely naked on a table, and feeling the full, weighted attention of the rest of the room's orcs, all of whom had left their work behind, and come to stand around the table.

"On your back," John said, soft, an order—and Rosa swallowed hard as she obeyed, lying her bare body back onto the smooth stone. Looking at his face, rather than the other orcs, though she could feel their eyes, close, prickling, unnervingly present.

"We have all studied our own kind at length," John said to her, stroking a gentle hand up her arm, leaving a trail of goosebumps behind. "So I shall show them the parts of you that differ from our own. Ach?"

Rosa nodded, fought to keep her breaths steady, to ignore the way her nipples had hardened in the room's cool air. But John had noticed, surely, giving them a brief, telling glance that seemed almost satisfied.

"Good pet," he murmured. "Now, open your mouth."

It took Rosa several seconds to obey, her eyes darting wildly at the watching orcs—until a gentle pinch to her side drew her gaze back to John again. He was waiting, patient, almost amused at her discomfiture—so Rosa finally opened her mouth, her heart thumping, and waited.

"You see her teeth," John's casual voice said, as though this—his pet naked on a table, with her mouth open, while a room full of orcs peered inside—was a perfectly normal, everyday activity. "They are small and blunt, with weak little fangs. They are not meant for tearing or killing, as ours are."

One of the orcs—perhaps Marcus—asked a question, something about pressure, and in reply John ordered Rosa to bite down on his finger, as hard as she could. A command that, again, felt surprisingly difficult to obey, but Rosa finally clamped down on it, with as much force as she could muster.

Earning not even the slightest glance of pain across John's eyes, but only a warm, approving amusement.

"See?" he said to Marcus, showing him the faint red indentation she'd made on his finger. "It is naught to speak of."

The other orcs seemed intrigued by this, and launched into a fascinating conversation about how jaw size might impact total bite pressure. After which John's fingers moved to Rosa's ears, stroking over her rounded tips, while the orcs discussed the accepted hypothesis that the altered shape provided a different hearing spectrum.

Next John showed the orcs where he'd bitten Rosa's neck, explaining how she had begun to heal, but far slower than an orc would have. Leading into an involved discussion about wound care, which went on long enough that Rosa had almost relaxed again—at least, until John's warm hand slipped downwards, and gently curved over her bare *breast*.

Her whole body stiffened, and John surely saw it, his brow furrowing, his eyes catching on hers. But yes, yes, she could do this, she *wanted* to do this—and at her fervent nod, his other hand obligingly dropped down to mirror the first, covering both her breasts in the heat of his large palms.

"Her teats are small," he said, "but well-formed. It pleases her to have them cupped and stroked, and their points pinched and teased."

Oh hell, he had *not* just said that—but now he was *demonstrating*, softly pinching at Rosa's already-peaked nipples, rolling them between his fingers. "One must yet be gentle," he continued calmly. "I should not bite these, or use claws, as I might with another orc."

Rosa's chest was suddenly heaving, her eyes narrowing, and John's gaze back was deceptively bland, his mouth quirking up. "And she is just as jealous as any mated orc, also," he said, with damnable coolness. "Though she does not like to admit this, ach, my pet?"

The bastard. Rosa made a face at him, even as her breaths came deeper—had he just compared her to a *mated* orc?—and almost didn't hear the next shocking question from the watching orcs, this time about whether her tiny teats would still be enough to *nurse an orcling*.

"Ach, I ken," came John's equally shocking reply, as he gave her nipple another gentle pinch. "They have already swelled larger than they were. I shall seek to fatten her further, also, before this comes."

Before this comes. And again, good gods, he was saying this. Saying it, with the quick, furtive glance of his eyes to hers, with that soft, quiet touch on her too-sensitive skin. "Do not fear, little pet," he murmured. "Orclings do not bite whilst they nurse, as you might have read."

Rosa was truly gaping at him now—yes, he was saying it, he might as well have been shouting it to the room. And the devious bastard damned well knew it, his eyes dropping like that, *hiding*, as his hand smoothed down Rosa's front with alarming, distracting purpose.

"Spread your legs, pet," he said, more curtly than before. "Next I shall show them your womb."

Rosa's numb body obeyed without thinking this time, her thighs willingly parting, her gaze still caught on his betraying, blinking eyes—at least, until those gentle hands purposefully, intently brought her feet up to the table, drawing her knees wide. Showing the entirety of Rosa's open crease to the room, to five more sets of orc eyes—

But John's glinting gaze had angled back to hers, again saying all the things he wasn't actually saying. *Please me. Let me flaunt you to them. Let me show them how well I care for you. How you seek to obey me.*

So Rosa nodded, even as her cheeks furiously burned, as John's hand slipped downwards. As those warm, familiar fingers glided along her crease, and then spread her swollen lips, showing all that was hidden between.

"There is much here to see, and learn," John said, his cool voice bearing perhaps just a shade of huskiness. "Here"—his claw touched, very gently, making Rosa gasp and shiver—"is where her pleasure pools from. It likes to be rubbed, both from outside, and within."

And then, curse him, he again *demonstrated*, sliding the pad of his finger up and down against it—and Rosa couldn't help another frenzied squirm, a choked, helpless moan. But John liked it, John *approved*, flashing her a brief, true smile before again dropping his eyes...

"And here," he continued, as his finger brushed lower, "is the way to her womb. It must be teased open, thus."

He was stroking it with gentle, purposeful intent, indeed guiding her further open, further apart. And in return Rosa's body was flaring back at him, clenching, greedy, exposed. Showing her swollen, shameful hunger to a room full of watching, judging orcs, and then—her whole body froze—spluttering out more of that familiar thick wetness, all over John's still-caressing fingers, all over the table beneath...

Rosa's eyes squeezed shut, her hands snapping up to her hot, mortified face, while John, the bastard, just kept doing it. Kept stroking, coaxing out more, his hand now wet and slick with his own damned seed, while five other orcs watched in utter, astonished silence.

"She oft soils herself, with my spent seed," John's voice said, as his wet, clawed finger carefully, gently began to slip up inside. "She is shamed by this, but it pleases me to witness her little messes, and clean her with my tongue."

Oh. Oh, fuck. The room felt charged, suddenly, sparking with the heat of Rosa's rapidly rising hunger—but she held herself still, so still, such a good pet, as that finger slipped deeper, smooth, approving. He liked it. It pleased him to witness this...

She scarcely heard one of the orcs ask, a little stilted, whether she wasn't afraid to be breached by a claw like that—but John's low answer only ramped up more hunger, more craving. "She knows I shall do this with the greatest care," he said. "It has taken time, but I have gained her trust. And in return, she has bent fully to my will, and has learnt to welcome my taking, however I might wish to use her."

Rosa's breathless moan escaped on its own, catching a dark, heated look from John's watching, half-lidded eyes. Good gods, he wanted this too, he was doing this on *purpose*, he was bragging about her, flaunting her, showing her off to a room of staring hungry orcs—

"Surely she cannot handle *all* your use," said one of the orcs, from somewhere very far away. "Her little openings all seem far too small for this. Even the captain's mate can scarcely sheath him, and she is a far larger woman."

It sounded like a challenge, Rosa's flailing thoughts shouted, and surely, *surely* John wouldn't—but gods curse her, curse *him*, because he was looking at her, his eyebrows raised, and his tongue had slid out, slow, brushing against parted lips...

"I shall prove this, should you all wish to see," he said, his voice silken, deadly. "If she agrees."

But Rosa was already nodding, furtive but urgent, because yes, she wanted this, needed this, she was a good pet, she needed him to flaunt her, use her, any way he wished...

Clearly the orcs hadn't objected, surely there was no possible objection. And John silently lifted Rosa bodily up, turned her over, and after pulling out a fur from somewhere, placed her onto her trembling hands and knees on the suddenly soft table. And then strode around to stand before her face, his tented groin almost in line with her stunned blinking eyes—

And then he tugged down his trousers, and drew out that scarred, veined, dripping hardness. Exposing himself not only to her, but to a room full of silent, intently watching orcs.

"*Sjúga mig*," he ordered her, husky. "*Djúpt.*"

Suck me, it meant. *Deep.*

And before Rosa could follow, nod, speak—*yes, yes, of course, my lord*—that slick, dripping head was spreading her lips open around it, sinking smooth and steady inside. Deeper and deeper, without stopping, sweetness swarming her tongue and her breath, opening her up—until he was buried all the way, her mouth flush to the thick vibrating base of him, his sleek head rammed deep into her throat.

"*Gott*," he breathed, or perhaps choked. "*Horfðu á mig.*"

Look at him. Rosa was looking, blinking wide-eyed up at his face, drinking in the dark, dangerous pleasure in those watching, approving eyes. And as she desperately swallowed, he slowly, purposefully drew out again, all the way. Until she was just suckling at the very tip of him, soft, sweet—and then he thrust back inside, harder, opening up her mouth and her throat with fluid, uncompromising ease.

"You see?" he said to the watching orcs, his voice damnably even. "I am sunk to my bollocks. My seed drips straight into her belly."

Rosa's answering moans were helpless, strangled, caught on a huge prodding orc-prick, and thank the gods he drew out again, let her breathe again. And another orc had asked a question, one Rosa hadn't heard through the rushing in her ears, but it prompted John to slide in again, slow, devastating, merciless, until her mouth was again flush to his groin, her throat frantically convulsing around his thick, implacable invasion.

"It feels better than aught else I have ever known," John said, quiet, and Rosa's screaming brain registered that it was in answer to a question, whatever the orc had asked. "It is true joy, to wield such command over a tight little human throat, and to feel it choke and spasm upon you."

Gods damn the bastard, he had not just *said* that about her, to all these orcs—and somehow, lost in the whirling spiralling furious craving, Rosa—*bit* him. With her *teeth*. Something she'd never once dared to do before, with anyone, let alone an *orc*, her *lord*—and the shame and chagrin surged with ruthless force, her eyes wide and suddenly terrified on John's astonished, blinking face. Fuck, she hadn't meant to do that, but he was such a damned *reprobate*, to say such things to them and not her, what if he punished her, what if she'd displeased him, what if he changed his mind...

He drew himself out of her, slowly exposing that new red line of her teeth across his shaft, and Rosa realized, with true shock, that his other scars down there—scars that she'd never actually asked him about, maybe because she hadn't wanted to know—all looked much like this one. Like he'd been *bitten*. Repeatedly. Perhaps even in retaliation for obnoxious actions just such as this...

And he *had*, he *liked* it, his eyes even hungrier than before, his hand circling close and threatening and delicious around Rosa's exposed neck. "Foolish pet," he purred, husky, breathless. "When you dare to bite your lord, little rose, you *know* you shall be punished."

Rosa's nod was instinctive, compulsive, *madness*. "Yes, my lord," she whispered. "Thank you, my lord."

He groaned aloud at that, and his other hand dropped down to brush against her new mark on his shaft, stroking at it, his fingers reverent, almost disbelieving. "Good," he said, so soft, his eyes blinking down toward it. "You must tell me if I truly alarm you. Or if you wish me to stop."

They were the same words he'd said to her that very first night, in the library—and it almost felt like they were back there again, tentative, watchful, exploring. Learning each other, testing each other, alone in the room, in the world. No falsehoods.

Rosa nodded, her eyes desperately blinking on his, and he nodded too, jerky, uncontrolled. And then walked away from her, away from her face, around to stand behind her. Yanking her bodily back to the edge of the table, thrusting her legs wide apart.

But Rosa didn't care what he saw anymore, what they saw. Only tilted her arse up, out, exposed, waiting—and when John's first slap came, swift and purposeful, it was a sharp, perfect jolt of unimaginable, indescribable pleasure. Setting her arching, howling body aflame with sudden, crackling heat—and then ratcheting higher, tighter, as that demanding hardness jutted between her parted lips, waiting, waiting...

And then he slammed inside, all the way. Strong enough that Rosa's teeth chattered, her whole body trembling, nearly falling off the table—but John had her, John held her safe, skewered and pinioned on his huge, throbbing prick, even as his hand delivered another swift, stinging, *magnificent* slap to her bare arse.

"You shall learn, pet," gasped his voice behind her, as he drew himself out, slow—and then again slammed inside, in time with another stinging slap of his hand. "You shall know what it is to displease an orc. An orc who wishes to bare you"—another slap—"and mark you, and make you his. *Forever.*"

His. Forever. And Rosa was nodding, shaking, fighting to control this, her arching back, her shivering body. Desperately needing to show him, prove to him, spread herself wider, take him deeper, welcome every smarting strike of that warm, familiar hand. Speaking so firmly, so fundamentally, of his regard, his affection—*forever*, he'd said—even as he roughly grasped her stinging arse-cheek, and yanked it further open, apart.

And that was his other hand, gripping at the other side, fully exposing the last of Rosa's hidden places to the room, to his taking. And of course he should, he had every right to use her however he wished, she was a good pet, a worthy mate, and she wanted this, all of this, so primal and powerful she was on the edge of weeping—

"Yes, my lord," she choked out, through her dragging breaths. "Forever. Please."

And John was saying it back, with one more slap of that hand, gentler this time. With the equally gentle settling of his huge, dripping-wet cockhead to that vulnerable pucker of skin. As he slowly, gently, mercilessly bore down, splitting her open upon him, cleaving her in two, filling her with sheer power and need and *love*.

The thought recoiled and rebelled, even as it kept rising, kept sinking, until it was locked, trapped, all the way. Pulsing and flexing, straining and squeezing, her lord caught with her, within her, his pet, his mate, his librarian, his *love*.

The next slap of his hand trembled, skittered, shouting just as loud as that strength buried inside her, and Rosa cried out, brutalized, broken by an orc. An orc who'd bared her, marked her, claimed her as his own. An orc who was ravishing her, commanding her, flaying her raw on the altar of his rule—

Her release flared, flashed, exploded. Consuming her with stark screaming ecstasy, with her whole self exposed and bared and *owned*—and flooded, suddenly, with burst after burst of sheer, swarming euphoria, as her lord sprayed himself out again and again. Filling her with his essence, his promise, his truth. Forever. Safe. *Home*.

Rosa drifted in that truth, lost in the sparkling, glittering, impossibly peaceful wonder of it. In the sound of her mate's heaving breaths behind her, in the aftershocks that seemed to be running through them both at once, lingering bursts of pleasure beneath their joined skin.

And then John collapsed against her, heavy and hot and sweaty, his chest pressed to her bare back. And his face was here, close beside hers, his eyes blinking hard, his lips parted, his cheeks flushed redder than Rosa had ever seen them.

"Are you well," he whispered, breathless, into her ear. "Did I truly frighten you. Or harm you."

It was impossible to find coherent words, in this moment, so Rosa only shook her head, quick, forceful. And then revelled in the answering shudder of that warm body against her, the added weight of its unspoken relief on her skin.

"Clever, *foolish* little pet," he murmured, so soft, into the curve of her neck. "You ought never to bite your orc, lest you *wish* to hurl him into a frenzy, before all his kin."

Wait. Rosa's floating, contented brain had completely forgotten about the orcs—oh gods, the medics, *watching*—but when her head jerked up, her eyes frantically searching, they were gone. Vanished. As if they'd never been there at all.

"I sent them away," John said, with a low chuckle. "You did not even notice, ach? Too lost in your squalling and flailing, I ken."

Rosa attempted an elbow up toward him, but failed miserably, to which John carefully drew her loose hair back from her neck, and pressed a soft, warm kiss against her marked skin. "Ach, this pleased me," he whispered. "You are a worthy pet, my little rose, and a brave, clever woman. I could never have thought"—she could hear his swallow—"you could be this. For an *orc*."

There was a twinge of that familiar bitterness in his voice, and Rosa fought to focus on it, to find words in the swirling miasma of sheer, sated *happiness*. "For *you*, John-Ka," she breathed. "*You*. Orc. Scholar. Leader. Lord. Rightful Priest of Orc Mountain. Best fuck in the realm. And"—she hauled in a breath—"raging, devious *reprobate. You.*"

The stillness echoed for an instant, ringing through his

form above her—and then settled again, into another unbearably soft kiss of those warm lips against her neck. Speaking again, as loud as a shout, without speaking at all.

Rosa didn't know how long they stayed there together, the world spinning and swaying with impossible contentment— but she blinked fully awake at the feel of him finally pulling out of her, away. And then deftly mopping up the mess, before drawing her back to seated again.

"You must hunger," he said, his eyes not quite meeting hers in the guttering lamplight. "Mayhap I shall take you to bed, and fetch you some supper?"

His face was still unaccountably, adorably flushed, his shaky hand rubbing at his mouth, and Rosa's own mouth was already giving him a slow smile, brimming with warmth and affection. "I *am* hungry," she confessed. "But instead of bed, maybe we could go to the library? And read together, for a while?"

The warmth surged higher at John's jerky answering nod, and even higher as he silently dressed her again, braided her hair, and then snatched her still-tingly body up onto his hip. And then carried her through the corridors, stroking gently at her neck—until he suddenly reeled back a step, as an orc sprinted straight down the corridor toward them.

"John!" the orc called, and Rosa realized it was Baldr, his eyes wide with urgency. "The captain needs you, now. They've finally agreed to meet."

They. The *men*, he had to mean, and the snap of tension all through John's form confirmed it, his mouth gone thin and grim. "Ach," he said. "Grant me one moment, brother."

With that, he spun and sprinted down the corridor, Baldr close at his heels, until they burst into the library. Tristan was already there, turning around to blink toward them, and John strode over to place Rosa in her usual chair, his fingers gently, regretfully, angling up her face.

"You stay here and read with Tristan, little pet," he said. "I shall return as soon as we are done."

Rosa's heart was thumping with unaccountable irregularity, and she grasped for his hand, held it close. "Can't I come with you? Please?"

She didn't miss the shadow that crossed John's gaze, or the swift glance he shot Baldr over his shoulder. "Not this time," he said. "But I shall tell you all that we learn. Ach?"

He followed that with a hard, fervent kiss, his lips hungry and hot on hers, and when he drew away Rosa felt herself nodding, her body relaxing, her mouth tilting up. "Then good luck, John-Ka," she murmured. "See you soon."

He smiled back, small but true, and gave her cheek a firm little pat before turning and striding off, leaving Rosa to smile hazily at his retreating back, at the lovely taut curve of his arse. And when she finally blinked, glancing belatedly at Tristan, he was watching her with quiet, unmistakable approval.

"You and John-Ka have settled matters between you, ach?" he asked, and at Rosa's answering nod, he smiled, slow and stunning. "It pleases me to witness this, Rosa-Ka. My brother has wished for a mate for so long."

Rosa-Ka. A *mate*. The warmth swirled again, the happiness swelling to thrust away nearly all else—except, of course, for that one last, constant, unfinished truth, thrown again into sharp relief with this damned sudden meeting. The men. The atrocities. The *war*.

Lord Kaspar.

Rosa drew in a heavy breath, let it out. She could do this. She wanted this. She was safe. Home.

"If I write a letter to Dusbury, Tristan," she said, "is there a way to send it there, from here? Now?"

Tristan nodded, again with that telltale approval in his eyes, and promptly passed over a fresh sheet of paper. Which Rosa stared at for a long, twisting moment, before she pulled out her quill, and began to write.

It was a short letter, but it said all she needed to say. And once she'd blown the ink dry, and silently handed the letter back across the table, there was only a hushed, shuddering *relief.*

Tristan took it without speaking, but he was again smiling at Rosa, warm, approving. "I shall take this to Eyarl now," he said. "He oversees such matters, and shall send it out tonight. I shall soon return."

Rosa gratefully nodded, and once he'd left, she sagged back into her chair, her eyes glancing around at the familiar, lovely library. It had already become so dear to her, so much like home, and even the thought of leaving it now—leaving John— was almost acutely painful.

But she didn't have to leave now. They'd—*settled matters,* like Tristan had said. John had asked. She had answered. She'd pleased him, earned his approval and his praise and even his *name.* She would be the pet—and the partner—he'd always dreamed of. He would see.

But it was at that moment that two orcs walked by, speaking in Aelakesh together. Two orcs who were entirely unfamiliar— but that wasn't what made Rosa sit up in her chair, her gut twisting, her hands gripped tight to the table.

They were talking about *her.*

"*Er þetta konan?*" one of them said. "*Sú sem Lord Kaspar kom með heilan her fyrir?*"

Is that the woman, it meant. *The woman Kaspar has brought his army for.*

Wait. The woman *Kaspar* brought his *army* for?!

Rosa's heart kicked and flailed, her brain screeching in her skull, and her suddenly jittery, prickling body lurched out of her chair, dashed to the door. And desperately, fervently listened, through the wild clanging in her ears.

"Ach," the other orc said. "*En John-Ka neitar. Hann vill hafa hana hjá sér.*"

Yes. But John refuses. He wants to keep her.

The orcs were still walking, their voices fading into the darkness—but behind them, it was like something had stabbed Rosa straight through the stomach, and crushed her flat against the doorframe.

Lord Kaspar had brought the army. For *her*?! And was that what John's meeting with the men had been about? Was he meeting with *Lord Kaspar*? Was Lord Kaspar truly *here*?!

There was no air, suddenly, only empty dragging gulps, scraping into Rosa's throat. No. It couldn't be true. It couldn't. Surely John would have told her the truth. They'd agreed on this. They'd settled matters. No more secrets. He wanted her to stay...

But Rosa's panic just kept jolting, louder and louder with every strangled breath. *I will try*, John had told her. He'd hinted at the future, yes, at sharing all his secrets with her—but had he actually *said* any of that? Surely he had?

Rosa's brain was frantically casting through memories, grasping and discarding, finding only more hints, more meaningful looks and silences. And John had never actually even said who was leading the men, he'd said they were waiting, *is there aught more you wish to ask me...*

Rosa felt on the verge of screaming, and she groped at the doorframe, groped for rational thought. No. There still had to be some mistake. Because surely, Lord Kaspar would never have come to Orc Mountain. Not with an army, not for her. He was a scholar, not a fighter or commander, he was travelling, he was busy, far too busy to care about his librarian's whereabouts...

And Rosa hadn't even told him, in that first letter she'd left, where she was going. She'd only written that she was taking time to better research, just as he'd suggested. There was no way he could have found out, no one had even *known* there was an orc in the Dusbury Library that day...

Or had they. Because *Susan* had known. Good gods, Susan had known, and she'd even said to Rosa, that morning, *maybe he's here for you...*

Rosa only faintly registered the sight of another orc striding up the corridor—but wait, it was Simon, *Simon*—and Rosa rushed out toward him, grasping unthinkingly at his huge, solid arm. "Simon," she choked out. "Is Lord Kaspar here? At Orc Mountain? With an army? For *me*?"

Simon gazed down at her, unblinking, and Rosa gave his arm a frenzied shake, fought to ignore the sudden wetness welling behind her eyes. "Please, Simon," she begged. "I need to know. The truth. Is Lord Kaspar here for me? Is John meeting with him right now? *Please.*"

Simon's eyes on her didn't change, and for an instant, she thought he would push her away. Laugh. Call her a stupid, foolish woman, caught in a bond, believing all that a lying Ka-esh orc said—

But then Simon nodded. *Nodded.*

"Ach," he said. "This is truth."

28

This is truth. *Truth*.

John was *lying*.

The dark corridor had slowly begun to spin, Rosa's knees actually knocking together. Her breath coming in short, high-pitched little gulps, Lord Kaspar was *here*, with an *army*, John was *lying*...

She only vaguely felt Simon's huge hand on her elbow, steadying her, keeping her upright. The touch surprisingly gentle, and Rosa's head snapped up, her eyes frantically blinking at his frowning face. He'd known too, he'd known this whole time, and maybe—maybe he'd even tried to *warn* her—

"Would you," she gulped at him, "take me to John? Now? *Please*, Simon?"

The irritation visibly flared in his eyes, he didn't want to, of course he didn't, he'd never been able to stand her—and Rosa gulped back a sob, and shoved away from him, staggering down the black corridor. She would find someone. Anyone. Please...

The sudden grip of a hand on her elbow made her jump, her arms flailing—but it was only Simon again. Simon, who despite the still-present look of visible annoyance on his face, had begun steering her bodily down the corridor.

Rosa's feet moved on their own, fighting to keep up, staggering into the darkness. She'd entirely forgotten the lamp, still burning back there in the library, and the pitch-black corridor felt narrow, claustrophobic, thoroughly disorienting. Simon's stride was far larger than John's, and the corridor seemed to follow a twisting, erratic path that her rough mental map couldn't at all place, but maybe that was due to the continued screeching in her skull, the earsplitting thud of her heartbeat.

Lord Kaspar was *here*. John had *lied*.

There was a rising clatter ahead of them, voices and commotion filling the darkness, and suddenly light blasted across Rosa's eyes. From a *torch*, that was somehow burning in Simon's hand—and up ahead multiple orcs had thrown their arms in front of their faces, several of them loudly cursing.

But John was among them, he'd been walking close beside Nattfarr, though his form had stilled mid-step, his hand also shielding his eyes. And with them was also the captain, and Jule, and Baldr and Drafli and Olarr, all blinking at Simon and Rosa's clearly unexpected appearance.

"Rosa!" Jule said, with genuine-seeming surprise. "What are you doing here? Were you supposed to be at the meeting? I'm so sorry, we just finished."

The meeting. Rosa's eyes darted reflexively toward John, searching his face—and yes, yes, oh gods, it had been a meeting with *Lord Kaspar*, John was *lying*...

"I just," Rosa's voice choked, sounding like someone else's. "Needed to see John."

No one argued, of course, and John abruptly stepped away from the group, striding over toward her. But his face, his eyes, he didn't like that she'd come here, he was frustrated, annoyed, *disapproving*—

"Can we talk?" Rosa managed, through her too-thick tongue. "In private? Now? Please?"

John's head nodded, curt and quick, and he wordlessly grasped the torch from Simon's hand, and then gestured in the opposite direction of the group, the movement sharp. As if he were truly angry, at Rosa, when he'd been the one who'd been *lying* to her, all this time. And with Rosa's rising shock and incredulity, there was a quivering, unsettling *hurt*.

But John didn't seem to notice, he was ushering her into a strange new room, one that—Rosa's head whipped around, her eyes wide—had actual *shackles* embedded in the walls, and chains coiled like snakes across the stone floor.

It was a—*prison*.

Rosa stared at John, at how he'd roughly thrust the torch into a wall bracket, and spun to face her. His arms crossed, his entire form emanating anger, frustration, disapproval.

But he didn't speak, he was waiting, for her. For her to explain her actions, maybe, and Rosa gulped for breath, for coherency. *He* was the liar here. He had no right. *None.*

"When were you going to tell me," she choked, "about Lord Kaspar? Coming here? For *me*?"

John's arms flexed over his chest, his lip curling, his narrow eyes glittering in the torchlight. "I should have told you this," he said, the words crisp, "when you asked me."

Rosa's feet wrenched sideways beneath her, pitching her toward the stone wall, and she clutched for it, dragged in air. It was true. Good gods, it was true, maybe it had been true, all this time...

"You *lied* to me," she heard her voice say, frayed, trembling. "Again. You've lied about *everything*. The bond. The war. The men. Lord Kaspar. Even your clan's secret *debauchery*. We *agreed* on this, John! You *swore* you would tell me the truth! No falsehoods! You *said*!"

The anger surged again across his eyes, bright and

inexplicable. "I said I should *try*," he replied, his voice clipped. "I gave you leave to ask me further of this. Ach, I *urged* you to this. You did not. I thought, mayhap"—his jaw twitched—"you did not *wish* to know."

"Of *course* I want to know!" Rosa shouted back, shrill. "Of course I want to know that my *patron* of nine whole *years* has brought an *army* to Orc Mountain to *rescue* me!"

The words came out sounding wrong, somehow, and before her John faintly, visibly flinched. But didn't speak, just kept looking at her with those wrong, glittering eyes, while Rosa's heartbeat knocked louder and louder against her chest.

"How long has Lord Kaspar been here," she heard herself say, from somewhere far away. "The *truth*, John."

His eyes briefly closed, his mouth grimacing. "He came with the first band of men," he said flatly. "Eleven days past."

Eleven days. Dear gods, Lord Kaspar had been here almost the *entire time* Rosa had been, while John had pretended there was no war, no men, nothing. While he'd seduced her, toyed with her, distracted her with his library and his affections and his *lies...*

"And has Lord Kaspar been asking for me?" Rosa's hollow voice whispered. "All this time?"

John didn't move, didn't even pretend to bother to answer, but as usual his non-answer spoke for him, as loud as a piercing, spine-clutching shout. Lord Kaspar *had* been asking for Rosa. For *eleven days.*

And that—the realization cracked through Rosa's skull with deafening power—*that* was why the men hadn't been attacking. *That* was why it had felt wrong, why it hadn't quite fit. The men were supposed to be waiting for the peasant rebellion, yes, and maybe they still were. But *these* men—these two regiments—had only come for *her.*

"You utter *prick*," Rosa spat at John, almost breathless with the lurching, overpowering rage. "You deceitful arrogant *swine.*

How *dare* you hide something like that from me. And"—she gulped back a breath, while more comprehension swirled— "what the *hell* have you been telling Lord Kaspar about me, all this time? Have you told him you'll torture me, or kill me, if he tries attacking you? Or some other orc *rubbish*?!"

John's body twitched again, and she could almost feel his own anger roiling, surging through the room, crashing to match hers. And it made no fucking sense, he shouldn't be angry, he had *no right*, not when he'd done this to her…

"We have told this man," John replied finally, his voice so cold, someone else's, "all that you have told me. What you claimed as your truth. That you did not wish to return to him. That you hated him. That you felt only relief, to be free of him, and that you never wished to meet him again."

Rosa's eyes squeezed shut, her teeth gritting so hard it hurt. "You had," she breathed, "no right to tell him that, on my behalf. I told you that *in confidence*."

"You also told this to Tristan," John growled back. "And to the captain's own mate. Was all this *in confidence*, also?"

Rosa fought the urge to snarl at him, and clenched her hands to fists. "So what did Lord Kaspar say," she demanded. "When you told him all that."

And why was there hope, suddenly, hope that John would say, perhaps, that Lord Kaspar turned around and left, never again to return—but no, no, John had lied to her, nonstop, for *weeks*, and now he was speaking to her like this, yelling at her like this, so soon after they'd supposedly settled things, but maybe that was a lie too. Maybe this had all been a lie, to keep Rosa away from Lord Kaspar, because…

"This man said," John replied, every word a dropping, devastating stone, "that he will only believe this when he sees you. Alone. When you speak this to his face."

Something was clawing inside Rosa's belly, fighting and scrambling to escape, and for a long, painful moment she couldn't answer, couldn't breathe. "You didn't—*agree* to that," she somehow said, her voice a whisper. "Did you?"

The anger shuddered and flashed in John's eyes, in his fist abruptly slamming out, punching against the solid stone wall behind him. Hard enough that she could hear his gasp of pain, could see the blood forming in the fresh welts on his knuckles.

"The captain agreed," he said, hoarse, a monotone, dropping his bloody hand back to his side. "You shall go speak thus to Lord Kaspar. Tomorrow. Alone."

Rosa would go to Lord Kaspar? *Alone*?! The room juddered starkly around her, and suddenly there was panic, flailing, *destroying*.

"And then," she gulped, "what happens?"

John stared at her, for an instant too long, while the walls seemed to buckle and twist—and then he *laughed*. The sound harsh, bitter, and he hadn't laughed like that in so long, he wasn't supposed to laugh like that anymore, it was *wrong, everything* was wrong—

"You tell me, *pet*," he said, and he was smiling at her, all deadly sharp teeth. "You tell me. What do you say, when you are alone with this man tomorrow? What do you do?"

There was no answering this, no possible way, even as a distant part of Rosa began chanting, or perhaps screaming. They wouldn't truly leave her alone with Lord Kaspar, they *couldn't*, and if they did, what *would* she say, what would she do? *I've found several possible atrocities, now please take me home, and make me a student like you promised? Please, use me to start your war?*

No, no, *fuck* no, even the thought was sickening, revolting, recoiling painfully in Rosa's gut. But what the hell else was left to do, to say, to *be*? *I want to stay here, in Orc Mountain? Where the orc I thought I was mated to has lied to me for weeks on end? Lied to me, again and again, used me, manipulated me, from the first damned day of our acquaintance, because, because...*

John was prowling closer, his movements fluid, deadly. "Why do I taste your fear, pet," he said, so easy, with a swift little flick of his tongue into the air. "I have not even touched you. I have not growled or bared my prick. I taste no scent of your hunger. What causes this, woman?"

The words felt like a slap across the face, Rosa's trembly body backed against the wall, her hands frantically grasping at the cool stone. She should say something, why couldn't she say something, he could never, *ever* know…

"You are afraid to answer me," John continued, prowling closer, snapping out a sharp finger to gently tilt up her chin. "Why is this, pet? What is it about this man, and this war, that you are afraid to speak to me?"

His claw-tip trailed down her throat, slow, while he again smiled, showing all those teeth, wrong, *wrong*. "Speak this to me, pet," he purred, as his hand slid around to curve, close and familiar and exquisitely awful, against her trembling neck. "*Why do you hide all these things? Why can't you tell me?*"

They were her own words, Rosa realized, with a clanging jolt of dread, spoken even in a parody of her own accent, her own voice. And her mouth was opening, closing, but nothing came out, nothing, she was lying, he was lying, everything was a lie…

John's strangely clammy hand circled closer around her neck, and for perhaps the first time ever, Rosa felt the true strength of it, the real danger behind it. The flash of awareness that he could kill her, so easily, it would only take a moment…

"Stop this, John," her wavering voice said, from somewhere very far away. "This isn't you."

His laugh was hard, brittle, agonizing. "Ach, but this *is* me," he said, his eyes glinting in the torchlight. "I am an orc. I have said this to you, again and again, and you have said you wished for this. For *me*. For John, of Clan Ka-esh. But"—his chest heaved—"this was not truth, was it, my pretty rose? *Is it*?"

Oh gods, oh gods, the fear was screeching, scraping, scoring deep inside. Because John was waiting for an answer, he was going to make Rosa answer, and then—

"You do *not* truly wish for this," he growled, with a jerky wave down at his body, himself. "You do not wish for an orc who is not all patience and pleasure. You do not wish for an orc who longs to frighten you, and conquer you, and *punish* you. You do not wish for an orc who was raised to doubt, to mix hunger and fear, to know that power shall always win over reason, and humans shall always lie, and cheat, and scheme for yet more *war*. No matter how much an orc strives to give them!"

He was shouting at the end, his voice ringing through this dark and terrifying room, his fingers digging into Rosa's neck. While the fear screamed and ricocheted, crushing all else beneath its force, he could kill her, *John* could truly *kill her*—

Suddenly he stumbled backwards, staggering, as though he'd been shoved—but Rosa hadn't moved, hadn't spoken. Only stared at him, at John, *her* John, who'd somehow become *broken*, his bloody hand rubbing at his mouth, his eyes glittering with pain.

"Since it seems you shall never speak of this, little *pet*," he said, so smooth, so biting, so dead inside, "then mayhap I shall. You shall meet with Lord Kaspar tomorrow. You shall tell him"—his chest heaved again—"that you have excelled at the task he has given you. You shall tell him you have unearthed some new scandal of Orc Mountain, mayhap of dark magic, or orcs mating together, or chains and beatings. You shall then help him spread the word of this, so he may spark yet more fear and hate against my kin."

Rosa stared, stunned, horrified. Words crashing, colliding, jamming chaotic into her skull. John—*knew*?! About the assignment, the spying, the *atrocities*?!

No. No. *No.* John couldn't know. He couldn't have known. It *wasn't possible*, he could *never know*—

"W-why," Rosa stammered, so far away, "do you say such things. Did Lord Kaspar t-tell you that. He *lies*, John."

Something unfamiliar flashed across John's eyes, and for an instant, there was the thought, brief, distant, wildly hopeful, that maybe there was still an escape. Maybe Rosa could still blame everything on Lord Kaspar. He *did* lie, that was true, everything was his fault, please, please, she could still salvage this, there was still a way out...

"Foolish woman," John replied, finally, his voice a bitter, furious croak. "Do not play-act with me. I have known this truth from the start. From the first day we *met*. You are here to spy upon me, and spark a *war*."

29

John *knew*. He'd known from—the *start*?!

Rosa's whole self had spasmed into numbness, poured too full of shock and terror even to breathe. Only able to stare at John's furious face, while her heartbeat pummelled an odd, flashing white behind her eyes.

He'd known. The entire time. About Rosa's mission. That she'd come here to spy on him, and his brothers, and his *home*. To help start a *war*.

And John saw her shock, perhaps even tasted it, because he laughed again, the sound an ugly, chilly rasp in Rosa's ears. "You thought yourself so clever, foolish woman," he gritted out. "With your stack of books and treatises. With how you offered yourself to me that day. As if I should not see past your foolish play-acting with a single *sniff* of you."

Rosa's mouth had fallen open, the disbelief thudding, dazed, dragging. He'd known, all this time. It was impossible. Impossible...

"And then, this *letter*," John spat at her, ruthless, relentless. "This letter from this man, coming in the night, urging you to do this, in trade for his *rewards*. This letter with his seal, which you then open, and thrust into a book, with your scent heavy upon it—and next you leave me alone with this, whilst you fritter about your library. As if I could not smell? Or *read*?!"

Oh. Oh, gods. Rosa couldn't think, couldn't understand, what was happening, why, why, *why*…

"Why," she somehow gulped at him, barely audible, "did you do it, then. Why did you"—she choked for air—"agree. To touch me."

John barked another laugh, thin, hateful. "As always, *pet*, with the pointed questions, ach?" he sneered. "Mayhap I wished to frighten you. Mayhap I wished to teach you your place. Mayhap I longed to see Lord Kaspar's foolish, smug, *favourite* little wench stuck and screeching and *begging* upon an orc-prick!"

Dear gods, this couldn't be true, John couldn't be saying this, this couldn't be happening, *why*. And he couldn't mean— he *couldn't*—

"You didn't," Rosa whispered, her heart racing, her breaths short and shallow. "Come to the library, just to get at Lord Kaspar. Just to seduce me. To take me away from him, and ruin my future. Did you?"

Something flashed across those eyes, something like disbelief, or maybe even pain. But he didn't answer, didn't move, and why did Rosa feel so desperately and precariously on the verge of weeping, her eyes hot and wet and blinking—

"But you," she panted, over the lurking sobs in her throat. "You brought me here. You were *kind* to me. You made me your pet. Your—your—"

She couldn't say it, suddenly, couldn't bear to hear him say it hadn't been true, and John whirled away from her, his hands pressed against his face.

"Ach," he said, and it almost sounded like a sob, too. "And *I* was the fool, in this. I *knew* not to trust you, I *knew* to keep you apart, to hide our truths from you, until this foolish, *foolish* mistake of our son could be dealt with. But—"

But. Rosa was waiting, choking on her lurching breaths, staring helpless, shivering, at his back. "But *what*, John."

"But you are cleverer than you seemed," he said, in a voice she'd never heard before. "You made me believe you had changed. You went to such lengths to sway me to this. You took me with such eagerness, you were so warm and sweet, you laughed and spoke and played with me. You did good work in my library and wrote out this world-altering book for me. You gave me full leave to rule over you. You showed me no judgement for what I was. You showed me you were a *scholar*."

Rosa's arms had tightly wrapped against her waist, her body rocking back and forth, and when John slowly turned around again, his eyes were there too. On her waist. On—on—

"I knew you spoke false when I asked you of this man, and this war," John said, so quiet, his gaze unseeing, unblinking. "But then you said you wished to risk all to bear my son. I"— his throat convulsed—"I longed for this with such foolish ardour, that I chose to look beyond your falsehood. I chose to believe you truly grieved your past deeds, and now wished for this. For me. For *him*."

Him. Their *son*. Rosa couldn't speak, could only rock in place, her arms clutching at her waist. He didn't mean that. He couldn't. He hadn't said. He'd *lied*...

"When were you," her voice choked, "going to tell me? About him? Our"—she had to force the words out—"our *son*?"

John's eyes were still on her waist, still glittering with some- thing that might have been hatred, or longing, or both. "I did tell you," he said, and for an instant he sounded almost— pleading. "Do not play-act with me, woman. You *knew*."

And maybe she had, but it was still rubbish, he'd still lied, he'd *lied*. "Did I?" Rosa shot back. "Since *when*, John? How long has this been—have I been—"

She couldn't say it, she could scarcely stand upright at this point, and John was still looking at her waist, still with that awful agony in his eyes. "Since this night, two days past," he said. "When you showed me this book you made, and took my seed into your womb again and again, and made me believe—"

He didn't finish, and thank the gods there was anger again, shouting, rattling inside Rosa's skull. "Oh, of *course*," she said, her voice thick, mocking. "You've known about this for days, too. You kept my own *pregnancy* a secret from me. I'm shocked, John, *shocked*."

John growled, his claw jabbing in the air toward her, his eyes bitter, glinting misery. "You *knew*," he breathed. "You *did*. I saw you. I smelled you."

"Yes, and you still didn't tell me!" Rosa shouted back. "Again! Again, and again, and again! You never said *anything*, John! Not about our son, not about the war, not about Lord Kaspar. Not about our future, or what was supposed to happen after this, or even what the hell all this really was, between us! You said *nothing*!"

And here, vivid and horrible, was the memory of Simon. Saying, over and over again, how the Ka-esh lied. How they didn't speak vows, because that meant there was nothing to break. And Rosa had seen it with her own eyes, in how Salvi had treated Tristan, just assuming that he'd be forgiven for throwing him over for a woman, without either of them actually saying a fucking *thing*.

"You knew," John said again, lurching a sharp, dangerous step closer. "You are not a fool. You *knew*. You *said* you would stay, when I asked."

"No, you *prick*, I didn't know!" Rosa shouted back, and was that true, maybe, *maybe*. "I'm a human! I'm not an orc, I don't run around lying, and fucking with other people's affections, and *beating* on people I'm supposed to care about! I'm a human, for fuck's sakes, I'm not a *monster*!"

The words rang through the room, vicious and powerful, enough to snap John's head sideways, away from her, his eyes squeezed shut. As though Rosa had just hurt him, struck him across the face, but he deserved it, she was pregnant with his deadly *child* and he fucking deserved it—

But then his head turned back toward her, so slow, so inhuman, so lethal. His eyes alight with bitterness, with rage, with *anguish.*

"Mayhap I *am* a monster," he said, his voice cracking. "Mayhap it pleased me to rule over you, and stoke your fear and your hunger. But I have *never*"—his mouth twisted, his chest hollowing—"taken a hurt, eager, fatherless *child* out of her school, against her will, so I could use her alone as I pleased. I have *never* starved a child, so she might stay small and weak and girlish for me. I have *never* fathered a son and then *forgotten* him. I have never taken a clever woman's work, and claimed it as my own. I have *never*"—he came a sudden step closer, his anger rising, fusing—"used my power as the last of the Ka, or as a would-be Priest, to *use* those who do not wish for me, or imprison those who *fear* me!"

His claws were still at his sides, they *were,* but it felt like he'd dragged them deep down Rosa's front, carved bloody trails in her skin. Like he'd flayed her whole, exposed everything that had been so safely hidden within, and Rosa wanted to weep, to vomit, to disappear. He was the monster. He *was.* He had to be...

"You—you *are,*" Rosa's voice sobbed, as she cowered against the wall, trembling all over, her arms wrapped tight. "You are, you are, you *are!*"

And he *was,* he'd trapped Rosa in this room, to yell and mock and scorn her, to make her unworthy, unknown, unloved, uncared for. And anything else had been a delusion anyway, he didn't care, she wasn't his pet, she was nothing, he was a *monster*—

He was staggering backwards, away, his hands pressed to his face, his head shaking. "Then go," he rasped. "Then *leave* me!"

It came out a roar, a command, raw and brutal and terrible. A lord's final strike at his defeated pet's bare bleeding heart...

And Rosa obeyed. Clutching for her wounds, choking back her sobs, she fled.

30

osa stumbled into the dark corridor, clinging to the forbidding stone wall, her breaths shallow and panting and desperate. Go, he'd said, but how, why, *where—*

"Rosa," came a voice, close and terrifying—and she yelped, cringed back, clutched her hands over her waist—

"Rosa," the voice said again, quieter, more soothing. "It is me. Tristan. I will not harm you."

Oh. Rosa's eyes squeezed shut, her trembling body sagging against the wall, and suddenly there was the stupid, *stupid* hope that John was here too, that John would run up, and take her in his arms and say all the kind, meaningless things she so wretchedly wanted to hear. *I'm sorry I frightened you, I'm sorry I hurt you and used you, I'm sorry I'm such a compulsive insufferable liar...*

But there was nothing, only the very faint sound of Tristan's breath, and Rosa groped frantically for thought, for words. "J-John," she gulped out, "t-told me to go. To *leave* him. C-can you help me?"

She could feel Tristan's hesitation, could hear his slow

exhale, could even picture the uneasy look on his face. "You ought not to take all John-Ka's words as truth," he said, quiet. "Most of all when spoken in anger. You are welcome to stay here, Rosa, as long as you should wish."

"Am I really?" she shot back, her voice cracking. "Even if I came here to spy on you? To help start a *war* against you?!"

She'd somehow begun weeping again, the water streaking down her cheeks—and Tristan's stilted silence in the darkness was suddenly just as loud as any reply. Because he'd known too, damn these lying Ka-esh he'd *known*, and he'd still taught her his language and answered all her questions and treated her with nothing, *nothing*, but kindness.

"I c-can't stay," Rosa croaked, through the misery, the guilt, the *shame*. "I can't, Tristan. Not now. Please."

There was another instant's stillness, another slow sigh in the darkness. "Where do you wish to go?" he asked, his voice very even. "Back to this man?"

This man. Lord Kaspar. And Rosa's head was wildly shaking, hard enough that sparks flashed behind her eyes. No. Not Lord Kaspar. Never. The man who'd taken a child out of school, and *starved* her, because...

"Back to my library," she managed. "To Dusbury. Without"—she swallowed—"Lord Kaspar knowing it. Or following me. *Please.*"

Tristan was silent for another breath, and there was the sudden, rising certainty that he would say, *no, I can't, you're worthless, useless, you deserve to go back to this man—*

"Ach," he said, the word a shouting, shuddering relief. "We shall go."

31

Tristan led Rosa through the corridors in silence. While a dark, desperate misery descended upon her, dripping from her eyes in a steady, bitter-salt stream. John had lied. He was a monster. She was *leaving*.

But the tears only dripped faster, Rosa's feet staggering on the smooth stone below, her body kept upright only by the hard clench of her hand to Tristan's solid arm. She would go back to Dusbury. And then...

"Little teacher?" cut in a voice, deep and vaguely familiar. *Simon's* voice. "Where go you?"

"North," Tristan replied, clipped. "I take Rosa back to Dusbury tonight."

Simon's growl was immediate, feral, sending more fear scattering up Rosa's spine. "You no do this," he hissed. "Break captain *rule*. Men lie in wait. Men *attack*."

"Then we shall stay underground, until we have passed the men," Tristan said testily. "This is important, Simon. To John-Ka. To *me*."

He sounded surprisingly fierce, suddenly, and his body against Rosa's didn't even flinch at Simon's harsh, answering growl. "Then I come," Simon replied, voice flat. "Keep little teacher *safe*."

Tristan huffed out a breath, his hand clenching against Rosa's arm. "You may only come," he snapped, "if you go find Salvi, and bring him with you. And tell him to bring a lamp, and human food, and a warm cloak for Rosa. Ach?"

Simon muttered something back in Aelakesh, something about false medics and useless humans who couldn't survive a one-day journey without coddling—but Tristan snarled again, and finally Rosa could hear Simon muttering his assent, and loping off into the darkness.

And then it was just more walking, endless miserable walking for what felt like an *age*, while the tears kept streaking down Rosa's face, dripping off her chin. John had lied to her. John had never truly cared about her. John was a monster.

She had never been worthy. She had never been cared for. It had all been a lie.

She only faintly registered a rising clatter behind them, a distant dance of light—and suddenly Simon appeared again, jogging through the corridor, a gleaming scimitar slapping against his side. Close behind him was Salvi, tall and grim-looking, with his huge pack strapped to his back, his narrow eyes fixed to Tristan's face. To where Tristan looked wan and tired in the lamplight, but also unmistakably relieved.

"Hey, *sæti*," Salvi said, his voice rough, as he strode straight toward Tristan, and yanked him bodily into his chest. "You're all right. Ach?"

Tristan's eyes briefly closed, his claws curling into Salvi's tunic. "Ach," he murmured back. "But we need to take Rosa-Ka to Dusbury. Tonight."

"I have heard," Salvi said, into Tristan's hair. "These women causing us nothing but trouble. Again."

Rosa's cold, numb-feeling body had already backed against the nearest wall, blinking between Simon and Salvi, shivering with more jolting, rising fear. Because maybe they knew too, and what if they yelled at her, or overpowered Tristan, made him change his mind—

"Peace, woman," Salvi said, his eyes flicking toward her over the top of Tristan's head. "You have naught to fear from us. Now, put this on, before you catch a chill, and thus gain us John's undying wrath."

His free hand threw something toward her—a cloak, Rosa realized, grasping for it, staring blankly at its thick wool weight. *John's wrath.* But John didn't care. Not anymore. She wasn't worthy. Wasn't wanted. He'd *lied.*

"John won't care," she heard her hollow voice say, even as she somehow yanked the cloak on, curling herself into its scratchy warmth. "He wants me to leave. With good reason, because"—she gulped in air, scrubbed at her face with the cloak, she could say it, they had to know—"I was here to spy on you. To help start a *war.*"

But there wasn't a trace of surprise in Salvi's eyes, or even Simon's. And good gods, they *had* all known, all this time?

"Ach, woman," Salvi said, as he hooked his arm around Tristan's neck, and began drawing him down the corridor. "You ken we didn't guess why a powerful lord's cleverest, most favoured wench was suddenly so eager to serve an *orc*? Why she could never stop quizzing us about our mountain, and our ways? Why she fought so fiercely to worm her way onto John's prick, and thus into his cold dead heart?"

He actually *winked* at Rosa over his shoulder, as if to soften the blow of those shocking words, but it still felt like he'd struck her straight in the chest, knocked all the air from her lungs. They all knew, and they thought—they truly thought—

"But I just—I only asked questions because I wanted to *learn,*" Rosa said, her voice abominably plaintive, wavering, again on the very verge of weeping. "And I *liked* John. I *cared* about John."

No one answered, not even Tristan, and finally Simon grunted from where he was walking behind Rosa with surprisingly silent steps. "Caught in bond," he said, voice flat. "Like all women. There is no *care*."

Rosa's trembly body flinched, and she whirled around to face him, the misery catching, choking. "I did care," she shot back. "I *did*. John is an obnoxious lying *prick*, but he's also determined, and thoughtful, and *brilliant*. And he's had to put up with way too much, from all of you, from the men, from"— she dragged in air—"from *me*. And I told him I would stay, I *agreed* to be his mate, I *agreed* to have his son, even if it might still *kill* me, because I *know* how much it fucking *means* to him!"

The words rang through the corridor with painful shrillness, with astonishing fervency. With all three orcs hesitating to turn and gape at her, Simon with disbelief in his eyes, Salvi with confusion, and Tristan with—with *approval*. With a small, careful smile.

"Ach, I told you," he said, soft, glancing up at Salvi. "She wishes for their son, also."

She did? But oh, good gods, maybe she *did*, and beside Tristan Salvi was frowning at Rosa, his head tilting, as though she were a puzzle he couldn't quite solve. While Simon only snorted again, the sound harsh, bitter, angry.

"Woman *lie*," he growled. "She *leave*. Next she kill son. Ka-esh *way*."

Rosa's still-wet eyes snapped to glare at him again, her hands clutching against her waist, the answer erupting all on its own. She wanted this. She wanted this?

"I *do* want my son," she gulped at him. "I *do*. And I will do everything within my *power* to see him born. John will *not* be the last of the Ka, even if I never speak to him *again*."

Simon didn't move, just stared at her for a long, twisting moment. As Rosa's fingers spread a little wider on her waist, confirming it was true, it was real. John was a monster, and yet she wanted to bear a monster's son, an *orc*, and what did that mean, what the hell was *wrong* with her—

But here, swarming her thoughts, was the memory, vivid, acutely painful, of lying in John's bed, in John's warm arms.

I ought not to feel shame for the deeds of others, he'd said. *My deeds, and my wishes, are my own.*

It hadn't felt like a lie, it hadn't, and at the time Rosa had been sure—*sure*—that he'd meant it about her, too. About her shame, and her choices. Telling her, maybe, that her choices were valid. Worthy. Just because they were hers.

Rosa fought to stamp the thought down, away, deep inside where it belonged—but it wouldn't seem to budge. Speaking so strong, so relentless, that she swallowed hard, wiped at her face, lifted her chin—

"I want my son," her voice said again, firm, clear, into the stillness. "I want him. I want John to have him."

It made no sense, none of it made sense anymore—but this was true, this was her own, and Rosa was clinging to it with all her strength. And Simon's eyes on her were glinting, accusing, unnerving, almost... uneasy.

"I scout above," he said abruptly, spinning on his heel, and leaping up onto a little ledge in the rock Rosa hadn't noticed before. "Mayhap past men now."

His big body shoved up again, moving with surprising ease through what seemed to be a tiny crack in the rough-hewn rock above. Leaving Rosa standing there blinking after him, her breaths heaving, her fingers still spread wide on her waist.

John had lied. He'd shouted at her, and frightened her, and used her, and hurt her. And now she was foolish enough, pathetic enough, to try to please him again? To impress him again? To bind him to her, maybe forever, with this child?

But her head was shaking, suddenly, her hands fluttering up to press against her still-wet eyes. *My deeds, and my wishes, are my own.*

Her own.

She wanted this. With John, or without John. Just the same way she wanted to read. The way she needed to learn. The way, even, she wanted to be taken care of. To be—*mastered*.

That unsettling thought was broken by a loud, bloodcurdling howl. Deep and vicious and harrowing, hurling chills up Rosa's back, snapping her stunted, blinking gaze to the hole in the ceiling. That had been *Simon's* shout, Simon had gone up to scout for men, and wait, wait—

The howl sounded again, rippling with rage and pain. And beside Rosa Salvi leapt up, swiping for a nearby flat rock to hold above his head, while hauling his huge pack higher onto his shoulders. "Stay, *sæti*," he breathed at Tristan. "*Ég elska þig.*"

With that, he hurled his lean form up toward the hole above, ignoring the choked sound from Tristan that might have very well been a sob. "*Wait*, Salvi," Tristan said, his voice hoarse. "*Elskan!*"

But there was no answer, just a faint thumping noise from above—and then a chorus of distant, rising *shouts*. It was men, Simon and Salvi were being attacked by *men*, and Rosa's sudden scraping fear was crushed by the sheer, hunted terror in Tristan's wide eyes.

"*Helvíti*," he breathed, shouted. "*Salvi!*"

He threw himself up toward the hole, and Rosa's unthinking hands clutched for him, yanked back at his arm. "*No*, Tristan," she gasped. "You need to stay. It's not *safe!*"

Rage flashed across Tristan's eyes, and for an instant Rosa thought he might scream at her, or hurl her away—but instead he reeled backwards, his body visibly trembling, while a keening sound tore from his throat. His grief and fear seeming to strike into Rosa's very soul, and she felt her stomach heave, her hands clutching tight against it.

"You can't, Tristan," she gulped at him. "You *can't*. You have to stay safe. You can't get hurt or die, *ever*, this war can't touch you, this war is unjust, and cruel, and *wrong!*"

Her voice echoed through the corridor, pinging off the walls—and once again she was struck still by her own words, by the force with which she meant them. *This war is unjust, and cruel, and wrong.*

There was a loud thump above them, closer than before, and Tristan rushed toward the hole in the ceiling. Toward where Salvi was suddenly leaping down, and lugging something behind him. Something huge, and limp, and covered with blood. *Simon.*

For a long, horrible moment, Rosa could only stand there, fighting for breath, fighting to shove away the blackness prickling at the edges of her eyes. She'd never seen so much blood in her *life*, and it was pouring from Simon's body, streaming thick and red down his front, down his thigh. Filling her nostrils with sharp bitter iron, even pooling at her *feet*—

He wasn't dead. Was he *dead*?!

Tristan lurched to Salvi's side, helping him settle Simon's limp bloody mass onto the stone floor—movement that dragged a deep, strangled sound from Simon's mouth. But he was alive, oh gods he was alive, and finally Rosa could move again, staggering toward them, her hands fluttering uselessly in the air.

"What happened?!" she choked. "What can we *do*?"

"Fucking crossbows," Salvi shot back, his bloody hands frantically digging through his pack. "And he yanked the bolts out of his *arteries*, the fool, and *sæti*, find the bindings, *please*, we have to *move*—"

Salvi's body wrenched back to Simon, pressing his bare hands hard against Simon's spurting shoulder and thigh, as more thick blood streamed between his fingers. While Tristan turned and began yanking things out of Salvi's pack, strips of leather and cloth, and then thrust them toward Salvi, who then had to jerk his hand away from Simon's shoulder, blood spraying wide—

"Fuck," Salvi gasped—but thank the gods, Rosa's brain had jolted into action again, and she darted forward, and shoved both her hands against Simon's shoulder, just where Salvi's had been. Feeling the hot, sticky, sickening blood pulsing out under her fingers, but it was helping, somehow, freeing Salvi to grasp for Tristan's cloth, and to begin binding it around Simon's bloody thigh. Tying it off, grabbing for another one, Tristan helping this time, yanking the knots tight.

The binding was already pooled full of red, but Salvi's bloody hands had now thrust Rosa's away, and began doing the same to Simon's shoulder. "Hold his arm up," he ordered her, so she did, struggling against the astonishing weight of it, until they'd tied another bandage tight around Simon's shoulder.

Simon's head had begun lolling sideways, his breaths loud and shallow, and Rosa flinched at the sight of Salvi slapping him across the face, hard. "Up, you great lout," he snapped. "Now."

And that, Rosa realized, with another stab of horror, was because there were *voices* above. *Men*. The men knew they were close, the men were going to find the tunnel, the men were going to come down and *kill* them—

But Tristan and Salvi were conferring in rapid Aelakesh, and somehow, impossibly, Salvi had dragged Simon's massive body up onto his feet. And though Simon badly staggered, grunting with pain, he was up, he was moving, he was *alive*.

"Grab the pack, Rosa," Salvi gasped at her. "And *run!*"

32

Rosa obeyed without thinking. Dashing to hoist up the heavy pack onto her back, racing to grab the lamp, to catch up to Salvi—and then realizing, suddenly, that Tristan was still behind them. And he was alone, his clawed hands scrabbling wildly at the stone wall, as the sound of men's voices above rose louder, louder—

"Come *on*, Rosa!" Salvi's thin voice hissed, as Tristan reeled away from the wall he'd been digging at, and began sprinting at full speed toward them. His eyes wide, his braid streaking out straight behind him, his hand grasping for Rosa's, dragging her after him—

When inexplicably, impossibly, the whole earth trembled. So powerful that Rosa staggered sideways, nearly crashing into the wall—but the wall was shaking too, and Tristan had her, his fingers clamped tight and strong around hers as they ran, as thunder boomed behind them, dust and dirt streaming through the air—

Tristan had *collapsed the tunnel.* To stop the men. To keep them *safe.*

Rosa ran like she'd never run before, slipping and sliding

on the stone, coughing and choking on the thick, swirling dust. Ran, and ran, for what felt like hours, until her legs could scarcely stay upright anymore, her lungs barely able to breathe—

Until, suddenly, it stopped. Stopped, in what appeared to be a small, cramped stone room. With a stone door that, after a powerful shove from Tristan, crunched shut, blocking out the noise and the dust behind it.

Rosa heaved in choked, bracing breaths, sagging against the nearest stone wall, her bloody hands gripping painfully against her knees. They were alive. And against all reason, somehow, they were *safe*.

Or were they, because Salvi's taut body had lunged toward Rosa—toward the pack that was still on her back, her twirling thoughts registered, even as she jerked away from him, the terror again choking in her throat.

"Sorry," Salvi said with a grimace, as he carefully pulled the pack off Rosa's shoulders. "Didn't mean to frighten you. I'm only a bit twitchy, ach?"

Rosa's mouth made a sound that might have been a laugh, or a sob. And once Salvi had darted away again, kneeling over Simon's limp—but still visibly breathing—form, Rosa slid all the way down the wall, buried her head into her knees, and fought to find air again.

They were alive. She was alive. Because these orcs—the orcs she'd come to start a *war* with, the orcs she'd *betrayed*—had kept her safe. They'd collapsed their own tunnel, and taken *crossbow bolts*, to keep her safe.

When she blinked up again, Tristan and Salvi were both hovering over Simon. Tristan ripping off Simon's tunic, seemingly inspecting him for more wounds, while Salvi unwrapped the bandage on his thigh. Which was still oozing thick dark blood, though perhaps less freely than before.

"Will Simon be all right?" Rosa asked, her voice far too high-pitched in the small room. "He won't—*die*, will he?"

The sudden, twisting misery of that was almost too powerful to bear—until it was broken by the distinct sound of a hoarse, disapproving grunt. *Simon's* grunt, to which Salvi gave a wry laugh, a shake of his dark head.

"It'll take more than a few crossbow bolts to kill this bastard," he said, as he pulled out what seemed to be a water-skin from his pack, and poured it over Simon's thigh, and then over his own hands. "As much as we all might wish otherwise, ach, *sæti*?"

He shot a quick, sharp-toothed grin toward Tristan, and Rosa could see Tristan relaxing, his shoulders sagging. "We do *not* wish Simon to be killed," he countered weakly. "And if you are sewing that, Salvi, you ought to give him a drink for the pain."

Salvi, who had indeed fished out a curved needle that looked much like Rosa's book-binding one, huffed an exasperated sigh, but accordingly dug in his pack and pulled out a small bottle, yanking the stopper free before thrusting it toward Simon. And to Rosa's vague surprise, Simon took it without complaint, using his good arm—which still seemed slightly shaky—to dump it full down his throat.

"Ach, that is better," Simon said after a moment, his voice thick and gravelly. "Thank you, sweet teacher."

There was a beat of stillness, during which Tristan faintly winced, and Salvi shot Simon a dark, irritated glare. "Oh, stop it, you great arse," Salvi snapped, as he rapidly threaded his needle, and then dunked it into another bottle Tristan had produced from the pack. "You don't think I haven't noticed you macking on Tristan for weeks now? He's *mine*, you prick, and he's just too damned nice to tell you off, and I'm getting fucking *sick* of it."

His voice wavered at the end, suggesting that maybe he

wasn't quite as composed as he seemed, and he jabbed the needle into Simon's thigh with surprising force, enough that Simon's entire body jolted with visible pain.

"Teacher not *yours*," Simon said, through laboured-sounding breaths. "You lie. You betray him. Leave him to make son. Then you allow false Priest to *kill* son, and betray own *kind!*"

Salvi's shoulders visibly stiffened, though his eyes stayed intent on his work, on his hand pulling the thread through Simon's raw, bloody flesh. The movement gentle, careful, at total odds with the furious look on his face.

"Oh, fuck *off* with this, Skai," he said, his voice again wavering, a shade too high-pitched. "That is *not* what happened."

"Then what happen," Simon said, between breaths. Giving Rosa the distinct impression that talking was a distraction, a welcome one, to counter the pain of his wounds, and what Salvi was doing to his leg. "Tell me *true*, liar Ka-esh."

Salvi actually snarled, though his hands kept carefully stitching. "You want some truth?" he hissed, toward Simon's thigh. "Ach, here's some truth. John didn't betray his own kind when he did that, because I fucking *asked* him to do it. Hell"— Salvi drew the thread tight, making Simon grimace—"I *made* him do it."

The room seemed to snap back into silence, sudden and quavering—while both Tristan and Simon stared at Salvi, Tristan's gaze wide and unblinking, Simon's hazy, disapproving.

"You *make* John kill son," Simon repeated, his voice slurred. "How. *Why.*"

For an instant, Rosa thought Salvi surely wouldn't answer—but then he sat back on his heels, his threaded needle still carefully poised in his fingers, while he rubbed at his face with the back of his other hand. His eyes held not on Simon, but on *Tristan*.

"Look, I know all orcs are supposed to—to want sons," Salvi

said, wooden. "Our people are dying. Our *clan* is dying. So we're supposed to give up everything for sons, right? But"—his chest expanded—"I didn't want a son. I didn't want my mate. *None* of it. At *all*."

The silence skittered thicker, deeper, and no one spoke, or moved, apart from Tristan's wide, rapidly blinking eyes. And now Salvi was blinking too, his sharp white tooth visible against his lip.

"I just wanted you back, *sæti*," he said, in a whisper. "Fuck, I missed you. The way you *looked* at me, when I was with her. Gods, it was *torture*. And to see you turn to fucking *John*—"

Tristan's eyes shut, briefly, and Rosa could hear Salvi's inhale, rattling in his throat. "And she *knew*," he continued, hollow. "She told me she didn't want to have a son with someone who didn't love her like that. I could have tried to convince her, hide it better. But I didn't. I was just so fucking *relieved*."

The silence kept spinning out, wider and wider, until Salvi audibly swallowed, his throat convulsing. "So I went straight to Efterar," he said, quieter, "and of course, the bastard refused. Wouldn't even consider it. Because sons are everything, ach? So then I went to John, and when he refused too, I pushed it, I pushed him. I told him it was either that, or he loses me. *You* lose me. *Forever*."

Tristan's face spasmed, but he still didn't speak, and Salvi barked a laugh, low, bitter. "And John probably would have even let me off myself, if it came down to it—but we both know the way to make him do *anything* is to fuck with the people he's taking care of. To fuck with *you*, *sæti*. So he managed it all for me. Managed the captain, Efterar, *her*. Took all the heat for it, probably burned all his chances of becoming Priest for good. Because of *me*."

There was more stillness, broken by an odd gulping sound in Salvi's throat, his gaze snapping back down to his own slightly trembling fingers, again carefully drawing the thread through Simon's thigh. "And I hid it from you, *sæti*," he said, so quiet. "I didn't tell you, because I didn't *ever* want you to think it was your fault. It wasn't. It was *mine*."

Tristan still didn't answer, though there was visible wetness streaking down his cheeks in the lamplight, and Salvi still wasn't looking at him, his fingers pulling the thread through again, again.

"So there's your truth, Simon," he said, his voice bleak. "John was just taking care of our kind, beautiful, *incomparable* little teacher. Just like he's always done. Even if"—he barked another bitter laugh—"it means he has to take it up the arse from Skai pricks like you. *Again*."

The stillness felt different, suddenly, even heavier than before, as if that last statement had been some kind of—*challenge*. A challenge Simon didn't seem to want to meet, somehow, his eyes dropping to Salvi's slow, methodical stitching on his thigh.

"Ach, don't pretend you didn't know, Simon," Salvi continued, rough, raw. "It was the Skai scouts' favourite secret stop for *years*. The far eastern camp with the three weak, pretty, fatherless Ka-esh, with their smooth faces and easy words. Almost like women, weren't we?"

Rosa had almost felt somewhere else, someone else, as Salvi's voice had spoken—but with those last words, so pointed, so *broken*, it was as though the horror had smashed through the blunted distance of her thoughts, coiling deep in her gut.

That couldn't be true. Not about Tristan and Salvi. Not about *John*. But he'd said—hadn't he said—*wait*—

"Skai *wrong*, to do this to you," Simon said finally, forcefully, his gaze still on his thigh. "I never allow such wrong. Not since I am Enforcer. I maim any Skai who have *whisper* of this. Whether this wrong done now, or many summers past."

Salvi barked another brittle laugh, and bent to bite off his thread, spitting the loose end onto the stone floor. "That's true," he said, as he again grasped for the waterskin, pouring it out over what now appeared to be a small, clean red line across Simon's thigh, a vast contrast from the bloody gash it had been before. "I'll give you that, Simon, for free, because you *have* done all that. But what about the *actual* women? What about the women hidden in your own camps? The women you pretend don't exist, who keep *dying* bearing your sons? Many of them with no fucking *need*, just because you're too fucking stubborn and stupid and *paranoid* to let us give them any proper medical care that isn't fucking *magic*?!"

Salvi's voice had risen as he spoke, bellowing through the room. Enough that even he looked shocked, and in a single shaky movement, he hurled away the rag he'd begun scrubbing his hands with, and leapt to his feet.

"Fuck," he gasped, whirling toward the door. "*Fuck*, I need a run, a hunt, I just—"

But behind him Tristan had jerked to his feet too, bodily lurching toward him—and Salvi whipped around, just in time to catch Tristan, to fold him close into his heaving chest.

"Ach, *sæti*," Salvi breathed, into Tristan's hair. "You ought to scream at me. Scorn me. I have held back all these truths from you. For *so long*."

But Tristan didn't yell, didn't scorn. Only buried his face into Salvi's tunic, his shoulders shuddering, his hand clenching at Salvi's back. "You are a fool, *elskan*," he whispered. "A stupid, *stupid* fool."

Salvi's whole body seemed to sag into Tristan's, his arms wrapping tighter around him, his head bending into his neck. "I know," he replied, soft. "*Ég elska þig, sæti minn. Fyrirgefðu mér.*"

I love you, my sweet, it meant. *Forgive me.*

Tristan was nodding fervently into Salvi's chest, his leaking eyes squeezed shut. Dragging in multiple long, deep breaths, until he finally drew backwards, wiping at his face.

"Now go hunt, *elskan*," Tristan said, flashing Salvi a small, twitching smile. "Well away from any humans, ach? And I shall be waiting here when you come back. As always."

It sounded like a promise, like something that extended far beyond just this moment, and Salvi seemed to know it too, his head giving a jerky nod, his eyes unusually bright.

"And I shall always return," he said, as his trembling hands fumbled for Tristan's face, tilting it up toward his. "Always, *sæti*. To you. Only you. For as long as you'll have me. This, I"—his throat convulsed—"I vow to you, Tristan of Clan Ka-esh."

Tristan nodded back, his eyes locked to Salvi's, another streak of wetness slipping down his cheek—and then Salvi ducked his head, and kissed him. Hard, thorough, desperate, as though all the world depended upon it, and maybe, in this moment, it did.

When they pulled apart again, Tristan looked stunned, dazed, blinking—and also happier than Rosa had ever seen him, his mouth curving into a slow, truly stunning smile. "Thought you were going for a hunt, *elskan*," he murmured, his hands sliding up Salvi's chest to curl around his neck. "Bring me back a taste?"

"Ach, I'll bring you more than a taste, my hungry *sæti*," Salvi said, with a wink, and a purposeful grasp of his hand against Tristan's arse. And after another hard kiss to Tristan's mouth, Salvi spun around with surprising speed, shoved open the stone door, and took off. Leaving Tristan standing there, flushed and smiling, with a visible bulge in his still-bloody trousers.

It was almost as though Rosa's happiness had risen throughout all this, blooming to match theirs—but suddenly, the sight of Tristan's trousers, of all the foolish things, set her heart plummeting again. Tristan and Salvi had—settled matters, maybe. But she was still unsettled, unwanted, uncared for. John had still seduced her, and used her, and then thrown her away, for good.

He'd still *lied*, just like Salvi had. He'd still made all those promises, those vows with no words, and *broken* them. He hadn't *cared*.

Rosa distantly felt something warm sink down beside her—Tristan—and his knee bumped against her own, companionable, kind. "How fare you, Rosa-Ka?" he asked. "I am sorry to have drawn you into all this."

Rosa's mouth made a strange noise, something like a laugh. "Don't apologize, Tristan," she said, her voice thin. "I'm so happy for you both. And you didn't draw me into anything, I'm the one who dragged *you* into this whole mess. I should have"—she pulled at her hair—"I should have thought. Done it properly. I should have gone to Jule, and gotten supplies and scouts and things, I know she would have helped me, I should never have put this kind of thing on *you*—"

Tristan's knee bumped against hers again, harder this time. "Stop this, Rosa-Ka," he cut in, his voice firm. "You are one of us. You are John-Ka's mate. We are glad to help you."

But Rosa felt perilously close to weeping, and she shook her head, wrapped her arms around her knees. "You shouldn't, Tristan," she choked. "You shouldn't, because I'm *not*. I *lied* to John. I betrayed him, and I betrayed *you*. And in return, he betrayed *me*. And maybe"—she gulped back air—"I might have even *deserved* it, Tristan."

Tristan didn't answer this time, didn't offer approval or condemnation, so Rosa kept talking, feeling her way, seeking her truth. "Because I just kept on lying to him," she whispered. "He asked me. He gave me a chance to tell him. He *wanted* me to tell him. And I didn't. I just kept hiding. *Lying*."

Tristan still didn't speak, just listened, and Rosa scrubbed at her wet eyes. "I just wanted to pretend," she breathed. "I wanted to believe it was real. That he really cared, and I was really his—his *pet*. That it wasn't just about me spying. Or him not wanting my *blood* on his hands."

Beside Rosa Tristan made a huffing sound, his shoulder nudging against hers. "John-Ka is not one to oft speak of such things," he said, his voice soft. "But I am sure it was not only this, for him. He would not have tended to you as he did, had you meant naught to him. He would not have allowed you into his library. He would not have granted you such freedom in our home, or answered so many of your questions. He would *never*"—his shoulder bumped hers again—"have traded away a fortnight of his own suppers, to gain you *honey* for a single breakfast."

Rosa couldn't help a tentative, darting glance toward him—*surely* John hadn't done that?—but the look in Tristan's eyes clearly suggested otherwise. "John-Ka will give much for those he cares for," he said, resolute. "He will give *all*."

Rosa's eyes clenched shut, thinking of Salvi's words from earlier, and she knew Tristan was thinking of it too. "John-Ka gave all for me, and for Salvi," he continued, his voice lowering. "I know he shall do the same for his mate, and his son."

Rosa twitched a convulsive grimace, a frantic shake of her head. "He sent me away," she said, her voice frayed, pleading. "He said he would make me meet with Lord Kaspar. Alone. He"—she shivered, her head ducking closer into her knees— "he threw Lord Kaspar in my face. I *told* him what Lord Kaspar did to me, I *trusted* him with that, and he—"

She couldn't finish, couldn't bear to, and beside her Tristan let out a sigh, slow, regretful. "John-Ka ought not to have done this," he said. "I cannot excuse this. But"—he sighed again— "this is also, mayhap, all he has known. To defeat a monster, John-Ka throws its truth back in its face. He wins his battles not by strength, but by *knowledge*."

Knowledge. Knowledge, to defeat a monster. A monster like Lord Kaspar. The Skai. Rosa. *Himself.*

Knowledge informs new choices, new actions. Knowledge changes us, if we'll accept it. Knowledge changes everything.

Rosa's head was shaking, her eyes welling with prickling dangerous heat. She couldn't. She *couldn't.* John had lied, he hadn't cared, he'd yelled at her and betrayed her and chased her away from him.

And without John, without Lord Kaspar, what *was* Rosa? *Who* was she? A cheap strumpet with a ruined future, a prattling pest who asked too many questions, a bald-faced *liar.* And now, apparently, the foolish, would-be mother of an orc's son, lost and worthless, when the orc himself had promised no falsehoods, had promised to keep her safe, and then—

It was too much to bear, too much knowledge, thick enough to choke and *die* on—and Rosa finally bowed her head, covered her eyes, and wept.

33

It was a long, dark, dismal night. Broken only by Rosa's bitter, muffled sobs, erupting out of her without pattern or warning, while she fought and failed to find some semblance of sleep on the hard stone floor.

Salvi returned sometime in the night, bringing both Tristan and Simon huge chunks of raw meat, and once they'd finished eating, Salvi had pushed Tristan down, and licked the blood from his lips. And then they'd lain there together, whispering and casting occasional meaningful glances toward Rosa, until she'd finally fallen asleep again, her body curled tight in her cloak.

When she next awoke, there was a faint stream of light shining through a distant crack in the ceiling, and Simon was sitting up beside her, drinking from a waterskin. He was still coated with a thick layer of crusty-looking blood, but he otherwise looked well enough, and after gazing at Rosa for a moment, he actually passed her the waterskin, his eyes unreadable.

Rosa couldn't help giving it a dubious look, but she *was* thirsty, so she drank her fill, and even managed a nod of thanks. Earning a nod in return that seemed almost approving, before Simon leaned back against the wall, and purposefully flicked his eyes across the room. Toward where Tristan and Salvi were wrapped together under a cloak, Salvi's bare shoulders rippling as he rocked over Tristan, their faces buried in one another's necks.

They hadn't seemed to notice that Rosa had awoken, and her bleary eyes couldn't seem to move away from the sight. From how Salvi's throat was slowly, leisurely swallowing, pulling gentle draughts from Tristan's neck, while Tristan's long eyelashes fluttered, his claws softly scoring Salvi's bare back, his breath coming in hoarse little gasps.

"Kind teacher so sweet, in his joy," Simon said to Rosa, with surprising mournfulness. "*Wasted* on loud, rude healer."

Salvi's hand snapped out of the cloak to give Simon a lewd gesture, even as he kept sucking on Tristan's neck—but Tristan's eyes had flown open, his ears rapidly turning pink, his head jerking toward Rosa. Again being so considerate of her, as always, and Rosa's rueful smile at him felt warm, surprisingly genuine.

"Don't you dare stop on my account, Tristan," she said. "Simon's right. You two are lovely together."

Beside Rosa, Simon let out a loud, disapproving growl—to which Salvi raised his head from Tristan's punctured neck, and dragged his bloody tongue against his swollen lips, slow, deliberate, taunting.

"He's *mine*, Skai," he said, with vicious satisfaction, rolling his hips against Tristan's under the cloak, wringing a harsh, hungry gasp from Tristan's throat. "Watch, you great arse, and *weep.*"

Simon snarled back at him, but he didn't actually argue—not even as Salvi hurled away the cloak altogether, baring their lean, powerful bodies to the room's cool air. And as Rosa watched, oddly breathless, Salvi's hips again ground between

Tristan's parted thighs, while Tristan arched up toward him, meeting him, his arms and legs clutched tight against the rippling lines of Salvi's back, against his rounded muscular arse.

"This pleases you, ach, *sæti minn*?" Salvi murmured to Tristan. "You like being fucked slow and deep by your bonded mate? By the first prick you ever had, and now your last, also?"

This was said with a dark glance toward Simon, but Tristan's clawed hands turned Salvi's face back to his, their long black tongues twining together as Tristan's hips arched up, meeting Salvi's circle down, again, again, again. As though this were an easy, fluid, familiar dance they'd long ago learned, their joined bodies rocking, rising, flowing as one.

And when Salvi drew back to his haunches, dragging Tristan's lower half up onto his lap, they didn't miss a beat, still circling, parting, meeting again. Though the sight of it was far more vivid now, with Tristan's bare front entirely exposed, his lean muscles flexing and relaxing, his long, slim, dripping cock flaring straight up with every thrust of Salvi's hips.

Beside Rosa Simon had let out a strangled groan, his huge hand clutched against his own tented groin, and in this moment Rosa could almost feel it too, the longing licking hunger, lighting the room as a flame. Sparking higher and stronger with every breath, as Salvi's strokes became harder, longer, as Rosa could now see his slick, thick length, plunging with depth and power beneath Tristan's thighs.

"Fuck, *sæti*," Salvi gasped, his half-lidded eyes roving up and down Tristan's bare front, lingering on his smoothly flaring cock, then on his reddened cheeks, his parted lips, his long-lashed blinking eyes. "Fuck, you're beautiful. Feels so fucking *good*."

Tristan replied with a quivery flick of his fingers, the movement at total odds with the fluid thrusts of his hips, the steady ooze of white from his pulsing cock. And at the sight Salvi groaned, his grip shifting on Tristan's thighs—and then he rolled onto his back, drawing Tristan's arching body up with him. So that Tristan was now the one straddling him, shaking loose his long black hair as he settled his hands to Salvi's heaving chest, their hips still rolling, meeting, writhing in their fluent, unbroken rhythm.

But the sight of this was even more obscene, especially with Tristan's flushed, steadily leaking length now bobbing blatant and rock-hard over Salvi's rippled abdomen—and with how Salvi's hands were sliding down into the pooling liquid with something almost like reverence. As one slick, clawless hand then caressed all the way up to Tristan's mouth, slipping two fingers between his parted lips, while the other hand circled familiar, gentle, around the base of Tristan's pulsing prick. And then sliding up, milking out more spluttering white, in perfect time with his own slow, smooth, sensuous thrusts inside.

Tristan's back had arched, his mouth sucking on Salvi's fingers, his face reddened and rapturous—and Salvi kept going, working Tristan with his hips and his hands, his hooded gaze glittering, intent on Tristan's face. And when Tristan's eyes fluttered fully closed, Salvi swiftly curled himself up, bending his upper half almost double, so he could somehow— impossibly—suck Tristan's slick, leaking cockhead into his mouth.

Tristan's shocked, guttural moan hissed through the room, his eyes flying open, drinking in the raw, thrilling sight of his lover fucking him, sucking him, stroking him, and plundering his mouth, all at the same time. Not once losing their rhythm, their own mesmerizing dance, and beside Rosa Simon muttered a low, frustrated curse, his eyes fixed on Tristan's bobbing cock, now plunging in and out between Salvi's tight sucking lips.

"Braggart healer," he said, with deep disapproval. "Skinny body make easy. *Spoil* pretty teacher thus."

But Rosa couldn't at all begrudge Tristan's being spoiled, not if it made him look like this, sound like this. His body lean and smooth and rippling, covered with a faint sheen of sweat. His thick black hair swinging out behind him, falling long over his shoulders. His cheeks and pointed ears brightly flushed, his mouth desperately sucking on Salvi's fingers, his hips rocking to meet Salvi's with such fervent, fluid grace. And his throat moaning, dark and deep, as his cock swelled fuller between Salvi's lips, his hands sinking into Salvi's hair—

And suddenly Tristan's moans rose, sharp, almost a scream—and the rhythm paused, frozen in place, as his whole body seemed to light up, crackling with warmth and fire and sheer sparking craving—

His shaft abruptly, visibly pulsed, clearly flooding Salvi's mouth full of his hunger, while Salvi's throat thickly, greedily swallowed, his own hips wrenching up once more, hard, vehement—and then he was moaning too, frantically swallowing, even as his groin shuddered and strained against Tristan, pouring himself out deep inside.

There was one last instant's stillness, held there, hanging—until finally Tristan sank down, as Salvi deftly uncoiled, quick enough to catch Tristan's limp-looking weight in his arms. And then they sagged to the floor, Salvi on his back and Tristan sprawled on top, their heavy breaths rising and falling together, like a sweeter, softer dance that still belonged only to them.

Salvi's hands had begun stroking Tristan's back, his hair, his face—and when Tristan made a soft whimpering sound, Salvi bared his own neck, and gently bent Tristan's head toward it. A silent offer that Tristan immediately accepted, his teeth clamping down, his eyelids fluttering as he swallowed.

"Take all you like, *sæti minn*," Salvi murmured, his hands still stroking, soothing, caressing. "Anytime you like. You sweet, stunning creature. Fuck, I adore you."

An answering shiver rippled down Tristan's back, hard

enough that Salvi's visibly softened length slipped out of him entirely. Exposing first Tristan's used, stretched-open body, and then a thick stream of white, streaking down his muscled arse-cheek.

Tristan didn't even twitch, as if he didn't even care that Rosa and Simon were seeing such shocking things. As if there was truly no shame in being fucked, flaunted, *satisfied*. And Rosa couldn't stop staring, suddenly, while beside her Simon huffed out another low, strangled-sounding groan.

"*Wasted*," he said again, voice flat. "Though I grant this to healer, he know how to please teacher. He *cherish*, as he should."

Rosa silently nodded, but beneath the shock and the whispering hunger, there was, again, the misery. The misery that had been her constant, awful companion throughout this entire journey, twisting deeper with every hour that passed. With every hour that John wasn't there to touch her like that, or look at her like that, or even show her off like that, because he'd sent her away. Because she'd lied to him. And he'd lied to her.

And looking at Tristan's languid, beautiful body, Rosa couldn't help another dark thought, surprisingly bitter. John had done this with Tristan, too, hadn't he? And Tristan had looked like that, and maybe they'd had their own secret rhythm, and John might have slapped his pretty arse, made him obey—

"Ach, Rosa, I can smell you vexing," Salvi said, out of nowhere, his head turning, his hazy eyes fixing to her face. "Don't worry, Tristan was *never* this good with John. Right, *sœti*?"

He spoke with surprising arrogance, and Rosa blinked at the sight of Tristan's fervent little nod of agreement. Though his eyes still hadn't opened, his mouth not budging from Salvi's neck.

"He was always pushing you too much," Salvi said, his gaze

back on Tristan's messy dark head, his hands still gently stroking. "Always wanting to be in charge, put you in your place. Never following your lead."

Tristan nodded again, still not opening his eyes, and Rosa's twisting brain assessed the truth of that, of what she'd just seen. It hadn't been Salvi dominating, or pushing. It had been Tristan setting the pace, without words, and Salvi meeting him, matching him. *Tristan will weep*, John had said, *if I even…*

And blinking toward them, Rosa's jealousy seemed to settle again, even as the misery surged higher to take its place. Because unlike Tristan, she'd liked that about John. Gods, she'd *loved* that about him. His easy, commanding authority, so instinctive, so assured. Wanting to dominate her, wanting to show her off, to make her obey. Wanting to be her lord.

And she'd wanted it too. Wanted to be directed, flaunted, used, *enjoyed*. Wanted to be his pet.

"Although," Salvi continued, a little darker now, his eyes flicking toward Simon, "maybe we can't really blame John for that, can we? Considering who all *taught* him to be that way?"

Simon visibly winced, and Rosa winced too, her gaze dropping to her hands. Her thoughts swarming, suddenly, with another truth, bitter and uncomfortable and… surprising.

John's desires had, maybe, been shaped by his own past, too. By horrible, unjust things that hadn't been in his control. But he hadn't given way to guilt, or shame, for who he was now. *I ought not to feel shame for the deeds of others*, he'd said. *My deeds, and my wishes, are my own.*

Rosa could hear Simon's slow sigh, heavy with regret. "Even Enforcer," he said, "cannot put right all past wrongs. But"—he sighed again—"after this, I seek to sway Skai, of women in camps. Seek to grant Ka-esh leave to come, and give care."

Salvi's head twisted to fully stare at Simon, his eyes wide with genuine astonishment, and even Tristan had briefly stopped swallowing, his dazed eyes blinking at Simon's face.

And Simon wasn't looking at either of them, his gaze fixed intently on his thigh, still exposed through his ripped-apart trousers. Still showing the red line of his wound, held together by Salvi's neat stitching.

And here, suddenly, was more understanding, filtering into Rosa's brain. Simon was afraid, too. Afraid, maybe, that the Ka-esh might take revenge for what the Skai had done to them. *We no show our women no pretty, smooth-speaking Ka-esh. So you no steal.*

"Would it help," Rosa said, stilted, "if another woman came along, too? To meet your mates, and help care for them?"

Simon's glance at her was narrow, suspicious. "Not help," he snapped, "if woman *kill* own son. If woman next offer this to others."

His frowning gaze flicked to Rosa's waist, and she rolled her eyes at him, even as her hand stole to her belly, her fingers spreading wide, almost protective. "I already told you," she shot back, "my son isn't going anywhere. Also, maybe you need to accept that not every woman is going to want to go through with a terrifying and potentially deadly birth—and that's probably *never* going to change. But the safer you can make them, and the better partners you can be to them"—she jabbed her finger toward Simon—"the more likely they'll be to want to bear your sons. And, according to our research, the more likely they are to survive it, too."

Simon was still frowning at her, but he almost seemed to be considering it, his head tilting. "Then why *you* wish for son?" he demanded. "*John* good partner? Make you *safe*?"

It sounded like a taunt, like he was mocking her, because clearly John had sent her away, and then they'd been chased by men, and nearly *killed*—but Rosa swallowed back the thickness in her throat, and nodded. "He was," she said, her voice a whisper. "He was so thoughtful, and thorough, and *kind*. He made me feel safe. Wanted. Worthy. At *peace*."

No one spoke, and Rosa rubbed irritably at her blinking, prickling eyes. The misery rising and swerving again, this time dragging up her own words, her own shame, the awful things she'd thrown in John's face.

I'm not an orc. I don't run around lying, and fucking with other people's affections, and beating on people I'm supposed to care about. I'm a human, for fuck's sakes, I'm not a monster.

And worst, maybe, of it all: *No, you prick. I didn't know. You said nothing. You didn't tell me.*

But Rosa *had* known. About her pregnancy, about John wanting her to stay, wanting to make her his mate. He hadn't said it aloud, no, but he'd still made it very clear. And rather than asking the simple question to make it even clearer, Rosa had stayed silent. She hadn't spoken truth, either. Just like Salvi, she hadn't made a vow, because then there was nothing to break.

You only do not like to admit such things, John had told her that day, in his bed. *Thus it is not your truth to bear.*

Rosa's eyes were fully leaking now, streaking yet more wetness down her cheeks, and she didn't wipe at it this time. Just let it come, let herself face all the miserable, painful truths she'd been hiding from. Truths not just about John, but about herself.

She'd spied. She'd lied. She'd betrayed. She'd taken the secrets of someone she cared about, and used them in anger to hurt him. She'd been afraid. Afraid of her past, her future.

And yet, too, she'd cared. She'd learned. She'd gained incredible, impossible amounts of knowledge. She'd found a new library, new friends, new ideas she'd never before considered. She'd even found the courage, maybe, to start facing her truths. She wanted to learn. She wanted to be mastered. She wanted to seek her joy, without shame, without regret.

Knowledge changes us, if we'll accept it. Knowledge changes everything.

"Do not fear, Rosa-Ka," cut in Tristan's voice, and when she blinked up, he was looking at her with genuine concern, his brow furrowed, his lips still stained a deep red. "John-Ka shall not stop caring for you, even if you are now parted. He shall never stop."

He said that with utmost certainty, knowing it because he'd *lived* it, and Rosa took a shuddery breath—and nodded. Agreeing, finally, because even now, this room, this moment, with these orcs—even the fact that Rosa was still alive, still safe— would be because John still cared.

And maybe—maybe—it was high time for someone to care for *him*.

"Are we close to Dusbury now?" Rosa asked, lifting her chin, wiping at her wet cheeks. "Will we get there today?"

"Before noontide," Simon said, his voice curt. "If woman's little legs keep up."

Rosa flashed him the same lewd gesture Salvi had used earlier, but felt her head again nodding, her determination circling tight. John had made a mess of this, but so had she. And she was going to take care of it. She was going to take care of the people, the home, the *life*, they both cared about.

My deeds, and my wishes, are my own.

"Good," she said firmly. "Then I want you to take me to the north side of town. I'm paying a long-overdue visit to Lady Scall."

34

I   f Lady Scall was shocked by the sudden appearance of a muddy, bloody librarian in her fine sitting-room, she certainly didn't show it.

"To what do I owe this... call?" she said, once she'd shut the door behind them, and glided to sit in an overstuffed chair across the room. She was wearing a simple riding-dress, rather than the exquisite confection she'd sported last time they'd met, though the look on her face was perhaps just as pinched, just as disapproving.

But Rosa had spent weeks in Orc Mountain, dealing with unnerving and cantankerous orcs on a daily basis. And after that, it felt almost easy to hold her eyes to Lady Scall's, to speak.

"I need to talk to you," she said. "About Lord Kaspar."

Lady Scall's eyebrows arched up, her manicured hands folding together in her lap. "Do you."

"Yes," Rosa said firmly. "You ought to know that Lord Kaspar's been sleeping with me. Since I was fifteen. He came to my school, and"—she took a deep breath—"told the headmaster he needed someone small and unobtrusive to help him in his library. He picked me out of a *lineup*."

Lady Scall's face was a mask, suddenly, impossible to read, but this was Rosa's truth, she was speaking it, she could. "At first, I thought he loved me," she continued, with a bitter little laugh. "He let me believe that—wanted me to believe that. But then I learned the truth. I was just one of many, many women. He sleeps with his housemaids. With his acquaintances. With courtesans. He has multiple mistresses. Multiple illegitimate children that he refuses to recognize or support."

Lady Scall still hadn't moved, or acknowledged any of this, and Rosa drew in more breath, more truth. "But I *am* still special to him," she said, quieter. "Enough that he told me, that day he brought you to the library, that he would never give me up once he married you. Because"—Rosa swallowed hard, she could say it—"I'm small, and obliging, and good with my mouth. But most of all, because I've been researching and writing most of his academic papers for the past half-decade."

Lady Scall's face had begun to look rather pale, but Rosa wasn't done. "I recently went on an unexpected journey," she said, "without telling Lord Kaspar exactly where I'd gone. And do you know what he did? He somehow rustled up two entire regiments, and rode there to rescue me. Not, I assure you"—she grimaced at the floor—"because he missed me that much. But because I was supposed to be writing the biggest paper of his career."

It almost hurt to say that last bit, because even now, part of Rosa had hoped that Lord Kaspar had truly cared, in some small way—but she'd had far too much time to think these past days, and to put together just what must have happened. Susan must have told Southall of John's appearance in the library, and then Rosa's sudden disappearance. Rosa's research—her books, her treatises, her papers—had all been left behind. And while Rosa's letters had sought to explain the situation, they'd been admittedly vague, and hastily written, and had likely been easily dismissed as being penned under duress. At the command of a cruel orc kidnapper, determined to foil Lord Kaspar's research, and his war.

Which had, perhaps, been at least a partial truth. Perhaps John *had* come to the library with the express intent of seducing her. And while the thought of that still clutched painfully in Rosa's belly, she couldn't even seem to muster the outrage anymore. This war was unjust. The men had been breaking the treaty, again and again, and had done so before Rosa's very eyes. And John would give all to keep safe those he cared for.

"The last time Kaspar wrote me," Lady Scall's voice finally said, very even, "he told me he'd been sent to *Orc Mountain.*"

Her eyes were narrow on Rosa's, the challenge of those words clear in the air between them, and Rosa nodded, slow. Truth.

"Yes," she said. "I indeed went to Orc Mountain. Would you like to hear how it happened?"

Lady Scall gave a jerky shrug, which Rosa took as a yes—so she sucked in a breath, and launched into the whole tale from the start. Finding John in the library. Her research, their frantic pleasure together, the bitter reality of the next morning. The escape. The mountain.

She spoke with as much coherency and urgency as she could muster, almost as though this were another scholarly presentation, perhaps the most crucial one of her life. She needed to convince Lady Scall. She needed to take care of John. She *needed* to stop this war.

When Rosa finally finished, maybe a full hour later, her face felt flushed, her breath shallow, her hands clutched instinctively to her waist. But Lady Scall had listened without interruption, her gaze now intent, searching, piercing.

"You know, I might not have believed you," she said abruptly, unexpectedly, "or even entertained you, or such a mad tale. If not for"—her hands twitched toward her dress pocket, and drew out a folded piece of paper—"for this."

She jerked up to hand it over, her steps not quite steady on the plush rug, and Rosa accordingly took the paper, and unfolded it. It was a letter from—Jule?

And yes, yes, it was, and it was dated to just the day before. And it was—Rosa's eyes scanned the page, her disbelief rising—it was a request for Lady Scall's *help*. It called upon their past friendship, and alluded to altered allegiances, and the atrocities committed by the men against their own treaty. It even introduced Rosa, suggesting that she may soon return to Dusbury, and that she was a dear friend of Jule's, as well as a bright and clever scholar—and might Lady Scall grant her the favour of a call, and keep an open mind toward whatever she might have to say?

"It appeared on my doorstep this morning," Lady Scall said, settling in her chair again, smoothing out her dress. "I haven't heard from Jule in over a year, though of course I'd heard the rumours, and hoped she was still alive and well. And now—"

She waved a wobbly hand toward Rosa, her mouth tight, her eyes bright—and suddenly Rosa realized that she appeared almost on the verge of weeping. This poised, rich, beautiful woman, looking just as bared and broken as Rosa felt.

"I'm so sorry to have upset you," Rosa said, quiet. "And I'm sorry I didn't tell you earlier. But I thought it was important for you to know. Because knowledge changes *everything*."

Lady Scall nodded, once, and visibly squared her shoulders, and met Rosa's eyes.

"I agree," she said. "Now, tell me what you need."

35

A week later, Rosa unlocked the door of the Dusbury Library, and stepped inside.

She wore an old but well-made dress—a castoff from one of Lady Scall's nieces—and clutched a stack of crisp papers to her chest. And her heart was thumping loudly and erratically, her gaze darting around at the familiar stacks, searching for any sign of movement or voices or breath—

But there was only silence. She was alone. For now.

Rosa sagged back against the closed door, shutting her eyes, clutching her papers tighter. It was her first time stepping foot into the library since her return to Dusbury—in fact, her first time out in public—but today was the day. Her three-week deadline had finally arrived, and today was when Lord Kaspar had promised to return.

And if Lady Scall's sources were correct, Lord Kaspar had indeed ridden into town just the night before. And soon, surely, he would come.

Rosa shoved her shaky form off the door, toward the familiar lending desk. Toward where—she froze, blinking—

her stack of orc research still sat, unmoved. Untouched. As if it had been awaiting her return, all this time.

The memories swarmed with sudden, vicious force, trampling past her eyes. John's sharp finger, dragging down the edge of the stack. His eyes, as he'd torn her dress down the middle, and thrown her onto this very desk. His voice, as he'd said all those words, those threats, those *promises*.

We mark you. With our claws, our teeth, our scent. We make you ours. Forever.

Rosa's eyes were prickling, for what felt like the thousandth time that week, and she squeezed them shut, fought to draw in breath. She'd stayed in regular contact with Tristan these past days, by means of a basket hidden in Lady Scall's garden—but there hadn't been a single mention of John in Tristan's letters, let alone any word from John himself. Even as the truth of what they'd made inside Rosa had begun to grow stronger and surer each day, between the quiet constant nausea, her increasingly tender breasts, and the unfamiliar hardness low in her belly.

Rosa's only foolish, desperate hope, of all things, had been the milk. The sweet, distinctive milk John had so consistently given her at the mountain, and which had continued to appear in their secret basket each morning. Hinting, perhaps, that John was arranging for them. Perhaps, somehow, he still cared.

But the more Rosa had ruminated over it these past days, the more despondent she'd become. She'd lied to John, again and again. She'd taken advantage of his hospitality and kindness. She'd had the audacity to castigate him for not sharing all his secrets, when she'd gone to his home with the express purpose of starting a *war*.

And at this point, all she could do was try. She could show John that she cared. She could do everything within her power to make amends for what she'd done.

Which meant—Rosa looked around at the library, and

drew in another bracing breath—she could face the truth. She could face Lord Kaspar.

She set her new pile of papers neatly on the lending desk, squaring off the edges, squaring her shoulders. She'd worked with an almost manic intensity this week, frantically writing and revising, pouring as much fervent persuasive truth into her words as she possibly could. She had a plan. This was her chance.

But suddenly—Rosa's head snapped up, her body struck still—there was a sound. A small, barely perceptible sound, from the back of the library. A sound like—like a *page turning*.

The fear stuttered and choked, Rosa's hands gripping desperately at the desk, because maybe—surely—it was Lord Kaspar. Lord Kaspar, already here, back in his little room, waiting for her. Perhaps even reading in bed, undressed, expecting her to come in, climb aboard, and—

Rosa had to clamp her hand over her mouth, drag in deep lungfuls of air, fight back the surging nausea. She could do this. She could face this.

She grasped for her stack of papers again, and then forced herself to step out from behind the desk, and down the aisle between the stacks. Step, after step, closer, closer, while the fear and the dread scraped and screamed—

But when she turned around the last shelf, it was like the world had skidded to a halt, teetering on a cliff-edge. Because it *wasn't* Lord Kaspar.

It was an orc. In the library. Reading.

It was *John*.

36

For a long, faltering moment, Rosa couldn't move, breathe, *think*. John was *here*. In the *library*. Reading a *book*.

His dark head was bent over the book, his face hidden in shadow—but as Rosa stared, frozen, he slowly lifted his head, and met her eyes. Looking unusually tired, with deep smudges under those eyes, faint lines around his mouth, an even sharper cut to his jaw and cheekbones. And his clawed hands closing the book, setting it aside, didn't bother to keep his place, as though he hadn't really been reading it at all.

Rosa's stomach was dangerously lurching, dragging her unsteady hand down to press against her waist—a movement that drew those eyes downward, too. Almost as if they could see through the papers she was still gripping, through her clothes and her very skin, to what was hidden beneath.

To their *son*.

John's gaze felt almost agonizing, suddenly, and Rosa clutched both hands back to her papers, and hauled in a shaky, stilted breath. John was here. John was *here*, good gods, she could say something, *something*—

"Um," she said, her voice thick. "You're here."

It was the stupidest comment, completely inane, but thankfully John didn't curl his lip, or roll his eyes, or any of the other things he might very well have done. Only nodded, quick and curt, as he crossed his arms over his chest, his fingers tight and pale against his grey tunic.

"Ach," he said finally. "Have you been well, woman?"

His voice was just as it had always been, low and even and smooth, but in this moment it felt more like a shout, or a slap. So painfully, brutally familiar, so close, and still so far away. Rosa had lied to him. Hurt him. *Betrayed* him.

"I've been—all right," she made herself say, though she couldn't quite hold her eyes to his stark, shadowed face. "I, um, I went to Lady Scall. Lord Kaspar's almost-fiancee, you know. And she's been shockingly kind, she's put me up in her home all this time, and fed and clothed me, and told everyone I'm her long-lost cousin who's gotten into some, um, trouble"—she gave a vague, stuttery wave at her waist—"so everyone's mostly left me alone, which has been such a *relief*. And she's even helped me stay in touch with Tristan every day, and she hasn't been judgemental at *all*, and it's so *foolish* that I hated her so much, when really—"

Rosa was babbling, she realized, too late, and as she forcibly clamped her mouth shut, she also realized she *knew* the way John was looking at her. So blank, so intentionally careful, but still somehow betraying that none of this was new to him. And wait, that meant he knew *everything*, and of course he did, he was *John*, and—

Rosa's eyes were prickling again, and she impatiently scrubbed at one, and dragged in another bracing breath. She could do this. She could.

"I'm sorry, John," she said, her voice cracking. "Gods, I'm so sorry. For spying on you. Lying to you. For"—she gulped in more air—"for saying all those horrible things to you, the day I left. For calling you a *monster*."

John didn't speak, didn't move, and Rosa hugged her papers closer, grasped for words, for truth. "I was wrong," she said. "I was wrong to judge you, and throw your past in your face. I was wrong to accuse you of lying to me, when I'd been lying to you the entire time. I was wrong to pretend I didn't know things you'd made very clear to me."

John's dark lashes blinked, once, but his eyes were still flat, distant, a mask. Meaning, maybe, he truly didn't care anymore, maybe it was too late, but Rosa had to keep going, keep getting it out. "I *knew*," she said, through the growing lump in her throat. "I knew you wanted me to stay. I knew I was pregnant. And of course I knew you weren't a monster, you were so gods-damned *kind* to me. You fed me and bathed me and clothed me. You gave me important work and the freedom to do it how I wished. You helped me learn and grow. You called me a *scholar*."

Nothing changed or moved in his face, and Rosa's nausea roiled again, her eyes dropping to the table before him. She could say this. She could tell him the truth.

"And you taught me," she managed, "how to accept my desires, rather than being ashamed of them. You taught me to face my past, rather than pretending it didn't happen. You showed me I was still worthy, despite all that. You gave me—*peace*."

There was only more silence, shuddering bleak and pained around them, and Rosa forced her eyes back up, back to his unreadable face. "You were a brilliant lord, John-Ka," she whispered. "I *loved* being your pet. I'll never, *ever* forget it."

A streak of wetness escaped her eye, slipped down her cheek, and she dashed it away with a trembly hand. "I'm so sorry," she choked out. "*Mér þykir þetta svo leitt.* I hope, someday, you might be able to forgive me."

And that was it, that was everything she'd needed to say, and she held herself still, dropped her blinking eyes back to the table. Waiting, bracing herself, for him to say something, anything, and what if he didn't, what if he was truly done, what if this was just *goodbye*—

"Ach," John said finally, and when Rosa's eyes darted up, he was rubbing his mouth, his eyes shifting, glimmering with something she couldn't name. "Ach, pet. I—"

His words broke at the sudden deafening bang—the library *door* slamming open—and Rosa jumped, her heart reeling, her skin crawling with a surging, trammelling fear. It couldn't be. Not yet. Not now. Please…

"Rosa!" called a familiar, gut-churning voice, laced with unmistakable anger. "Come out and explain yourself. At once!"

37

Lord Kaspar had arrived.

Rosa's eyes squeezed shut, and for a horrible, hurtling instant, she didn't know whether she might faint, or scream, or vomit all over her feet.

Lord Kaspar was here. She would face this. She would.

Before her John's seated body had stiffened, his eyes narrow, glinting, dangerous. And wait, there was an *orc* in the library, and Lord Kaspar was here, if he found out there would be guards, blood, *death*—

But John didn't move from behind the table. Only raised a single finger to his lips, his meaning very clear—so Rosa swallowed hard, gave a jerky nod, and then forced her heavy-feeling feet to move. To walk back through the stacks, her hands shaky and sweaty on her papers, her heart jamming her throat.

Lord Kaspar stood beside the lending desk, facing away from Rosa, his fingers tapping impatiently against his thigh. He was dressed in travelling-clothes, his boots smeared with mud, and his dark hair had grown longer than usual, curling over his ears. And in another world, another life, Rosa might have stolen up behind him, slipped her arms around his slim waist, and said, *how might I serve you, my lord?*

But today, Rosa felt her feet scrape to a stop a good distance away, well out of Lord Kaspar's reach. While he slowly turned to face her, tall and imperious and undeniably beautiful, and flicked a tight, chilly glance all the way down her body, and back up again.

"You did return, after all," he said finally, calmly, though palpable anger glinted in those lovely grey eyes. "You'd best have something *very* impressive for me, love. And one *hell* of an explanation."

His gaze felt like a tangible force, and Rosa fought against it, raised her chin. "What do I need to explain?" she asked, with creditable steadiness. "You ordered me to research the orcs, and take whatever measures were required. So I did."

Lord Kaspar's mouth spasmed, barking a sound that might have been a laugh. "So you *did* go voluntarily to that hellhole," he said, his voice thick with contempt. "Good gods, Rosa, I thought you were *kidnapped*. Because surely even *you* couldn't possibly be fool enough to believe a *lord* would ever order his *mistress* to go to *Orc Mountain*, for *research*!"

His mistress. *Fool* enough. Words that shouldn't have been a surprise, but still crackled with a misery that took Rosa's breath away. Enough that her own words felt locked in her throat, her body pinned in place, as Lord Kaspar came a swift, dangerous step closer.

"So if you truly *chose* to go to Orc Mountain," he said, very evenly, as he reached into his coat pocket, "then what the *fuck* did you mean by *this*?!"

This. It was a letter. One that looked very familiar, and when Lord Kaspar snapped it open, Rosa's heart clenched at the glimpse of her own script, written in neat lines across the page.

"*To Lord Kaspar*," he read aloud, in a crisp voice. "*I write to inform you that I will not be returning to Dusbury, or to my work at the library. I have found a new life, with new work, new friends, and a new partner who truly respects and cares for me. I do not expect we will meet again. Farewell."*

Rosa swallowed, but didn't move, and Lord Kaspar tossed the letter onto the lending desk, and came another step closer. "I've spent almost *two weeks* camped at that hovel, trying to *rescue* you," he hissed. "And for my *extraordinary* efforts on your behalf, I get this?! What the hell kind of game are you playing, Rosa! Did the orcs *force* you to write that?!"

There was a slight waver in his voice, something Rosa couldn't ever recall hearing from him before, and she made herself hold his gaze, take a thick breath. She could tell the truth. She could.

"The orcs didn't force me to do anything," she said, quiet but sure. "The letter was true. I was happy there. I wanted to stay."

Lord Kaspar's eyes goggled at her, his mouth dropping open, and he sharply shook his head, as though he'd badly misheard. "You wanted to *stay*," he repeated, enunciating each word. "With the orcs. With this—*partner*. An *orc*. Who, I presume, has also been *fucking* you this entire time?!"

Rosa wasn't talking about that with Lord Kaspar, she would *not*—but the look on her face must have spoken anyway, because he gaped at her for another hurtling instant, the disgust and disdain flaring across his furious eyes.

"Good gods, Rosa," he said, as he lurched another step closer. "Have you lost your fucking *mind*? You deliberately misunderstand my orders, you humiliate me, you waste two weeks of my *extremely* busy life—and now you spout off with this utter *insanity*?! You wanted to leave me, a *lord*, so you could go live in *Orc Mountain*, and fuck a disgusting illiterate *beast*?!"

His hand snapped out as he spoke, grasping tight at Rosa's chin. "Last chance, you fool wench," he said flatly. "You need to get on your knees, right now, and *beg* me for my mercy. And you also need to present me with a research paper so explosive, it will blow that entire fucking mountain to *ash*, without my lifting another fucking *finger!*"

The fear that had been pooling in Rosa's belly was steadily rising, clanging against her chest—but deeper still was her own determination, her own fusing contempt. And beyond that, somewhere, was—John. John, still here, in the library, hiding, listening, waiting. And no matter what happened here, John would keep her safe. He *would*.

"Look, I'm sorry if I've alarmed you, or wasted your time," Rosa said finally, to Lord Kaspar's furious eyes. "But I will not beg you for *anything*. Because"—truth, *truth*—"this needs to be over, between us. It should have been over long ago, once I realized what it truly was. You've been manipulating me, and taking advantage of me, for years. It's *finished*."

The shock in his eyes felt visceral, truly aghast, as though no one had dared speak such things to him before—and before he could counter it, Rosa kept going, getting it out. "And I don't have a research paper for you," she said firmly. "I don't have any new information, any new atrocities or scandals. The orcs are not what we say they are. They are different, yes, with a different culture, a different language, a different way of living together. But *none* of it was worth a war. *None* of it is worth breaking this treaty."

Lord Kaspar was still staring, his hand gone slack on Rosa's chin, and she drew in more breath, more courage. "We *humans* are the ones breaking the treaty," she said. "I saw it with my own eyes. I witnessed multiple acts of unwarranted aggression against orcs, and heard reliable accounts of many more. It needs to stop. *You* need to stop it."

There was a strange twitch on Lord Kaspar's face, in the clutch of his fingers on her skin. "Do I," he replied, his voice thick. "Do explain *how*, Rosa."

A sudden, skittering hope whispered in Rosa's gut, and she held his eyes, made her voice as convincing as she could. "You need to go to your father," she said, "and the other lords on that Council, and tell them just what I've told you. There are no atrocities. There's been no new aggression from the orcs. *We're* the oppressors. *We're* the ones who have been breaking the treaty. This foolish attempt at another war is a complete waste of your time and money, and there are far more important matters to address. Like"—she squared her shoulders—"taking care of the peasants like me across the realm who've been suffering for *years*, thanks to the nobility's neglect and injustice and cruelty and greed. *That* is the true atrocity here. *That* is the scandal. *Not* the orcs."

Lord Kaspar's face convulsed again, twisting into something Rosa didn't recognize, and for another hurtling instant the hope rose, stretched, spread wide—and then spattered into dust, as Lord Kaspar laughed. *Laughed*, with true, brilliant, callous mirth dancing across his lovely eyes.

"Oh, *Rosa*," he said, between guffaws. "You truly have lost your silly little mind. I suppose the orcs fucking you likely broke your sanity altogether. I should have known better"—his laughter faded, his head tilting—"than to expect true mental fortitude from an ill-bred peasant woman, no matter how clever you pretended to be."

His eyes had narrowed slightly, his hand gripping tighter on her face. Sparking the fear again, raw and virulent, shuddering under Rosa's skin.

"But," he said slowly, "perhaps you could still be of use to me, after all. Perhaps I could present you as an exhibit of what happens when a woman is stolen and brutalized by orcs. Perhaps *you* can be my atrocity, my empty-headed little darling. And surely"—his other hand came up, and brushed at her lips—"your deep little throat still works, I presume? As long as the orcs haven't broken that, too?"

His voice was light, like this was all suddenly a good joke. Like *Rosa* was a joke, a tool, an empty vessel for his amusement. Which, perhaps, she always had been, all this time.

"Why don't we give it a try, darling," he said smoothly. "Gods know I need a decent blow, after all this. And who knows, maybe a good deep-throating will clear some of the fog from your pretty little head."

He roughly released Rosa's chin, in favour of reaching to pluck the papers out of her slack, trembling fingers. While also dropping his other hand to unbutton his trousers, even as his eyes swept up and down Rosa's front, settling narrow on the slight swell of her breasts.

"What the fuck have you been eating?" he asked, voice testy. "Gods, Rosa, you're starting to look like a fucking *matron*."

The fear and the bile both surged in Rosa's throat, and somehow, thank the gods, her frozen body jerked backwards, away from him, away from that suddenly repulsive sight at his exposed groin.

"No," she choked out. "I am not touching you, Lord Kaspar. Never again. I told you, it's *over*."

But he only laughed again, advancing closer, one hand on his swollen bared cock, the other still holding her papers. "Are you sure, Rosa darling?" he asked. "Oh, I think you could be convinced. Maybe I'll make you a student. Maybe I'll even make you my *wife*. Will that do, for now?"

He was *mocking* her, Rosa realized, with a jolting, sickening misery. He was saying he would never have given her such things, he would *never* have made her a real student, let alone his wife. Her future had always been just—*this*. Trapped serving this horrible empty man, until he tired of her, and threw her away.

"You need to be *thankful*, Rosa," he continued, almost conversationally. "You're lucky you can be of any use to me at all anymore. Especially after the *hell* you've put me through these past weeks, without a single fucking *paper* to show for it!"

Rosa's body had begun shivering, backing toward the nearest shelf, her heart clanging, her breath gulping. "*You're* the one who's fucked, Kaspar," she gasped. "You lying entitled *swine*. Don't *touch* me!"

But he was reaching for her, gripping at her shoulder, shoving her back against the shelf. "Oh, don't play coy with me," he snapped. "We both know you like a bit of force with your fucking anyway, don't we? Now get on your knees, before I knock you out and *put* you there."

The fear was shouting, scrabbling, and Rosa hurled herself away from him, grasping at the shelf behind her. For the book she knew was there, had to be there—and she gulped as she dragged it out, her hands skittering against its heavy weight. It was the *Annals of the Realm*, full of pomp and blather and *lies*, just like Lord Kaspar himself—and Rosa flung it toward him with all her might. Not at his head, as her initial impulse might have been—but instead straight at his exposed, swollen groin.

It made impact with a vicious-sounding *crack*, and Lord Kaspar shrieked with satisfying shrillness, his face contorting with agony as he staggered back onto the floor. Sending Rosa's papers flying everywhere, wafting through the air, settling down all around his sprawled, moaning body.

"You devious little *bitch*," he croaked, clutching both hands to his groin. "You will fucking *pay* for this, you—"

His voice abruptly broke, as if it had been strangled— because he was blinking, gaping, at the paper. The single sheet of paper that had settled onto his thigh, its block letters clear, blatant, glaring. Shouting, striking, into the sudden deadly silence.

LORD KASPAR'S BASTARDS, it read. *The Shocking Truth Behind the Realm's Most Acclaimed Gentleman Scholar.*

"What. The. Fuck," hissed Lord Kaspar, his voice poisonous, "is *this*."

Rosa felt her chin lifting, her composure and conviction rising, her body straightening to its full height. "Oh, that?" she said, with surprising coolness. "That's my latest treatise. Quite a compelling title, don't you think? I've arranged for a thousand copies to be printed, with wide distribution to begin next week."

Lord Kaspar gawked open-mouthed at her, his eyes round and bulbous, his face gone a sickly shade of white. "You have *not*," he gasped. "You would *never*."

Rosa felt herself smile at him, cool, bitter. "Oh, wouldn't I?" she said. "Just the same way you wouldn't start an unjust war, or make promises you never meant to keep, or force yourself on someone who doesn't want you? Someone who's only done her best to *please* you, these past nine *years*, despite everything you've done to her?!"

Lord Kaspar's mouth was opening and closing, his throat working, his eyes suddenly darting around at the other papers scattered all over. Many of them full of neat typeset text—courtesy of one of Lady Scall's many connections—and several more with large titles, printed in the same thick block letters.

INSIDE ORC MOUNTAIN: A True Account, one read. *ORCS ON TRIAL: Myths and So-Called Scandals*, read another. And then, *THE REAL ATROCITIES OF THE REALM: A Firsthand Account of a Lord's Ruin of an Innocent*.

And then, the last one, Rosa's own pet project—*ORCLING BIRTH: A Summary of Best Practices for Protecting Women's Health*.

Lord Kaspar looked like he'd been struck in the groin—again—and his dazed eyes blinked at the titles, again, again, as if he truly couldn't believe they were real. And with a jolting, jerky movement, he grasped for the nearest paper, and ripped it to shreds with visibly shaking fingers.

"You will *not*," he said, his voice hitching as he clutched for another sheet, and tore it again and again, "*dare* to besmirch a lord's *impeccable* reputation with such foul, unfounded *falsehoods*. You will *not*."

But Rosa was smiling again, hard and grim. "You misunderstand me, Lord Kaspar," she said flatly. "I will do this, whether you approve of it or not. I will *only* reconsider if you do as I asked, and speak to your father and the Council, and *beg* them to stop this unjust war."

Lord Kaspar was goggling at her again, and Rosa snatched up the nearest paper—another title page for *Lord Kaspar's Bastards*—and held it up toward him. "And while you're at it," she said coldly, "you will seek out your children—including the girls—and give every one of them your support, and a proper education. Then, and *only* then, will I refrain from distributing these treatises. Otherwise, I will use every means at my disposal to deliver copies to every town, village, and library in the *realm*. You have one week."

A sheer, maniacal hatred had flashed across Lord Kaspar's blinking eyes—and in a burst of movement, he leapt to his feet, and launched himself at Rosa. His clammy, sticky hands finding her neck, and clamping tight.

The panic soared and screamed, Rosa's entire body kicking and writhing against him, against the horrifying force of that shocking, dangerous pressure. Entirely unlike anything she'd ever felt before, unlike anything John had *ever* done, and her vision was already spotting, sparking black holes in Lord Kaspar's handsome, leering, furious face.

"You will not," he gasped, through his heaving breaths. "Because you'll be *dead*. Killed at the hands of an *orc*, who dared to come into *my* fucking library, and try to steal what's *mine*! You want to start a *war*, my stupid little bookworm, *here's* how we start a war!"

No. *No*. Rosa's feet were slipping, her vision stuttering, Lord

Kaspar was going to kill her, everything was for nothing, everything, *John*—

John. Rising up behind Lord Kaspar, like a huge, violent, avenging god. His eyes glittering with fierce, inhuman rage, as his powerful arm snapped over Lord Kaspar's head, and crushed hard against his neck. Dragging Lord Kaspar away from Rosa altogether, his pale face suddenly contorted with pain, his eyes bulging, his mouth screaming with no sound.

"She is *mine*, vile human," John hissed, deep, close in Lord Kaspar's ear. "And for this, you *die*."

38

For a choked, careening instant, Lord Kaspar fought and flailed against John's deadly grip, his arms frantically swatting and swinging.

But John only yanked tighter, the muscles flexing in his powerful arm, and Lord Kaspar's movements gradually, visibly slowed. Becoming more sluggish and erratic, his eyes rolling back, his mouth falling open.

And as Rosa watched, blinking, strangely detached, there was the awareness, unnerving but certain, that she didn't care if Lord Kaspar died. That he'd been truly horrible, both to her and the orcs, and to everyone else around him. John could kill him, with her blessing.

But then, a bang. Loud, pointed, from the very back of the library. Almost like a door slamming open, and Rosa's dazed, blunted brain finally leapt back into motion, more panic surging and soaring. What if it was armed men. What if Lord Kaspar had somehow called for guards. What if there was a brawl in the library, what if John was found out, captured, *killed*—

But it was—Tristan? Yes, Tristan, sprinting, bodily leaping

over a table with surprising ease, while Salvi dodged around after him. And instead of going for Lord Kaspar's rapidly sagging form, as Rosa might have expected, they both launched themselves toward—John?

"*Stop*, John-Ka," Tristan hissed, grasping with clawed fingers at John's arm, still clamped around Lord Kaspar's neck. "You must not. *Please.*"

Salvi had grabbed for John's other arm, yanking it backwards, and John barked a growl at him, shook him off with a hard jerk. "I *shall*," he snarled at Salvi. "This vile man is *owed* this death. Did you not witness what he sought to do to my *mate,* who bears my *son*?!"

"We heard," Tristan said, his voice low and soothing, his hands still tugging at John's arm, his black claws sunk into John's skin. "We know. But you must not kill him. You shall thus break our treaty. The captain shall *never* make you Priest, after this."

"This alters naught," John spat at him, though his grip on Lord Kaspar's neck seemed to have loosened slightly, allowing Lord Kaspar to renew his wild flailing. "The captain shall never make me Priest *now!*"

But beside Tristan, suddenly, there was—Simon. Towering over all of them, and glowering down at Lord Kaspar's thrashing form with palpable loathing. "Captain may," he said, his deep voice flat. "If Skai ask. But John rage at me for sitting on *rock*, when he *kill* stinky little man? Skai *never* ask, after this."

That seemed to finally catch John's attention, his narrow eyes angling toward Simon—and when Tristan yanked John's arm again, he abruptly released Lord Kaspar, hurling away his coughing, staggering form with vicious force.

"Foul, cheap, selfish *fool*," John spat at Lord Kaspar's back. "You shall never touch Rosa or frighten her *again*. She is *mine*, and she has *bested* you, and you shall do *all* that she asks!"

Lord Kaspar's teetering, shuddering body had turned to face the orcs, his visibly trembling hands buttoning up the front of his trousers. "I'll call the guards and soldiers," he gasped. "I will have you all *killed*."

"No, you will *not*, Kaspar," said another voice, smooth, clipped. And when Rosa whipped her head around, following Lord Kaspar's astonished eyes, there was—*Lady Scall*. Standing in the aisle with her hands on her hips, her expression one of utter, merciless disdain. And wait, had she been hiding in the back room, too? With Tristan, and Salvi, and *Simon*?!

"I have heard far more from you than I would have preferred to," she said to Lord Kaspar, in frigid tones. "I shall not countenance an unwarranted massacre under my nose, and certainly not at the behest of such a scheming piece of *scum*. Why I ever entertained a marriage proposal from the likes of you, I cannot *fathom*."

Lord Kaspar had begun speaking, babbling words no one was listening to, and Lady Scall raised a cool, imperious hand. "Silence," she snapped. "And you shall agree to all Rosa asks, in compensation for your *reprehensible* behaviour toward her. At *once*."

For an instant, Lord Kaspar blinked at Lady Scall with something almost like awe—but then his eyes flicked back toward Rosa, and she could see the rage kindling, stoking, flaring. "I will *not*," he hissed. "After everything I've done for her, this *peasant* used me, and lied to me, and betrayed me with an *orc*"—he cast a baleful, hateful look toward John—"and now she has the audacity to *blackmail* me?!"

John was again trying to escape Tristan and Salvi, who at some point had again latched onto each of his arms, but Lord Kaspar didn't even seem to notice, taking two lurching steps toward Rosa. "You will *never* be a student or a scholar," he said to her, grating and triumphant. "You will never step foot in a library *again*. Without me, you will end up living impoverished on the *streets*, sucking *cock* for your supper!"

Rosa was backing away again, toward the safety of the bookshelf, and she blinked at the sound of John laughing, hard, grim, almost diabolical. "She shall *not*," he spat. "She shall be kept fat, and happy, and content. She shall run her own library, and pursue her work as a scholar, and write as many treatises as she pleases. She shall *destroy* you with every page from her pen. She shall *forever* be known as the saviour of countless women's lives, and the fair, clever mother of the last of the Ka!"

The words rang through the room, firing a strange, twisty ripple straight to Rosa's groin. And though she could vaguely hear Lord Kaspar speaking again, it sounded dim and garbled, and her eyes were only held to John's cruel, beautiful, furious face.

"You are a *fool*, to speak such lies," John continued, every word sure and fierce. "We all know the truth of this. You had a kind, clever, eager woman, who seeks to obey and please with such stunning sweetness, and who boasts mayhap the deepest throat in the *realm*. And you spoke false to her, and truly frightened her, and trapped her here as your *servant*. You allowed her to become chilled and gaunt and weak. You taunted her with true learning, but all the while kept this just out of her reach, and instead claimed her good work as your own. You did not even listen when she spoke of how to protect your own priceless *library*. You ought to *drown* in your sheer *disgrace*."

John had wrenched out of Tristan and Salvi's arms as he'd spoken, and he took a sharp step closer to Lord Kaspar. His taut, muscular body looming tall and powerful over Lord Kaspar's cowering, suddenly small-looking form.

"You shall meet her terms," John growled, extending his hand toward Rosa, clawed fingers outstretched. "Or you shall yet *die*."

No one seemed willing to argue this time, not even Lord Kaspar, and Rosa's eyes were caught on John's hand. Reaching toward her, waiting, in a silent but steady offer—

And in a jerky, twitchy movement, Rosa took it. Lurching toward him, and finding herself abruptly clutched tight against him, her back pressed to his warm familiar chest, his hands spread wide and protective against her waist.

This close she could feel his heartbeat, thundering strong and reassuring into her back, and she felt herself sag into it, into the warm, wonderful, fundamental *rightness* of it. Of her mate, here. Holding her, keeping her safe in his arms, even as he eviscerated her greatest enemy with his truth.

Tristan and Salvi had both begun to advance toward Lord Kaspar, their claws and teeth bared, and Rosa's whirling brain pointed out just how *little* Lord Kaspar looked. Even Tristan, who in Rosa's thoughts had somehow once seemed small, towered a full head over him, and Rosa could see Lord Kaspar's answering shiver, his eyes darting up and around, lingering desperately on the closed front door.

"We shall not allow you to leave," Tristan said, his voice oddly frightening in its smooth, biting certainty. "Not until you comply."

"You cannot *do* this to me," Lord Kaspar spluttered. "You're breaking your own *treaty!*"

This time it was Salvi who laughed, showing his sharp white teeth. "We are not, you *helvítis fáviti,*" he said, "and you know it. Now stop wasting our time, and get the fuck on with it. Unless you truly want to be forever known as"—he reached down and snatched up one of Rosa's strewn-about papers— "'the cruel, careless, and callous despoiler of countless naive women.'"

Lord Kaspar's body was angling toward the door, a hunted expression flaring across his eyes. "No one will believe the word of an *insane* peasant woman over *me. No one!*"

"Oh, I beg to differ," interjected Lady Scall, who'd continued to watch all this with chilly disgust, her arms crossed over her chest. "I think the public will be very curious about these revelations. *Especially* if they are widely known to have originated with another member of the nobility, who has a *great* deal of firsthand knowledge upon this particular subject."

A choking noise escaped from Lord Kaspar's throat, his eyes now gaping at Lady Scall's hard face. "You would not," he said, "publicly *endorse* this."

"I *would*," replied Lady Scall, with finality. "I have not taken kindly to your dedicated pursuit of my hand in marriage, under such thoroughly fabricated pretences. You are an absent father, a false scholar, and a *cheat*."

The rebellion kindled again in Lord Kaspar's eyes, and his lip curled, his mouth opening to speak—and then went slack again, because this time, it was Simon striding toward him. His steps heavy, menacing, his massive body towering over Lord Kaspar as he purposefully cracked his huge knuckles, one by one.

"Fool man too proud to learn," he said, his voice deep with scorn. "Or too stupid. Enforcer shall better teach."

Lord Kaspar's face drained of all colour, his eyes wide and terrified on Simon's fists, as a sudden pool of wetness stained the front of his trousers. Earning a derisive snort from Simon, and a cold, terrifying laugh from John.

"You are conquered on all sides, you cheap fool," John hissed. "Now yield. At *once*."

Lord Kaspar finally seemed to wilt, his shoulders dropping, his lips mouthing uselessly, his bulging eyes still fixed to Simon's huge fists. "I—" he choked. "Fine. I—I concede. I'll do it."

Rosa exhaled, harsh and shuddery, the relief so visceral she felt herself collapse back into John's solid strength. Lord Kaspar would do it. He would try to stop the war. She'd *won*.

At that very moment, the library's front door flew open behind him—and in strode Susan, the library's morning maid. Looking blithe and bright-eyed as she shut the door behind her—until she turned around, caught sight of the four orcs, and screamed.

It was shrill, deafening, piercing through the room. And at the sound, Lord Kaspar's already-swaying body tilted, swerved, and staggered—and then dropped to the floor in a dead faint.

39

The next few moments were pure chaos. Consumed by Susan's bout of hysterics, Salvi's frantic attentions to Lord Kaspar's limp body, and Simon's loud, uncontrollable guffaws of laughter.

Rosa focused on calming Susan, a task which proved deeply infuriating, particularly as Susan kept threatening to call various guards and regiments to forcibly oust the orcs from the library. A vision of blood and ruined books that still curdled Rosa's insides, and even her sternest scolding wouldn't seem to shut Susan up, especially once she realized that the prostrate form on the floor at the orcs' feet was none other than Lord Kaspar himself.

Finally Salvi managed to revive Lord Kaspar, who then proceeded to vomit onto Lady Scall's expensive shoes. Earning in return a fierce, eloquent earful from Lady Scall about pathetic lords who couldn't control themselves, or accept when they've been defeated, or stop contributing to the unholy stench that emanated from this damned odious library.

Lord Kaspar soon sat up, clutching his head, and yelled at

Susan to stop screaming, unless she wanted to be bodily hurled under the wheels of the next passing wagon. Which gained them all a moment's respite, at least until Lord Kaspar fainted again, and Simon broke into more hoots of uproarious laughter, while Susan launched another chorus of ear-splitting wails, and John—who was standing beside Rosa, his arms crossed tight over his chest—appeared on the verge of tearing someone's head off, probably Susan's, or Simon's, or Lord Kaspar's, or all three.

"You should go, John-Ka," interrupted Tristan's voice, close behind John. "We shall address the rest of this from here, ach?"

John's angled glance down at Tristan was sheer, unabashed gratefulness, and he immediately nodded, his hand clasping at Rosa's arm. "I thank you, my brother," he said, low and fervent. "Come, pet."

Rosa twitched and blinked at him—*come, pet*, he'd said— and his taut form seemed to brace even tighter, his eyes briefly closing. "I ought to say," he amended, his voice thick, "should you wish to come with me, Rosa, I should be honoured to bring you home. To our mountain."

Home. To our *mountain*. Every word a deep striking bell, ringing turbulent and powerful, and Rosa stared at John, at the bared, naked uncertainty in his eyes. Waiting for her to speak. To—*choose*.

Rosa's eyes kept blinking, prickling, and her head somehow jerked a nod, all on its own. Flaring a surge of unrestrained relief across John's face, and within a breath he snatched her up into his arms, close, warm, *safe*.

"I shall meet you at the mountain, brother," he said to Tristan. "Again, I thank you."

Tristan only beamed at them with unmistakable satisfaction, and then turned back toward Salvi, who was currently cursing at Lord Kaspar's still dead-eyed face. A sight that made

Rosa grimace, and thankfully John abruptly spun away, hoisting her closer as he strode for the door.

Rosa watched him open the door a careful crack, smelling the air beyond, waiting—and then he sprinted them out into the sun. Into a world that had felt surprisingly bleak and empty, earlier that very morning, but suddenly looked lush and alive, flickering bright with *hope*.

John didn't once falter in his stride, careening straight for the cover of trees. And as he dodged and leapt, darting over rocks and under branches, it was almost like time had slipped, reversed, turned back and forward and back again. All the way down to the familiar firm grip of John's hand against Rosa's arse, the relentless grind of his hip between her spread legs.

But it was different, this time. John carried no books. There were no more secrets. And this wasn't a wild rescue mission, or a reaction against a night's ill-thought weakness, or a foolish attempt to research a war. It was—*what*?

John's gaze slanted down at Rosa, at where she'd been openly searching his harsh profile. And it was almost as though he could see her very soul, the awareness flickering across his narrowed eyes.

And with a hard jerk of his body against her, he stopped. Halted entirely, here beneath the dappled morning sunlight, caught in the forest's whispering, watching silence.

"Ach, pet," he said, his voice cracking. "I must—speak with you, I ken."

Rosa blinked at him, her thoughts flashing back to Hanarr's words that first day. *We Ka-esh do not oft offer vows. One's mouth may speak any number of empty words, but one's acts speak only truth.*

And John's actions today had surely spoken any number of surprising things. He had come to the library. He had been there when Rosa had faced Lord Kaspar. He'd nearly *killed* Lord

Kaspar, to keep her safe. And he'd helped her conquer Lord Kaspar, his truths fierce and blistering alongside hers.

And, too, he'd said those things to Lord Kaspar. All those lovely, impossible things, about Rosa being kept safe, and running her own library, and pursuing her own interests as a scholar. About her being the mother of the last of the Ka.

But he hadn't said such things to *her*. Good gods, the last time they'd truly spoken, they'd both said all those awful things to each other, and he'd hollered at Rosa to *leave* him.

She could see the awareness of that in John's eyes, and he shifted her in his arms so that she faced him head-on, her legs twined around his back. His chest rising and falling, gently heaving her along with it.

"You ought to know," he said finally, uneven, "the truth of why I first came to your library. I did not come to woo you, or harm you. I only came"—he sighed, and squared his shoulders—"to learn more of this foul man. We have long sought to research all these lords and their spoilt sons, and I have long wished to visit this library. So thus, I went."

He'd gone to the library for *research*. And if it hadn't been so ridiculous, Rosa might have laughed—but she couldn't even seem to breathe, caught on the look in John's eyes, the unsteadiness of his voice.

"And this library," he said, "reeked of *you*, pet. You were upon every last book and paper. Upon even the quills and ink bottles. And most of all upon the tables and desks, and this *bed*. All the places where this foul man took you."

Rosa swallowed hard, waiting, and John choked a laugh without warmth. "I could scarce even *read*, for the strength of this," he continued. "And then you came to me. You did not collapse or shriek or weep at the sight of me. Instead, you argued with me. You asked me questions with clarity and cleverness. And next you heard my words, heeded them as truth, and granted me leave to stay. You—surprised me."

Oh. Rosa felt her mouth reluctantly twitch up—only John would express such approval at having been *argued* with—but his eyes were grave, his hands tightening against her. "And next," he said, his voice lowering, "you *offered* yourself to me. And I knew the truth behind this, I *knew* you wished to use me to gain your own ends, and yet"—his eyes closed—"I longed for you, pet. I brooded upon you for the whole of this day. Your hunger tasted so sweet, your yielding was so eager, and your *fear*—"

He grimaced, his head snapping away, as though he couldn't bear to admit that, in this moment—but Rosa's hands had cupped to his face, bringing it back, drawing those eyes back to hers. "It aroused you," she whispered. "I know. It aroused me, too."

There was a glimpse of his tongue, flicking between his lips, and he choked out another curt laugh. "I longed for this," he said. "I *craved* this. I cared not if I filled you with my son. I cared not about this foul man whose reek tainted your scent. My only thought was my need to have you. To fuck you until you screamed and spurted for me. To *own* you, pet."

The shame tainted his eyes again, heavy with regret, but Rosa kept her hands on his face, her gaze steady on his. Refusing to judge his desires, or condemn them, in just the same way he'd refused to judge hers.

"I *gloried* in this," he whispered. "In ploughing you senseless upon this table, where you read all these foolish lies, and sought in such earnest to undo my kin. I had *never* tasted hunger or power such as this. But after it was done—"

He broke off, once again grimacing, but Rosa watched, waited, until he spoke again. "I swore, that night, that I would address this, and not again yield to your call. But I could not stop. I did this again, and again—and each time there were new secrets to learn, new joys to find. Each time you trapped me deeper under your spell."

One of his hands shifted from her arse, lifting up to brush against her lips, his clawed finger nudging between them. "I fought against this with all my will," he breathed. "I fought the bond we had forged. I fought *you*. But I failed."

The words seemed to settle deep into Rosa's gut, filling in all those empty spaces, brimming with warmth, with longing. Even as John's eyes darkened again, flicking away from her, his finger dropping from her lips.

"I could not bear to lose you to this man, when he came for you," he continued, wooden now. "So I held this from you. I chose to believe your words of hate toward him, rather than seeking your truth."

Oh. John's face was slipping into the old mask again, chilly and distant, his jaw rigid under Rosa's touch. "I failed you, in this," he said. "And I failed you again, when I struck you unawares with the truth of what this foul man had done to you. And then again when I did not see the strength of your fear of this man, and faced you with meeting him, without me. And then *again*"—his jaw ground tighter under her fingers—"when I raged at you, and sent you running from me, and cast your care upon my kin, and a *Skai*. When I thrust you and my son into true danger, where I could not keep you safe."

The words wouldn't seem to come, suddenly, caught in the clutch of Rosa's throat, and John's chest swelled against her, hollowed again. "I ought never to have done this," he said, his voice so low, so bitter. "I was a fool. I allowed my grief and my rage to swallow me. I bowed to the fear of forever losing you, and my son, to this man. I did not see. I did not learn. I did not"—his eyes flicked to Rosa's, brief, chagrined—"trust my own *mate*."

His own *mate*. That loaded, deadly word, actually spoken from his own mouth, the truth of it glittering in his own eyes. Rosa had been his mate. She *was*.

Rosa felt her head lurch up and down, her fingers skittering on his skin. Her eyes searching his, seeing again that bitterness, the blame. "But I didn't trust you either," she whispered, over the lump still clogging her throat. "I lied to you the *entire time*, John."

John's shoulder shrugged, jerking Rosa along with it. "Ach, but I knew all your lies," he replied, hoarse. "I knew what you stood to lose, and how deeply this man had harmed you. You were yet my mate. You yet carried my *son*. I ought to have kept you safe."

His eyes were again blinking beyond her, blank, unseeing, and suddenly Rosa couldn't bear the sight of it, of her beautiful, powerful mate lost in such misery, such regret.

"You *did* keep me safe," she said, giving his head a purposeful shake. "You *knew* I was with Tristan. Didn't you?"

John's gaze darted toward her, shifting, as he nodded, once. Confirming what Rosa had already known, and she somehow even smiled at him, blinking her own too-wet eyes. "You trusted Tristan to keep me safe," she said, "and he did. He's *wonderful*, John. And his loyalty to you is absolute. But I'm sure you know that, don't you?"

John nodded again, quick and grim, and Rosa nodded too, her hands stroking at the hard lines of his face. "He told me what you did for him and Salvi, all those years ago," she whispered. "And Salvi told us what you did for him, with his mate. You kept them safe. And you *knew* they would do the same for me."

John's throat convulsed, but there was another nod, and Rosa attempted another smile, and jabbed a weak-feeling finger into his chest. "You know, I *hated* fighting with you, and being parted from you, you great *reprobate*," she said, as lightly as she could. "But in the end, I think it worked out. Don't you? I—needed time, I think. To come to terms with you, and with me. To face my own past, and my own truth. To understand my own actions toward you. The ways I lied to you. How I wanted to make amends to you."

She was babbling again, maybe, but John didn't seem to mind, and his mouth even twitched, his shoulders sagging. "This was not *amends*," he said, husky. "This was a full battle, set and staged and won. This was—*brilliant*, my clever little pet. It was a play well worthy of a Ka. Of—*you*."

Warmth coursed through Rosa's belly, thick and rich and full, and she flashed him another quick, genuine smile. "Well, it wouldn't have worked without you," she said, and she meant it. "Thank you for being there, my lord."

His eyes felt almost painfully intent on hers, and his nod was slow this time, determined. "I knew I would never again leave you to face such trials alone," he murmured. "I swore to keep you safe, and I *shall*."

The warmth bubbled again, fuller and brighter, so much that Rosa felt herself beaming at him, her legs tightening around his waist, her arms curling around his neck. "Even if I'm not tall or hearty or serene?" she asked. "Like that other woman you wanted?"

She didn't quite know why she'd asked it—maybe because it was the last, little nagging whisper, dragging against her happiness—and John was looking at her oddly, his eyes blank. "Who?"

Rosa tried for another smile, but didn't entirely manage it this time. "Oh, you know," she said, as offhandedly as she could. "The woman you told me you wanted that day, when you tied me to the bed. The one who doesn't sell herself, or prattle constantly, or pretend to be cleverer than she is."

John blinked at her, true astonishment flashing across his face—and there was the comprehension, slow and incredulous. "You ken I *meant* that?" he said, and suddenly he barked a too-loud laugh. "*Helvíti*, woman. After this you took my *claw* in your womb, and begged me to spew my seed upon you, and licked your pretty face clean of me, and *thanked* me. And then smiled at me the whole of the day as if I were a *god*, all whilst reeking of my fresh scent. You ken I should think of *aught* other false woman, after you fell me with *this*?"

Oh. The warmth was trickling back in, shuddering its relief so powerfully that Rosa felt faint—though John was still frowning, his eyes still dark with disbelief. "I wish for *you*, woman," he snapped. "You are quick and curious and clever. You have read more than aught other I know. You are a *scholar*. You have studied five languages, one of these my own. You found a book that alters the future of my kind, and freely granted this to me, and next wrote a treatise upon this to share with the humans, so that all may gain from your knowledge. You may have stopped a *war* today, with your pen, and your insights, and your truth. And"—he inhaled, his voice deepening—"your throat is a *marvel*, your tight little womb drips orc-seed for *days*, and when I push and frighten you, this *excites* you, and you beg me for more. And now you carry my son, and have sworn to my kin that I shall not be the last of the Ka. How could I not crave you, and a son from you, with the whole of my *being*?"

Oh. There were no possible words, no possible ways to speak—so instead, Rosa thrust herself closer against him. Clutching at his solid body with all her strength, burying her face in the rapid pulse of his neck, feeling her eyes leaking against his skin.

"You devious scoundrel," she whispered. "Gods, John-Ka, I *love* you."

She could feel him wrench still against her—and suddenly there were familiar clawed hands, tilting her wet face up. His own wet, long-lashed eyes blinking hard, searching hers, waiting. Wanting her to say it again, wanting to see her say it—so she did.

"I love you, John-Ka," she breathed. "My lord. Make me your bonded mate? And your loyal, obedient pet?"

And in those eyes, there was life, joy, *wonder*. Warmth unlike any Rosa had ever seen there before, and when they finally smiled at her, so slow, so affectionate, she thought she might shatter with the strength of it.

"Ach, my lovely rose," he whispered, as he bent to seal it with a kiss, sweet, soft, hers, *forever*. "I shall."

40

The rest of the trip to the mountain passed in a whirl of warmth and light and colour. Of John actually smiling, actually laughing, perhaps with more ease than Rosa had ever seen, and tormenting her mercilessly with every steady grind of his hip between her legs.

"Ach, my poor pet is so hungry today," he purred, once he'd paused to feed her a generous quantity of dried meat from his pocket, and she'd then begun eagerly sucking on his fingers. "You have deeply missed your lord's care and feeding, have you not?"

Rosa didn't even pretend to deny it, squirming back against the capable strength of his body, her greedy hand slipping down to cup at his tented groin—but even as he hissed a heated growl, he caught her back up into his arms, and again kicked into a run.

"Soon, pet," he said, as he darted and leapt, back in this lovely familiar frolic, this dance. "As soon as we have you safe."

Because of the men, Rosa realized, who were still likely lurking, waiting to attack at any moment. Though maybe not for long, if Lord Kaspar truly followed through on trying to persuade his father, and the Council, to abandon their foolish attempts at war.

And he would, Rosa thought firmly. His reputation and standing had always been Lord Kaspar's highest priority, well above his family or any political squabbles, and Lady Scall had in fact already had all Rosa's treatises printed, ready to distribute at a moment's notice. Tristan had also reassured Rosa, in their letters leading up to today, that from henceforth the Skai's scouts and spies would have Lord Kaspar closely monitored, and would surely know of any attempts at double-dealing.

The sun had almost set when Orc Mountain finally loomed before them, huge and craggy, streaming its smoke to the sky. And looking up at it, rather than the fear Rosa had felt last time, there was only relief. Anticipation. Excitement, sheer and bright and breathtaking.

"Welcome home, pet," John said, his voice thick in his throat, as he eased them in the same way he had last time, crunching the stone door shut behind them. A sound that should have been unsettling, perhaps, especially combined with the sudden pitch-darkness—but again Rosa only felt more warmth, more excitement, more *peace.*

"Thank you, my lord," she whispered, into his neck. "*Ég fíla þetta.*"

His hand gripped gentle and approving to her arse, his breath exhaling into her hair, as if he were about to speak—but then there was a clatter up ahead, and the distinctive dance of firelight.

"John-Ka!" shouted a vaguely familiar voice, and when Rosa blinked toward it, it was Aaron. And Brandr, and Marcus, and Gary, and Hanarr, and a half-dozen other Ka-esh, all grin-ning and speaking at once. And among them were also Jule and Grimarr, and Baldr and Drafli and Nattfarr—and within a breath John and Rosa were surrounded by a crush of loudly chattering orcs, demanding how the operation had gone, and welcoming Rosa back to the mountain, and offering their enthusiastic congratulations.

John, to Rosa's vague surprise, betrayed no outward signs of annoyance at the sudden melee, and actually began to regale the mass of orcs with a brief summary of the day's events. Speaking with clarity and unmistakable pride of Rosa's clever treatises, and her brave upstaging of Lord Kaspar, and the depths to which this fool man had been reduced under her deft handling.

And then, to Rosa's continued rising surprise, John carefully set her down, turned to Grimarr and Jule, and bowed, his hand in a fist over his heart. "I thank you, Captain, Lady Captain," he said, "for your clever planning and support of my aims. And I must also"—he turned to Drafli's tall, silent form, and bowed again—"thank the Skai, for the many scouts and spies they have freely granted me these past days, and for the ongoing loan of your Enforcer. You have kept me, my mate, and my kin-brothers safe. I am grateful. *Ég er þakklátur.*"

With that, he nodded over his shoulder, to where three more tall, rangy-looking Skai were silently striding up behind them. From outside, from where they—and apparently also Simon—had been *following* John and Rosa? Spying? Keeping them *safe*? Not only today, but all this past *week*?

But yes, that had to be what John had meant, because before them Drafli had inclined his head, his own hand fisting over his chest in the exact same gesture. While his other hand gave a few quick, pointed flicks, his dark gaze slanting toward Baldr beside him.

"Drafli says, 'The Skai see this praise,'" Baldr said, with satisfaction. "'We are honoured to keep safe our wise Ka-esh kin.'"

John bowed toward Drafli again, to which Drafli returned a nod. And soon the murmurs all around rose back into full-on chatter and shouts, during which multiple orcs peppered John with more questions, and Jule strode over to pull Rosa into a tight, warm embrace.

"We're so *happy* you've returned," Jule said firmly as she drew back again, flashing Rosa her broad, contagious smile. "Amazing work dealing with Kaspar. I hope it wasn't all too horrible?"

Rosa shrugged and smiled back, her eyes angling up toward John, who was still deep in conversation with Baldr. "Some parts were," she said truthfully, "but Lady Scall was so helpful, and so surprisingly kind. I'm so grateful to you for soliciting her assistance, as you did."

Jule waved it away, her eyes sparkling. "It was the least we could do," she said. "And to be quite honest, none of us wanted to live with *him*"—her head jerked toward John—"after you left. I truly had no idea Ka-esh could be so damned *malevolent*. It was like he was *possessed*."

John had clearly heard that, his gaze snapping toward Jule, his lip balefully curling—and Jule laughed aloud as she shooed Rosa back toward him. "Good gods, it's *still there*," she said. "Go fuck it out of him, Rosa, please, for all our sakes."

Rosa's face flooded with heat, but the idea was suddenly, desperately appealing—a sentiment that John seemed to share, his hand abruptly clenching to her arse, and guiding her through the crowd.

"Now, where do you wish to go, pet?" he asked, once he'd snatched a lamp from someone, and they'd moved beyond the worst of the noise. "To bed? Or mayhap your library?"

Both those options sounded truly delightful, though Rosa felt herself belatedly frowning up at him, her head tilting. "*My* library?"

"Ach," John said, with a shrug. "You have given up your own library for my gain, and you know more than any other in this mountain how best to take care of one. It is only fitting that you should now have mine."

Have his. This orc was giving her a *library*, coolly, easily, as if it were nothing. But in staring at him, searching that watchful wary distance on his face, Rosa knew it *did* mean something. It *did* matter. This was a monumental gift, it was John handing over perhaps his greatest treasure, to *her*. Showing his truth through his actions, as he always had, since the first day they'd met.

Rosa flung herself toward him, her arms clamping around his waist, her face thrust into his warm chest. "*Thank* you, John," she whispered. "No one's ever given me *anything* so lovely."

John's arms had closed around her, clutching so tight it stole her breath. "Foolish pet," he murmured, though the words were thick with emotion. "You shall not be so thankful when you truly see all the work this shall bind you to. Not only this, but also your teaching, and your Aelakesh studies, and your writing. All whilst your tiny body also grows my *orcling*. And because of all this"—his voice hardened—"you shall forever lose your dream of studying at this university."

But the warmth was so bright, it felt like Rosa might burst with it, and she drew back to meet his gaze, both hands spreading wide against his chest. "I don't need to be at a university to learn," she whispered. "I want to be here, John-Ka, learning with *you*. And also"—she twitched a grin at him—"serving you, as your loyal pet."

Something stuttered, shifted in those eyes, and he wordlessly gripped Rosa's hand in his, and led her down the corridor. Toward his room, Rosa realized, and once they were inside he again turned to face her, his eyes oddly unreadable in the flickering light.

"I have one more gift for you," he said, very quiet. "Should you choose to accept it."

Rosa felt her brows rising, but she nodded, waited—and from beneath the stack of clothes on his nearby shelf, John drew something out. Something smooth, bright, gleaming gold and silver.

It was—a necklace. Or, more accurately, a *kraga*. One of the ones from the Ka-esh forge, like the ones Rosa had seen in the pleasure-den. But far smaller and thinner than those had been, made of delicate shards of gold and silver beaten together. And when Rosa blinked closer, drinking up the utter loveliness of it, she realized it also had *script* written on the inside, all beautiful flowing Aelakesh.

"Can you read it to me?" she whispered, gently tracing her finger against it. Feeling the detail of the etching, the impossible, unreal beauty of the metalwork, crafted with astonishing care and skill. A gift. For *her*?!

"Upon it is written, 'I belong to John, of Clan Ka-esh,'" John said, his voice very quiet. "'He vows to keep me safe, and fed, and fulfilled, so long as he is able.'"

Oh. Rosa's wide eyes jolted to John's face, searching those damned blank, distant eyes—and still reading them, somehow, as easily as if they were written on a page.

This was his vow. This was his promise. This was John admitting, without words, that he'd had this made for her, specifically for her, and hadn't Gary said one of these took *days*—

Rosa's throat clamped in on itself, and her fingers traced over that damned telling line, suddenly screaming at her with the bare, violent force of its truth. *Ég er John's. I belong to John.*

"Once I close this around your neck," John's voice said, hoarse, "it shall not again open. It must then be broken off, or melted."

Rosa's eyes couldn't stop blinking, first at the power of those words, and then at his face. His face, so blank, so wary, so—*afraid*.

"It is a foolish orc custom, I ken," he said, very quickly, as he abruptly lowered the *kraga* to his side. "Or, rather, a Ka-esh one. A silly wish to fully claim another, and flaunt this to one's kin. It means naught, I ken, when one can so easily use one's scent and one's teeth for marking, and mayhap I shall set it aside, until—"

He was babbling, Rosa realized, with a sudden, jolting affection so heated it seemed to melt her insides—and John was turning *away* from her, he was hiding it back on his shelf. And after an instant's shocked speechlessness, Rosa bodily launched herself toward that arm, that *kraga*, before it could possibly disappear forever—

"Stop," she choked at him, her hands scrabbling, her nails actually scratching gouges into his skin. "Don't you *dare* put that away, my lord. It is *mine!*"

Her breath was heaving, her body tingling all over, and against her John had snapped into stillness, his eyes intent on her face, his nostrils flaring, his teeth bared. A low growl burning from his throat, and the thrill of desperate, wonderful fear was so visceral, so powerful, the very stone staggered under Rosa's feet.

"You are an orc," she hissed at him. "And you aren't foolish, your practices aren't silly, your culture is yours, and you're *you*. And you're a marvellous devious *reprobate*, and I *love* you, I've already told you I'll be your pet and your mate and the mother of your *child*—so of *course* I want to wear such a beautiful gift, for the love of the *gods*, John!"

She was nearly shouting at him, and also truly on the verge of weeping—until it all broke off at once, shattering into stillness, as John's hands circled close around her throat.

He was still growling, and the gleaming *kraga* was thrust up onto his arm, freeing both his hands for this. For fully enclosing Rosa's neck with such purpose, such checked power, such tenderness.

Rosa had fully frozen in place, not moving, not thinking, and John's head curtly nodded his approval, his growl rumbling lower, almost to a purr.

"*Gott*," he breathed. "Then you shall undress for your lord, pet."

Heat sparkled under Rosa's skin, streaking to her belly, her groin, her heart—and she wordlessly reached behind her for the dress' row of buttons. They were small and plentiful, running in a long line down her back, and Rosa's shivery fingers fumbled against them, her gaze trapped on the deadly hunger charging across her mate's impatient, imperious eyes.

"Foolish woman," he sneered, as his hand dropped from her neck to her collarbone—and with a swift, vicious yank, he tore Rosa's *dress*. Ripping it straight down the middle, slicing through seams and trim and lace with breathtaking force. Until the dress fell from Rosa's body onto the floor, leaving her standing there naked, fully exposed, before her lord's greedy staring eyes.

And he was staring, his hooded eyes sweeping up and down, his tongue slipping out to brush against his lips. His gaze lingering, suddenly, on the slight new swell in her waist, the unmistakable new fullness in her tingly-feeling breasts.

John's groan was raw, guttural, and in a flare of movement he was here, close against her. His hands roving over her skin, cupping her belly almost whole between them, and then curving against her breasts with soft, astonishing reverence.

"My lovely little rose finally blooms for me," he breathed. "You are so fair, and so sweet, and so brave, my clever Rosa-Ka."

He was giving her his name, Rosa's thoughts wildly whispered, along with his vow and his praise—but she ignored the rising thunder in her heart, and obediently waited, held herself still, fixed her eyes to his stark, beautiful, impossibly tender face.

His hands slightly shook as they gripped the *kraga*, guided it gently to Rosa's throat. Settled its cool light weight against her vulnerable skin, against the roaring beat of her pulse.

His eyes never once left hers, perhaps searching for hesitation or fear, but there was none. Only a sudden, jubilant craving as the *kraga* slipped closer, slow, careful, safe—until at the back of her neck, she heard a deep, definitive *snap*.

John's hands drew away, visibly trembling now, and in their place, Rosa could feel the cool, light kiss of the *kraga*. Not tight, not painful, not constricting in any way—but most definitely there. Speaking of John, whispering John's name, brushing John's vow soft against her skin.

John's eyes were locked on the sight, gone blacker and hungrier than Rosa had ever seen them, and she lifted a shaky finger to trace against the cool metal, feeling the delicate weight of it, but also the strength. The way—her finger traced up, around, behind her—there was indeed no seam that she could feel, no easy way out.

But it wasn't a curse. It wasn't a trap. It wasn't like Lord Kaspar, with his frilly dresses and empty promises. It was a reflection of what already was, of the path Rosa had already chosen.

She'd faced her truth. She wanted John, and she wanted this life. She wanted to accept her joy, her desires, her choices, without shame, without regret.

Knowledge changes everything.

John was still gazing at her, so hungry Rosa could taste it, his eyes sweeping up and down her bared body. His own form was huge and taut, his hands gripped to fists, and his trousers were massively tented, twitching, boasting a rapidly pooling spot of wetness.

"What do you think, my lord?" Rosa finally managed, as lightly as she could, one hand still smoothing shivery against the cool circle of her *kraga*, her other clutching against the soft swell of her bare belly. "How do I look?"

His growl was throaty, helpless, his eyes fluttering, his cheeks and ears flushed with red. "Foolish pet," he croaked. "You look as though you need a pretty little chain, for your pretty new *kraga*. And a night of good hard fucking, upon the prick of your bonded mate and lord."

The hunger was a tidal wave, a towering teetering catastrophe, held in check only by the strength of that vow on Rosa's throat, its truth kissing her skin. She was his. He was hers. She was home. *Safe.*

"I couldn't agree more, my lord," she whispered. "So please, take me to your pleasure-den, and ravish me."

41

Rosa had never once imagined feeling the kind of hunger that trampled over her as her fully clothed mate—her lord—silently led her naked, marked, pregnant body through the dark corridor, and into the heated, firelit Ka-esh pleasure-den.

She could hear the slaps and moans fading as John ushered her across the floor, as all the room's shocked watching eyes seemed to prickle at once upon her bare skin. But it didn't matter, nothing mattered, only John, only the hunger, as he wordlessly grasped for something from the wall, and clipped it to Rosa's *kraga* with a smooth flick of his hand.

It was a *chain*, it truly was, a thin golden line that now snaked from Rosa's neck, and into the easy grip of his palm. And as Rosa gaped, her mouth bone-dry, John slipped the chain through his fingers, weaving it between them with astonishing ease, as though this were something he'd done a hundred times before.

And the reason for it—that hand gripped for Rosa's chin, tilting it up to meet his glittering eyes—was so he could still use the hand as he pleased, without once losing his hold on the chain. And too, perhaps, so his pet could feel the strength of that gold wrapped on his knuckles, the whisper of its silent danger on her skin.

"When a Ka-esh chains a pet," his voice rasped, "the pet kneels. At once. Always."

A helpless groan escaped Rosa's clogged throat, but she instantly nodded, and dropped to her knees. The floor below her was thankfully covered with soft fur, but she scarcely noticed, not with the tall, powerful form of her lord now looming over her, his groin close and visibly swelling under his trousers, the sweet, dangerous scent of him filling her mouth, her breath.

Rosa's tongue licked her dry lips, and her trembly, tingly hand reached toward that beautiful, desperately tempting bulge—until a light, but very pointed, tug on her *kraga* stilled her fingers in midair, her eyes darting up to his face.

"And you do not touch," he breathed, gazing down at her through hooded eyes. "You do *naught* but look at me, and breathe my scent, until I grant you leave for more."

Another choked groan burned from Rosa's throat, but she frantically nodded, and clasped her fingers together on her bare lap, leaning back onto her heels. Fuck, she wanted to touch him, she needed it so much it *ached*, and she had to bite her lip as she risked another glance up at him, at the cool, easy command in those watching, imperious eyes.

"*Gott*," he said. "Now speak to me, pet. In my own tongue."

His fingers flexed on the chain wrapped between them as he spoke, suggesting an actual *threat* if Rosa failed—and the thrill of mingled fear and longing and craving was so breathtaking, she could scarcely find the words.

"*Ég vil vera þín, John-Ka*," she breathed, enunciating as clearly as she could. "*Ég er þín.*"

I want to be yours, John-Ka, it meant. *I belong to you.*

John's tongue slid out, his nostrils flaring, hinting at perhaps a stutter in his cool control—so Rosa gulped in more air, kept her eyes locked to his. "*Ég elska typpið á þér, John-Ka. Ég elska bragðið af þér.*"

I love your cock, John-Ka. I love how you taste.

"Please let me see you, my lord," she whispered. "I need to see you. *Please.*"

And John liked that, he wanted that, the approval and the affection and the sheer *need* flashing across those eyes—and Rosa shuddered all over at the sight of his hands slowly, indulgently dropping to his groin, and drawing himself out.

And *fuck*, he was huge. Swelled and inflamed fuller than Rosa had ever seen him, thick and scarred and flushed, and dripping from that sleek head in a steady stream of white. The sight and the smell of it so damned magnificent that Rosa was oddly, acutely aware that they weren't alone in this room, this room was full of *orcs*—some of which John had clearly had before, maybe like this. And his beauty and his power were supposed to be hers, only hers, and a furtive glance around indeed showed many orcs looking, watching, seeing her mate's spectacular cock, some of them even *licking their lips*—

Another light tug of her chain dragged Rosa's gaze back up to John's face—but she couldn't hide her wince, her chagrin, her sudden surging jealousy. Perhaps, even, her *shame.*

There was a hanging instant, John's head tilting—and in a quick jolt of movement, he was crouching before her. Slipping his chain-studded hand gentle against her neck, his hunger simmering behind something that looked almost like—*concern.*

"Pet," he breathed. "My rose. Are you well."

A quavering shiver wrenched through Rosa's kneeling body, and John's eyes searched hers, digging deep, so powerful it felt like he was brushing at her very soul. "What vexes you, pet," he whispered. "Speak to me. We may stop, or leave, at any moment, should you wish."

And the offer of that, the fierce potent *care* of that, somehow brought a wavering smile to Rosa's mouth, as another staggering surge of hunger shot through her groin. "No," she gasped. "Please. It's just"—she darted a helpless glance at the watching orcs—"they can all *see* you. And you're *mine*."

Comprehension flared across John's eyes, along with an unmistakable relief. "Ach, I am," he said, the coolness creeping back into his voice. "I am your bonded mate. I am the father of your son. And thus, I shall never again touch another. But"—those claws traced, soft, against her *kraga*—"I am yet an orc. I am yet the last of the Ka. And should we stay, I shall flaunt my hunger, and my good seed, and my power over you. I shall flaunt my pretty, obedient pet, as you suckle and scream and spurt upon me."

It was a warning of what was to come, Rosa's flailing brain realized—but it was also John speaking his own truth, perhaps even accepting it. *I am your mate. I am an orc. The last of the Ka.*

And there hadn't been the faintest trace of reluctance in it. The slightest hint of shame. It had been spoken with smooth, unbroken ease, with the threat of a *chain* still brushing against her throat.

"But should you wish to go, pet," he said, quieter, "we shall go. And it shall alter naught between us. Ach?"

And that, Rosa thought, with a sudden, wild certainty, was truth too. His truth. He was an orc, and he viciously defended those he cared for, even from himself—and in this, he would not deviate or falter. He was hers, and he always would be.

The hunger was bubbling up again, crashing against a pure, raging *devotion*. The need, almost overpowering in its force, to serve such a strong and kind and powerful lord, who so thoroughly deserved one's loyalty, and one's affection, and one's trust.

"I understand, my lord," Rosa whispered, her hand raising on its own to touch his face—but then stopping in midair, just in time. "Thank you. But I would rather stay here, and serve you, as you wish."

John's eyes briefly closed, almost as if in pain, or relief—and after another gentle scrape against her neck he rose again, swift and graceful, towering over her. His hard length had flagged slightly as they'd spoken, but now it visibly swelled again, flaring and filling before Rosa's wide, greedy eyes.

And before the eyes of all these watching orcs, too—but the awareness of that felt far less overwhelming, less meaningful than it had before. Especially with John looking down at her like that, with such warmth and hunger and pride in his heavy-lidded eyes. *Hers.*

"May I touch you?" Rosa whispered, without at all meaning to. "Or taste you? Please, my lord?"

Something wicked flashed across his face, and his chain-wrapped hand smoothly moved to his thick hardness, gripping close around it—and then he slowly, deliberately, stroked up. Milking out a long, oozing string of white, dangling down slick and viscous before Rosa's eyes.

"You may not yet touch me," he purred, with deadly satisfaction. "But you may open your little mouth, and drink this."

Rosa could only blink at it for an instant, her cheeks burning hot. Until a gentle tug on the chain drew her forward—and somehow, her heart desperately pounding, she obeyed. Leaning toward him, and tipping her head back, her mouth opening wide, so that she might catch the dangling string of her lord's seed between her hungry parted lips.

The taste of it exploded on her tongue, so succulent and sweet that she moaned, loud and ragged, the sound echoing across the too-quiet room. A sound that was answered by *laughter*, not only from John above her, but from several orcs around them—but Rosa's shame was startled, broken, by another gentle, purposeful jerk at her *kraga*. Drawing her attention back up to her lord, who was leisurely, generously pumping himself again. Oozing out more of that thick, luscious seed, into a shiny-slick rope that stretched from his slit, and pooled on Rosa's rapidly lapping tongue.

"Catch every drop, pet," came his voice, low, commanding. "And after, mayhap, I shall allow you to suckle from me."

Fuck, the words and his voice and the promise of it, shattering straight to Rosa's swollen-feeling groin, wringing another fervent moan from her greedy swallowing throat. Not caring anymore what this looked like, what she must look like, kneeling naked before an orc with a ring around her neck, her nipples peaked and tingling, her open mouth desperately gulping the thick string of white pumping steadily from an orc's scarred, gorgeous prick.

And she was being such a good pet, the approval and the triumph glittering in John's watching gaze as he jerked the chain upwards, in another silent command. One that Rosa immediately obeyed, rising higher up onto her knees, keeping her mouth open and swallowing, even as that swollen heft flared just before her eyes, so *close*—

His finger dropped to her lips, opening her mouth wider with a firm brush of his claw. And then his chain drew her closer, closer—until he finally filled her open mouth with the silken, rounded head of his swollen, dripping cock.

Rosa's moan was sheer, soaring ecstasy, and she didn't care who saw, who heard. Because all that mattered was this, her lord's prick *finally* in her mouth, where it was supposed to be, where she could lavish and worship it—and she willingly plunged it deep, almost all the way. Earning an immediate, unmistakable groan from John above her, and even several gasps of surprise from the otherwise-silent room.

Rosa sucked at him with as much strength as she could

bear, eagerly gagging on the invasion thrusting into her throat, and her fluttery hands lifted on their own, meaning to grab at his arse, to give herself leverage to go deeper—but then she moaned in sheer, strangled frustration, her hands frozen in midair, her teeth clenching slightly upon the thick shaft between them.

John laughed again, low and rich, his eyes crinkling with true mirth, his heavy hand caressing against her hair. "Foolish pet," he murmured. "I grant you leave to touch me, but only so that you may suckle me deeper. And I have warned you about your teeth, have I not?"

Fuck, yes, he had, which was why Rosa let them scrape again, harder this time—a shocking, incomprehensible action that made John's eyes flare, his thick length gouging with far more strength than before. And yes, yes, that was just why Rosa had done it, and she clutched her hands to his gorgeous arse, and yanked him closer. So deep she could scarcely breathe, kissing and suckling at the very base of him, her face thrust into his scratchy, sweet-smelling hair, while he dripped smooth and steady down her throat, straight into her hungry belly.

"Ach, this suits you, my pet," John said, his voice faltering as he ground against her convulsing throat. "You are so pretty, with an orc's *kraga* and chain upon your little neck. With his prick stretching out your little lips, wedged down your deep little throat."

Rosa shivered all over at the praise, even as she felt her eyes narrow up at him, her moans darkening. He wasn't goading her again, wanting that again, or was he—

"It is such deep joy," he continued, his eyes alight with fiendish warmth, as his hand sank deeper into her hair, his hips grinding his cock deeper into her throat. "To see my helpless pet struggle and suck with such hunger. To know that you shall not ask me a single silly question, so long as I keep filling your little mouth, and clogging your little throat with the whole of my prick—"

Gods curse the bastard, because he surely *was* doing it again. Provoking her, pushing her, his black tongue sweeping against his lips, his gaze glittering with such dark, deadly *greed*. And Rosa was going to do it, fuck, she was going to do it—

She bit down, hard. Harder than she'd ever imagined biting another living being, let alone this one—and in return John actually howled, his head rearing back, his claws scraping sharp on Rosa's scalp. Not making the slightest move to pull away, not even as Rosa's mouth swarmed with the taste of his *blood*, thick, tangy-salt iron, seeping against her tongue.

Good gods, what the *fuck* had she just done, and Rosa belatedly drew back, shaky, licking at her lips—and stared, frozen, at the thin red line she'd left behind. Nearly at the very base of him, further up than any of the others, very like she'd *marked* him. Flaunting how deep she'd taken him, staking her claim upon her bonded mate...

John was looking too, blinking, tracing an unsteady claw against it—and when his head lifted, slow, his eyes were blazing with rage, and with hunger, and with *pride*.

"I warned you, pet," he hissed, heated, deadly, his voice vibrating straight to Rosa's swollen, starving groin. "Do *not* bite your lord. Most of all before his kin."

His thumb had jerked to her lips, yanking them open, perhaps looking at the sight of his blood in her mouth—and in a sudden, furious flare of strength, he yanked Rosa bodily up, whirled her around, and pressed her face-first to the nearest wall. Her feet finding purchase on a little ledge she hadn't noticed before, raising her up to John's level, and just above her—Rosa gulped aloud—hung a heavy steel *chain*, with two shackles attached.

But yes, yes, John was going there, dragging up her arms with fluid, ruthless force. And then grasping at an innocuous-looking length of fabric that had been hanging on the wall, and wrapping it quick and deft around her wrists, before jerking the steel shackles close, and clamping them shut with a powerful, gut-wrenching *snap.*

"Fuck," Rosa gasped, trying and failing to yank her hands away from that iron hold, and behind her John gave a dark, diabolical laugh. His hand teasing, stroking up her bare thigh, gripping at her bare exposed arse—

And then that hand drew away, intent, deliberate—and *slapped* her. The sensation bright and screaming, exploding a shocked, helpless moan from Rosa's throat, her body shivering all over, her breaths ragged and choked—

"Ach," John growled, tugging her head backwards by the chain, so he could look at her, hold her frantic eyes. "Is this what you wish for, my disobedient pet? To take the punishment you deserve, for *daring* to provoke your lord thus?"

Oh gods, oh *fuck*, because his hands were yanking her arse out behind her, thrusting her trembling legs apart, and showing the watching room everything, *everything*—and then he again struck her bared, bent-over arse with another cold, stinging, purposeful slap.

Rosa shouted and keened, twisted and writhed, her eyes wide and wild as they drank up the smug righteous fury on his cruel, triumphant face. "You devious reprobate," she panted, craving, revelling in the instant answering heat flaring across those eyes. "I just want you to *fuck* me."

A deep, thoroughly frightening growl burned from his throat, and that hand slapped again, soaring showers of sparks beneath Rosa's already-tender skin. "Foolish pet," he snarled. "You must *earn* a fucking from your orc. You must eagerly yield to my command, and *show* me your hunger for me."

The sheer frenzied need was bellowing, blistering across Rosa's body, skittering with the next firm slap of that hand. And even as a distant part of her screamed to keep fighting him, to see just how far he would go, his hand struck again, even harder—and then, oh hell, slid down against her dripping-wet heat. Taunting her, tormenting her, slipping into what was *his,* where he *belonged*—and when it drew away again, leaving her empty and untouched, it felt like the craving was about to burst, lost in the sheer, screaming *need.* In Rosa's fierce, fundamental need to please him, to feel him, to accept, to *be. My deeds, and my wishes, are my own.*

She felt her head frantically nodding, her body shivering, sparking, gulping for air—and then she somehow spread her trembling legs wider, jutting her stripped, stinging, reddened arse out further. Baring the shameful, greedy clutch of her empty heat straight toward John, toward the open room. More exposed than she'd ever been, at any point in the entirety of her *life,* silently pleading for her mate to look, to know, to take what was his, to give what was hers.

"Please, my lord," she gasped. "*Ríddu mér. Ég vil þig.*"

Fuck me. I want you. The words landing like stones, rippling into silence, into the audible noise of her swollen clenching lips—and then, the sudden, shameful, thoroughly shocking trickle of her own wetness, streaking down her thigh.

"Please, John-Ka," she choked, into the taut stillness. "My lord. My Priest. I'm yours. Your pet, your mate, your *worshipper.* However you want to use me. I need you"—she heaved for breath—"to take me, and plough me, and fill me until I *burst.*"

She could *feel* the intensity of John's attention upon her, the weight of the silence in the still, watching room—and there was no shame left, no hesitation, as Rosa thrust her legs even wider, exposed herself further, felt the proof of her hunger actually dripping straight down from her, pooling onto the stone floor.

"Please, my lord," she whispered. "*Ríddu mér. Ég elska þig.*"

Fuck me. I love you.

The stillness closed, hung, shimmered—and finally, *finally,*

John moved. His body jerking forward, until—a shout tore from Rosa's mouth—she could feel the slick, smooth strength of that cock, brushing against her clenching, wide-open heat. Swelling and flaring and reaching toward her, almost as if seeking her, finding its way. While her swollen, desperate body strained back to meet him, convulsing upon the head of him, pleading, fighting for more—

His slam inside was brutal, furious, deadly—and in that single, devastating thrust, Rosa's pleasure coiled, gripped, and exploded. Her mouth truly screaming, her hands uselessly yanking at her shackles, while that huge, rock-hard prick drove home again and again and again. Splitting her in two upon it, flaying her apart, juices spurting and dripping, while her scream kept tearing through the room, her release still throbbing, still clinging, still shouting its fervent worship to her mate, her priest, her lord. The sole owner of this iron driving prick, these pointed claws sunk into her hips, these vicious teeth scraping at her throat, and Rosa arched back, bared her neck to him, begged and babbled and broke—

The teeth clamped down, as his cock locked into stillness, his bollocks bulging—and then, with a choked roar, he *burst*. Blowing out seed with so much force that it blasted him straight back out of her, the spray spattering across her reddened arse, down her bare legs, while those sharp teeth still kept hold of her neck, his greedy swallows thick and audible in Rosa's ear, his throat moaning with heated, broken ecstasy.

Rosa somehow stood there, revelling in the floating, sighing pleasure, still so fiercely powerful it was almost unbearable—at least, until the intensity of John's bite finally faded into the feel of a gently lapping tongue, and softly kissing lips. As Rosa's distant, whirling brain vaguely noted that he also had her *kraga* in his mouth, he'd bitten her *over* it, maybe just to feel its strength upon her neck as he'd done it. Just the same way as— her body prickled, keened under the touch—his hand had slipped downwards, sliding almost eager into the utter mess he'd made of her. His wetness still streaming down her spread thighs, dripping liberally off her exposed, reddened arse.

But her legs had begun badly trembling, her exhausted body dragging against the shackles' hard grip on her wrists—and suddenly John was here, holding her up. Supporting her full weight with one strong, gentle arm, while the other deftly unfastened the shackles, and drew down her wrists. Carefully pulling off the cloth, and then turning over one hand, and then the other, clearly examining them for any hint of damage.

Next he began smoothing the cloth against her, cleaning up his sticky, slippery mess with soft, silent intent. Working down Rosa's back, stroking against her loose hair, and then moving to her arse, her legs, even down to where he'd somehow gotten it on her *feet*.

Only then did he turn her around again, propping her against the wall, boxing her in with his arms. Almost as if to now hide the sight of her away from the room—or maybe to hide the truth of his own swollen mouth, the flushed heat of his cheeks, the glittering brightness in his blinking eyes.

"Are you well, pet," he whispered. "Have I harmed you. Or truly frightened you."

But Rosa's thoughts only swarmed with warmth, with contentment, with a rapt, rising elation that felt far too close to triumph. "Of course not," she whispered, soft. "I wanted it. I *loved* it, my lord."

The words were vaguely familiar, like something she'd said long ago, and John's eyes briefly widened before squeezing shut, his breath expelling in a single harsh huff. "No false-hoods," he whispered, like he still didn't quite believe her—so Rosa wrapped her trembly arms around his neck, dragged him close. And kissed him with lips and teeth and tongue until he was kissing her back, so sweet and reverent it sang deep in her soul.

"I would have yet stopped," he breathed, once they pulled apart, his forehead bent to hers. "If you had once asked. Or smelled of true fear."

"I know," Rosa whispered, and she did know, her hands spreading against his chest, feeling the thud of his pounding heartbeat—and, also, feeling fabric. His *tunic.*

"Wait," Rosa said, yanking back to blink at him, seeing him for what felt like the first time. "You were still *dressed* this entire time?! And"—she scrabbled around for his braid, and held up its shiny black neatness before her eyes—"your hair still looks like this? You sprayed your *seed* in mine!"

The last traces of unease had entirely pooled away from John's face, and in its place was a tender, twitching impishness. "I did not hear you complain, pet," he murmured. "Too busy squalling and flailing to notice, I ken. *Again.*"

Rosa tried for an elbow at him, but she was far too staggery and slow, and in a sudden whirl of movement, John snatched her up into his arms, and then unhooked the chain from her *kraga.* Tossing it off to someone else, and then barking an order in rapid Aelakesh before grasping for his lamp, and striding from the room.

"You are sure you are well, pet," he murmured into her hair as he walked. "I wish you to swear this to me."

"I swear, John-Ka," Rosa said, with a roll of her eyes toward him, but she was still smiling up at him, all the same. "I was a good pet for you, wasn't I?"

John nodded down at her with utter seriousness, and hitched her a little closer. "You were—*joy,* my pet," he breathed. "You are all I could have dreamt of. So eagerly longing to be bared and marked and used. So hungry to serve your lord. I shall"—his throat convulsed—"I shall forever cherish this night, my sweet rose. I shall forever cherish *you.*"

The warmth was about to burst out of Rosa's chest, threatening to erupt in either gales of laughter or hysterical happy weeping, and she hurled her arms close around his back, and thrust her leaking face hard into his neck. "I love you too," she said, hoarse, muffled. "Even if you are a merciless, clothes-wearing reprobate. Who secretly gets off on being *bitten*, in places where teeth have *no right* to be."

She could feel the slight return of his unease, the trace of stiffness under his skin. "You—caught this, then."

Rosa couldn't help a strangled laugh, an affectionate little nip at his delectable-smelling throat. "I think everyone in the room caught that, John-Ka. Everyone in the mountain, probably. And *especially* the woman with your cock in her mouth, who you *really* wanted to bite you."

John barked a chuckle too, and then turned, striding into the familiar warmth of his bedroom. Setting the lamp on the floor, before easing her naked body onto the soft furs of his bed.

"It is another—orc way, I ken," he said, quiet, as he slid himself in beside her. "I should not blame you, pet, if this shocked you, or repulsed you."

He turned away for an instant, and Rosa realized that someone had handed him a basket—Hanarr, she vaguely noted, as he gave a cheerful wave, and strode away again—and it was full of delicious-looking meat and cheese and bread, and another distinctive bottle of that milk. So wonderfully, suddenly familiar that Rosa's heart seemed to swell in her chest, and she immediately yanked out the stopper and drank it dry, while John watched with quiet, affectionate approval in his eyes.

"You cannot repulse me, John-Ka," Rosa said, wiping her mouth, flashing him a warm, wry smile. "I keep telling you, don't I? You're just—you. Scholar. Leader. Lord. Orc. Rightful Priest of Orc Mountain. Devious bastard who likes to be bitten. Reprobate. It's all good. All *you*."

John's eyes were blinking at her again, almost dazed, as

though she couldn't possibly be real—at least, until there was a sound from the bed opposite. A snort, Rosa realized, and when she and John both jerked to look, it was Salvi. Lying fully naked on Tristan's bed, with an equally naked—and very aroused— Tristan curled in his arms.

"And soon the *real* Priest of Orc Mountain, too," Salvi said, as his hand stroked smoothly, blatantly, up Tristan's bobbing length. "Thanks to *me*, for giving Simon a much-needed tongue-lashing on your behalf, while also sewing up his huge and"—he shuddered—"*very* hairy leg."

Tristan made a weak noise of protest, his eyes darting help- lessly between John and Salvi, even as Salvi stroked up again, making him quiver and keen. "It was not just that, *elskan*," Tristan gasped, "and you know this. I have been teaching Simon, all this time. Rosa-Ka earned his respect for her work, and she was the one who proposed these new classes in common-tongue. And we heard of your public thanks to the Skai today, John-Ka. Very heartfelt, I am told."

It was astonishing, Rosa distantly noted, how all these orcs seemed to always know about everything—and even John was looking entirely nonplussed by this revelation, frowning narrow-eyed across the room toward them. "Has Simon yet spoken to the captain of this?"

"Tomorrow," Tristan replied, though his voice sounded increasingly frayed, as Salvi's hand kept up its smooth, familiar strokes. "He swore to me he would."

"Ach, my sneaky little *sæti*," Salvi said, with an exaggerated grimace. "Wrapping that horrid, thick-witted lout around your pretty little claw. *Anything* for *John-Ka*."

"Oh, hush, *elskan*," Tristan purred, as he languidly arched closer into Salvi's touch. "You would too. Harder. *Ach*."

John rolled his eyes and settled back onto the bed beside Rosa, though a curious, satisfied little smile played on his mouth. "Eat, pet," he said, nudging the basket of food closer against her. "You have a Ka to grow, you ken. We must do all within our power to ensure you birth him safely."

Rosa meekly obeyed, but she couldn't seem to stop eyeing him, smiling too. "You really think they'll make you Priest?" she asked, between bites. "Because you'd be so brilliant, John-Ka. Imagine what you could do, if you had a whole *mountain* to take care of."

The smile still lingered on his mouth, warm, hopeful, beautiful. "Ach, as if I do not have enough to care for now," he said coolly, even as he settled her closer, tucking her under the weight of his arm, his claws gently tickling at the *kraga* on her neck. "Now rest, pet, and listen."

He'd reached over her for a book—*The Lady Bright*, Rosa realized, with a true jolt of shock. Because it was *still here*, and had they truly now *stolen* all those books from the Dusbury library?!

"Wait," she said, her voice shrill. "Are we book thieves?! Good gods, John, we're *book thieves!*"

John's glance down at her was amused, his eyebrows rising, his claw flipping the book open to the last place they'd read. "Of all you have faced these past weeks," he said, with damnable calmness, "*this* is what most vexes you?"

Rosa just kept glaring at him, even as her mouth abominably twitched, and John drew her still closer against his solid warmth. "Foolish pet," he purred. "I am an orc, ach? And thus, I raided this library, and stole away what I wished. These books are now *mine*. Just as you are, with your pretty new *kraga*, and your full little womb."

Rosa could have argued, she supposed, but she still couldn't seem to stop grinning at him, drinking up the gods-damned *triumph* in his gleaming, satisfied eyes. "Devious *scoundrel*," she murmured. "I'm truly starting to wonder if there isn't some truth to everything I read about you orcs, after all."

His slow, sharp-toothed smile back was sheer,

unadulterated joy, all the world's rightness wrapped up in his beautiful, beloved face. In Rosa's own lord, her own bonded mate. Her priest, wise and wicked and worthy. Her orc.

"You ought not to heed *all* you read," he said, his claws brushing gentle against her neck, before reaching down to turn the page. "Now rest, my little rose, and *learn*."

BONUS EPILOGUE

After more than a year in Orc Mountain, Rosa still found the orcs' parties a bit... overwhelming.

It wasn't that they weren't fun—in fact, they were a wild, chaotic delight—and as Rosa glanced around the echoing Ka-esh muster-room, she felt her mouth twitching up in genuine amusement. It seemed like every orc in the mountain was in attendance, all talking and drinking and eating at once, and there were drums thudding in one corner, a sparring-match in another, and a variety of intensive games and contests, complete with loudly cheering audiences to spur them on.

It was home, it was everyone Rosa loved, but at the moment it was also... *loud*. Very, very loud, clanging into Rosa's slightly aching head, and she shot a rueful smile down at the whole cause of the party, and indeed, her headache. The plump, adorable grey orcling on her hip, blinking his long-lashed eyes at the hubbub all around. Her son. Thorin.

They'd named him after an ancient hero in a Ka-esh tale—now one of Rosa's favourites—and in Thorin's six months of life so far, he'd proven himself more than worthy of the name. He was stubborn, eager, quick to mimic and learn, and thoroughly devoted to his favourite people. To Rosa, of course, and also to Tristan and Salvi, who had instantly assumed the role of additional parents—an arrangement no one had actually discussed, but which had proven highly agreeable to all.

But without question, Thorin's favourite person in the world was John. And even in this moment, his little black eyes were blinking up toward John, who was currently standing tall and silent beside them, and frowning out toward the party. And as John kept standing there, his fingers tapping impatiently against his thigh, Thorin's tiny clawed hand snapped up, grasped the end of John's dangling braid, and gave it a forceful, purposeful little yank.

John's answering glance down toward his son was immediate, increasingly affectionate, and he dropped a hand to gently tug at Thorin's own tiny braid—earning in return a sudden, vicious-looking clamp of Thorin's sharp little teeth against his finger. To which John laughed, his crinkling eyes darting brief and approving toward Rosa's, his mouth curving up with easy, tolerant warmth.

And though Rosa should probably have protested—one should *not* be pleased when one's offspring showed such fondness for biting, right?—she felt herself rolling her eyes back at John, and tickling her fingers at Thorin's little grey chest. Making him wriggle and squirm, his mouth clamping tighter on John's finger, while John made an impressive face of mock agony, and Rosa grinned at them both with a rising, tilting tenderness.

It was—odd, being a mother. It was something that, despite all her obsessive research on pregnancy and childbirth, Rosa still hadn't in the least felt prepared for. This almost agonizing affection, clutched in a permanent knot in her chest, competing with the constant exhaustion and the spiking elation and the pure, devastating terror that one day, it might all disappear.

But it hadn't, yet. In fact, despite Rosa's frequently exhausted state, this past year had been without question the most delightful and intriguing of her entire life. Even when factoring in her childbirth—a well-supported yet still horrendous trial that she far preferred not to think about—she had never even imagined feeling so content, so stimulated, so amused. So *alive.*

And over the past year, she had indeed accomplished any number of surprising things. She'd become nearly fluent in Aelakesh. She'd almost doubled her library's holdings, and translated all its Osadan books into common-tongue. She'd met more than a dozen other women bearing orc sons, and had helped inform and support their choices, no matter what those choices were. And she'd successfully grown and birthed a whole *son,* and John was no longer the last of the Ka—and many months before, John had also been fully, finally proclaimed Priest of Orc Mountain, in a raucous, massive celebration that had closely rivalled this one.

"How fare you, pet?" came John's voice, close and low in Rosa's ear. "Mayhap I shall fetch you another drink, or aught more to eat?"

Rosa shot him a grateful smile, but shook her head. "I'm fine," she said, at her normal volume, knowing that John—being an orc—could somehow still hear through the hubbub. "Just a bit tired. Likely because of *you* barely sleeping last night, you hungry *litla skrímsli.*"

She shot a wry smile down at Thorin as she spoke, and he blinked back at her with adorable, utterly convincing innocence, his teeth still gnawing on John's finger. Until John swiftly drew the finger away, instead using it to tilt Rosa's face up toward him, his eyes narrowing. "This is not the only cause, pet," he said. "You know you—"

But his words were drowned by a shrill, ear-splitting howl, piercing through the room. It was Grimarr, raising his hands high into the air, while his own young son Tengil clung to his thigh. "Peace!" Grimarr bellowed, though his eyes were warm, his mouth grinning a terrifying smile. "We must welcome our new Ka-esh son, and then further rejoice!"

The room accordingly settled into a steady murmur of voices, and suddenly almost every eye in the room had turned toward them. Toward John and Rosa and Thorin, waiting together at the front of the muster-room—because this was indeed a celebration of Thorin. A long-standing orc tradition, Rosa had learned, to hail an orcling's first half-year of life, and fully welcome him into the clans.

Grimarr snatched up Tengil into his arms, and then, with Jule close at his side, strode across the room toward Rosa and John. He was followed closely by Baldr and Drafli, and then by Silfast and Stella, and Simon and his new mate Maria—a very lovely, yet very stubborn woman who had more than proven herself Simon's match. And last of all were Nattfarr and his cheerful mate Ella, who, despite her distaste for all things scholarly, had quickly become one of Rosa's closest friends.

They settled into a loose half-circle around John and Rosa and Thorin, and it was Nattfarr and Ella who stepped forward first, both smiling at Thorin's watching little face. "*Okkur hefur verið gefinn sonur og í dag fögnum við,*" Nattfarr said, his low voice carrying through the room. "A son is given to us, and today we rejoice!"

There were more shouts and cheers, and once they'd finally subsided again, Nattfarr gave a fluid, flourishing little bow toward Rosa and Thorin. "A gift for Thorin of Clan Ka-esh, from the Grisk," he said. "Welcome, little brother."

With that, he held out his hand—and upon it was a glinting, sparkling *bracelet*. A piece Rosa had never seen before, but which was clearly a marvel of Grisk craftsmanship, made up of hundreds of gold links, all woven together into a shimmering, breathtaking whole. And as Rosa carefully took it into her fingers, she realized it was flexible enough to fit Thorin's little arm now, while also expanding along with him as he grew.

"It's *lovely*," Rosa said, blinking back the wetness prickling behind her eyes. "Thank you. All of you. *Við erum svo þakklát.* We are so grateful."

John thanked them too, speaking smoothly and eloquently of the Grisk's warmth and generosity, while also somehow ignoring the fact that Thorin had made another mad grab for his finger, and was chewing forcefully upon it. To which Natt-farr only flashed John a knowing grin, and then strode with Ella back to their own Grisk kin. One of whom was currently wrangling their own tiny, squirming son, an active, adorable little hellion named Rakfi.

Jule and Grimarr stepped forward next, and after some prompting from Jule, Tengil carefully held out a gift from the Ash-Kai—a delightful little pair of drums painted with colourful patterns. And after another heartfelt thank-you from John and Rosa, Simon and Maria stepped forward, handing over the Skai's gift. A set of wonderful little carved wooden figures, depicting both humans and orcs wielding tiny, intricate scimitars and axes.

"Help little Ka learn of battle," Simon said firmly, rustling his huge hand against Thorin's head. "Learn of Skai ways, as we learn of Ka-esh."

John answered that with equal gravity, giving Simon a brief but sincere smile, after which Silfast and Stella came forward, holding out the Bautul's gift—a cleverly carved, perfectly balanced tiny wooden sword. A gift that Thorin eagerly and immediately clasped into his little hand, prompting Silfast to begin guffawing with laughter, loudly proclaiming—much to John's visible chagrin—that perhaps this little Ka-esh would become a warrior, after all.

And finally, Tristan and Salvi stepped forward, clearly on behalf of the Ka-esh—and in Tristan's hands was a *book*. One of those distinctive, beautiful little devotional books, neatly bound in embossed leather. And Rosa only vaguely noticed herself passing Thorin over to John, so she could reach for the book, and flip through its crisp new pages.

And it was—stunning. Full of intricate block letters and illustrations, accented with shimmering gold leaf. And its even, elegant, handwritten script was Tristan's, fully and entirely Tristan's, page after page after *page*.

"Good *gods*, Tristan," Rosa said, choked, blinking up at his warm watching eyes. "This is incredible. It must have taken you weeks. *Months*."

Tristan easily waved it away, as if this one book didn't represent appalling amounts of secret, painstaking, tiring work. "I was happy to do this," he said firmly, "to welcome our new son, and begin to teach him of his clan, and his home. Ach, *krúttið mitt*?"

He was giving Thorin his slow, dazzling smile, to which Thorin loudly gurgled, flailing his little arms toward Tristan's face. And when John willingly handed him over, Thorin latched onto Tristan with his usual immediate enthusiasm, butting him in the chest with his tiny head.

Tristan laughed aloud and curled Thorin close, brushing his black hair away from his face. "*Ég elska þig, krúttið mitt*," he said, soft. "Welcome to your home, and your clan, and your kin. And as your fathers, we vow to care for you, and guide you, and keep you safe. For as long as we are able."

Thorin blinked back at him, quiet and watchful, as though listening to every word, and Salvi hooked an arm around Tristan's neck, drawing them both close. "And you better appreciate that, you wee *menace*," he said, gently jabbing a claw into Thorin's chest. "Not every orcling gets three devoted and utterly *brilliant* fathers like us."

Simon, who had still been standing nearby, huffed a loud snort, earning sharp glares from both John and Salvi. And before the situation could devolve any further, Grimarr abruptly stepped forward again, and rested his huge hands against Thorin's tiny shoulders. "*Við blessum þig, litla barn,*" he said, his deep voice resonating through the room. "We bless you, little one. Welcome home."

The words felt like a bell, ringing deep into Rosa's bones, and into the growing swell of cheers and claps and stomps. An entire mountain rising in celebration, welcoming her cherished, adored son as their own.

The room rapidly spiralled into chaos after that, and Thorin was soon surrounded by yet more well-wishers, offering jokes and funny faces and warm congratulations. All of which he seemed to take in stride, blinking with visible curiosity at all who approached, and only occasionally hiding his little face in Tristan's chest.

Rosa watched it all with a rising, reckless-feeling reverence, and had to keep wiping at her eyes, brushing the steady stream of wetness away. Until she shot a watery, wavering smile up at John, who was looking back at her with sudden, careful intensity. And within a breath, he'd handed off all their lovely gifts to Hanarr, who'd been standing nearby, and gripped Rosa's wrist with warm, powerful fingers.

"Come, pet," he said, in his tone that brooked no argument. "You must now rest for a spell. We shall be in our room, brothers."

This was spoken loudly toward Tristan and Salvi, who both nodded back, their eyes briefly intent on John's. Knowing, without any of them saying it at all, that they would take devoted care of Thorin in John and Rosa's absence, and alert them at the first sign of the slightest concern.

With that, John's fingers tightened around Rosa's wrist, and he promptly marched her out of the bustling room.

Thoroughly ignoring her halfhearted attempts at protesting, in favour of plucking her up, and settling her into her usual place on his hip.

"Do not seek to sway me, pet," he said flatly. "You have been weary and overset all this day. All this *week*. I shall not see my mate's health uselessly squandered upon my brothers' ceaseless need for roistering."

Rosa felt herself reluctantly smiling at John's profile, illuminated sharply in the warm light of the corridor's new lanterns. "It was a party for our *son*, and I'm not *that* weary," she countered, jabbing weakly at his chest. "Also, did you just say *roistering*?!"

John fully ignored all of these entirely valid points, and stalked into their bedroom with single-minded purpose. "Ach, I did," he said coolly. "And you shall shut your pretty mouth, pet, and stop fighting me, lest you earn a harsh and painful punishment from your bonded mate and lord."

The shudder vibrated deep and reflexive in Rosa's chest, and her gaze on John's face was wide and intent, her mouth bone-dry. Gods, it had been so long since he'd done that, days, *weeks*. Out of concern for her safety, Rosa well knew, but the loss of it had become a slow gnawing ache—and suddenly she craved it, needed it, so fiercely the room seemed to judder and whirl around her.

"I shall *not* shut my mouth, you great *reprobate*," she hissed, jabbing at John's chest with far more force than before. "You have no right to steal me away from my own son's party. *None*."

John didn't even blink, though Rosa caught the brief, unmistakable twitch of relief, flashing behind his eyes. "I do," he said, "and I have. You are *mine*, pet, and thus, I shall do whatever I wish with you."

Rosa had to bite back her moan, especially as John yanked off her tunic, hurled it to the floor, and then eased her naked, wriggling form down onto their bed. "And if I should wish to punish you, or use you as I wish," he breathed, as he loomed over her on the bed, his body taut, his eyes flashing, "I *shall*, foolish pet."

"I am *not*—" Rosa began, with creditable clarity—at least, until John grasped for a nearby rag, and stuffed it *into her mouth*. Not deep enough that she couldn't spit it out, but enough to say just how far he was going with this—and Rosa's body gave another one of those deep, bone-wrenching shudders, shattering her from the inside out.

"Better," John said, with damnable coolness, as he gripped one of Rosa's wrists, and yanked it up toward the corner of the bed. Clamping it firmly into one of the padded, perfectly sized cuffs he'd had installed into the stone wall, before grasping for Rosa's other wrist, and securing it in the opposite corner with a decisive *snap*. And then he snatched up the exquisite gold chain embedded in the wall between the two cuffs, and clipped it to Rosa's *kraga* with easy, deadly efficiency.

It left Rosa stark-naked, gagged, leashed, and cuffed to a bed, while her fully clothed lord knelt over her, oozing power and insolence and a chilly, smug satisfaction. "Ach, silly pet," he purred, as he plucked at her peaked, reddened nipple, and roughly thrust her legs apart. "Now you shall lie back, and accept your lord's care for you. You shall now please me, and *obey*."

Rosa frantically shook her head, fighting to narrow her eyes at him, knowing he wouldn't stop—gods, he *couldn't* stop—and in return he laughed, cold and mocking. And then, with one strong, forceful forearm, he shoved both her thighs up and back, nearly bending her double, exposing her arse to the air. Holding his insolent eyes on hers, his eyebrows raised, as if to say, *Ach, you know what I shall do, you know what you deserve*—

Rosa kicked and writhed at him, her previous tiredness entirely lost beneath the sudden screaming need—but John was far too strong, too determined, too *everything*. And he was *enjoying* this, revelling in this, raising his clawed hand with visible, drawn-out menace, a low growl burning from his throat—

And then he *slapped* her. Harsh, stinging, *glorious*, straight on her exposed arse, firing pain and pleasure, streaking bright under her skin.

Rosa bucked and flailed, her legs wildly kicking, but John easily caught them again, gripping both her ankles together in one forceful hand. And then smiled at her, placid and dangerous, as he bent her lower half further back—and slapped her *again*. His palm stinging, his claws scraping sharp, digging against tender pale skin.

"What do you say, pet," he said, utterly unaffected, as he palmed at her with his lingering hand, letting her feel the danger of those claws. "Shall you now accept my care, and beg my forgiveness?"

Rosa shook her head, manic and desperate, even as he spread her legs apart again, his gaze casually dropping to the sight between them. And rather than kicking, fighting, hiding from him, she felt her legs spreading further, her swollen wetness clenching, begging, pleading for more—and John knew, he *obliged*, dancing those deadly claws against her greedy, wide-open heat with taunting, deliberate purpose.

Rosa could hear herself moaning through the gag, could feel her hungry, spread-apart body squeezing out its wetness. *His* wetness, left there just last night, and now spurting thick and hot and obscene onto his teasing, waiting fingers.

"Messy little pet," John purred, rubbing those fingers into her, spreading it, revelling in it. "Always piddling your lord's good seed, ach? I ought to have instead blown this good load down your deep little throat, where it should have at least stayed where I put it."

Oh *gods*, Rosa's moans were nearly drowning out his voice, her trapped, beleaguered body spurting out even more, proving the bastard right, *wanting* him to be proven right.

Wanting him to bring up that sticky, messy hand, just like this, and stroke it slowly, affectionately, mockingly, down the side of her face.

"Ach, my helpless, foolish little plaything," he breathed. "Shall you now seek your lord's forgiveness?"

It felt harder to shake her head this time, but Rosa somehow managed, and John's answering slap to her arse was swift, immediate, so forceful her whole body wrenched, her eyes rolling back. But gods it was good, so damned good, everything, and Rosa needed more, more—

And thank the gods, John gave it. First with a steady, rising series of hard, powerful slaps, leaving her bared arse raw and stinging, while his eyes never once left hers—and then, as Rosa quivered and moaned, with the cool, easy setting of two deadly, clawed fingers against her dripping-wet heat, and then sinking them slow and proprietary inside.

He was an expert at this by now, often using up to three fingers at once, without even touching the head of her womb, or drawing a single drop of blood. But in this moment, with Rosa gagged and cuffed and leashed to his bed, her legs thrust wide and back, her flayed arse throbbing, the fear was rising, sharp and overpowering and *wonderful*. Obliterating all else but the bare, shocking truth of her huge, stunning, growling lord bent over her, using her, punishing her, and piercing her whole upon his sharp, deadly claws.

Rosa's body had begun desperately writhing, begging for escape begging for more, but John stilled her with a deep bark, a warning flex of those fingers inside. Firing her back to immediate stillness again, as his fingers sank deeper, and her moans rose louder, and her hunger sought to claw its way out of her skin—

Her release was close, so close she was almost sobbing, her body stiffening, her arms and legs violently trembling—and curse the prick, but he yanked himself out, away, apart. Leaving her there cuffed and gagged and untouched, wholly at his mercy, pleading without words, without thought, for his touch, his use, his rule.

But he only gazed back at her, his eyes glinting and deadly, his black tongue flicking out to brush against his lips—and then he brought up his wet fingers, and slowly, leisurely licked them off, one by one.

"What do you say now, pet?" he asked, raising his eyebrows at her, his voice velvety smooth. "Shall you beg me?"

Fuck yes, gods fuck everything, and this time Rosa was fervently, furiously nodding, so hard it hurt. Enough that John's strong hand came to her face, stilling it, the disapproval flaring across his eyes, even as he gently drew the gag out of her mouth.

Rosa gulped back jagged breaths, her eyes frozen to his, and she fought for words, for thought. "*Mér þykir þetta svo leitt, John-Ka,*" she gasped, her voice hoarse. "*Ég er þín. Ég elska þig. Að eilífu.*"

I'm so sorry, John, it meant. *I belong to you. I love you. For always.*

John's answering nod was short, sharp, approving—and Rosa's reward, oh hell, was in his hands dropping to his groin, and drawing himself out. Showing her his scarred, beautiful heft, so familiar now, but still an awe-inducing marvel of force and power and pleasure.

And at the base of it—his clawed thumb stroked there with soft, unconscious reverence—was Rosa's mark. One she'd been working on for the whole of this year, teeth slicing in the same place again and again, because apparently human bites didn't scar the same way orcs' did. But John certainly didn't seem to mind, and in this moment there was a jolting, incongruous urge to beg him for that, *please, my lord, let me taste you, let me feel you between my teeth—*

But no, no, because he wasn't undressing any further, was

only going to give her this—and suddenly that was the urge obliterating all else, the sheer screaming need, Rosa's hands again jerking at her restraints, her eyes blinking hard at the prickling wetness behind them.

"All of you?" she choked out. "Please, John-Ka? My lord?"

And these words were different than the others, spoken with a raw, breaking-hot urgency—and above her John's body seemed to still, his throat convulsing, once. Almost as if to say, *not this time, pet*, as he had the last few times now. As he so often had for the whole of this past year, particularly if they had an audience. And while this was something Rosa now deeply understood—for John, being unclothed, undone, also meant being vulnerable, exposed, unshielded—she also still craved it, with an intensity that sometimes felt almost agonizing in its strength.

"Please, my lord," she breathed again, as she purposely spread her legs wider, felt his seed again seeping from inside her, streaking down her bared, raw, reddened arse. Showing him her own vulnerability, her submission, her reverence. Her worship.

There was a moment's stillness, John's glittering eyes held to the sight between her legs—and then, oh hell, he did it. Yanking first for his tunic, dragging it off, hurling it to the floor—and then shucking his trousers, and tossing them aside, too. And then—Rosa moaned, loud, unfettered—he even reached for his ever-present perfect braid, tugging it apart, shaking out the shining sheet of blackness around his face.

Fuck. Rosa was audibly whimpering, her chest heaving, her ravenous eyes drinking him up—and then she moaned, deep and guttural, as his clawed hand stroked up the length of his scarred, rock-hard prick, milking out a thick, delectable string of white. Drizzling it straight down into her parted, clenching, greedy wetness, and watching with intent black eyes as she hungrily sucked it up, enfolding it deep inside.

He liked that, she knew, and the feel of his hot, slippery seed pooling into her was melting all conscious thought, so she babbled and begged, bucked and brandished, sucking in every drop—and then shouted incoherently as he finally leaned closer, his hard sleek head twitching and shuddering, almost as if seeking to chase its seed inside. And when it finally touched her, kissed her, acknowledged her, Rosa's shout rang through the room, her whole body screaming and on fire, *please my lord please ríddu mér please please please—*

He sank inside like a hammer, like a perfect strike to the heart, and Rosa arched to meet it, dragging him in, taking him whole. Feeling his strength and his power wedged so deep within her, locking them together, making her so thoroughly and entirely *his*—and when his hot, sweaty bare body collapsed down to cover hers, hiding them in the fall of his silken black hair, it was even better, it was all the world coalescing into sheer, exquisite pleasure. Shattering brighter and deeper as he began to thrust, pummelling her with the pure, piercing power of his massive, feverish orc-prick.

And it was perfect, *perfect*, and even more so when his head bent down, almost as if on its own, seeking its familiar place over her *kraga*—and his teeth sinking deep made Rosa scream again, her whole self clenching flaring shouting on fire, her lord's tongue sweetly stroking as his throat greedily swallowed, as his hand scraped down her cheek down her side all glorious pain and heat and sheer bracing longing—

His seed pumped into her like a flood, pouring out from the head of that gorgeous, thrilling cock inside her. Filling her, marking her, claiming her as his own—and Rosa's answering release felt like a knell from above, like a maddening trampling ecstasy, like the whole world was swinging and surging and shouting her master's name. John-Ka. Her lord. Her priest. *Hers.*

The truth of it soared and sang, reverberating deep into

Rosa's belly, into her heart. Into the fundamental, still-shivering reality of her lord locked against her, his prick between her legs, his teeth in her neck, his claws sunk deep and piercing into the skin of her hip.

But one of the glorious things about the biting, Rosa had learned, was that it also dulled pain. And as her lord slowly detached his bloody mouth from her neck, and then drew up his bloody claws to blink at them, she only felt warm, smug, *satisfied*.

"*Helvíti*," John groaned, squeezing his eyes shut, even as his black tongue slipped out to caress his dripping-red lips. "*Fyrirgefðu mér*, pet. I ought to have taken better care, most of all when you have been so weary of late. *Ach*."

But Rosa darted her head up, pulling against her *kraga*'s chain just enough to reach him. "Stop it, John-Ka," she murmured, as she pressed a long, heated kiss to his lips, tasting the tang of iron and salt. "That was"—she exhaled, heavy, contented, *safe*—"everything, my lord. *Thank* you."

But she could feel his rising resistance, the tension slipping into his bared body against hers. "I ought yet to take you to Efterar," he breathed. "We must be sure you—"

But Rosa kissed him again, biting off the words with a light nip of her teeth. "No," she hissed at him. "And I will happily fight you on this until you punish me again, John-Ka. I needed that. And you knew it, you gorgeous, devious *reprobate*."

He was finally kissing her back, careful, thorough, and when he pulled away he looked adorably conflicted, uncertain—and also shockingly, breathtakingly beautiful, fully bared to the room, his hair pooling over his shoulders, his muscles glinting with sweat. And when he gently drew out of her, despite the loss of him—and the immediate surging mess—it was even more beautiful, his cock still bobbing and dripping white as he blinked at her with those dazed, long-lashed eyes.

"Ach, but *pet*," he began, though the words seemed to break in his throat, and he bent down to softly kiss at Rosa's belly. At the already visible swell within it, growing surer with every passing day. With Rosa's firmly held promise to him, to the world, that if she had her way, there would never, *ever* again be a last of the Ka.

But even as John so clearly longed for this, Rosa knew that Thorin's birth had deeply affected him, too. Its lethal, devastating power had been so far beyond his control, beyond any care or affection or mastering he'd been able to give. And Rosa had never before seen him the way he'd been that day, weeping even as he'd desperately sought to hide it, speaking fierce comfort to her, gripping her screaming body safe in his shuddering arms, and roaring at Efterar, his brothers, his ancestors, the *world*, until his words had faded into broken croaks and silence.

"Hush, John-Ka," Rosa murmured now, her voice easy and soothing. "None of this will harm our son in the least, and you know it. And the happier I am, the happier he will be. And second orcling births are almost always easier than the first. Right?"

John couldn't argue any of those points, thankfully—they were all assertions from the orcling birth manual, which had indeed proven highly accurate to date—and instead he kept blinking at Rosa's belly, and pressing soft, sweet kisses against it. Slowly slipping over to where he'd punctured her hip, his tongue brushing careful and reverent against the broken skin.

"This shall scar, pet, should you not go to Efterar now," he said, finally drawing back again, his gaze suddenly distant, unreadable. "Will you not come?"

But Rosa shook her head, firm and decisive, and despite all John's fretting, she could see the answering flare in his eyes, too. The dark, wicked side of him that *liked* leaving marks on her, and liked it even better when they spoke of some occasion. Like the claw-marks on her other hip, when he'd first taken her in the pleasure-den. Like the bite-marks high on her thigh, earned the day he'd been made Priest. And like the marks of his hands over her breasts, ten perfect punctures, made the night he'd given her a ring before another priest, a human one, and vowed to make her not only his mate, but his *wife*.

"I like having your marks on me," Rosa whispered now, quiet, not even a little ashamed. "Thank you, my lord."

She could see him swallow, could see the hunger surge across his eyes—but then his gaze darted away, the tension flicking back into his shoulders. Not much, not something Rosa would have noticed a year ago—and again, something that again had taken time and observation to fully understand. John didn't often succumb to the shame anymore, or to memories of his past—but there were still moments when he seemed to struggle to just *be*, as though he was uncomfortable, or even afraid, in his own skin. And this moment, with his scars bared and his hair down—and with him going against all his own instincts to keep his mate safe, and then meekly obeying her wishes, rather than commanding them—was surely one of those.

So Rosa squirmed against her restraints, abrupt and forceful enough that John instantly obliged, releasing her wrists and her neck, and then immediately launching into his usual survey, making sure he hadn't damaged anything. And then, frowning, he even tugged open her lips, looking for any signs of pain or chafing from the gag, while Rosa obediently held her mouth open, and waited until he seemed satisfied.

She didn't argue when he reached for his clothes again, or when he swiftly tied up his hair. And instead, she fumbled for the book he'd been reading—the book he'd barely been reading, of late, what between her and Thorin and his still-constant work—and thrust it into his hands. And though John blinked at her, he silently obliged, shuffling to lean back in his usual place against the bunk's wall, his legs askew, his eyes dropping to the open page.

But between his spread legs, he was still rock-hard, still streaking wet against his trousers—so Rosa slipped down, and drew him out again. Curling up her naked, dripping, freshly marked body between her lord's thighs, and sucking his swollen, leaking cock deep into her throat.

She sucked him eagerly but silently, swallowing every drop he gave her. Proving herself a good, non-disruptive, obliging little pet, entirely in thrall to her lord, her priest, her master. Not caring in the least if he was fully ignoring her, if he kept turning the pages of his book with maddening steadiness, if he barely even gasped as he surged her mouth full of hot, thick sweetness.

But he still hadn't drawn away, and at some point he'd carded his claws into her hair, so Rosa sucked him back to hardness, and did it all again. Until he'd filled her mouth with another blast of thick, delectable seed, and Rosa heard someone else come into the room—but John didn't move, didn't twitch, so she just kept suckling, taking him deep. Serving her lord as he wished, even as she could feel more of his wetness dripping from between her legs, streaking down to pool on the bed below.

"Ach, brother," John's low voice said with perfect, unaffected smoothness. "Is aught amiss? How is our son?"

"Oh, you know," came a wry voice, Tristan's voice. "Being doted upon by the whole of Bautul, at the moment. Though I ken he shall begin fussing soon if he does not nurse, so should you like us to feed him, or...?"

The last word was non-committal, and Rosa knew Tristan meant it—he would keep Thorin distracted and amused for as long as they needed it—but she could feel John's shrug, his hand carding a little deeper into her hair. "Ach, bring him," he replied, still with astonishing casualness, for someone who was still getting his cock sucked. "I am almost done feeding my pet. Her belly and womb are now full, and her teats ought to be full also."

He was right, damn him, and Rosa sucked him deeper, letting him feel just the slightest scrape of teeth—to which the bastard only chuckled, and then asked Tristan some other inane question about their latest communication from Lord Otto. Leading into a detailed political discussion that Rosa couldn't follow in the least, not with the hard cockhead currently boring into her throat, swelling even fuller—

He spurted into her mid-sentence, without so much as a hitch in his voice, and finally Tristan took his leave, promising to return within the quarter hour. A grace period that John seemed perfectly willing to take full advantage of, his hand briefly flexing on Rosa's head, holding her there, while she heard the distinct sound of a page turning.

She did bite him that time, earning a low, tolerant chuckle, and finally he drew her up again, his fingers easy and gentle on her skin. And his eyes on hers were warm, grateful, brimming with visible, palpable affection, as his thumb brushed soft and reverent against her swollen, aching lips.

But he still didn't speak—still couldn't, perhaps—so Rosa kissed his thumb, and then nipped at it for good measure. "Thank you, my lord," she murmured, smiling at him, slow. "I truly needed that. I feel *so* much better. And *very* full."

She gave her rounded belly a self-satisfied little pat, drawing John's gaze down toward it. And after setting aside his book, his hand dropped to cup beside hers, feeling how he'd so thoroughly filled her with himself, made her wholly and entirely his own.

"Although," Rosa continued firmly, jabbing him in the chest, "after your pregnant, obedient pet has sucked you off *three times*, John-Ka, it might be nice to give her *some* acknowledgement. Maybe a little 'this pleased me, pet'. Or maybe, 'I will find some time in my excessively busy schedule to finally show you the new passage dig that's been consuming my life of late.'"

John's brows lifted up, but there was the smile, slow and tolerant, tugging at his mouth. "There is naught about this to amuse you, little rose. Only muck and rubble and angry orcs, and a tunnel that refuses to fully drain."

"I don't care," Rosa countered. "I want to see it, John-Ka. Please. Tomorrow."

His hand had begun gently stroking at her belly, his eyes so patient, and still so damnably *concerned*. "You are sure you are not too weary for this, pet."

"I am not weary or overset at *all* anymore, John-Ka," Rosa replied, giving a haughty toss of her head. "I just needed to rest for a spell, that's all."

John actually chuckled aloud at that, his eyes crinkling. "Ach, is that so," he said coolly. "I should never have guessed, foolish pet."

Rosa poked her elbow into his stomach, drinking up that beautiful warmth in his eyes, and eagerly complied as he maneuvered her down against his side, tucking her under his arm, and yanking the fur up over them. Saying, without saying it at all, that he loved her, and he'd needed this too, and that he truly would take her to his passage dig tomorrow, and that all was right in the world again.

And the rightness only struck deeper, truer, as Tristan and Salvi strode into the room, Salvi carrying an audibly fussing Thorin—but upon catching sight of John and Rosa in bed, Thorin immediately gurgled and squirmed, reaching his chubby grey arms toward them.

Rosa and John welcomed his wriggling form with smiles and pats and kisses, and soon he was curled upon them, happily nursing at Rosa's breast, while John's arm circled tighter around them both, his hand gently caressing at Thorin's back. And it was quite possibly the most contented feeling in the world, being held so safe in the arms of one's mate and husband and lord, with one's beautiful son in one's arms, and a second son growing in one's belly.

Rosa massively yawned, earning a gentle pat from John's hand to her head, tucking it back down against his shoulder. A silent order that she all too willingly obeyed, snuggling closer against him, blearily blinking as he again reached for his book, and flipped it open to where he'd been reading.

But there was a lingering little smile on his mouth as he read, not even a trace of tension in his form or his face. And Rosa drew it in, treasured it, *cherished* it—and then closed her eyes, and drifted into a deep, dreamless sleep.

THANKS FOR READING
AND GET A FREE BONUS STORY!

Thank you so much for coming along on this Ka-esh adventure with me!

If you'd like a little more orc fun, join my mailing list at www.finleyfenn.com for extra content, including some fabulous artwork from *The Librarian and the Orc*, and a free Orc Sworn story. I'd love to stay in touch with you!

FREE STORY:
OFFERED BY THE ORC

The monster needs a sacrifice. And she's naked on the altar...

When Stella wanders the forest alone one fateful night, she only seeks peace, relief, escape. A few stolen moments on a secret, ancient altar, at one with the moon above.

Until she's accosted by a hulking, hideous, bloodthirsty *orc*. An orc who demands a sacrifice—not by his sword, but by Stella's complete surrender. To his claws, his sharp teeth, his huge muscled body. His every humiliating, thrilling command...

But Stella would never offer herself up to be used and sacrificed by a monster—would she? Even if her surrender just might grant her the moon's favour—and open her heart to a whole new fate?

FREE download now!
www.finleyfenn.com

ACKNOWLEDGMENTS

I am so deeply grateful to my readers (thank you!), and my incredibly generous and insightful beta readers and advance reviewers. I love you all!

I'm especially thankful for the kindness, encouragement, and guidance of Jennifer N., Jesse, Jen R., Marcia, and my ever-wonderful Amy. And a special shout out to Ann for all the orcling expertise, and to Þórey H. for all her fabulous help with the Aelakesh (a.k.a. Icelandic) translation!

I'm also SO grateful to my lovely Facebook group members at Finley Fenn Readers' Den (come join us, they are a DELIGHT), for helping me name my new Ka-esh orcs, and bringing so much joy into my life these past months. I also remain awed and honoured by the kindness and generosity of my fellow authors online. Thank you!

Finally, as always, my fiercest love and devotion to my own grumpy mate, who also loves to be left alone to read... until he's foiled by my incessant writing obsession (and other things, heh). I love you, my lord.

ALSO BY FINLEY FENN

THE LADY AND THE ORC

He's the most feared monster in the realm. And she's what he needs to win his war...

In a world of warring orcs and men, Lady Norr is condemned to a childless marriage, a cruel lord husband, and a life of genteel poverty—until the day her home is ransacked by a horde. And leading the charge is their hulking, deadly orc captain: the infamous Grimarr.

And Grimarr has a wicked plan for Lady Norr, and for ending this war once and for all. She's going to become his captive—and the perfect snare for Lord Norr.

There's no possible escape, and soon Lady Norr is dragged off toward Orc Mountain in the powerful arms of her greatest enemy. A ruthless, commanding warlord, with a velvet voice and mouthwatering scent, who awakens every forbidden hunger she never knew she had...

But Grimarr refuses to accept half measures—in war, or in pleasure. And before he'll conquer Lady Norr's deepest, darkest desires, she needs to surrender *everything*.

Her allegiance.

Her wedding ring.

Her future...

And with her husband's forces giving chase, Lady Norr can't afford to play such a dangerous game—or can she? **Even if this deadly orc's plans might be the only way to save them all?**

ALSO BY FINLEY FENN

THE DUCHESS AND THE ORC

She just traded herself to a new lord. And he's the most brutal orc in the realm...

In a world of recently warring orcs and men, Maria is desperate to escape her gilded cage, and her cruel duke husband. So she plots the perfect plan: she'll run away to Orc Mountain, and offer herself to the first orc who agrees to keep her safe.

But the first orc she meets is *Simon*. The huge, hostile Enforcer of Orc Mountain. The biggest, most dangerous orc in all the realm.

Worst of all, Simon hates humans. Especially wealthy, pampered women like Maria. And when she makes him her offer, he answers with vicious fury, and a proposal of his own...

He'll protect her, and share his home with her. But only if she gives him *everything* in return.

Her defeat.

Her dignity.

Her devotion...

Surely, a duchess wouldn't dare agree to such a shameful deal... or would she? Especially if her surrender to Orc Mountain's mighty Enforcer might spark another war... **or break both their hearts?**

ABOUT THE AUTHOR

Finley Fenn is "the queen of dark orc romance" (Virgo Reader), and her ongoing Orc Sworn series has been praised as "sexy, romantic, angsty, and captivating ... utter brilliance" (Romantically Inclined Reviews).

When she's not obsessing over her stories, Finley loves reading, drooling over delicious orc artwork, and spending time with her incredible readers on Patreon, Discord, and Facebook. She lives in Canada with her beloved family, including her very own grumpy, gorgeous orc husband.

For free bonus stories and epilogues, special offers, and exclusive Orc Sworn artwork, sign up at www.finleyfenn.com.